The Sidhe didn

Suddenly Sam w in flames, head to toe.

His heart contracted with fear, spasming painfully; he lost his breath, and he choked on a cry —

And in the next moment was glad that he hadn't uttered it. The flames, whether they were real, of magical energy, or only illusion, weren't touching him. There was no heat, at least nothing he felt, although Thoreau yelped, turned tail, and ran for the shelter of Sam's bedroom.

He remained frozen for a moment, then the true nature of the attack penetrated. *It can't hurt me, no matter what it looks like.* After a deep breath to steady his heart, Sam simply folded his arms across his chest and sighed.

"Is this supposed to impress me?" he asked mildly. A snide comment like that might have been a stupid thing to say, but it was the only attitude Sam could think to take.

The Sidhe's face twisted with rage. *"Damn* you, mortal!" he cried. And this time he *did* gesture.

A sword appeared in his hand; a blue-black, shiny blade like no metal Sam had ever seen. A small part of him wondered what it was, as the rest of him shrieked, and backpedaled, coming up against the wall.

"Not so impudent now, are you?" the Sidhe crowed, kicking aside fallen books and moving in for the kill, sword glittering with a life of its own.

Sam could only stare, paralyzed with fear, as his hands scrabbled on the varnished wood behind him —

BORN TO RUN

A NOVEL OF THE SERRATED EDGE

MERCEDES LACKEY
LARRY DIXON

BAEN

BORN TO RUN

Copyright © 1992, by Mercedes Lackey & Larry Dixon

A Baen Books Original

Baen Publishing Enterprises
P.O. Box 1403
Riverdale, NY 10471

ISBN: 0-671-72110-0

Cover art by Larry Elmore

First Printing, March 1992
Second Printing, February 1993

Distributed by Simon & Schuster
1230 Avenue of the Americas
New York, NY 10020

Printed in the United States of America

Dedication:

Dedicated to J.R. and Shirley Dixon, Ed and Joyce Ritche, and to all parents with the vision to listen to what kids *really* wish for — and help them find it.

Thanks to the music of Icehouse (and to Iva Davies for being the visual inspiration for Tannim), a-ha, Midnight Oil, Rush, Kate Bush, Alan Parsons, Thomas Dolby (hope you get the keys to her Ferrari), Edvard Grieg, Shriekback, David Bowie (past and present!), Billy Idol (for visceral fight-scene music), Mannheim Steamroller, the Floyd, Michael Hedges, and the entire Narada Artists catalogue, especially David Arkenstone and David Lanz — we could never have done this one without you!

Special thanks also to Kevin Barry's Pub and Acadia Restaurant (run by none other than the sparkling Trish Rodgers!), Trish Rodgers herself, the Buccaneer Region SCCA, Roebling Road raceway, Professor Russ Barclay (for drilling grammar into Larry's thick artsy skull lo these many years ago), and the faculty, staff, and students of Savannah College of Art and Design (for backing a long-haired hippy-freak dark horse).

● CHAPTER ONE

A dark red Mustang perched beside the ribbon of highway, alone but for the young man resting against its door. It was an unusual sight for such a place, here where the shallow water of the wetlands reflected moonlight, and endless silvered marsh grasses whispered in the breeze. The cicadas didn't care if the man was there, nor did the night-birds, nor the foxes and raccoons — they were used to the comings-and-goings of men in their loud machines, and would avoid him. There would seem to be no reason for him to be stopped here — no smoke or steam poured from beneath the nostrilled hood, no line of shredded rubber marked a newly departed tire. A highway patrol officer would have been very interested — if there had been one anywhere within twenty miles. And that, too, was unusual; this close to Savannah, there should be police cruising this stretch of road.

"One of these nights," griped Tannim to no one in particular, "I'll have a normal drive, with nothing chasing me, pestering me, shooting at me . . . no breakdowns, no detours, no country-western music, no problems. Peace, quiet, and the road. No place to go, no one to save, no butts to cover except my own."

Tannim pulled himself up onto his old Mach 1, faded black jeans *shush*ing over the hood. Its cooling engine tick-tick-ticked, radiator gurgling softly as it relaxed from its work, the warm old American sheet metal satin-smooth and familiar. He ran a hand through his long brown hair, catching fingers in his uncountable ratty knots of curls, and snorted in cynical amusement. Casting his eyes skyward, scratching at his scalp, he said wistfully, "Man. They keep telling me, 'Y'knew the job was dangerous when ya took it.' Thanks for giving me the job description *after* I've signed the contract, guys."

The cicadas answered him by droning on, unimpressed.

The road was deserted, the air clear, the bright country sky shining off of the curved fenders. Tiny pinpoints of light twisted into sweeping contours only to be swallowed up in the flat black intakes of the hood.

The beauty and peace of the evening softened his mood. *No finer job in this world, though. When it works out — wish Kestrel were here to help. He's better at this than me.* Tannim thought about his old friend from high school back in Jenks, Oklahoma, with more than a twinge of regret — regret for Derek's curious blend of talents, compassion, and guts. Derek Ray Kestrel was gifted not only with a sexy name but with a knack for magic that just wouldn't quit. Deke spent his time with his cars and guitars, now, and didn't do road work anymore. *Guess he didn't have the stomach for it. It can get gross enough to freak a coroner. Damned if he didn't have more than just talent, though.*

He gave up on his hair and adjusted his jacket, a third-hand Battlestar Galactica fatigue he traded a Plymouth carburetor kit for. Both he and the other kid thought they'd gotten the better deal. They were both right. Tannim didn't know from carbs then, and had let go of a rare five-hundred-dollar sixpack. Deke had sure given him a hard time about that! The other kid had no idea how hard the battle-jackets were to get. *Live and learn.* He dug around in one of the many pockets he'd sewn inside the jacket, and pulled out a cherry pop, whistling along with the Midnight Oil tape on the Mach 1's stereo, occasionally falling into key.

Decent night for a job, though. Not raining like last time, and no lightning to dodge, either. Tannim was a young man, but he was not inclined to die that way, despite the reckless pace he kept up. *Better to run towards something than away,* he'd always thought, but the scars and aches all over his wiry body testified that even a fiery young mage can be harmed by too much running. Or perhaps, not running hard enough . . . He had been self-trained up to age twenty, and then someone from *elsewhere* had taken him in and really shown him the ropes of high magic. Their friendship had built before their student/teacher relationship really began, Chinthliss admiring the boy's brazen style, wicked humor, and dedication to the elusive and deadly energy of his world's magic. That was, in fact, the reason Chinthliss had taken Tannim on in the first place; it had not escaped the young mage that he and his mentor were a great deal alike in many ways. There were a lot of words to describe the two of them, the best of which were creative, crafty, adventurous, virtuous — well, maybe not virtuous — but their many critics had other choice adjectives, none flattering. Tannim had a way of taking the simplest lesson and turning it around to befuddle his "master," who in turn would trounce the boy with the next one, and giggle about it for a week. It was Chinthliss who had given Tannim his name — it meant "Son of Dragons." It fit, especially since he thought of Tannim as he would his own offspring.

Eventually, the lessons simply became jam sessions of experimenting, and Tannim began teaching Chinthliss a thing or two. What was about to occur on this lonely stretch of road was something he'd come up with himself years ago — something that had scared the scat out of Chinthliss. It was the kind of "job" he had done a couple of times with Deke Kestrel in tow. He unwrapped the cherry pop and began chewing on it absent-mindedly, humming along with the tunes. He crumpled the wrapper and slipped it into a pocket, and his humming became a chant through clenched teeth.

He pulled his shoulders back and stretched, neck and back popping from road fatigue, and let in the rush of energy that heralded a major spell. Around him, the cicadas rose in pitch, to harmonize with Peter Garrett and the young man's chanting. Harmonizing with Garrett was no small feat, and he noted it as a good omen. He kept his arms raised toward the crescent moon overhead, and his eyes perceived a subtle change in the starlight as he entered his familiar trance.

His body went rigid, as if rigor mortis had suddenly frozen him in place.

To say that Tannim died then would be misleading — although he was not precisely alive anymore either. The trance he entered was protected well, and he was being monitored by otherworldly allies, but the young mage's soul was now connected to his body by the thinnest of threads — *much* more tenuous than anything most mages ever depended on during out-of-body work. Most of them would have been terrified at the notion of trusting their lives to so fragile a bond. But most mages weren't Tannim. *He* had been trusting his life and more to far more fragile bonds than this for a long time now.

As he stabilized his spirit-form, there was the sensation of everything being well-lit and dark at once, and of infinite visibility — the dizzying effect of mage-sight in the now-and-then hereafter.

He "felt" completely normal, right down to the candy tucked in his cheek and the feel of the Mach 1 beneath him. He tapped his worn black high-tops against the chrome, focusing his thoughts and getting comfortable, teeth gnawing on the pop's soggy stem as he drew energy up from the earth through the frame of the Mach 1, tempering it through the sheet metal, grounding the wild-magic resonances into the engine block, radiating the excess through the window glass.

Good so far; now to find him.

With that, he pulled his spirit away from his body, his shadow-image standing upright, stretching, and adjusting its jacket while his body remained seated on the hood, connected to it by a shimmering field of gossamer threads, the only traces of the spell visible to the trained eye. He stepped away from his anchor, and crossed the gravel shoulder.

A figure wavered and coalesced before him, a fortyish man in a plaid workshirt and chinos, standing with his hands in his pockets, looking away from the road. There was a half-smoked cigarette hanging slackly from his lips. He was an ordinary man, the kind you'd see at any truckstop, any feed store in the southern belt, lines etched into his face by hard work, bright sun, and pain endured. The only thing that set him apart now was that he was edged by a soft yellowish glow, which seemed to fill in every shadow and crease in that face, and followed him as he stepped towards Tannim.

His brows furrowed, as if trying to remember something. He took a drag off the cigarette. It glowed, but did not burn down. Smoke curled up around his face, a bright blue and violet. "Haven't seen you here before," the man said. "Hiya. Canfield, Ross Canfield. . . . " The man stepped forward, reflexively offered a hand. Tannim bit his lip, stepped forward again, and grasped his hand. *Well, I've got him. Oh God, I thought this was going to be easier. He doesn't know.*

"Hello, Ross," he said. "I'm Tannim."

Ross nodded; he seemed distracted, as if he wasn't entirely focusing on the moment at hand. "Tannim? Good ta meetcha. That a first name or a last name?"

"Only name," Tannim replied cautiously. "Just Tannim. How are you? I mean, you look a little stressed, Ross; are you all right? How do you feel. . . ? "

If Canfield was surprised about this atypical show of concern from a stranger, he didn't show it. "Been better. Strange night." Ross took a pull off of his cigarette. Its tip glowed again, but still didn't shorten. Its smoke wisped up violet and vanished above his head, and he blew smoke from his nostrils in a wash of reddish-purple.

"Mmm. As strange as usual." Tannim smiled inwardly at the oxymoron. "Where you from, Ross?"

Canfield focused a little more on him as the question caught his attention. "Louisiana. Metairie. You?"

Tannim moved a little farther away, unobtrusively testing the energies coming from Canfield. "Tulsa."

Now Canfield's attention was entirely focused on the young mage. "Why you ask?"

"Just curious; I wondered if you were local." It was time to change the subject. "You know, Ross, you seem like a friendly fella, laid back, able to handle 'bout anything. Got something kinda serious to talk to you about."

"Uh huh." Ross Canfield set his jaw, and the glow around him turned a rich orange. Not a good sign. Red would be worse, much worse, but orange was not a good sign.

"Ah, look, Ross, I have some bad news for you, so don't get mad at me. . . . " *They always blame the messenger, don't they?*

"Bad news?" Another drag on the cigarette, which now glowed a fierce red — echoing the glow of energy swirling around him. "My wife just left me, kid, and you say *you've* got bad news?"

Abruptly, Tannim was no longer the focus of Canfield's anger. "That sonuvabitch Marty Lear tore the hell outta my lawn with her in that goddamn Jap pickup of his and — and — took her away — "

So; there was the reason for it all. *Uh oh. Fast work, boy, you hit it right the first time.*

Tannim's eyes narrowed, and he took the mangled pop stick out of his mouth. Power fluctuated around them, silent and subtle, but there. Tannim noted their patterns, setting up buffer fields with a mental call. He saw a fan of lines spread around them both, channels waiting to be filled if needed.

"What did you do?"

Canfield did not take offense at what should have been considered a very personal question. "Went after 'em. We was fightin' and she'd already called the bastard; he showed up and she jumped in. Caught up to 'em. Have this ol' 'Cuda, hot as hell . . . "

"Had."

Tannim was the focus of Canfield's attention again; he felt the hot glare of Ross's stare. "What?" Canfield asked.

He isn't going to like this. "You *had* a Barracuda. I'm sorry, Ross, but . . . that's the bad news I have for you."

"What you talkin' 'bout, son?" Ross Canfield looked pale for a moment, then his glow pulsed cherry red and his face began to twist into anger. He exhaled bright red smoke from his nostrils, jaw set, threads of energy coalescing around his feet and fists.

Now a quick deflection. "Ross, walk with me a minute, will you?" Tannim started along the roadbed toward the overpass a hundred feet away. "How long would you say you've been standing out here, Ross? An hour, maybe? A couple?"

Ross hesitated, then followed Tannim. The tiny traces of reddish energy crackled and followed his steps.

"Ross, you remember stopping here? Getting out of that car? Lighting that cig?"

Ross absently pulled the cigarette from his mouth and looked at it, brow knotted in concentration.

Tannim stood next to the overpass abutment. It was gray concrete, scarred and cracked, with patches of cement covering half its surface. Bits of glass and plastic glittered in the starlight. Tannim picked up a razor-edged sliver of safety-glass an inch long. *Barrier's in place; might as well tell him straight up. He hasn't taken the hints.*

"Ross . . . this is all that's left of your 'Cuda. You hit this bridge doin' one-forty, and you never walked away from it."

The cigarette slipped from Ross' fingers and rested in the dry grass. It smoldered, but didn't set fire to the grass it landed in. The energy field around Ross Canfield crackled like a miniature thunderstorm, apparently invisible to him.

"Ross, look over there." Tannim pointed at the Mustang, and at the man still sitting on the hood. "That's me."

Ross took a deep breath, stooped to pick up his cigarette, and returned it in his mouth.

Here's where it hits. I can handle it; he's not too powerful . . . I hope. Tannim built up his defenses, preparing for a mental scream of rage. . . . Or worse. *Sometimes they don't just blame the messenger, they kill the messenger. I hate this part.*

Ross bit his lip, shock plain on his face as he realized the meaning of Tannim's words.

"Never . . . walked . . . away. . . . "

Tannim nodded, ready to strike back if Ross broke and gave in to the rage building in him. "So I'm dead, huh?"

Tannim could feel the energies arcing between them, screaming for focus. . . .

Hoo boy. Now so am I.

"That's right, Ross. You died three years ago, right here. I'm sorry, really. . . . "

Ross Canfield pulled himself up to his full height, towering over Tannim by almost a foot, eyes glowing red with fury as he seethed. His fists clenched tighter, then relaxed slowly and finally opened. His broad shoulders slouched as his aura dimmed to orange, red tinges slithering away into the ground. He inhaled one massive breath, pulled a hand back through his hair and said—

"Well, *shit*."

Tannim heard mental giggles from his guardians, felt them skitter away to other business, pulling his borrowed energy reserves with them. He heaved a sigh of relief and lowered his guard against a strike.

Ross swayed as if drunk, then stared at Tannim's spirit-form like he was trying out newly bought eyes.

"So, this is what it's like to be a goddamn ghost," Ross said to Tannim as they stood beside the Mustang. "Just my damn luck. I should've expected something like this to happen to me. What the hell do I do now?"

Tannim stood at the hood, beside himself. "I'll tell you in a second." He drew up the Walking spell's reserve energy and stepped back into his body, trusting his instincts that Ross was not going to disturb his transfer. Back at home, he opened his eyes, stretched and stood, rubbing the ever-present kink in his left leg.

"Just for the record, you could have hurt me pretty bad back there, Ross. Just now, I mean. Stepping into and out of a body is a vulnerable time. I trusted you that you wouldn't — thanks."

"Uh huh. What was I gonna do, rattle my chains at ya?" Ross snorted. "And, uh, if it's not too much trouble, what the hell good is this gonna do me? What am I s'posed to do? If I'm dead, where are the angels?"

Tannim paused, and walked to the door of the car. "Get in; I'll tell you."

Ross reached for the door-handle, and his hand passed through it, a tracing of fire around the point of entry. "That's lesson one, Ross. You're only partially in *this* land of the physical. You can choose whether or not to interact with it. Lotta advantages to being a ghost; I don't get the option of deciding if I want to be hit by a bullet or no." Tannim grinned. "You do. Or rather, you will. You're not up to that yet."

"That's spooky as shit," Ross observed, watching his forearm disappear completely into the door.

"Normally you wouldn't be able to do that to this particular car. As a ghost, that is. It has some powerful defenses. I'm lowering the ones against spirits for you, keyed to you and you only. Otherwise, you couldn't get within a foot of that door. Also, another thing: if you get near my tape collection, I'll kill you." Tannim smiled. "You can fry magnetics with a touch — tapes, computer disks, that sorta thing. The tapes are in that red box there. Please don't touch it."

Ross looked through the window at the red fabric case, and read "NO GHOSTS OR POSSESSIONS WITHIN 10 FEET" embroidered into a panel on its lid. The caution was surrounded by arcane symbols. "Yeah, I see. What are those, spells or something?"

Tannim chuckled and leaned against the roof. "The runes? They're from the back of Led Zeppelin Four. Scares most of the ghosts bigtime, except the metalheads, they just give me a high-sign and say 'Duuuude!'"

Ross laughed, and pulled his arm free of the door. He shoved his other hand in his pockets, and dragged on his ever-present cigarette. The smoke wisped away, disappearing as blue this time.

"That's another advantage, you can see things living people can't, like that warning. It's for spirits only. Your vision should be changing soon, now that you've realized . . . ah, what you are now. Things'll start getting pretty weird . . . people will have funny glows around them, colors that show how they feel emotionally, the brighter they are the more intense they are. I see that way all the time, it's called 'mage-sight' — that's how I can see you now. Watch out for blind spots, they mean trouble every time. They stand for something you can't see, something someone won't let you see, or something you don't *want* to see."

Ross appeared grim for a second, then turned his head to face the overpass.

He looks like he's seen a . . .

Well, he turned very pale.

"I can't see . . . I never noticed that before. That's where I died, and I can't see it at all." Ross looked visibly shaken, and began walking towards the overpass.

Would he be able to see it? Should Tannim even encourage him to try? But he seemed ready. "The trick is to look past it, and bring your field of focus into it. Concentrate on seeing the road past it, then pull back until it appears; the more you want it, the sooner it will come."

Tannim watched him walk up to the place where he'd died, and stop.

"Ross . . . " he said softly, "you don't have to do this, if it's making you uncomfortable, at least not right away. There are ghosts in this world who haven't been able to come to grips with their own deaths for centuries. It's not easy."

"How th' hell would you know?" Ross snapped, and then immediately looked embarrassed.

"I've helped almost a hundred move on to their next destination," Tannim said. "Not always willingly, but . . . it's for the better."

Ross faced him, skepticism warring with a touch of awe. "You're not — an angel, are you?"

"Me?" Tannim laughed. More often, he was mistaken for something else entirely. "Not hardly. Not even close. I'm just a man who can tell you a thing or two about magic, about dying, and what comes after it. Angels live far cleaner lives, and have far cleaner consciences."

"There are angels, then? And Heaven?" Ross pulled a long drag on his cigarette.

"I guess." Tannim shrugged. "Hell, I don't know what your definition of Heaven is, so I can't say. But I will tell you that not everyone who dies waltzes through the 'Pearly Gates' of their choice; they still have things to do. A lot of 'em love this world, and don't want to leave. They don't have to, at least, not right away."

"They don't?" Canfield looked surprised — and bemused.

"Nope. Not if they still have things to do, things on their minds." Tannim leaned up against the Mustang. "Most move on to whatever suits them, pretty much right off. But some, it takes a while to find out what it is they want. You're probably that way. It's a whole different ball game when you're dead; conflicts that were big guns when you were alive don't count for much. You meet all kinds of people from all times. Plenty to talk about. Hell, the drone of sports talk at Candlestick Park from a hundred thousand dead fans is enough to put you over the edge!"

"Uh huh." Ross pulled the butt from his mouth. "So I'm gonna be this way for a while?"

"Yeah, probably." He looked up at the clear night sky for a moment. "Since you didn't — go on, when you really understood what had happened to you. I guess you must have some things to do. The way you are — it's kind of a way to live again, with your senses enhanced and a new way of looking at things. Kind of gives you a second chance."

"I guess it isn't all bad," Ross observed after a moment of thought. "Guy could do a lot, see a lot, like this. Things he never got a chance to."

Tannim nodded. "There's a big tradeoff to it; if there's something you need to take care of, that tie will hold you to a place. Even without that, there's ties to your family. Most ghosts build up a sort of 'monitoring' of their families and loved ones, so they know what they are doing, and can be there to lend support from beyond if they can, while they're still ghosts. Native Americans in particular have a strong tie with their ancestors, and their spirits fill everything around them. If I were you, I'd travel a bit and reconcile your feelings about everyone you've ever loved or hated. Then visit your gravesite. After that, it's up to you whether to stay or to move on."

"Well, ain't this a helluva turn. Life after death is just as big a pain in the ass as living." Ross planted his hands on his hips, and stared towards the bridge. "I can kinda see it now, Tannim. And I can see . . . my 'Cuda. Holy shit . . . I really did buy it good." Ross shuddered, and swore again. "Damn. I loved that car."

Tannim nodded. "Yeah, I can relate. I've lost a couple of good ones myself. . . . Thank it for its services and offer it its own afterlife. Even cars can develop spirits, believe me. Honor everything you knew, Ross, then you'll be happy again."

Ross looked down at his feet. "I . . . I loved her too, more than the car, more . . . " he said, and Tannim didn't have to ask to know who he was talking about. "I cried like a goddamn baby every time I couldn't tell her how I felt. It was easier to drink the booze than to find the words. And I chased after her drunk . . . hell, I didn't even know what road she was on. I couldn't even get dying right. . . . "

Better intervene before he starts getting caught in a downward spiral. "Uhhh, Ross, I've met a lot of spirits in my day, and there've been a lot of them who died 'good deaths,' real 'blaze of glory' stuff. Every one of 'em mentioned how stupid it was after all, you know, big picture stuff. I don't know if there *is* a right way to die. But, they all have had regrets about their lives . . . the real heroes and the regular joes."

"Hmm. Yeah, well, I guess I have a lot to think about, and a lot of time to do it." Ross turned, and pulled the cigarette from his lips. "So now I get the chance to change things, huh? Fix what I shouldn't have been in at all. Fine." He threw the cigarette down and ground it out. "I've wanted to quit smoking for twenty years now, and never could. I'll be damned if I'll do it when I'm dead. Don't start drinking or smoking, boy."

Tannim smiled and said, "Yeah, the stuff 'll kill you."

Ross bent down before the concrete pillar, and reached a translucent hand towards a sparkling shard of glass. He crouched there a moment longer and smoothed the dirt over it, then strode towards the Mustang, leaving his death behind him.

The Alan Parsons Project's "Don't Answer Me" played on the tape deck as the wind rushed past the Mach 1, its engine thrumming in mechanical symphony. The breeze from the open windows made the young driver's hair stream back against the seat-covers, and that same breeze blew right through his passenger.

Ross Canfield put his hand to his chin, shifted to lean his arm against the sill, and put his arm through it. He withdrew and tried again, this time successfully resting his arm against the vinyl. "Shit, this is gonna be hard to get used to."

Tannim chuckled and leaned forward to tap a sticking gauge. "You're doing fine, Ross. Just remember, things in my world may or may not affect you. It's mostly a matter of what you want to be influenced by; for instance, you could, if you wanted to, fall right out of this car doing seventy now by simply deciding that seat won't affect you. Then, you may choose for the road not to affect you, and you wouldn't be hurt by the fall. But you missed the armrest just now because you forgot to 'want' it to affect you. Tricky, huh?"

"Kinda like — what'd they used to say? Mind over matter?"

"Exactly." He nodded with approval. "Now, until you learn spirit-traveling, you're limited by your old human abilities. One day, you may be able to fly cross-country by will alone, but for now, if you fell out of the car, I'd have to stop and pick you up, 'cause you couldn't run fast enough to keep up with me."

Ross chuckled. "Yeah, but I can run faster now that

I'm dead. No wheezy lungs from smoking, no beer gut."

"Yeah, and you can play tennis with dead pros to keep in shape."

Ross and Tannim both laughed. "You know, I never thought being dead would be so damned entertaining. And it seems like I should be more upset about it."

Tannim kept his eyes on the road, but he smiled to himself. Ross Canfield was coming along very well — a lot faster than Tannim would have thought. "Well, seriously, Ross, there are a lot of ways to deal with it, but you're running on instinct. Your subconscious was aware you were dead, but your superconscious wasn't ready to accept it, so you stood there sucking a butt for a couple of years. Now, it's kind of a relief that it's out in the open, and you're able to get to the decisions you've been building towards all this time. And as for it being entertaining, kissing a bridge at lightspeed drunk off your ass is a grim thing, but there are a lot of things about being a ghost that are damn funny, no matter what the circumstances are."

"Like fallin' through doors," Ross supplied.

"Uh huh. So, deal with it now with a laugh, because there are plenty of things in the future that'll make you cry, make you scream — " now he turned to look at Canfield out of the corner of his eye " — and make you wish you were more dead than you are."

"Huh. As you can tell by the two-year wait, I don't *spook* easily." His face cracked with a smirk.

"Ross! I'd never picked you for a punster!"

"Yeah, well, that's why I'm not in Heaven right now."

Tannim grinned and thought about the turn of a friendly card. Maybe they were both lucky they'd met.

"Seriously . . . what do I do now? How'm I supposed to learn all these ghost things, and how do I get outta bein' one? This shit's gonna get old eventually." Now Ross looked uncertain. "I don't suppose you'd teach me— "

Tannim shook his head. "I can't, Ross. The best I can

do is what I just did — break you out of the stalemate you were in and get you started. Like most things, Ross, you have to get out and practice. Learn by doing. Talk to other ghosts, pick up the tricks. I can't show you what you need to know; I've got too many other irons in the fire, and I've got problems enough with people trying to make *me* into a ghost."

At first Ross snorted; then he looked around, and squinted. His eyes widened, and Tannim figured he had started to see some of the protections on the Mustang. It was enough to impress him — even if he wasn't seeing more than a fraction of the magics Tannim had infused the Mach 1 with. "There are a couple of other things I can tell you: just like you can let the rest of the world affect you, with practice, you can influence what happens in the physical world — or, more accurately, the world I'm in right now. Like back there, when you touched that piece of glass, buried it . . . there's a lotta different kinds of 'physical.' Making a change in this one means discovering how to make yours interact with it. That thing with the magnetics is an example of one you can't control; there are others you'll pick up soon enough."

"Got some simple tips?"

"Sure. Stay away from things that make you tired, don't fiddle with walls that won't let you pass, and if anything tries to eat you, *hurt* it."

"Tries to — eat me?" Ross's eyes widened again.

"There's a lot of unfriendly things out there, including some that used to be human. Remember, don't attack first. Until you have the experience to tell friend from foe, be cautious. It's always easier to hold a defensive position anyway. And there are a lot of things out there that aren't human at all; treat them fairly, they can become very close friends. My best friend isn't human. Pretty simple. Otherwise, things are similar to living. You can have sex as a ghost, ride in an F-15. Fly on the Space Shuttle if you want, if you can find room. It's very popular. Enjoy it, and learn. That's the key to moving on — knowledge and maturity are important."

"But, what about moving on? How —"

Tannim shook his head. "I can't tell you; it's different for everyone. You'll know when. If you didn't know how, you'd have never seen the bridge back there; that was an important move. It shows you're finally ready to accept what you are."

Ross was silent for a while, and the miles ticked away as the skyline of Savannah came into view. Finally he spoke. "Tannim . . . thanks."

"No thanks needed, friend," Tannim said, slowing as he approached the city limit. "You ready to take off on your own?"

Ross nodded. "If you need anything, call. I'll find a way to get there. I guess this is dangerous work you're doing, and I owe you for this," he said through teary spectral eyes. "I'd better get out there. I lost enough time to getting shit-faced before, and I want to see what I missed."

Tannim looked sideways at Ross Canfield, nodded, and turned his eyes back towards the highway, pulled to the shoulder and stopped. The city lights illuminated the car, the driver, and the empty seat beside him.

"Be sure to visit River Street while you're here, Ross. Always a party. Good luck. Here's your exit."

The ghost stepped through the door onto the shoulder, and Tannim watched him in the rearview mirror, an ordinary enough guy, watching the Mach 1's taillights recede into the night. Ordinary — except that only Tannim could see him.

And only Tannim could hear him, as clearly as if Ross still sat beside him.

"You need me, you call."

glamoric behind their words and a strong publicity

● CHAPTER TWO

"That was Georgia's own B-52s, with 'Rock
Lobster,' " said the radio announcer, his cheerful
voice murmuring from the sixteen speakers of Doctor Sam Kelly's home-built quadraphonic system.
"Next up, Shriekback, the Residents, the new
British release from George Louvis, and an oldie
from Thomas Dolby, but first . . . "

Sam hit the "mute" button, and the commercial
faded to a whisper. The timer would bring the volume
back up in another sixty seconds, and by then the station should be back to music. Doctor Samuel Sean
Kelly might have majored in metallurgy, but he had
minored in electrical engineering; sensing, even back
in the '40s, that the time would come when everyone
had to have some understanding of electronics. After
all, hadn't he grown up on H. G. Wells, and the science-
fiction tradition that the engineer was the man who
could and would save the universe? "Not bad, for an
old retired fart," he chuckled to his Springer Spaniel,
Thoreau, who raised his head and ears as if he understood what his master was saying. "I liked Elvis in the
'50s, I liked the Stones and the Fuggs in the '60s, and
now, sure, I'm on the cutting edge — right, boyo?"

Thoreau wagged his stub of a tail and put his head
back down on his paws. He didn't care how eclectic his
master's taste in music was, so long as he didn't crank up
those imposing speakers to more than a quarter of their
capacity. When Sam retired from Gulfstream, he'd held a
party for his younger colleagues that was still the talk of

the neighborhood. There had been complaints to the police about the music from as far away as five blocks, and poor Thoreau had gone into hiding in the back closet of the bedroom, not to emerge for three days.

The desk-top before him was preternaturally clean, with only a single envelope cluttering the surface. Sam fingered the letter from "Fairgrove Industries," as the radio volume returned to normal, and Thomas Dolby complained of hyperactivity. He sat back in his aging overstuffed recliner, surrounded by his books, frowning at the empty room and wishing wistfully that he hadn't given up smoking. Or that he hadn't agreed to talk to this "Tannim" person.

It had seemed very harmless when he first got the letter; this "Tannim" — what sex the person was he hadn't known until the phone call came confirming the evening appointment — wanted to talk to him about a job as a consultant. He had offered Sam an amazing amount of money just to *talk* to him: fifteen hundred dollars for an evening of his otherwise idle time. Sam had said yes before he thought the consequences through — after all, how many retired metallurgists could boost their income by that much just by talking to someone? But later, after he'd had lunch with some of the youngsters at Gulfstream and heard some of the latest news, he began to wonder. There was a lot going on over there right now; the joint project with the Russians, a lot of composite development and things being done with explosive welding and foamed aluminum. None of it was exactly secret, but there was a lot of proprietary information Sam was still privy to — and more he could get clandestine access to, if he chose. What if this "Fairgrove Industries" — which was not listed with the Better Business Bureau, and not in any industrial database that Sam had access to — was just a front for something else? What if this Tannim was trying to set him up as a corporate informant, or looking for some "insider trading" type information?

Sam had loved his job at Gulfstream; they were, as he joked, a "growing, excited company." He liked the people he worked with enough to socialize with them, even now, when he had been retired for the past several months. He wasn't interested in doing anything that would hurt the company.

Sam tapped the edge of the envelope on his desk and made up his mind about what he *was* going to do, now that he had realized the implications. "Well, Thoreau, if this young fella thinks I'm some kind of senile old curmudgeon he can fool with a silver tongue and a touch of blarney, he's going to be surprised," Sam said aloud. "If it's looking to make a fool of me he is, I just may be making a fool of him."

If this Tannim *was* trying to set him up as a corporate informant, Sam decided, this old man would turn the tables on him. There was a break-in camera under the eaves; it took snaps when the burglar alarm went off, but it could be operated manually. Very well, then, he'd snap pictures of the man's car and license tag when he arrived. First thing in the morning, he'd call his old bosses, give them the number and the young man's description, and let them know exactly what had gone on. Looking for a corporate informant wasn't illegal, exactly — but the fellows at Gulfstream could certainly put a stop to anything shady.

And Sam would still have the fifteen hundred dollars.

Not bad, when you stopped to think out all the implications first, rather than backtracking in a panic. Assuming of course, the check didn't bounce.

But planning ahead in case things did go wrong was what had made Sam one of the best in his field.

"Or so I like to tell myself," he said aloud, smiling at his own conceit.

The doorbell rang, and Sam reached automatically for the modified TV remote-control that, through the intervention of an old Commodore microcomputer, handled gadgets throughout the house. The poor old thing was useless even as a game machine these days, but it was perfectly adequate to mute the radio — or take pictures of the young man and his car before Sam even reached the door. He made his way to the door with a shade of the limberness of his youth, and opened it, catching the stranger in a "listening" pose that told Sam the man had been trying to catch the sound of his own approaching footsteps.

"Doctor Kelly?" The man at the door was il-luminated by the powerful floodlight Sam had used to replace the ridiculous little phony carriage-lamp that had been installed there. And he was a *very* young man, much younger than his deep voice had suggested. He nodded in a noncommittal fashion and the man con-tinued. "I'm Tannim — we had an appointment —"

He was carrying a dark leather folder. Sam first took in that, then the wild mop of curly hair, cut short in front and long in the back, the way a lot of kids on MTV cut theirs — a dark nylon jacket, with a good shirt un-derneath, and a soft scarf instead of a tie — dark slacks, not jeans — boots — the first impression was reasonable. But not exactly fitting the image of a cor-porate recruiter. The face was good; high cheekbones, determined chin, firm mouth, fine bone-structure and curiously vulnerable-looking eyes. The kid looked like a lot of the hotshot young engineers Sam worked with. But not like what Sam had been expecting.

"I remember," Sam replied cautiously. There was something about the young man that suggested trustworthiness, perhaps his eyes, or the curious sense of *stillness* about him; but Sam knew better than to trust his first impression. Some of the biggest crooks he had ever known had inspired that same feeling of trust. And some of them had been just as young as this man.

"Can I come in?" A quirky grin spread across the

man's bony face, transforming the stillness without entirely removing it. "Or would you rather earn your retainer standing here in the doorway? Or would you like to go somewhere else entirely?"

Well, it wouldn't hurt to let the youngster in. Sam moved aside, and Tannim stepped across the threshold. Sam noticed that he walked with a limp, one he was at pains to minimize; that he moved otherwise with a catlike grace at odds with the limp. Sam was no stranger to industrial accidents and their aftermath. This was someone who had suffered a serious injury and learned to cope with it. That moved him a little more into the "favorable" column, in Sam's mind. Con artists tended to emphasize injuries to gain sympathy — con artists tended *not* to get injured in the first place. "Follow me, if you would," Sam said, leading the way to his office. This was going to be more interesting than he had thought.

Tannim cocked his head to one side as he entered the office, and caught what was playing softly over the speakers. The playlist had migrated to the outré. His eyes and his smile increased a trifle. "Doctor Kelly — I'm pleasantly surprised by your taste in music."

Sam shrugged, as the Residents gave forth their own terrifyingly skewed version of "Teddybear." He took his seat in the recliner behind his desk and waved at the two identical recliners in front of the desk.

But Tannim didn't take a seat; instead, he put the folder he had been carrying on the desk, and beside it, a set of I.D. cards he fanned like a set of playing cards.

"Before we talk, Doctor Kelly, I'd like to assure you of something. Fairgrove Industries is a brand new entity insofar as the rest of the world is concerned — but we've been around a long, long time in the private sector." Sam looked up to see that Tannim's smile had turned into a wide grin. "We've been around a lot longer than anyone knows. I know what you've probably been thinking; that I'm a corporate raider, that I'm a front-man for industrial

espionage, or that I'm looking for information on your
former employer. Actually, I don't usually do this for
Fairgrove, but the folks back at the plant thought I'd be
the best person to approach you."

"Oh?" Sam Kelly replied. "So — just what is it that
this Fairgrove does that they want from me?"

Tannim tapped the folder with one long finger. "We
build racecars, Doctor Kelly. We have nothing to do
with aerospace, and I doubt very much we'll ever be involved in that business. But you have skills we very
much need."

Sam looked back down at the top photo I.D.,
which was, unmistakably, Tannim. And listed only
the single name, oddly enough — no initials, no first
or last name. It was an SCCA card, autoclub racing,
sure enough; beneath it was a SERRA card
(whatever that was), an IMSA card, an I.D. card for
Roebling Road racetrack, and beneath that was his
Fairgrove card. That particular piece of I.D. listed
him as "test-driver/ mechanic," which Sam hadn't
known was still possible. Not these days, when either
profession required skill and training enough to
overwhelm most ordinary people.

But Tannim didn't give him any chance to ask about
that — he opened the folder, and began describing just
what it was that Fairgrove wanted from him, *if* he
would take the job.

"We need you as a consultant, Doctor Kelly," he said,
earnestly. "We're working on some pretty esoteric tech-
nologies here, and we need someone with a solid
background who is still flexible and open to new ideas. You
were one of the best metallurgists in the country before
you retired — and no one has ever accused you of being
stuck in a rut, or being too old-fashioned to change."

That surprised him further, and embarrassed him a
little. He was at a loss for a response, but Tannim was
clearly waiting for one. "Oh, I would'na know about

that," he said, lapsing briefly into the Irish brogue of his childhood.

"We would," Tannim said firmly, nodding so that his unruly mop of dark, curly hair flopped over into one eye, making him look, thin as he was, like a Japanese *anime* character. "We've looked very carefully at everyone who might suit us, and who could legitimately work with us without compromising themselves or their current or past employers. You are the best."

Sam felt himself blushing, something he hadn't done in years. "Well, if you think so . . . what's the job, anyway?"

"Metallurgy," Tannim told him. "Specifically, fabricating engine blocks and other high-stress parts of non-ferrous materials." He flashed that grin again, from under the errant lock of hair, calling up an answering smile from Sam. "Like your music, we're on the cutting edge."

"I don't know," Sam replied, slowly, as Tannim finally took his seat, leaving his host free to leaf through the Fairgrove materials. Most of them had the look of something that had been produced on a personal computer, the great-great grandchild of the one that helped Sam run his house, and the cousin of the one on the workstation behind him. The specs Fairgrove had on their "wish list" were impressive — and as unlikely as any of H. G. Wells' dreams of Time Machines. "I don't know. Engine blocks — you're talking about a high-stress application there. You want a foamed aluminum matrix for internal combustion, with water-cooling channels, air-cooling vanes, and alloy piston sleeves? In five castings for the main block? I don't know that it's possible."

"Ah, but you don't know it's *not* possible, do you?" Tannim retorted. "We aren't going to pay you on the basis of whether or not common wisdom says it's possible — we're doing research. Applied research, yes, but when you do research, you accept the fact that some of your highways may turn out to be dead ends. That's life. And speaking of payment — " He reached into his jacket, and pulled out an oak-tree-embossed envelope, which he laid on top of the Fairgrove folder.

Sam thumbed it open. There was a cashier's check inside, made out on his own bank, for fifteen hundred dollars. Until this moment, Sam had not entirely believed in the reality of this retainer. Now, holding it in his hands, he could find no flaw in it — and no real flaw with what Fairgrove, in the person of this young man, proposed.

Except, of course, whether or not what they wanted was a pipe-dream, a Grail; desirable, yes, but impossible to achieve. . . .

Or was it? These people certainly had a lot of money to wave around. And there *were* some problems you could solve by throwing money at them.

"I suppose I could take a look at this place," he ventured. "I could at least see what you people have to work with."

If anything, Tannim's grin got wider. He spread his hands wide. "Sure! How about — right now? We're all night owls over there, and it isn't that far away."

Now? In the middle of the night? That wasn't an offer Sam expected. Did they expect him to come? Or did they expect him to say no?

If he showed up now, surely they wouldn't have time to put on a big display for him . . . and that might be all for the best, really. He'd see things as they were, not a dog-and-pony show. As for the lateness of the hour, well, one of the advantages of being retired was that he no longer had to clock in — and he didn't have to follow the company's time schedule. He'd always been a night owl by nature, and although this was the "middle of the night" to some people, for him the day was barely halfway through — one reason why he'd set this appointment long after a "normal" working day had ended.

And besides all that, if he was going to take a look at this place, he wanted to see all of it. That meant the metal shops, too. This early in the fall, daytime temperatures were still in the nineties, and no matter how good their air-conditioning was, the shops would be as hot as Vulcan's forge during the daylight hours. Metal shops always were, especially if these people were doing casting work.

"All right," he said, shoving himself resolutely out of his chair. "Let's go. No better time to see this miracle place of yours than right now."

"Great!" the young man answered, sliding out of his chair and getting to his feet with no more than a slight hesitation for the bad leg. "Want to take my car? We've used it to test out some SERRA-racer modifications; y'know, suspension mods, rigidity, a little composite fiddling. It's street-legal — barely."

There was something challenging about his grin, and Sam decided to take the dare. "Sure," he replied, taking just enough time with his remote to tell the house to run the "guardian" program. He slipped the remote into his pocket as an added precaution; without that, no one would be able to disarm the system. Not even cutting the power would make a difference; the house had its own uninterruptable power supply, and a generator that kicked on if the power stayed off for more than half an hour. He'd installed all that during the Gulf War terrorist scare, when high-level people at a lot of industries, including Gulfstream, had been warned they might be targets for kidnapping or terrorism. He'd gotten into the habit of arming it whenever he left or went to sleep, and it didn't seem an unreasonable precaution still. Maybe he was paranoid, but being paranoid had saved lives before this.

Thoreau sighed as he saw Sam reach for his jacket. Sam reached down and ruffled the dog's ears, promising that even though "daddy" wasn't going to be around to beg a late-night snack from, there would be a treat when he got back. Thoreau accepted this philosophically enough, and padded alongside, providing an escort service to the front door.

There, Sam was briefly involved in locking the door, and wasn't paying a great deal of attention to the car behind him. Then he turned around.

Sam had been around hot-rodders all his life; seemed to him that for every four techies at Gulfstream who were indifferent to automobiles, there would be one who cherished the things. Now he was looking at a machine that would impress any of them. It was parked with the front wheels turned rakishly, and he made note of its distinguishing features. Dark metallic red; three antennas. Scuffed sidewalls. Dark windows. It was hardly the "company car" he was expecting.

Tannim was wearing that sideways smile of his, and thumbed his keyring. The Mustang rumbled to life, and its doors unlocked and opened a crack. Despite himself, Sam's face showed his interest in the electronic gimcrackery. Tannim gestured to the open passenger's side door with a flourish, and went around to the driver's side as Sam pulled the door open and got in.

Sam pulled the seatbelt snug as Tannim slid into the driver's side, noting as he did so, that these were *not* standard American windowshade seatbelts, which tended — in his opinion — to allow far too much freedom of movement for safety. And as Tannim closed the driver's side door, he noted something else. . . .

Something besides the door had closed, sealing them inside the protective shell of the Mustang. It had sprung into being the moment Tannim's door closed, and covered car and occupants. It wasn't tangible, like the seatbelts or the roll-cage — it wasn't even visible to ordinary sight. But it was there, nevertheless. Tannim pushed a worn tape into the dash deck, and turned down or switched off most of the suite of other instruments there — the CB, high-end channel-scanner, an in-dash radar detector, and — what was this, a police-repeater sensor? Sam looked over the interior a little more, noting the various boxes in the back seat. Some more electronics gear. Hmm. There was also a trash-box stuffed with candy wrappers, a tissue box, allergy tablets, fire extinguishers mounted next to crowbars, two first-aid kits . . . and an embroidered tape-case. As he peered at it, Sam thought he could almost see words in the threads, and familiar symbols. This vehicle was not just a very unusual car; there was more to it than that. There was a great deal of power under the hood — and there was far more Power of a different sort infused into it.

The differences might not be visible to normal eyes, but Sam had a little more to use than what his granny had called "outer eyes." Sam had not been gifted with the ability the Irish referred to as "the Sight" to neglect using it, after all. Nor had becoming a man of science interfered with that. If anything, he was too much of a scientist to discount a gift that had granted him knowledge he might not otherwise have, with fair reliability, over so many years.

Interesting. Very interesting.

"So," he said, as Tannim pulled out smoothly onto the darkened highway, the headlights cutting the darkness ahead of them into areas of seen and half-seen. "Tell me about Fairgrove. Why did they decide to get into manufacturing? And why nonferrous materials?"

Tannim fiddled with the tape deck for a moment before replying. He had put in a Clannad tape, and made a show of ensuring that the volume exactly matched that of the radio in Sam's office, stalling a little. Sam knew a stall when he saw one.

"Before I tell you about Fairgrove, I have to explain SERRA," he temporized, paying closer attention to the road ahead than it really warranted. "In some ways, they're almost the same entity. Virtually everyone

working for Fairgrove came out of SERRA, and the
president and board of Fairgrove actually helped
found SERRA. Uh, their families did."

Sam was pretending to watch the road, but he was
really watching Tannim out of the corner of his eye.
And that last, about the board founding SERRA, had
been a real slip. Tannim hadn't meant to say that. But
what made it a slip?

"So? What's this SERRA?" he asked.

"South Eastern Road Racing Association," Tannim
replied promptly, and with enthusiasm he didn't try to
conceal. "It's an offshoot of the SCCA — Sports Car
Club of America. Part of the problem for us was that
SCCA doesn't allow the sort of modifications we
wanted, and the folks in SERRA wanted to push the
envelope of sportscar racing a bit more, more
'experimental' stuff. Fairgrove also supports an IMSA
team, running GTP, but that's for pro drivers, guys
who don't do anything but drive, and we've only just
started that circuit. Some of us — like me — still race
SCCA, in fact, I drive for the Fairgrove team. There's
things to like about both clubs, which is why Fairgrove
still maintains a team in both."

"You don't drive in the Fairgrove SERRA team?"
Sam said. Tannim shrugged.

"We've got some drivers as good as I am on the
SERRA team, drivers who can't race SCCA cars. Since I
could do both, I opted for the SCCA team, and left rides
for the other guys." He grinned. "Don't worry, I get
plenty of track time in! If I had the time, I could spend
every weekend and most weekdays racing."

Sam had no doubt that Tannim was a professional
driver in every sense of the word, despite the disclaimer;
the way he handled this car put Sam in mind of an expert fighter pilot, of the way the plane becomes an
extension of the pilot himself, and the pilot can do things
he shouldn't be able to. There was an air of cocky com-

petence about the kid, now that he was behind the wheel, that was very like a good pilot's too.

"That's not cheap, fielding several teams — " Sam ventured.

"Three teams, each with several cars, and no, it isn't cheap," Tannim admitted cheerfully. "The founding families started out independently wealthy — inherited money that survived the '20s crash — but they've been making racing pay for itself for a while now. Not just purses and adverts — they've been farming out their experts — " he grinned again " — like yours truly, and opening up their shops for modifications to whoever was willing to pay the price. But that could only go so far. *Now* we'd like to hit the bigtime. Indy-style, Formula One, that kind of thing. Getting right up there with the big boys — maybe even have the big boys come to us. But to do that, we have to have something better than just mods. We have to have original advances. That's where you come in."

He braked, briefly, and Sam caught the flash of a bird's wings in the headlights. An owl; a big one. Most drivers wouldn't have known it was going to cut across the car's vector. Most drivers wouldn't have bothered to avoid it.

"Maybe," Sam replied, feeling his way. "I don't know; this sounds like it could be very risky business. . . ."

"Your part won't be," Tannim promised. "Fairgrove will pay half your consultation fee up front, before you even pin on a badge, and put the other half in escrow in your bank." Then he named a figure that would have given Sam cardiac trouble, if not for watching his diet and cholesterol. It was considerably more than his salary at Gulfstream had been. Of course, one of the disadvantages of staying with a firm for years was that your salary didn't keep pace with the going rate for new-hires with similar experience, but — this was ridiculous; they couldn't want him that badly! Could they?

"What about disclosure?" he asked, when he could speak again.

"We've got a tentative non-disclosure clause in your contract, but we can modify it if you feel really strongly about it," Tannim said. "We based it on the non-disclosure clause at Gulfstream, but we made one modification, and that's in the area of Research and Development in safety. Anything that's a significant advance in safety is immediately released, and patents won't be enforced. Think you can live with that? Even if it means a loss of income?"

Since that was the one area where Sam had himself had several heated arguments with his own bosses over the years, he nodded. "Some things should be common knowledge," he said grimly. "That's in a Mercedes ad, but it's true for all of that."

He asked many more questions over the course of the next fifteen minutes, and although Tannim never refused to answer any of them, he kept getting the feeling that the young man was doing a kind of verbal dance the whole time — carefully steering him away from something. It wasn't where the money was coming from; at least, this wasn't the kind of youngster or the kind of operation Sam would have associated with money laundering and organized crime. And car-racing wasn't the kind of operation that would lend itself to that sort of thing anyway. It wasn't what he would be expected to accomplish. It was nothing that he was able to put a finger on. But there was some skillful verbal maneuvering going on here, and Sam wished strongly that he could see at least the shape of this blind spot, so he could guess at what it was hiding.

Tannim pulled off the highway onto a beautifully paved side road, and stopped at a formidable gate, punching in a code on the keypad-box just in front of it. The gate-doors retracted —

And just on the other side of the gate, a miniature traffic signal lit up — the yellow light first, then the green, and the radar detector under the dash lit up. Tannim turned toward his passenger with a sparkle in his eye, and a grin that bordered on maniacal. "Did you know that there's no speed limit on private driveways?" he said, conversationally. Then he floored the accelerator.

Once again, it was a good thing that Sam had been watching his diet for years — and that he was well acquainted with "test pilot humor." As it was, by the end of that brief but hair-raising half-mile ride, he wasn't certain if Tannim had *added* years to his age, or subtracted them by peeling them off, with sheer speed as the knife-blade. One thing was sure; if Sam's hair hadn't already been white, the ride would have bleached it to silver.

Tannim pulled up to a tire-screeching halt beside another miniature traffic light. As they passed it, Sam noted — faintly surprised that he still had the ability to notice anything — that going in the opposite direction, the light was red as they passed it. It turned yellow well after they passed, then green a moment later. A wise precaution, if people used the driveway as a dragstrip on a regular basis. A board lit up with numbers, and Tannim laughed out loud. "Elapsed time and speed, Sam." He cocked his head sideways like an exotic bird. "Not my best run, but not bad for nighttime, and with a passenger weighing me down."

They rolled up to a driveway loop at a sedate pace. In the center of the circular cut-out was a discrete redwood sign reading "Fairgrove Industries." The building itself looked like Cape Canaveral before a shuttle launch, with hundreds of lights burning. Evidently these people *were* night owls.

Tannim pulled the Mustang into a parking slot, between a Lamborghini Diablo and a Ferrarri Dino. "Expensive neighbors," Sam commented. Tannim just chuckled, and popped his seatbelt.

He led the way through a series of darkened offices; the clerical staff was evidently not expected to keep the same hours as the techies. The offices themselves gave an overall impression of brisk efficiency with a touch of comedy; although the desks were clean and orderly, there were toys on all the computer terminals and desks, artwork and posters on the walls, and so many plants Sam wondered if someone had raided a greenhouse. Most of the artwork and toys had something to do with cars. These people evidently enjoyed their work. And these were working offices; had been for some time; there was no way you could counterfeit that "lived in, worked in" look. Whatever else Fairgrove was, it *had* been in existence for some time. This was no facade thrown up to delude him.

Tannim brought him to a soundproof wall — Sam recognized it as the twin to one at Gulfstream, that stood between the offices and the shops — and opened a door into bright light and seeming chaos.

There were cars in various states of disassembly everywhere, each one surrounded, like a patient in intensive care, by its own little flotilla of instrumentation and machinery. There was a *lot* of expensive equipment here: computer-controlled diagnostic devices, computer-controlled manufacturing machinery behind the cars on their little islands of activity —

There must have been several million dollars in cars alone, and about that in equipment. Oddly enough, though, no one seemed to be using any of the latter; they all seemed to be working directly on the cars. The machinery itself was standing idle. In fact, given the sheen of "newness" on all that expensive gimmickry, most of it hadn't ever been fired up.

Why buy all that stuff if you weren't going to use it?

Tannim was looking for something, or someone, craning his head in every direction. Sam was unable to get his attention, and really, didn't try very hard. There was definitely something odd about this place. There was a facade — and it was in here, not out in the offices.

Finally, as a little group of people emerged from be-hind one of the cars and its attendant machines, Tannim spotted whoever it was he was looking for among them. He waved his hand in the air, and called out to them.

"Yo!" he shouted, his voice somehow carrying over the din. "Kevin! Over here!"

A tall, *very* blond man turned around in response to that shout, green eyes searching over the mass of machines and people.

And Sam felt such a shock he feared for a moment that he'd had a stroke. Those eyes — that face — they were familiar.

Hauntingly, frighteningly familiar, though he hadn't seen them in nearly fifty years.

He *knew* this man —

— who *wasn't* a man.

● CHAPTER THREE

It was the same face — not a similar face, the *same* face, the same man. Identical. There was no confusing it, nor those green, cat-slitted eyes.

Inhuman eyes; eyes that had *never* been human.

Sam fell back across the decades, to his childhood, and his home, and one moonlit, Irish night.

Sam stumbled along beside his father, miserable right down to his socks, and wanting to be home with all his five-year-old heart.

"Da — me tum hurts," Sam whined.

The full moon above them gave a clear, clean light, shining down on the dirt path that led between the pub and John Kelly's little cottage. A month ago, they wouldn't have been on this path. A month ago, Sam's mummy, Moira, would have made them a good supper, one that wouldn't have hurt Sam's tummy the way the greasy sausage-and-potato mix the pub served up did. In fact, a month ago, John wouldn't have been anywhere near the pub, and the pint of whiskey he had in his back pocket would have lasted him the month, not the night. He would've had tea with his good dinner, not washed bad roast down with more whiskey.

But that was a month and more ago, before Moira took a cough that became worse, and then turned into something awful, something called "new-moan-yuh." Something the doctor couldn't cure, nor all the prayers Sam and his Da had offered up to the Virgin.

She'd taken sick on a Monday. By the following

Monday, they were putting her under the sod, and the priest told him she was with Jesus. Sam didn't understand any of it; he kept thinking it was all a bad dream, and when he woke up, his Mummy would comfort him and everything would be all right again.

But he went to sleep at night, and woke up in the morning, and it wasn't all right. His Da was drinking his breakfast, and leaving Sam to make whatever breakfast he could on cold bread-and-butter and go off to stay with Mrs. Gilhoolie, since he was too young for school. John Kelly was going to work smelling like a bottle, coming home smelling like a bottle, and taking Sam to the pub every night for a bad supper and more bottles.

It was cold out, and Sam had forgotten his coat. "Da," he whined again, knowing that he sounded nasty, but not knowing what else to do to get his Da's attention. "Da, me tum hurts, an' I'm *cold.*" The wind whistled past them, coming around the Mound, and cutting right through Sam's thin shirt and short pants. The Mound was an uncanny place, and Sam didn't like to go there. The Fair Folk were supposed to live there, and they weren't the pretty little fairies in the children's books and the cartoons at the cinema; Sam's granny had told him about the Fair Folk, and she had never, ever lied to him. They were terrible, wonderful creatures, taller than humans, handsome beyond belief, and many were utterly unpredictable. The best a human could do was steer clear of them, for no human could tell whether a man or woman of the Folk was kindly inclined towards humans or dangerous to them. Even when they seemed to be doing you favors, sometimes they were doing you harm, the bad ones. And the good ones sometimes did harm with the idea of doing good.

But right now Sam had more immediate troubles than running into one of the Fair Folk. His tummy hurt, he was so cold his teeth chattered, his head hurt, his Da was acting in peculiar ways—

And oh, but he missed his Mummy —

"Daaaaa," he whined, holding back tears of grief. When his Da said anything about Mummy, it was to tell him to be a man, and not cry. But it was hard not to cry. The only way he could keep from crying, sometimes, was to whine. Like now. "Daaaaaa."

There was no warning, none at all. One moment he was stumbling along beside his Da, the next, he was sprawled on the cold ground beside the path, looking up at his Da in shock, his face and teeth aching from the blow his Da had just landed on him. The moonlight showed the murderous look on his Da's face clearly. Too clearly. Whimpering, with sudden terror, he tried to scramble away.

He wasn't fast enough.

His Da grabbed the front of his shirt and hauled him to his feet, then off his feet, and backhanded him. Sam was in too much shock to even react to the first two slaps, but at the third, he cried out.

There was no fourth.

John had his hand pulled back, ready to deliver another blow. Sam struggled fruitlessly in his father's iron grip, crying —

Then there was a tremendous flash of light; Sam was blinded, and felt himself falling. He flailed his arms wildly, and landed on his back, hard enough to drive the breath out of him.

He wheezed and rubbed his eyes, trying to force them to clear. The sound of someone choking made him look up, squinting through watering eyes, still trying to catch his breath.

What he saw made him forget to breathe.

A tall, terrible blond stranger, dressed in odd clothing, like something out of the pantomimes of King Arthur, was holding his father by the throat. John Kelly was white-faced and shaking, but was not trying to move or fight the stranger. This was no one Sam had seen in or near the village, and anyway, most of the people around here were small and dark, or small and red-haired. Not tall and silver-blond. The man looked down at Sam for a moment, and even though the only light came from the moon overhead, he saw — clearly — that the man had bright, emerald green eyes; eyes that looked just like a cat's. And long, pointed ears.

This was no man. This could only be one of the Fair Folk, the Sidhe; and the fairy-man's eyes caught Sam like a rabbit caught in the headlights of a motorcar.

Sam couldn't move.

John Kelly made another choking noise, and the stranger turned those mesmerizing eyes back towards his captive.

"John Kelly," the terrifying man said — with a gentleness made all the more terrible by his obvious strength. "John Kelly, you're a good man, but you're on the way to a bad end. 'Tis the luck of your God that brought you here tonight, within my reach and my ken, for if you hadn't struck your lad just now, I wouldn't have known of your troubles and your falling into the grip of pain and whiskey. Now get hold of yourself and get your life straight again — for if you don't, I swear to you that we'll steal this lovely boy of yours, and you'll never see him again, this side of paradise. Remember what your mother told you, John Kelly. Remember it well, and believe it. We did it once within your family, and we can and will do it again, if the need comes to it."

There was another flash of light. When Sam could see, the man was gone, and his father was sinking slowly to his knees. Sam still couldn't move, numb with shock and awe, and feelings he couldn't put a name to.

For a long, long time, John Kelly lay in the dirt, his shoulders shaking. Then, after a while, John looked up, and Sam saw tears running down his Da's face, glistening in the moonlight.

"Da?" he whispered, tentatively. "Da?"

"Son — " John choked — and gathered Sam into his arms, holding him closely, just the way he used to. Sobbing. Somehow that made Sam feel both good and bad. Good, that his Da was the man he loved again. Bad, that his Da was crying.

"Da?" Sam said again. "Da, what's the matter? Da?"

"Sam — son — " John Kelly wept unashamed. "Son, I've been wicked, I've been blind with pain, and I've been wicked. Forgive me, son. Oh, please, forgive me — "

Sam hadn't been sure what to say or do, but he'd given his father what he asked for. Forgiveness, and all the love and comfort he had.

Eventually, John Kelly had gathered his son up in his arms, and taken him home. And from that day until the day he died, he never touched another drop of alcohol.

It can't be — he thought dazedly, from the perspective of half a century away. *It can't be* —

Despite the Sight, he'd assumed for decades that the whole incident had been a dream, something his childish imagination had conjured up to explain his father's brief, alcoholic binge and his recovery.

He'd only been five, after all. But this, this tall, blond man striding toward them was the same, the very same person as that long-ago stranger. No matter that the long hair was pulled back into a thick pony-tail, not flowing free beneath a circling band of silver about the brow. No matter that the clothing was a form-fitting black coverall, incongruously embroidered with "Kevin" over the breast pocket, and not the tunic and trews of a man of the ancient Celts. There was no mistake.

Sam knew then that he must be going mad. It was an easier explanation than the one that fit the situation.

The man strode towards them with all the power and grace of a lean, black panther in its prime. As he neared them, he smiled; a warm smile that reached even into those emerald eyes and made them shine. "You've grown into a fine man, Sam Kelly," he said, stopping just short of them, and resting his fists on his hips. "A fine man, like your father John, and smarter than your father, to wash your hands of a dying land and seek your life on this side of the water. Now you know why we chose you, and no other."

"I see you've met," Tannim said, with an ironic lift of an eyebrow.

This man, this "Kevin" — he hadn't aged a day since Sam saw him fifty years ago. He'd looked thirty or forty then, which would make him what? Ninety? A hundred?

Either he had discovered the fountain of youth, or —

"You —" Sam said, finally getting his mouth to work. "You're — "

"One of the Fair Folk?" Keighvin said, with a lop-sided smile, and a lifted brow that echoed Tannim's. "The Lords of Underhill? The Kindly Ones? The Old People? The Elves, the Fairies, the Sidhe?" He chuckled. "I'm glad to see you still remember the old ways, the old tales, Sam. And, despite all your university learning, you believe them too, or at least, you're willing to believe them, if I read your heart aright."

In the face of a living breathing tale out of his own childhood, how could he not believe? Even when it was impossible? He had to believe in the Sidhe, or believe that someone had read his mind, picked that incident out of his childhood, and constructed someone who looked *exactly* like the Sidhe-warrior, and fed him all the pertinent details.

It was easier and simpler to believe in the Sidhe — the Wise Ones who had stolen away his granny's brother, because great-grandfather had beaten him once too often, for things he could not help. He remembered his granny's tales of that, too, for Patrick had been granny's favorite brother, and she'd told the story over and over. Poor Patrick; from the vantage point of near seventy-five years Sam knew what Patrick's problem had been, and it hadn't been willfulness or clumsiness. They'd have called him "dyslexic," these days, and given him special teaching to compensate. . . .

"We helped him," Keighvin said, as if reading his mind again. "We helped him, and sent him over the sea to this new land, and our kin here in Elfhame Fairgrove. He prospered, married a mortal girl, raised a family. Remind me to introduce you to your cousins, one day."

"Cousins?" Sam said, faintly. "I think I need to sit down."

". . . so, that was when the Fairgrove elvenkin got interested in racing," Tannim said, as Sam held tight to his cup of coffee, and Keighvin nodded from time to time. Sam sat on an overturned bucket, Tannim perched like a gargoyle on top of an aluminum cabinet, and Keighvin leaned against one of the sleek, sensuous racecars. Now that there was no need to counterfeit the noise of a real metal shop, things were much quieter, though there was no less activity. "Now roughly a fourth of the SERRA members are either elves or human mages. At first it was mostly for enjoyment. The Fairgrove elves in particular got interested in the idea of using racing to get some of their members out into the human world, the way things used to be in the old days."

"Aye," Keighvin seconded, leaning back against a shining, black fender, and patting it absent-mindedly, as if it was a horse. "In the old days, it could be you'd have met one of the Sidhe at any crossroads, looking for a challenge. You'd have found a kelpie at every ford — and on moonlit nights, the woods and meadows would be thick with dancing parties. Plenty of the Sidhe like humans, Sam; you give us a stimulus we sorely need. It was Cold Iron that drove us Underhill, Sam, and Cold Iron that drove us away, across the sea. It's deadly to us, as your granny doubtless told you."

"But—" Sam protested, gesturing with his coffee cup. "What about—that? You're leaning against Cold Iron."

Keighvin grinned, white teeth gleaming in a way that reminded Sam sharply that the man was no human. "That I'm not." He moved away from the car, and the car — twisted.

It writhed like something out of a drug-dream. Sam had to close his eyes for a moment; when he opened them, there was no car there at all, but a sleek, black horse, with wicked silver eyes. It winked at him, and stamped a delicate hoof on the concrete. Sparks struck and died.

"An elvensteed," Tannim said, with a chuckle. "That's how the pointy-eared smartasses got into racing in the first place. They transformed the elvensteeds into things that looked like cars, at least on the outside. But once club racing started having *inspections*—"

"I'd have found it damned difficult to explain a racecar with no motor," Keighvin supplied, as the elvensteed nuzzled his shoulder. "Rosaleen Dhu can counterfeit most things, including all the right noises for an engine to make, but not the engine itself. Only something that looks superficially like an engine."

Black Rose. She's beautiful. . . .

Tannim gestured at the lovely creature with his chin. "And *that's* how Fairgrove is setting the pace in aerodynamics, too. Put an elvensteed in a wind-tunnel, and alter the design by telling it what you want. No weeks of making body-bucks and laying fiberglass." Tannim gloated, and Sam didn't blame him. This was better even than computer modeling.

"But — you're still racing now, with a real team — " Sam protested. "With real cars — real engines — "

"With every part we can manage being replaced with nonferrous materials," Tannim told him. "That's what we started doing even before the inspections. It was no challenge to race an elvensteed that can reach half the speed of sound against Tin Lizzies. It *was* a challenge to try and improve on human technology."

Keighvin held up his hands, and only then did Sam notice he was wearing thin leather gloves, black to match his coverall. Sam also noted a black web belt and a delicate silver-and-silk-sheathed knife, more decorative than a tool. "And for those things that can't be replaced by something other than iron and steel, well, some of us have built up a kind of tolerance to Death Metal. Enough that we can handle it if we're protected — and we try not to work much magic about it." He patted the horse's neck. "I'll explain the Laws of it all to you later — and how we're breaking them."

Tannim jumped down off the cabinet, catching Sam's eye, and began pacing. Sam suspected he needed to ease an ache in that bad leg. "Racing and building cars was what lured the elvenkin out from Underhill," he said. "But racing wasn't the real reason that some of the elves wanted more of their company out in the human world, and to be more active in it."

"Some didn't approve — " Keighvin said.

"But most of Fairgrove did," Tannim interjected. "And now we have to get into some old history. That's Keighvin's subject."

The horse had turned back into a car again while Sam had been watching Tannim; Keighvin leaned back against its fender (flank?) and folded his arms.

"Do you have any idea why I confronted your father that night, Sam Kelly?" Keighvin asked. "Or what I was talking about, with your great-uncle and all?"

Sam blurted the first thing that came into his head. "The Fair Folk steal children — everybody knows that — "

A moment later he wanted to go hit his head against a wall. *Now you're for it, Sam Kelly. Why not go into a gay gym and tell the boys there that you've heard they seduce six-year-olds?*

But strangely, Keighvin didn't look the least bit angry. "Aye, Sam, we steal children. The Seleighe Court does, at any rate. To save them. Children bein' beaten within an inch of their lives, children bein' left cold and hungry and tied t' the bedpost all day, children bein' sold and slaved.... Oh aye, we steal children. Whenever we can, whenever we know of one in danger of losing life or soul, or heart, and we can get *at* them, aye, we steal them." Keighvin's expression was dark, brooding. "We used to do other things, too. There are some problems, Sam, that can be fixed by throwing money at them, as you yourself were thinking earlier. Not all of those problems are technical, either. Do you mind some of the other stories your granny used to tell? About the leprechauns, or the mysterious strangers who gave gold where it was most needed?"

"Aye," Sam replied, again falling into the brogue of his childhood, to match the lilt of Keighvin's speech. "But those strangers were the holy saints, or angels in disguise, sent from the Virgin, she said — "

Keighvin snorted. "Holy saints? Is that what you mortal folk decided? Nay, Sam, 'twas us. At least, it was us when there were hungry children to feed, and naught to feed them with; when there was no fuel in the house, and children freezing. When some mortal fool sires children, but won't be a father to them, leaving the mother to struggle alone. Our kind — we don't bear as easily or often as you. Children are rare and precious things to us. We're impelled to protect and care for them, even when they aren't our own."

Suddenly a great many of the old stories took on a whole new set of meanings.... But Keighvin was continuing.

"This isn't the old days, though, when a stranger could give a poor lass a handful of silver and gold in return for a kindness. For one thing, the girl would be thought a thief, like as not, when she tried to trade it for paper money. For another, someone would want to track down whoever gave it to her. We have to truly, legitimately, *earn* money before we can give it away."

Tannim shook his head in mock sadness. "Oh, now

that's a real pity, isn't it — you elves having to *work* for a living. What's the world coming to?"

Keighvin cast the young man a sharp glance. "One of these days, my lad, that tongue of yours is going to cast you into grief."

Tannim chuckled, uncowed by the fire in Keighvin's eye. "You're too late, it already has." He turned to Sam. "These boys can literally create anything, if they've studied it long enough beforehand. We've been making foamed aluminum engine blocks ever since Keighvin here got his hands on a sample from a Space Shuttle experiment." He hopped back up onto his cabinet, crossing his legs like a Red Indian. "I'm not even going into how we got that. But, we've been using the stuff in our cars — now, can you imagine what we could charge some of the big boys to duplicate *their* designs in foamed cast aluminum?"

Indeed, Sam could. And the major racing teams had a great deal of money to play with. "So that's why you set up this shop, Fairgrove Industries — but what do you need me for?"

"We need a front-man," Tannim said, leaning forward in his eagerness to explain himself. "We need someone who can give a convincing explanation of how we're doing all this, and show us how to create a setup that will at least look like we're making the things by some esoteric process and not by magic."

"But there isn't any process — " Sam began. "There isn't a firm in the world that could duplicate — "

Tannim waved a negatory hand in the air.

"It doesn't matter if no one else can duplicate what we do," he said blithely. "They'll expect us to have trade secrets. We just need someone who knows all the right techno-babble, and can make it sound convincing. As long as you can come up with something that's possible in theory, that's all we need. We'll keep on buying machines that go *bing*, and you leak tech reports to the curious."

Sam couldn't help himself; he started to laugh. Tannim and Keighvin both looked confused and surprised. "What's so funny?" Tannim asked.

"Do you know much science fiction?" he asked, through his chuckles. Keighvin shook his head. Tannim shrugged. "A little. Why?"

"Because a very famous author, Arthur C. Clarke — who also happens to be a one of the world's finest scientists and engineers — said once that technology that's complicated enough can't be told from magic."

"So?" Tannim replied.

Sam started laughing again. "So — sufficiently complex magic is indistinguishable from technology!"

Keighvin looked at Tannim for an explanation; the latter shrugged. "Beats me," the young man said with a lopsided smile, as Sam wheezed with laughter. "Sometimes I don't understand us either."

It was nearly midnight when they'd gotten the basic shape of a plan hammered out. By then, they'd moved into Keighvin's office — a wonderful place with a huge, plate-glass window that looked out into what seemed to be an absolutely virgin glade. The office itself was designed to be an extension of the landscape outside, with plants standing and hanging everywhere, and even a tiny fountain with goldfish swimming in it.

"Well, I'm going to have to go home and sleep on this," Sam said, finally. "Then get into some of the journals and see what kind of a convincing fake I can concoct before I can definitely say I'll take the job."

He started to get up, but Keighvin waved him down again. "Not quite yet, Sam," he said, his expression grave. "There's just one thing more we need to tell you about. And you may decide not to throw in your lot with us after you've heard it."

"Why?" he asked, a little surprised.

"Because Fairgrove has enemies," Tannim supplied, from his own nook, surrounded by ferns. "Not

'Fairgrove Industries.' I mean Elfhame Fairgrove, the Underhill Seleighe community here." He leaned back a little. "Keighvin, I think the ball's in your — ah — 'court.' So to speak."

Keighvin didn't smile. "Sam, how much did your granny ever tell you about the Seleighe and Unseleighe Court elves?"

Sam had to think hard about that. Granny had died when he was barely ten; fifty-five years was a long time. And yet, her stories had been extraordinarily vivid, and had left him with lasting impressions.

"Mostly, she told stories with — I guess you'd say — good elves and bad elves. Elves who wanted to help humans, at least, and elves who wanted only to hurt them. She said you really couldn't tell them apart, if you were a human child — that even human adults could be easily misled, and that sometimes even the good elves didn't know who was good and who was bad. She said the Unseleighe Court even had agents in the Seleighe Court. She just warned me to steer clear of both if I ever met either kind, until I was old enough to defend myself, and could tell a glib lie from the truth."

Keighvin nodded, his hair beginning to escape from the pony-tail. "Good enough. And that fairly sums it up. There's the Seleighe Court — that's us, and things like elvensteeds and dryads, selkies, pukas, owls, things that can pass as humans and things that never could. Oh, and there's creatures native to this side of the water that have allied themselves with the Seleighe Court as well. And for the most part, the very worst one of us wishes is that the humans would go away." The Sidhe looked out into the forest beyond the glass, but Sam had the feeling he was seeing something else entirely. "For the most part, we're interested in coexisting with your kind, even if it forces us to have to change. Many of us are interested in helping your kind. We have the power of magic, but you have the twin powers of technology and numbers. One on one — you humans are

no match for us. But population against population —
we've lost before we even start."

"All right," Sam agreed. "I can see that. What about
the Unseleighe Court?"

"They hate you, one and all," Keighvin replied,
somberly. "There are elves among them; and many,
many things straight out of your worst childhood
nightmares: bane-sidhe, boggles, trolls, things you've
never heard of. The Morrigan is their Queen, and a
terrible creature she is; she hates all things living, even
her own people." His eyes darkened with what looked
to Sam like a distant echo of pain. "They hate us, too,
for wanting to coexist with you; they're constantly at
war with us. They want you gone, and they're active in
fostering anything that kills you off. If you run across a
human conflict that seems senseless, often as not, they
have a hand in it. Not that you humans aren't adept at
creating misery for yourselves, but the Unseleighe
Court has a vested interest in fostering that misery, and
in propagating it. And they don't like the idea that
Fairgrove is a little further along the path of easing
some of it."

"All right so far," Sam said, a little puzzled, "but
what's that got to do with me?"

"We have agents in their ranks, just as they have
agents in ours," Keighvin told him. "We've gotten
word that some of their lot that can pass as human have
found out what we're planning, and are going to try to
expose us as frauds."

"It'll be Preston Tucker all over again," Tannim put
in, his own expression grim. "Without someone with a
spotless reputation fronting for us, they can do it, too.
They can claim we've stolen our samples, that the engine blocks aren't what we say they are, and that we
have no real intention of manufacturing the products.
It's happened enough times in this industry that
people are likely to believe it — especially with a bit of
glamorie behind their words and a strong publicity

campaign. Your actions will be the saving of us — as Keighvin's was of you and your father."

"No one's ever heard of us, except as a racing team," Keighvin said, leaning forward in his chair, giving Sam all of his attention. "But they know you. Your reputation can give us the time we need to actually build a few customers. Once we have that, it won't matter what they say. They'll have to come after us some other way. But there's the danger. They will. And not only us, but you."

Oddly enough, the threat to himself didn't bother Sam. In fact, if anything, it added a little spice to the prospect. Terrorists and fanatics who threatened folk just because they were American frightened him; there was no predicting people like that, and there was something cold and impersonal about their enmity. Give him a real, honest enemy every time. You knew where you stood with a real enemy; you knew whose side you were on. After all, hating a country takes away its faces, but hating someone because of what he did was something he could get a grip on.

"To tell you the truth," Tannim put in, "I'd have been a lot more worried before I saw how you've got your home defenses rigged. Even a creature with magic is going to have trouble passing them. And once I add my two cents' worth, I think you'll be in fairly good shape to hold them off if you have to."

"Your two cents' worth?" Sam asked quizzically. Tannim grinned and shrugged — and Sam remembered the odd protections around the car. This Tannim might not be one of the Fair Folk, but there was no doubt he held his own in their company.

More of Sam's granny's lore was coming back to him. There was, surprisingly, a lot of it. And the things he remembered about the Unseleighe Court were unpleasant indeed, especially when it occurred to him that she had undoubtedly toned things down for his young ears. Now he wondered how much she hadn't told him, and how important that information was.

And where she had gotten it from. The "missing" brother, perhaps? He made a mental note to ask Keighvin about that some time.

Still — here was a chance to see things very few other humans had seen. A chance to be useful again. He'd retired only because he'd had no choice. He had enjoyed the first few weeks of his vacation, but truth to tell, he was getting bored. There were only so many things he could do to improve the house. He hated fishing. He could only watch so much television before feeling the urge to throw something at the tube.

"All right," he said. "I'll do it. Full speed ahead, and damn the torpedoes. You've got your man."

The little that remained of the evening passed in a blur. Tannim took him home again—and this time did not treat him to a mini-race on the driveway. Neither of them said much, except to set a dinner meeting for that evening — since it was already "tomorrow," being well past midnight.

Tannim waited until he was safely sealed inside his little fortress before driving off; he wasn't certain if that was a wise precaution, or real paranoia. Surely the Unseleighe Court denizens wouldn't already know he'd agreed to help Fairgrove?

Then again, this was magic he was dealing with; as unknown in its potentials as a new technology. Maybe they could know.

Thoreau was lying beside the door, patiently but obviously waiting for his promised treat. Sam headed for the kitchen and dished out a tiny portion of canned food. Thoreau didn't need extra pounds any more than a human did, and these late-night snacks were the only time he got canned food. The rest of the time, he had to make do with dry.

Thoreau was one of the more interesting dogs Sam had ever owned. Instead of greedily gobbling down his treat, he ate it slowly, licking it like a child trying to make an ice-cream cone last. Sam left him to it and went to his library in the office, but didn't immediately pull down some of the reference materials he'd mentally selected.

Instead, he sat with hands idly clasped on the desk for a long moment, wondering if, when he did go to bed, he'd wake up in the morning to find that all this had been a dream.

Something crackled in his jacket pocket as he took it off, and he found the envelope with the check in it still in his breast pocket.

"All right," he said to Thoreau, as the dog padded into the study, licking his chops with satisfaction. "Maybe it is a dream. Maybe there are fairy checks as well as fairy gold. But it's here now." He planted the envelope under his favorite paperweight, a bronze replica of the Space Shuttle Challenger. "If it's gone in the morning, I'll know it was a dream. But for now, all we can do is try. Eh, Thoreau?"

Thoreau wagged his stub of a tail in agreement, and put his head down on his paws as Sam got up and began pulling books and bound magazines down off the shelf. He'd seen this before. He knew it was going to be a long night.

● CHAPTER FOUR

The Mustang purred happily as Tannim drove into Sam's driveway. There were times, especially lately, when Tannim wondered if maybe he hadn't instilled a little *too* much magic into the car. Or maybe he'd planted something else besides pure Power. Lately it had seemed as if the Mach 1 was almost — sentient. It certainly seemed to approve of Sam Kelly; there was a warmth to the engine's purr that hadn't been there before he turned into the drive, and the car had embraced Sam as if he belonged inside it.

Well, for that matter, Tannim approved of Sam Kelly. He was a smart, tough old bird, and too good to waste on retirement. Now, as long as he and Keighvin hadn't gotten the old man into more danger than any of them could handle. . . . His conscience bothered him a bit over that. Sam had brains and savvy, but what if he needed that and a younger man's reflexes as well?

He was taking Sam to dinner, after a couple of drinks at Kevin Barry's Pub in Savannah, on River Street. There were several Irish pubs in the area, but Kevin Barry's was the one Tannim preferred. He had the feeling that Sam would feel more at home, easier, in an atmosphere that reminded him of Ireland and all it meant.

He'd chosen a dinner meeting rather than a return to Fairgrove for a very good reason; he wanted Sam's first dose of Keighvin Silverhair to wear off before they talked again. Keighvin's formidable personality had been known to overwhelm far stronger personalities than Sam's, even without a glamorie at work.

Not that Keighvin would have used a glamorie on Sam Kelly. They wanted a willing ally, with all his faculties in working order, not a bemused dreamer.

Tannim wasn't entirely certain how old Keighvin was; certainly at least a thousand. That much living produced personalities that could easily bowl the unsuspecting over. If Sam was having second thoughts, Tannim wanted to know about it without Keighvin around to influence him.

The pub itself, however, was a good place to talk to Sam. The atmosphere, so strongly Celtic, should put Sam in the state of mind to remember and Believe, even though he was going to be completely in the "real world."

And there was no more "real world" a clientele than the bunch that frequented Kevin Barry's. Students from SCAD, business people, locals, artists, holdover hippies, folkies — you name it, and you would probably see it in Kevin Barry's. Except maybe yuppies; the place wasn't trendy enough for them.

Not enough ferns, or drinks with clever names and inflated prices. And no selection of forty-five mineral waters.

Sam must have been watching for him, for he was locking up even as Tannim arrived. He opened the passenger's side door and slid in beside Tannim as soon as the Mach 1 came to a full stop. He was amazingly fit for a sixty-five-year-old man; he looked as if he'd been getting lots of regular exercise and watching his diet — his build was a lot like Jacques Cousteau's, in fact, who at sixty-five had still been leading his own underwater expeditions. Maybe Tannim didn't need to worry quite so much about him after all.

"Am I in for any more impromptu racing today?" Sam asked, with a twinkle, as Tannim pulled out again. And there was no doubt of it; the Mustang was truly purring with satisfaction, a note in its engine he'd never heard before. The Mach 1 liked Sam.

Too bad I can't ever find a lover it likes that much, he

thought ironically. *Of course, if I do, she'll probably like the car better than me. I can see it now — my girl and my car, taking off into the sunset without me.*

"No, no racing today," he said, with a chuckle. "I'm taking you into Savannah. I had the feeling you probably haven't been downtown in a while."

Sam nodded. "Not for years," he admitted. "Never had a reason to. And to tell you the truth, I spent most of my time at Gulfstream. There wasn't much of anything I wanted to go downtown for."

"I may be able to change your mind," Tannim replied. "So, how are you feeling about our offer in the cold light of day?"

"Well — the check didn't disappear, or turn into a handful of leaves when morning arrived," Sam replied after a moment. "And my bank was perfectly happy to have it. I wasn't entirely sure it would still be there when I woke up this morning, and that's a fact. I was half convinced I must have dreamed the whole thing. Especially that car-horse-car."

"I don't blame you." Tannim chuckled, watching Sam out of the corner of his eye. "I know how I felt the first time I saw anyone working real magic."

There. The word was out in the open. Sam hadn't flinched from it, either.

"Magic," the old man mused. "The Sidhe, and magic. Maybe I've come into my second childhood, but — I think I could come to appreciate all this." He tilted his head to the side. "So, what happened the first time *you* saw magic at work?"

Tannim laughed. "I freaked. For the first few minutes, I thought someone had slipped me recreational pharmaceuticals without my noticing. Then, once I figured out that everything I saw was real, I just hoped that whoever was duking it out didn't notice *me*. I was — oh, sixteen or so — and I kind of got caught on the sidelines of a magic duel." He waited to see the effect of that revelation on Sam.

"Fair Folk?" Sam asked after a moment. "A duel between elves?"

Tannim shook his head. "No. A witch and a sorceress. The witch was the good guy — or rather, gal. I didn't know who the bad guy was, or that it *was* a female at the time. I was just glad the witch had a good sense of ethics and was trying to keep the mayhem to a minimum where the audience was concerned."

"A witch and a sorceress? Aren't they the same thing?" Sam asked, in a genuinely puzzled tone.

Again, Tannim shook his head. "Trust me, there's a difference between the two. The reason it was dangerous was because although the witch was being careful about innocent bystanders, the sorceress wasn't. And, like I said, in this case, the witch was the good guy. There's a lot of parallels between the Seleighe and Unseleighe Courts there."

Sam nodded thoughtfully, but made no further comments for a moment. By that time, they had reached Savannah proper, and the infamous brickwork streets. Quaint and picturesque, but hell to drive on.

They got a bit of relief at a stoplight. Tannim's leg ached distantly, from hip to ankle. "I keep forgetting about these damn streets," he remarked to Sam, who nodded.

"I remember now," Sam responded. "This was one of the reasons I avoided coming downtown. There wasn't anything down here that was worth having to drive this, and the cobblestones are worse."

Tannim sighed. "I guess it's because I like River Street so much I sort of forget what it takes to get there. I'm sure the tourists like this — but I swear, I know I'm going to have to put the car up and do an alignment when I get home."

"It's the tight suspension, I'd wager," Sam said through clenched teeth. "Makes you wish you had a Lincoln or a Caddy."

Tannim laughed. "Maybe I'll remember this next time I come here, and rent one!"

The Mustang coughed as though its carburetor had stuck, then settled once Tannim patted the dash.

Some things never change, Sam thought, as he watched a trio of black-clad art students walk by in the shade of the old, Spanish-moss-bedecked oaks. There seemed to be an unwritten rule that young artists had to wear black and act morose at least twelve hours out of every day. He'd seen that sort of thing, in a different way, with the Gulfstream engineers, who thought that if they wore blue cotton shirts, club ties, and Cross pens, they would be taken for Brain Trust. Sam had never been able to take that kind of thing seriously after watching a PBS documentary about mimicry in moths.

The art students were a constant source of amusement and amazement for the locals, but the kids always meant well. It tickled Sam that their school was slowly buying out the entire downtown, building by building. "Are those ninjas, or performance artists?" Tannim chuckled, nodding at a duo in black *gis* and black, absurdly baggy pants, like rappers wore on MTV. They lounged beneath a wrought-iron balcony that was old when their great-grandparents were their age. They reminded Tannim of similar sights in New Orleans, and the mix of cultures and ambience there.

"Poster kids for mousse abuse," Sam replied solemnly. "Ninjas would have better taste."

"Geez, you could hide aircraft in those pants," Tannim commented, after a second look. "Better keep them away from Gulfstream, Sam. Some of your planes might mistake them for hangars."

A blue-haired old lady under the trees of one of the dozens of tiny park squares nagged at her husband as the balding man focused his camera on a building across the street. "Wait until the kids are in the *picture,* George," she shrilled. "I want a picture with *art kids* in it. This is where the *art school* is, I want *art kids* in the picture."

The old man just grunted and made minute adjustments of the focus. The art students just ignored it all and continued drifting along in front of the boutique windows, expressions of studied *angst* decorating their young faces.

"Maybe he can't hear her," Tannim suggested. "His shorts are drowning her out." Indeed, the man was wearing possibly the most obscene pair of Bermudas Sam had ever experienced; an appalling print in cerise and chartreuse. He and his wife were completely unaware of the team of video students behind them — taping every move *they* made. Sam nearly died, choking down laughter.

They found themselves creeping along at five miles an hour, stuck behind one of the horse-drawn sightseers carriages. Tannim put up with it for a little, but finally muttered something under his breath and turned off their street at the next light, leaving the coveys of tourists and micro-herds of art students behind. After about a mile, Sam noticed they had left the glass-front boutiques and hole-in-the-wall shops behind as well. The buildings were neglected, now; paint cracked and peeling, windows broken and patched with tape and cardboard, yards full of weeds. The cars here were in the same shape as the houses. There weren't many businesses; what few there were had grates over the windows and rusted bars on the doors.

Sam would not have wanted to break down here, and now he recalled another reason for not visiting downtown. River Street was flanked by two bad neighborhoods. Even in daylight, Sam would not have wanted to be alone out here. The sullen expressions of the toughs lounging on the corners were not feigned or practiced, and their cold, dead eyes gave Sam the chills. He kept his eyes on the dashboard, and Tannim was uncharacteristically silent.

Finally the young man broke the silence. "This neighborhood's economy isn't depressed," he said grimly, "it's suicidal."

They turned another corner and drove for about half a mile, with the buildings slowly improving again. Finally they turned onto River Street itself, and as they hit the cobblestones and the punishment really began, Sam felt able to take his eyes off the dashboard. That was when he found that the dubious sorts weren't limited to the bad neighborhoods, either; there was a cluster of kids in front of a shop with a "for rent" sign in the window, and from the look of them, they were exchanging money for drugs. Sam watched the loitering toughs out of the corner of his eye, and remembered that this was yet another reason why he had avoided the downtown area in general. He certainly wouldn't want to come here alone at night, and maybe not even with someone. He knew he was tougher than he looked — yes, and a lot sprier than he let on — but he was no match for a street-gang.

And he was smart enough to know it.

A cop car rumbled down one of the cobblestone ramps from the street above River, and the gang evaporated, vanishing into the covered alleyways behind the River Street stores.

Well, maybe it wouldn't be so dangerous. The cops were certainly a presence. And then, again, there were a number of Irish pubs around here, and a lot of Irish on the street as well — the ones without the bags and cameras and look of tourists. If he *did* happen to find himself in trouble, it could be there'd be more help here than he first reckoned.

Tannim pulled into a parking place so abruptly that Sam was taken by surprise; cutting in right under the fender of a departing vehicle, and neatly getting the Mustang worked into the slot so quickly it seemed as magical as the car-horse. As the young man shut the engine off, he turned to grin at Sam. "You've got to be quick around here," he said. "Parking places go fast, and the god of parking has a short attention span."

To his surprise, since Tannim hadn't mentioned specifically where they were going, the young man led the way into one of those Irish pubs Sam had been eyeing. And to Sam's great delight, once inside, the place proved to be real Irish, not "tourist" Irish. It looked — and felt — homey and lived-in. There was a small stage in the restaurant section, against one wall, with a folk-group setting up on it, whose instrumental mix Sam also noted with approval. He liked mixing the old with the new, although one could do some quite amazing things with traditional instruments. One of his most cherished memories was of being in a club in Tennessee and hearing the Battlefield Band performing "Stairway to Heaven" on the bagpipes. . . .

Still, although *he* was prepared to spend several delightful hours here, this did not look like the kind of place that would suit his companion. Young Tannim looked as if he'd never encountered an acoustic guitar in his life; a rock'n'roller to the core. The Clannad tape notwithstanding, he couldn't imagine Tannim caring for any music that didn't come with amps and megawattage. It was to Sam's considerable astonishment that the lady bartender greeted his escort by name, and asked if he wanted "his usual table." At Tannim's nod, the lady waved them on, telling them that "Julie" would be with them in a minute.

As Sam took his place across from Tannim, he realized that, once again, he was going to have to realign all his previous ideas about the lad. And that was a discovery just as pleasant as the existence of this pub.

"Well," Tannim said, when the waitress had brought them both drinks, "ready for a little more business?"

Another surprise for Sam — not the question, but the drink. Tannim had stuck to pure cola. He was young enough to take delight in drinking because he could. Interesting.

"I think so," Sam replied cautiously. "You gave me a lot of information last night, but it was all in pieces. I'd like more of a whole picture."

"Fine," Tannim said agreeably. "Where would you like me to start?"

"With magic." Sam took a deep breath. "Just what is it? How does it work? What can you do with it — and what's it got to do with racing — "

Tannim held up a hand. "The discipline people call 'magic' is a way of describing an inborn talent that's been trained. It has rules, and it obeys the laws of physics. It uses the energy produced by all living things; it also uses the energy of magnetic fields, of sunlight, and a lot of other sources. It's a tool, a way of manipulating energies; that's the first thing you have to remember. It's not good *or* bad, it just *is*. Like, I can use a crowbar to bash your head in, or to pry a victim out of a wreck." He shrugged. "It's a tool; just a tool and nothing more. Some people have the skill to use the tool, some don't."

Sam nodded, since Tannim looked as if he was waiting for a response. "But — how does it work? And who has it? Can anyone work it if they've got the knowledge?"

Tannim chuckled. "Hard to describe, Sam. First of all, you have to be able to see the energies in the first place, or at least know that they're there. That's the key; if you can see them, you can learn to manipulate them with magic — which is basically a way of making your own will into that tool to manipulate energy." He licked his lips. "Here's where it gets complicated. If you've trained your will well enough, you can still use the energies without seeing them. Everyone could use some kind of magic, if they had the training — but most folks never come in touch with what they can use. Know anything more now than you did before I said that?"

Sam shook his head, ruefully. "Well . . . no. Not really. But I can believe in plasma physics without knowing exactly how *it* works. I suppose I can believe in magic too. So long as it follows rules."

"That's the spirit!" Tannim applauded. "Now, what Keighvin won't tell you, because like most elves, he's an arrogant sonuvabanshee, is that humans were applying magic to cars before the elves thought of it. A lot of times they didn't realize that was what they were doing, but a lot of times they knew *exactly* what they were doing, especially on the racing circuit. So when the elves came on the scene, they got a bit of a shock, because there were humans out there already, using magicked cars. That's when they decided it might be a good idea to try and join up with some of those humans." He spread his hands. "Voila — SERRA was born."

"But why racing?" Sam asked, still bewildered. "For the Sidhe, I mean. It seems so — foreign to what they are."

"Boredom," Tannim replied succinctly, tracing little patterns on the wooden tabletop with his finger. "They live — if not forever, damn near. But here's something else they won't tell you. The one thing they lack is *creativity*, as near as I can figure. Every bit of their culture, with the sole exception of who and what they worship, comes from humans." He looked up through his lashes, as if he were sharing a secret. "They can replicate what we do, and even improve on it, but I've never once seen one of them come up with something new and original. So they depend on us to bring new things to their culture; as far as I can tell, that's always been the case. They were bored, and racing gave them a chance to bring back some excitement to their lives, like the old combat-challenges used to give them. Brought them that element of risk back — " his face sobered " — 'cause, Sam, if you mess up on the track, sometimes it's permanent, and sometimes it's terminal."

Sam wondered if Tannim's game leg was evidence of the boy's own brush with just that.

"But they won't admit it, even if you confront 'em,"

Tannim said, with a crooked smile, making a figure eight. "That's the real reason they got into racing though, I promise you. Now as to why Keighvin took it farther, to where Fairgrove is trying to make mundane money — he's not lying, he wants to have that kind of mundane cash to kind of fix things for kids. I've got a hunch he wants to set up some safe-houses for abused kids that we can't take Underhill, starting here in Savannah. All elves have this thing about kids; Keighvin has it harder than most. If he could save every kid in the world from pain, hunger, fear — he'd do it. But he can't do it magically, not anymore." Tannim made a complex symbol that looked suspiciously like a baseball diamond. "For one thing, there's too much Cold Iron around for his magics to work down here in the cities."

"Huh." Sam nodded, but he had reservations. Not that he hadn't heard about all the supposed abused kids, on everything from Oprah to prime-time TV dramas, but he wasn't sure he believed the stories. Kids made things up, when they thought they were in for deserved punishment. Hell, one of the young guys at work had shown up with a story about his kid getting into something he was told to leave alone in a store, breaking it, then launching into screams of "don't beat me, Mommy!" when the mother descended like a fury. Embarrassed the blazes out of her, especially since the worst she'd ever delivered in the kid's life was a couple of smacks on the bottom. Turned out the brat had seen a dramatized crime-recreation show the night before, with an abused-kid episode. Sam was beginning to think that a lot of those "beaten kids" had seen similar shows, then had been coached by attorneys, "child advocates," or the "non-abusing spouse." Wasn't that how the Salem witch-trials had happened, anyway? A bunch of kids getting back at the adults they didn't like?

As for the runaways — they'd had a solution for that back when he was a kid. Truant officers with the power to confine a kid, and reform school for the kids that

couldn't toe the line at home. Maybe that's what they
needed these days, not "safe-houses."

But just as he was about to say that, he took a second,
harder look at Tannim, and thought back about what
Keighvin had said. Tannim might be almost a kid himself, but he didn't look as if he was easily tricked. And
Keighvin had known what was happening to Sam —
and presumably Sam's great-uncle — by supernatural
means. It wasn't likely that *they* were being tricked. . . .

They, the elves, had been right about Sam's great-
uncle. And who could say what might have happened
if Keighvin hadn't intervened that night, so long ago.
Would John Kelly have come to his senses before he'd
done more than frighten Sam? Or would the beatings
have continued, getting worse with every incident,
until Sam turned into a sullen, trouble-making creature like Jack McGee, with his hand against every man
alive, and every man's hand against him? Jack's father
was the mainstay of the town pub . . . Jack's mother a
timid thing that never spoke above a whisper, and always with one eye out for her husband, wore high
collars and long sleeves, and generally bore a healing
bruise somewhere on her face or neck. Now Sam was
forced to confront that memory, he wondered, as he
had not, then. What did those sleeves and collars
conceal?

Maybe the stories were true; maybe the elves were
right. . . .

Glory be. Am I thinking as if they're real?

He was. Somewhere along the line, he'd accepted all
this — magic, elves, all of it. He might just as well accept
the abused kids as well. . . .

"Have you people cast some kind of spell on me?" he
demanded. "Made me believe in you? Brainwashed me?"

Tannim laughed. "If we used magic to make you
believe in magic, to brainwash you, doesn't that mean
magic works?"

Well, the boy had him there.

"I suppose you could have brainwashed me some other way," Sam said, feebly.

Tannim shrugged. "Why?" he replied reasonably, as the waitress brought another round. "What's the point? By definition, someone who's been brainwashed is operating at less than his optimum reasoning capacity. Why would we want you brainwashed, when what we want is for you to be at your sharpest?" Tannim took a sip of his cola, and looked up at Sam from under a raised eyebrow. "Are you having second thoughts about all this, about agreeing to help Keighvin?" he asked. "If you are, Sam, it's nothing to be ashamed of. We need you, but not at the expense of forcing you to make a bargain you regret."

Sam sighed. "No. No. It's just that I find myself believing in the impossible, and it doesn't seem right, all my brave words about plasma physics to the contrary."

The young man took a moment to finish his drink before answering. "Sam," he said, slowly, gazing off into nothing for a moment, "when you were a kid, people said it was impossible for a plane to fly past the speed of sound, for polio and smallpox to be eradicated, for the atom to be split, for a man to walk on the moon. I don't know what's impossible. All I can say is that 'impossible' just seems to mean that nobody's done it yet. There's some people that still don't believe a man walked on the moon. And there's people who still believe the earth is flat. Nobody puts *their* names in the history books. I know it all seems fantastic, but we *are* based in reality. It's just a bigger reality than most people are used to dealing with."

"What *do* you know?" Sam found himself asking, his own meal forgotten for the moment. "You, who's magicked his car, who walks and talks with the Folk and treats them like mortals — what do you know?"

Tannim grinned. "Well — I know your beer's getting flat."

Sam laughed, and gave in.

Tannim finished his third cola with one eye on Sam, and another on the crowd. On the whole, the evening had gone well. Sam had weathered both his initial exposure and the period of doubt that always followed it in good form. Better than Tannim had expected, in fact. Of course, he'd had a dose of the Folk as a child; that tended to leave a lasting impression.

Sam had finally worked himself round to asking specific questions about the elves, and how they were functioning in the human world. And why.

The crowd-noise around them was not too loud for them to be able to talk in normal voices — or at least, it wasn't after Tannim did a little local sound-filtering around their table, a tiny exercise in human magic that was worth the energy he expended on it. "Well, this is something else Keighvin won't admit unless he's pressed. Essentially, the Seleighe Court is split," he said. "One group thinks they should all withdraw Underhill, and leave the world we know to the humans. The other group thinks that would be a major mistake."

"Why?" Sam wanted to know, his head turned to one side.

"Remember what I told you about them, that they can't seem to create anything?" Tannim reminded him. "Keighvin thinks that if they withdraw, they'll stagnate. That's something a little more serious to them than it is to humans. They call it Dreaming; they can be forced into it by caffeine addiction, or they can drop into it from lack of stimulation, and being cut off from their old energy sources by Cold Iron. That's happened to one group in California already. They managed to get out of it, but — it wasn't pretty."

He didn't like to think about that. They had all been *damned* lucky to pull out of their trap. And they wouldn't have been able to without the aid of humans.

He pulled his thoughts away; Elfhame Sundescending was all right now, and thriving. "Like the old story of the Lotus-Eaters; they lose all ambition and do next to nothing, sit around and listen to music and let their magic servants tend to everything, dance, and never think a single thought. Scary. I've seen it once, and I wouldn't wish it even on the Folk who'd be pleased to see me six feet under. Keighvin's got some plans to keep it from happening on this coast, and they involve all of us in Fairgrove."

Just then, his attention was caught by someone that didn't fit with the usual Kevin Barry's crowd. She was clearly underage; he guessed round about thirteen or fourteen. Fifteen, max, but he doubted it. She was tarted up like a bargain-basement Madonna in black-lace spandex tights, a black-lace skirt, and a cheap black corset; wearing entirely too much makeup, so that her eyes looked like black holes in her pale face, with a bad bleach-job that made her hair look like so much spiky dead straw. What in hell was she doing here? This didn't look like her kind of crowd. *God, she looks like Pris from* Bladerunner, he thought.

But then, Sam had been surprised that *he* was a regular here. Maybe she just liked the music.

"I can see that, and I can see why racing, now," Sam said, in answer to whatever he'd just told the man. "But what are they doing about Cold Iron? That's what drove them out of the Old Country, isn't it? Doesn't it bother them now?"

"How much real iron and steel do you see nowadays?" Tannim countered, raising his eyebrows. "Plastic, fiberglass, aluminum, yes — but iron?"

"Hmm. You have a point."

The girl had worked herself in towards the stage, with a look of utter fascination on her face. Tannim felt a twinge of sympathy; he remembered the first time *he* encountered really good Celtic folk-rock. It had been right here — and this band, Terra Nova. Kind of like having your first experience of pizza being Chicago deep-dish. And it wasn't often that the old members of Terra Nova got back together again for an old-time's-sake gig, what with Trish being so busy at the restaurant and all. No wonder this chick had shown up. Yeah, it looked like she was just a punker with Celtic-rock leanings. Too bad she was so young. This was supposed to be an adult club, what with the bar and all. She could get bounced in no time, if she got herself noticed.

Well, if she behaved herself, they'd probably leave her alone.

He watched her, still a little bothered by something, something not quite right. Then, as he saw her stop and talk to a businessman who shook his head abruptly — and ignore a SCAD student who half-made an approach, it dawned on him.

She was a hooker.

He'd thought he was beyond shock, but this stunned him. So damned young —

He watched her make her way around the floor, most of her attention on the band, but obviously a part of her keeping an eye out for a potential john. *Don't try and turn a trick in here, honey, please,* he pled silently with her. He might be wrong — but the more he watched her, the surer he became. At that age — out here on a school night, dressed like she was — it was long odds against her being on River Street for the fun of it. *If you get too obvious, or bother the customers, they'll throw you out. Stay cool. It's cold and mean out there, and if one of the soft-hearts sees you, they'll get you something to eat and you'll be safe a little longer. . . .*

Sam asked him a question, and he answered it absently. "Well, what's happening is that some of the elves — with Keighvin leading the pack by a length — are trying to build up a kind of immunity to Cold Iron — or a tolerance, at least. I can think of half a dozen, actually, who can handle it with a minimum of protection, and two that can actually tolerate it well enough to work on and drive a stock car."

Donal, he thought fondly. *Wish you were here, man. You could pick up this poor little chick and glamorie her into coming back to Fairgrove with you, tuck her away Underhill until you'd talked some sense into her. And if you couldn't your brother could.*

The more he watched the girl, the less comfortable he felt. She was wandering around the area of the stage, and although she wasn't making any full-fledged tries at picking up the customers, it was pretty obvious that if anyone that she thought had money responded to her tentative overtures, she wouldn't turn him down.

"Keighvin says the Folk have to adapt or die, it's that simple," he concluded, as the band finished a wild polka and went into a still wilder reel. "They haven't got a choice anymore. *He* thinks if they withdraw, they'll do worse than stagnate, they'll fade away. Just—disappear."

"Is that possible?" Sam asked, sounding surprised. Tannim pulled his attention away from the girl long enough to catch his eyes. He nodded, slowly.

"It's already happened," he said seriously. "Mostly in Europe, but even over here, there've been enclaves of the Folk that went Underhill and just vanished after a while. Nobody's heard from them, nobody can find them."

"Couldn't they just have closed themselves off?" Sam wanted to know. "If they became that anti-social, maybe they even got tired of other elves. I mean, what is this Underhill, anyway? We used to say the Fair Folk lived in the mounds, but what you're saying, it sounds more like Underhill is everywhere. Couldn't the missing Folk have just shut the door and turned off the phone, so to speak?"

Tannim shook his head. "Underhill doesn't work that way. It's hard to describe. It's kind of — another world, one magicians can touch, and sometimes get into. A kind of parallel world, I guess. Lots of magic; I mean, of power, and it's readily available, like electricity, only it's like — " He thought for a moment, as the crowd began clapping in time to the music. "It's like having all the power-stations and the power-grid in place and running, only there's nobody manning it, and no electric company to make you pay for what you take. It's yours for the tapping into. The only 'cost' involved is in tapping into it and in using it."

Sam shook his head, but not in disbelief, exactly. "Sounds like free lunch, to me."

Tannim looked around for the girl, but she'd gotten lost behind a screen of taller people. Not that *that* was hard, as tiny as she was. He thought he knew where she'd moved to, though, by the path of mild disturbance along the bar. "Not really; the cost to the individual of tapping in and using it is high, and you have to have the ability in the first place. Kind of like solar energy. Keighvin thinks that's where the power created *here* that doesn't get used leaks off to — if you think of it as bio-energy, the kind that makes Kirlian auras, you're close enough to the truth."

Sam closed his eyes for a moment in thought. "All right," he replied, opening them again. "That much I can believe in. What's it like in there?"

"Parts are likc a bad sf novel," Tannim laughed, without humor. "Like some of the old pulp writers described an alien planet. Parts of it are like an architect's wet-dream." He spread his fingers wide for emphasis. "Mostly it's a kind of chaos, a place where things are always changing, always dangerous, and that's where the Unseleighe Court creatures go. Then there's stretches of order, walled gardens or even small countries, and that's where the Seleighe Court enclaves are."

"And those?" Sam prompted.

Tannim sighed, but this time at the memories Sam's question invoked. "I've only been there a couple of times, and each time it was different. Figure every description you've ever heard of Elvenlands, Morgan Le Fay's castle, the Isles of the Blest — that's what those Underhill enclaves are like." He felt his eyes sting with remembrance and the inevitable regret that he hadn't stayed, and pushed the memory away. "Incredible —

and they require elven-mages of very high power and a great deal of will to force the chaos out, and the area into that shape. That means they leave a mark on the world of Underhill, very visible, like the Red Spot on Jupiter. When someone like Keighvin goes Underhill, he *knows* where all the other pockets are, at least the ones created by other Folk. Always. He might not be able to get into them without invitation, but he knows where they are."

Sam took a sip of his beer before replying. "So it doesn't matter if the Folk in that place don't want to be bothered, they can't hide themselves. At least not on purpose."

Tannim nodded. "Right. So with the ones that faded out, the places that have gone missing — well, they're not there anymore. Maybe they died, maybe they went to still another world, and maybe they just dissolved back into the chaos. Even if there are still Folk alive in there, nobody can reach them, and they can't find their way back to the rest of us, nor to the real world. Likeliest — according to Keighvin — is that they faded until they were easy prey for the Unseleighe Court critters."

Sam toyed with a napkin, looking troubled. "You mean — they — "

Right on cue, Terra Nova launched into "Sidhe Beg and Sidhe Mor," a tune that sounded lighthearted — but was about a war between elves of the Seleighe and Unseleighe Courts. The body count, as Tannim recalled, had been pretty high.

He raised an eyebrow at the band. Sam chewed his lip, as the meaning of the tune came home to him. "The Unseleighe Court plays for keeps, and every time they kill a Seleighe Court creature, or a human, they add his life-energy to their own power. Elves can die; they can be killed. Ever think about where the word 'banshee' came from?"

Sam's eyes widened. "Bane-Sidhe?"

"Right. 'Bane' or 'death' of elves. And it's not just a name." Tannim was just glad he'd not had any personal experiences with one. The descriptions were bad enough.

"The stories my grandmother told me — she said some banshees actually came for people." Sam looked a little embarrassed, as if he'd been caught believing in the bogeyman.

Who also exists.

"They do that too; they'll do their damnedest to scare you to death," Tannim said grimly. "That's how they get their energy; from your fear and from your dying."

"Oh." Sam blinked, as if he wasn't sure how to take that. He'd accepted danger last night — but that was with Keighvin, in Fairgrove territory. He was here now, the "real world," in the middle of a pub full of noisy people and a Celtic-rock band.

And a thirteen-year-old hooker.

She appeared again, this time giving up all pretense of working the crowd, just standing close to the stage and hugging herself, as Trish sang "Buachaill on Eire" with a voice an elven Bard would have paid any price to display.

A glitter of Trish's half-closed blue eyes, and the set of her chin, betrayed the fact that she was watching the girl too, and Tannim relaxed minutely. Trish didn't pick up on street-sparrows often, especially not now that she was managing "Acadia," but when she did, she was very kind to them. Like the way she'd adopted that monster wolfhound of hers, letting it take over her life to the point of buying a house just so the dog would be able to stay with her. She wouldn't let the girl get away without at least trying to see she got something to eat. With luck, she'd keep the child busy until Tannim could take over.

Maybe I can get her to Keighvin. I can't get him out of Fairgrove territory, not yet, but if I can get her to him, he'll take care of her. Not for the first time, he wished that he could just lie to the kid, get her into his car and make off with her, but to take her away from whatever life she had chosen, he had to have her consent, and she had to know what she was choosing. Conal and Donal wouldn't have worked that way, but they were Sidhe, and trickery was a part of their nature. Not his. It couldn't be by deception. Even Keighvin could work that way, but he couldn't; he was bound by a different set of rules. Self-inflicted, but nevertheless real. He hadn't liked being lied to, or manipulated, even with good intentions, when he was younger. He wouldn't do that to another kid. *Besides, small incidents have a way of turning around and biting my ass. If the wrong person saw me getting into my car with an underage hooker, it could mean big-time trouble later. Trouble we can't afford.*

As the band finished the set, he saw with relief that Trish definitely had her eye on the girl. As soon as they'd finished their bows — and before the child had a chance to escape — she was down off the stage and beside the kid. She made it look completely casual, and Tannim gave her high marks for her subtlety.

"What's wrong?" Sam asked, startling him. He tore his eyes off the girl for a moment to stare at his companion.

"What do you — "

"Oh, come now," Sam interrupted. "You haven't had more than half your attention on me for the past fifteen minutes. And you've got a frown on your face, so it can't be that you're watching a pretty girl, or that you're enthralled by the band. So what's the problem?" As Tannim paused, debating how much to say, he lost his half-smile and began to frown, himself. "Is it something I should know about?"

Tannim sighed. "Over there, with Trish, from the band. See that other girl?"

"The one that's made up like a cheap tart?" Sam asked, disapproval thick in his voice. "Girls these days — ah well. What about her?"

"She's not only made up like a cheap tart, she probably *is* a cheap tart," Tannim replied wearily. And before Sam could reply to that, added, "Take a good look under all the paint. She's not only underage, she's hardly gotten away from playing with Barbie dolls. What's a kid like that doing out here hooking? And more than that, why? She has to be a runaway — what's she running from that's bad enough for her to be turning tricks at fourteen?"

Sam started to make some snap reply, but it looked as if some of what Tannim had been talking about — the abused kids and all — had penetrated. Tannim could almost read his mind from the fleeting expressions that passed over his face. First, contempt — then disgust — but then a moment of second thoughts, followed by worry. "I don't like it," he said.

"Neither do I," Tannim told him, "but we're going to have to be careful about this. She could be bait in a trap; she could be a trap herself. Some of the Unseleighe Court things can look like anything they want. *I* don't See any magic around her, but that doesn't mean shc's not one of them, or even a human kid they picked up to use against me. This is one of my regular hangouts, and everybody knows it."

And they know my soft spots.

"So what do we do?" Sam asked. A frown line was forming between his brows. Obviously he wasn't used to the kind of the multitudinous layers of deceit the Unseleighe Court creatures used by habit.

"We let Trish handle her. If she's after me, she'll find a way to get Trish to bring her over here. If she's a real kid in real trouble, she'll act like one." He watched the two of them, without seeming to. It looked as if the singer was warning the girl against soliciting; Trish was nodding her head so emphatically that her black hair bounced, while the child blushed under all the makeup, and hung her head. But the singer didn't leave things there; she took the girl to a table in the corner, and got her a sandwich and a cola, standing over her and talking until the food arrived. By then, it was time for the next set, and Trish abandoned the girl for the stage.

The kid finished the food in about three seconds flat. Tannim had never seen a kid put away food so fast, and the way she cleaned up every crumb argued that it might well have been the first meal she'd had today. She lingered over the dregs of her cola until Trish was obviously wrapped up in her song. Then a look of bleak determination passed over her face, and she slid out of her seat; and without a single glance at Tannim or even in his direction, she went back to the bar.

Tannim sighed, half in relief, half in exasperation. *All right,* he said to himself. *She's genuine. Now what am I going to do about her?*

● CHAPTER FIVE

Just as Tannim asked himself that question, the girl found a mark.

It wasn't one of the regulars, and Julie hadn't even bothered to try to find the jerk a table. He was holding up the bar, more than two sheets to the wind, and up until the kid cruised by, he'd been insisting that Marianne, the barkeep, turn on a nonexistent television. He jumped all over her tentative overture, so much so that it was obvious to half the bar that he'd picked her up. The guys on either side of him gave him identical looks of disgust when they saw how young the girl was, and turned their backs on the situation.

Unfortunately, Tannim wasn't going to be able to do that. Not and be able to look himself in the mirror tomorrow. *Hard to shave if you can't do that. . . .*

Well, he knew one sure-fire way to pry her away from Mr. Wonderful. And it only required a *little* magic. With a mental flick, he set the two tiny spells in motion. With the first, a Command spell, he cleared people to one side or the other of a line between his table and her. With the other, a simple look-at-me glamorie, he caught her eye.

At precisely the moment when she looked his way, down the open corridor of bodies, he flicked open his wallet, displaying his Gold Card, and nodded to her. Her eyes were drawn to it, as if it was a magnet to catch and hold her gaze. Only after she looked at it did she look at him. She licked her lips, smiled, and started toward him.

Tried to, rather. The drunk grabbed her arm.

"Hey!" he shouted, rather too loudly. "Wa-waitaminit, bitch! You promised me some fun!"

All eyes went to the drunk, and none of the looks were friendly. Kevin Barry's was not the kind of pub where the word "bitch" would go unnoticed.

So much for taking care of this the easy way.

Tannim was up and out of his seat before the girl had a chance to react to the hand gripping her arm. He grasped the drunk's wrist and applied pressure. The drunk yelped, and let go. "I think she's changed her mind," he said, with deceptive gentleness.

The drunk yanked his hand away, and snarled aggressively, "Yeah? And what's a faggot artsy punk like you gonna do about it? Huh?"

His hands were balling into fists, and he swung as he spoke, telegraphing like a Western Union branch office. Tannim blocked the first blow with a little effort; the second never landed. Three patrons landed on the drunk, and "escorted" him outside. And that was all there was to the incident; Kevin Barry's was like that. Tannim was family here, and nobody messed with family.

And nobody even looked askance at Tannim, for guiding a kid barely past training bras back to his table. It would be assumed that, like Trish, his intentions were to keep the kid out of trouble, and maybe talk some sense into her. He caught Sam's eye as he made a show of pulling a seat out for her; the old man was anything but stupid. "I'll be at the bar," he said as Tannim sat down. "I can hear the band better over there."

That was a palpable lie, since the bar was far from the stage, but the girl didn't seem to notice. Sam vanished into the crowd, leaving Tannim alone with the girl. She looked around, nervously; tried to avoid his eyes.

But then, young hookers are always nervous.

"So, what's your name, kiddo?" he asked quietly, projecting calm as best he could, and regretting the fact that he wasn't an Empath.

"Tania," she said, so softly he could hardly hear her.

"Tania. Okay, my name's Tannim. We've both got the same first syllable in our names, that's a start." She looked up at him, startled, and he grinned. "Well, heck, it's not much of a line, but it beats 'Come here often? What's your sign?' "

She smiled back a little. "Wh-what do you want me to do?" she asked bluntly. "W-we could go to your car and — "

My car. So she hasn't even got a place of her own. The thought sickened him. How long had she been turning tricks in strange men's cars?

"What's your rate?" he asked, just as bluntly.

She didn't bat an eye. "Sixty an hour."

Right. You wish. And you'd take sixty a night. He raised an eyebrow, cynically. "Give me a break. That's for somebody with a little more experience than you've got."

She wilted faster than he expected. "Forty?" she said, tentatively.

He watched her over the top of his drink, as Trish belted out one of her own compositions, the notes sailing pure and clear above the crowd. "Sixty and forty. Okay, that makes a hundred. Let me tell you what you're going to do for a hundred."

She looked frightened at that, and she might have tried to get up and run except that he was between her and the door. He wondered if she'd gotten an "offer" like this before. And if she'd gotten away relatively undamaged.

Yes to the first question, from the look of fear in her eyes — and no to the second. It was all he could do to keep up the pretense; to keep from grabbing her hand and dragging her to his car, and taking her straight to Keighvin.

"No, I'm not a cop," he told her, "and I'm not going to bust you. I'm not into S and M and I'm not going to hurt you." A little of the fear left her eyes, but not all of it, not by any means. "I *am* a pushover."

He looked up long enough to signal Julie with his

eyes. She hustled over to his table as soon as she'd set down the other customer's beer. Tannim's tips were legendary in the River Street bars and restaurants, and that legend ensured him downright eager service.

"Julie, I need four club sandwiches with everything — to go." He nodded significantly and she winked at him, turning and heading towards the kitchen with the order. He turned back to Tania.

"Okay, that's a hundred dollars for tonight; the first time. You take it, you go home if you've got one. You get *off* the damn street, at least for tonight. You get a room if you don't have a home." He slid the five twenties he fished out of his wallet across to her. She looked at them, but didn't touch them. "Use what I gave you for seed money; start putting a real life together for yourself. I come here a lot. You find me here and ask me for help, you get another hundred to keep you going — but only if you aren't doing drugs. Believe me, I can tell if you are, better than any blood-test. Got that?"

She was just inexperienced enough to believe him, and experienced enough to be skeptical. "So what do you get out of this?"

He smiled crookedly. "I stop having to rescue you from drunks. I *told* you I was a pushover." He sobered. "Tania, it's harder to keep believing in dreams these days — but when you stop believing in them, you kind of stop believing in yourself. I still believe in them. And I'm just crazy enough to think that giving an underage hooker a hundred bucks just might make a difference to her. Maybe give her a chance to go out and build some dreams of her own."

"I'm not under —" she started to protest frantically.

He covered her hand, the one that was holding the cash, with his, just for a moment. "And you can start by not lying to me. Kiddo, you're underage even in Tennessee, and we both know it. Now there; one crazy, helping hand. This time, I pushed help off on you. Next time, you ask for help. All right?"

She nodded, speechless, as Julie arrived with the sandwiches. "Julie," he said, as he shoved the brown paper bag towards Tania, "I want you to start a tab for Tania here. Two hundred bucks' credit, food only. Put it on the card."

"Sure thing, Tannim," the waitress replied, plucking his credit card from his outstretched fingers, and flashing a sparkling smile. She winked at Tania, who clutched the paper bag with a dumbfounded look on her face, looking for all the world like a kid in a Halloween costume.

Yeah. "Trick" or treat. Poor kid.

"Now, you get hungry, you come here," he ordered. "Even if I'm not here, you can get fed. Okay?"

"O — okay," she said, letting go of the bag long enough to shove her money into her cheap vinyl purse.

He grinned again. "Go on, get out of here. It's getting nasty out there, and I don't just mean the weather." She whisked herself out of the chair, threading the crowd like a lithe little ferret, and vanished into the darkness beyond the door. Sam returned almost immediately.

"What the hell was all that about?" he asked, sitting himself down in the chair Tania had vacated.

Tannim sighed. "The first step in building trust," he replied. "I just put up a bird-feeder. If I'm really lucky, one of these days the bird will eat from my hand. That's when I can get her back to where she belongs — or over to Keighvin, whichever seems better for her."

Sam shook his head dubiously. "I don't know. You gave her money, didn't you? What's to stop her from blowing it all on drugs?"

"Nothing," Tannim admitted. "Nothing, except that she doesn't do drugs, yet. Kid like that probably doesn't turn more than a couple of tricks a week. I just gave her enough to stay off the street for a while, maybe even more than a week, and promised her more if she asks for it." Julie brought back his card and the credit slip; he signed it, and added a sizable tip for her. "And this gives her a two-hundred-dollar food tab here."

Sam frowned. "You're a fool, boy. She's going to be on you like a leech."

He let out some of his tension in a long breath. "I don't think so," he replied. "I know . . . I don't have a real reason to think that way, but I don't think she's hardened enough to see a potential sugar-daddy and snag him. And even if she did — well, I could insist she come stay with me, and hand her over to Keighvin that way. Frankly, Sam, I'm more worried she'll vanish on me; decide I'm some kind of nut, the Savannah Zodiac killer or something, and never come near me again." He looked up again at the stage, where Trish had just begun "The Parting Glass," a sure sign that the gig was over, at least for her. The rest of the band might stay, but Trish was calling it a night. "Enough of this. That's our signal to move along, Sam, and go find ourselves some dinner. How's tandoori chicken with mango chutney and raita sound? Or lobster with macadamia nuts?"

Sam gave him a look of pure bewilderment. "What in hell are you talking about?" he asked.

"Dinner, Sam," he replied, grinning with anticipation. "Pure gourmet craziness."

"Sounds crazy, all right," Sam said, as they wormed their way through the crowd, and out into the damp, fish-redolent air.

"Trust me, Sam," he laughed, as the mist began to seep across the street, the precursor of one of Savannah's odd, chin-high fogs. "Trish knows wine and food the way she knows music. It might be odd, but you won't be disappointed."

Tania Jane Delaney slipped up the warped steps to the apartment she shared with five other kids, her heart in her mouth. The entrance to the upstairs apartments gaped like a toothless mouth when she'd arrived, dark and unfriendly. The light at the top of the stairs had gone out again — or somebody had broken or stolen the bulb — and she shivered with fear with each step she took. Jamie'd been beaten up and robbed twice by junkies; Laura'd had her purse snatched. If anybody knew she had money — if there was someone waiting for her at the top of the stairs —

But there wasn't, this time, nor was there anyone standing between her and the door as she'd feared when she felt for the knob. She fumbled open the lock with hands that shook so hard her key-ring jingled. There were only three keys on it, and the little brass unicorn Meg had given her for good luck. One key for this place, and the two to the locks of the townhouse in North Carolina —

But she wouldn't think of that.

There wasn't anyone else in the apartment, which was all right. She really didn't want to share Tannim's largess with the other three kids that had the room with the kitchenette, anyway. They'd given her a hard time the last time she'd wanted to cook something, and she thought they were filching things from her shelf in the fridge. Not that there was much to filch, mostly, but there had been things she'd thought she had that came up missing. She and Laura and Jamie never gave *them* any trouble over using the bathroom, and never had any problem with making sure there was paper and soap in there.

Please, don't let them blow all their money on dope again, she pled with an uncaring God. *The rent's due in three days, and old man March sent his kids to collect it last time. I think they could wad us up like Kleenex without even trying hard. They could throw us out on our asses and we couldn't do a thing about it.*

She'd already eaten one sandwich, feeling guilty, but too hungry to leave it alone. She hadn't eaten anything yesterday but a cup of yogurt she'd shoplifted. But that still meant Jamie and Laura had a sandwich and a half each, plus all the chips. There'd been a styrofoam cup of bean soup in there too, and cookies; she'd saved the cookies for Jamie and his sweet-tooth, but she drank the soup, sitting on a stone bench in Jackson Square, watching the fog roll in, listening to the far-away music coming from a bar somewhere. It had been awfully good soup.

Mother had never made soup like that. Mother never made soup at all; she bought it from a gourmet place. And when she bought it, she bought weird things, like cold gazpacho or miso, things that didn't taste like soup at all. When she wasn't on some kind of crazy diet with Father, that is. When Tania ran away, they'd been on one of those diets; some kind of stuff that looked like rice with things mixed into it, and tasted like hay. They'd made Tania eat it too, and she was hungry all the time. She'd have killed for a candy bar or a steak, or even a hamburger.

"You only think about what tastes good," Mother had said, scornfully. "Just like every child."

The only time Tania had eaten real soup was when she was little, and she got it at school or the learning center. It wasn't called a "day-care" center, it was a "learning center," and she'd had lessons stuffed into her every day for as long as she could remember. French, math, music . . . she hadn't gotten bedtime stories, she'd gotten flashcards. She hadn't gotten hugs, she'd gotten "quality time," with quizzes about how well she was doing in school.

Like the Spanish Inquisition, with long talks about how if I really wanted to get into a first-class college like Yale I had to have better grades.

She left the food on her roommates' sleeping beds. Jamie and Laura had an old mattress, with the seams popped and the stuffing coming out. It had been so stained that Tania would have been afraid to use it, because of germs, but they didn't seem to mind. They had a pile of cargo pads stolen from a moving van for bedding, all spread neatly on top of it, plus the blankets and sheets Laura had taken out of the Goodwill drop-box, all different sizes, none matching. Tania had two thin foam mattresses she'd gotten from the open dumpster at the old folks' home, piled on top of each other, and some of Laura's leftover sheets and blankets. Laura had thought the idea of using the egg-crate mattresses was too creepy; they wouldn't have been out in the dumpster if their owner hadn't died, probably *on* them. But the idea of ghosts didn't scare Tania; she'd taken them, hosed them down real good in case the old person had peed on them or something, and she hadn't been haunted yet. In fact, a ghost might be preferable to some of the people who hung out around here.

She went to the bathroom to wash the makeup off. The makeup, bleach-job, the whole outfit was Laura's idea, but she wasn't sure it was working. On the other hand, any tricks she got looking like the way she used to would be real pervs. The makeup at least made her look older, and the outfit like she knew what she was doing. But it itched, and if she didn't wash it off every night, she'd wake up looking like Tammy Faye Baker after a good scam-cry. She saw as soon as she pulled the chain on the bare bulb dangling from the ceiling that somebody had been by the Hilton again; the toilet-tank lid was covered with little bars of soap, and matching rolls of paper sat on the cracked and grimy brown linoleum. It was probably Laura; she was really good at sneaking in, finding an unattended maid's cart, and sneaking out again. That was how they'd gotten their towels, too.

She ran some water into the sink, ignoring the rust that had stained the gray, grainy porcelain under both spigots. The hot water was actually hot tonight, and Tania decided impulsively on a bath. She had to clean the tub first, though, and by the time she was done, she was ready for a good long soak.

She went to the footlocker where she kept her things, got her tiny bottle of hotel shampoo, and discovered that there were lots more beside it. That clinched it; only Laura would have gotten shampoo for everybody. She silently blessed Laura as she stripped,

hurrying because the apartment was cold. She ran
some hot water into the tub to warm it, trying not to
think about her beautiful, antiseptic, sparkling-clean
private bathroom at home.

*It wasn't my home. It never was home. It was just a place to
live. They probably didn't even miss me when I was gone; I bet
they're glad I'm gone, in fact. Now they can buy another BMW
or a Porsche and take a trip to Bermuda.*

She washed her hair under the tap, kneeling in the
bottom of the chipped, scratched tub, then filled it to
the top with water as hot as she could stand. Mother
and Father had a Jacuzzi in their bathroom, but they'd
never let Tania use it.

She sighed, and sank back into the hot water. She
was so cold; when the fog came, it brought chilly air
with it, and Spandex wasn't very warm. She'd been out
longer than she'd intended after that strange guy gave
her all the money. She'd stopped to watch *Legend*
through the window of somebody's apartment after
she'd eaten the soup; the unicorns had attracted her attention, and she stayed when there didn't seem to be
anyone in the room who could see her peering in from
outside.

What a great movie. Altogether, it had been a good
night, and she felt a little happy for the first time in
weeks. First there'd been the music at that bar, then the
food the singer had gotten her, then the money for
doing *nothing*. That would have been enough, but
there was a two-hundred-dollar tab waiting for her,
and she'd be able to get one good meal a day for all
three of them until that ran out. She wasn't certain the
guy was for real, but the tab was. It would be easy
enough to avoid him, and still eat on his money.

The movie had put a cap on the night. She hadn't seen
it when it was first out, Mother and Father hadn't permitted it. They didn't let her watch any TV at all except
PBS, didn't let her see any movies, *ever*, but this had been
one film they would have really tossed a hissyfit over.

Fantasy. They said it like it was a cuss-word. If Meg's parents hadn't been one of Mother's clients, they'd have made her throw out the unicorn keychain. She wasn't allowed to read anything but schoolbooks, listen to anything but classical music, but *fantasy* was the ultimate slime, so far as they were concerned. She'd managed to read some at school, by keeping the books from the school library in her locker, along with the unicorn poster Meg gave her, and the dragon calendar. She'd also had a little cache of books she'd hidden under the springs of her bed, books Meg gave her when she was through with them, books full of unicorns, elves, magic . . . and that turned out to be a major mistake. Mother had found them.

You'd have thought it was kiddie-porn, she thought, angry and unhappy all at the same time. *Or drugs. You'd have thought they were Fundies and the books were about demon-worship.*

The way they'd carried on had been horrible; not yelling, no, yelling would have been a relief. No, instead they lectured her, in relays. About how the stuff was going to ruin her mind for logical thinking; about how it was wasting time she could have been using on extra-credit stuff to boost her grades and give her an edge. How they felt betrayed. How if the colleges found out she read this stuff, they'd never let her in. On and on and on—

And then they took it and her into the living room and burned the books in the trendy gas-log fireplace, right in front of her.

"No living in a dream-world for you, Tania," Father had said, as he fed the brightly colored books to the flames. "It's time to wake up to the real world."

Well, I'm in the real world now, Father, she thought at him, her eyes stinging. *It's more real than yours.*

They hadn't been able to do much to her, other than spend every minute they had to spare lecturing her. What could they do, after all? She wasn't allowed to "waste" her time on clubs, boyfriends, hobbies, music for pleasure — the only time she was ever outside the townhouse was when she was at school or at her after-school lessons: ballet on Monday, piano on Wednesday, tennis on Saturday. She didn't *like* any of those outside lessons; they couldn't punish her by taking any of them away. She didn't have any friends but Meg, she wasn't *allowed* to have any friends but Meg, and she only saw Meg on Saturday, at the club for tennis lessons.

Then she found one Saturday that there was still one thing they could do. They moved her lesson, from Saturday morning, to Saturday afternoon. She'd lost even Meg's tenuous friendship.

They told her Friday night. That was when she decided to run away.

Father always accused her of being unable to plan ahead, of forgetting about the future. *Well, he was wrong.*

She knew the combination of the safe, and how much money her parents kept in it. She went to it by the light of a tiny flashlight, opened it, and counted . . . she didn't dare take too much, or they might miss it if they happened to need money for something on Saturday, but she made sure she had enough for the fare. Then she packed her tennis bag, taking everything she could fit into it, stuffing it and her purse to bursting. Father was on the way to New York, Mother was seeing a friend of Meg's father, helping him find a house for a relocating veep. She did things like that for her clients; that was why she got so many accounts.

Too bad she didn't do things like that for her kid. Or maybe I was like a "declining account" to her.

When Mother dropped her off at the club, she'd gone around to the kitchen instead of to her lesson. She asked one of the busboys how to get to the city bus, figuring they'd know, if anyone would.

It was easier than she'd thought; many of the employees at the club used the bus as their primary transportation. She'd taken the city bus downtown, and from there it was a simple matter to get to the Greyhound depot. Before the four-hour tennis lesson was over, she was on her way to Savannah. There was no special reason to go there, it was just a place somewhere, anywhere, else. She'd picked it more-or-less at random, figuring if she hadn't known in advance where she was going neither would her parents. Research Triangle Park, North Carolina, vanished behind her.

If Father'd been more like Tannim. . . . She let a little more hot water into the tub, and sank back with a wistful sigh.

Money didn't last as long as she'd thought it would. Really, she didn't have any idea how much things cost. She made the mistake of buying a couple of nylon bags and a lot of t-shirts and things to wear so she didn't look so conspicuous. By the time she reached Savannah, she was down to her last twenty dollars, and desperate. The bus arrived after midnight, and had dumped her out on the street, cold and scared. Afraid to hang around the bus terminal, she'd wandered the streets, jumping at every shadow, expecting to get mugged at any moment.

That was when Jamie found her; she found out later he'd just turned a really good trick, and was a little high, and feeling very generous and expansive. All *she* knew was that this really cute guy came up to her, as she was sitting on a bench in some kind of little park, and looked at her kind of funny. Then he'd said, "You're in trouble, aren't you?" and offered her a place to stay.

If she hadn't been so exhausted, she'd have been horrified by the awful apartment. The place was musty, full of mildew, with stained ceilings where leaks had sprung. Two rooms, on the top floor of an old, unpainted building so rickety that it leaned. No furniture, cracks in all the walls, carpeting with about a hundred years of dirt ground into it, bugs crawling everywhere — she'd never seen a place like it before.

Laura had been waiting, and when she saw that Jamie'd brought Tania with him, she started to yell at him. But then she'd taken a second look, and just gave Tania a couple of blankets and a pillow, and said they'd talk in the morning.

They talked, all right. Or rather, Tania talked. When she was through, Jamie'd looked at Laura, and Laura had nodded slowly. "All right," Laura had said. "Y'all can stay. But y'all gotta pay your own share. We ain't got anythin' t' spare a-tall."

She'd thought it would be easy. She didn't know that no one was going to hire a fourteen-year-old with no experience, no phone, and no transportation. Not when there were so many SCAD students looking for jobs. After a week of filling out applications and getting turned down, she was getting desperate. If Laura and Jamie threw her out—

She asked Laura to get her a job where *she* worked. That was when Laura laughed, and told her what she, Jamie, and the other kids sharing the apartment did all night. And offered to show her how.

"It's easy," Laura'd said cynically, in her thick, Georgia-cracker accent. "They pay y'forty bucks, and y'just lie there. Half hour, and it's over, an' ya go find another john."

She'd had sex education; she knew about all of it, from contraceptives to AIDs. As desperate as she'd been, she hadn't thought it would be that bad.

So she'd been deflowered by some guy in the back seat of his car and gotten forty bucks out of the experience; he hadn't even known she'd been a virgin. It had hurt a lot, but she soaked away the pain in the bathtub, and went out the next night. After a while it stopped hurting — physically.

It could have been worse, she told herself. In fact, she'd been incredibly lucky, and she knew it. There were guys who hung around the bus station waiting for kids like her; they'd offer a place to stay, and the next thing the kid knew, she was hooked and he was her pimp. Jamie saved her from that, anyway. At least she wasn't doing drugs, her money was her own, and she could make her johns wear rubbers.

She sat up a little in the tub, thinking she heard the key in the lock. But no, it wasn't Laura or Jamie. It was getting awfully late, and she was beginning to worry.

Especially about Jamie. *He'd* started using drugs; he'd always smoked a little grass, hell, he was high when she'd met him. But she was pretty sure he'd been doing something harder than grass, lately, and she was afraid it was crack.

She couldn't blame him, in a way. She'd naively assumed that he was getting picked up by women the way she and Laura were hooking with men. Then she'd seen him in a car with one of his johns . . . and later, down on Bull Street, with the other cute young boys, cruising for another customer. Male customers.

"I'm not a fag," he'd said fiercely, when she mentioned she'd seen him. "I'm *not*. I'm straight, I'm just making the rent, okay? It doesn't mean anything."

"Okay," she'd said hurriedly, "I believe you." And didn't bother to tell him that it didn't matter to her if he was gay or straight. Her father had referred to one of her Fine Art Appreciation teachers as "queer as a football bat," and she'd always liked *him*. What mattered was that Jamie was careful; that he made sure all his johns wore rubbers, the way she did, and that he stayed *safe*. That he didn't start on heavy drugs, like the kids in the other room.

Because she'd seen what happened when you got hooked. Especially the guys; they wound up going to a pimp, one who'd keep them stoned all the time and take all their money, and when they got stoned, they weren't so careful anymore.

Laura wasn't much better about taking chances.

When Tania did anything besides in the guy's car, she never went anywhere with a guy except a motel room, and then she'd meet him there, and if he wasn't alone, she'd leave. She wouldn't do kinky stuff, either. Laura did things Tania never would; Laura took chances all the time.

But Laura was a lot tougher than Tania.

You'd have to be tough to take what she did. Getting raped by your stepdad, then thrown out of the house for telling . . . her mom saying she was a slut, and that she lied about it all. . . . I guess she figures she hasn't got a lot to lose. Except Jamie, I guess.

Laura spilled the same story every time she came home drunk, which was about once a week, even though she wasn't more than sixteen. Jamie didn't talk about *his* past. Tania figured it must have been worse than Laura's; sometimes she'd wake up and hear Jamie crying, hear Laura comforting him. She'd seen him nude a lot, and there were scars all over his body.

Tania was getting all wrinkly, like a raisin; she got out of the water reluctantly, and pulled the plug. As she watched the water run down the drain, making a little whirlpool, she remembered the PBS show bit about how you could tell what hemisphere you were in whether the whirlpool ran clockwise or counter-clockwise.

Gravity, Coriolis forces . . . her life was running out like the water. It was so hard to think of anything but the next trick, hard to plan past making the rent.

She used to have dreams, plans. When she first ran away, she was going to get a job, maybe learn to be a model . . . or get into a tech school and learn computers . . . or maybe see if her art teachers were right about her being good at drafting. These days, she watched the SCAD students with a kind of dull hatred. They had it all, and they didn't even know it. How *dared* they pretend they were so tortured, so tormented by art? They didn't know what torture was.

Torture was coming home with cigarette burns on

your arms, like Laura; having scars all over your body, like Jamie.

Torture was running fifteen blocks with a guy chasing you, hoping you knew a way to get away from him before he beat you up and took your money. Torture was not having enough to eat, ever; worrying about getting kicked out onto the street because the junkies in the next room couldn't afford their share of the rent.

Tannim had talked about having dreams. What had happened to hers?

She pulled on an oversized t-shirt and curled up in her blankets, waiting for the others to get home. Next week was the end of the month and the bookstores would strip books of their covers, turn in the covers for credit, and pitch the stripped pages into the dumpster. There might be some fantasy or science fiction in there, if she got there early enough. There had been, last month.

If she couldn't live on her own dreams, she'd take other people's. That would do. She thought again about that black-and-white TV she'd seen for ten bucks at the Goodwill store; maybe she could get it with a little of the hundred dollars. . . .

Meanwhile she'd wait for Laura and Jamie to get home, make sure they ate the food she'd brought, make sure they were all right.

They were all the family she had.

She must have dozed off, because she woke up with a start to the sounds of the kids in the other room coming in, all three together, higher than anything. Joe and Tonio were all over each other, and Honi kept telling them to hush in a voice louder than their giggles. Tania didn't know if Honi was a boy or a girl; Honi had awfully big hands and feet for a girl, and a prominent Adam's apple, but she never wore anything but tight black skirts and pumps and fishnet hose out on the street — and this grubby old bathrobe with tatty marabou trim at home.

Joe and Tonio were, according to Jamie, "queer as

football bats." Odd that Jamie and her father used the same expression. They said they were lovers, but whenever they got drunk — as opposed to high — they beat each other up something awful. Laura and Jamie ignored them, but Tania always stayed hidden in bed when they started on each other that way.

She glanced over at the other bed, almost by reflex, and saw one lump in it, with long, fire-red hair. Laura.

"Jeezus, ah wish the hail them queers'd take it outside," came a loud groan from the lump. Laura had deliberately made it loud enough for the others to hear, and Tonio just giggled harder.

"But baaaby it's cooold outside," Joe shrieked, and by the thump, fell onto the sleeping-bags he shared with Tonio. The overhead bulb went out in the other room, leaving the harsh light from the cracked ceramic lamp in the corner of their room as the only source of illumination.

Laura sat up, shaking her hair out of her eyes, and peered through the doorway into the other room. "Weahll, theah goes the rent," she said glumly. Tania pulled her blankets back and sat up too, her heart sinking.

But then Laura took a second look. The trio in the other room were already snoring. "Or mebbe not," she said thoughtfully, and slipped out of her bed to creep quietly into the other room.

She came back with a handful of something. "Damnfools didn't spend it all, this tayhme," she said grimly. "Got thutty from Tonio's pants, foahty from Honi, an' twenny from Joe. I got foahty put by. How 'bout you?"

Tania dug into her purse and came up with Tannim's five twenties, handing them over without a qualm. After all, she didn't have to worry about eating for a while.

Laura looked at her with a dumbstruck expression on her face. "Whut in hail did y'all do, gal?" she asked. "Ah found the sammiches. You go to a pahty, or didja get a delivery kid?"

Tania giggled, and shook her head. "No," she said, and the story of the strange guy in the bar spilled out under Laura's prodding. But to her surprise, Laura wasn't pleased.

"Jee-zus!" the girl finally exploded, tossing her tangled hair over her shoulders. "Whut in hail didja thank you was doin'? This ain't no fairy tale, girl! Man don' give away money foah nothin'! You ain't gonna go back theah, are you?"

"Not while *he's* there," she replied, resentfully. "But the tab's real, Laura; I saw the charge slip. I think we oughta eat it up before he changes his mind —"

Laura wasn't convinced, and she scowled, then interrupted her. "That's 'nother thang, now ah'm glad I didn' eat them sammiches — he prolly put dope in there. First taste is free, but —"

"Laura, they came straight out of the *kitchen*. He didn't touch them! Kevin Barry's is straight-edge, you dummy, they wouldn't do anything like that!" At Laura's continued scowl, she added, "Besides, I already ate one, and it was okay."

"*Jeezus,*" the older girl said explosively. Then, "I reckon it's all right. But don' go near him agin, you heah me? He's prolly a pimp, all that crap 'bout dreams and do-good bull. Only dreams man like that has come in white powdah, or lil' brown rocks. He jest wantsta get you off, get you stoned, an then he's got you."

Tania sighed, and bowed her head in acquiescence. It would have been nice to have somewhere to go for help. She had vague memories of a dream, where Tannim was some kind of warrior, in leather and blue jeans, and he fought monsters to protect her. . . .

But this wasn't a fairy tale or a movie; Laura was right. Nobody gave money away for free, and dreams had a way of vanishing when the rent needed to be paid. Laura was nibbling tentatively at a corner of one of the sandwiches, as if she expected to bite into something dangerous.

That much was real, anyway. Food today, and food for the next week or so, and just twenty more dollars from Jamie and the rent would be paid up.

"Where's Jamie?" she asked, and Laura stopped chewing. Her scowl turned to a frown of worry.

"Ah don' know — " she began, and then they heard the rattle of a key in the lock. From the sound of it, Jamie was having a hard time finding the lock.

When he stumbled through the darkened outer room, it was obvious why. He was even higher than the others had been. But this was a manic kind of high that made Tania sick inside. There was booze on his breath, but that wasn't all.

Crack. He's been smoking crack.

She sat in dumb silence, while Laura scolded him out of his clothes and into bed, holding out one of the remaining sandwiches. But even she went silent at the sight of rope burns on his wrists.

"Whut happened?" she asked, after a long pause. Jamie laughed and snorted.

"I did a party, baby. There was a birthday, and I was the favor. They got a little rough, but they made it up to me." He snatched at the sandwich she held, and devoured it before she could say anything; dove into the bag and got the cookies and ate them, then the second sandwich.

How? With dope and booze? Or did he get that after?

"How many?" Laura asked, finally, flatly. He gave her an owl-like stare, as the food made him sleepy.

"I don' know," he replied, his words slurring. "Four. Five. I wanta sleep."

"Did you make 'em use rubbers?" she snarled, as he lay down. When he didn't respond, she shook him. "Answer me, dammit! *Did you?*"

"Yeah. Sure. I'm gonna sleep now." And he pushed her away. He didn't so much fall asleep as pass out.

Frantic now, Laura scrabbled through his pockets, turning them out on the cargo-blanket and pawing through them. A pocket-knife, a butterfly-knife, assorted change. Keys. Three crumpled twenties. Gum wrappers and half a pack of gum.

Three condoms.

"He went out with six," Laura whispered, her voice tight with fear. "He had six."

Six; three gone — but Jamie had said there were four or five johns. And he had been at a party; no telling how many times each.

Laura started to cry, tears streaking her face with cheap mascara, rent money lying forgotten on the bed.

Tania went to her, hugged her, and held her, rocking, not able to say anything, only able to be there.

"It's all right," she said, meaninglessly. "It's all right. We'll take care of him in the morning, okay? It'll be all right. This isn't the first time this has happened, and he was all right before."

"Yeah," Laura sobbed, "but — "

"If they had the Plague, they wouldn't have partied together, right?" she said, trying come up with something that could soothe Laura's fears — and *not* mentioning her own.

Like, what if they had it and didn't know yet. Or what if they all had it and didn't care?

"But — " Laura couldn't get the rest out through her tears.

"Look. Whatever happens, we'll take care of it," she said, holding Laura and rocking her. "We will. We'll take care of it together."

● CHAPTER SIX

George Beecher sighed, pulled his raincoat a little tighter against the damp chill, and lit another cigarette. He moved out of the shadows, walking a little farther along the riverfront, and leaned on one of the cutesy gaslights, staring out at the river as if he was watching for something.

He was, but it wasn't out on the river — which you really couldn't see much of because of the creeping fog. What he wanted was inside that building behind him, in warmth and laughter and candlelight.

Well, the only way he was going to earn some of that for himself was to park out here, in the dark, fog and cold. And wait.

A lot of what a P.I. did was wait, although for the life of him, he couldn't imagine why the gal who'd hired him had wanted her hubby followed. Or what she figured he was doing on his nights out. He hadn't done anything at all this whole evening. He'd thought she was a little odd when the boss first talked to her; now he was sure of it.

The guy had shown up at the Irish bar, like she'd said he would — but it wasn't with a chippie, like he'd expected; it was with an old man, a guy that had that "white-collar worker" look about him. Retired white-collar. Nothing untoward there, either, the old guy was as straight as they came; George had a knack for picking out the bent ones no matter how far in the closet they'd buried themselves. The young guy just had an odd friend, that was all. No big deal. Plenty of guys were buddies with old guys — maybe this was somebody he'd worked with before the old man retired.

They'd listened to the band — along with the rest of the bar. The guy — kid, almost — hadn't even had anything to drink; it had looked to George like he'd stuck to cola the whole time.

Then a chippie *had* shown up, a free-lancer, and way out of place for the bar. For a little bit, it had looked like he was going to get a bite; the guy'd come real close to getting into a fight over the underage hooker.

But the fight never materialized. The rest of the patrons bounced the drunk, and the guy George was following had taken the kid back to his table. The old guy left them alone.

Once again, it started to look like pay-dirt, but he'd just talked to the kid; then got the girl some food, maybe passed her some money, then turned her loose. And when he and the old guy left, it wasn't to go party with the chick — it was to this second-floor restaurant.

They'd been there for hours. The girl had evaporated.

Nobody in his right mind would give a hooker cash and expect her to be waiting for him after dinner. Either the guy was really crazy, or —

Or the guy was a pushover for a sob story. Stupid, but nothing you could prosecute in a court of law. Unless wifey was planning on getting him committed. . . .

You'd need a lot more than giving a panhandling kid some dough to get a guy committed. He hadn't even started the fight in the bar back there — and he'd hardly laid a finger on the drunk. You'd need some serious shit to lock a guy up; some evidence that he was being more than just a pushover for a sob story, something really crazy. So far the guy hadn't obliged at all.

What was more, he didn't look as if he had enough money to make locking him up a profitable deal. He had a nice classic car, yeah, but nothing wildly spectacular, no Ferrarri, no fancy clothes, and he wasn't parading around with high-class types.

On the other hand, he *had* flashed a Gold Card. And

he *was* eating in a gourmet place. A lot of millionaires didn't look or act the part. Maybe —

Well, it wasn't George's business what she did with the information he got her. All he had to do was follow the dude around, and make his report, take his pictures. He'd gotten one of the guy with the old guy, and one going into the restaurant. Funny thing had happened; every time he wanted to get a pic of the guy with the hooker, somebody had gotten in the way. He had only his verbal report, and a picture of the kid as she came out of the bar.

No matter. Wifey would have what he'd gotten. Whatever she did with the full report after he turned it in was her own affair.

He dropped the cigarette on the cobblestones, ground it under his heel, and lit another. It was going to be a two-box night from the looks of it.

Aurilia nic Morrigan leaned over her stark ebony desk and flipped through the pages of the last detective agency's report one more time, frowning. This perusal, like the last, yielded nothing she could use. Bruning Incorporated certainly hadn't come up with much in three weeks of following Tannim around; hopefully the new agency she had hired would be a little more resourceful.

She slapped the folder closed, petulantly, and stared at her perfectly manicured nails. Aurilia wanted Keighvin Silverhair shredded, scattered over at least a continent, preferably by those same perfectly manicured nails. But Keighvin had formidable protections, and at least the grudging backing of Elfhame Fairgrove. She and Vidal Dhu were the only Folk of the local Unseleighe Court who wanted Keighvin's skin; they had *no* backing if it came to an all-out war instead of minor skirmishing. So she and Vidal were reduced to hide-in-corner strategies; one thing she had never been particularly good at. Right now, the only way to get Keighvin, at least so far as she could tell, was through this "Tannim" character. The problem was, she had discovered that beneath a veneer of commonly known information, there wasn't *anything* to give her a clue to the human's nature.

She sighed, tossed the bound folder onto the filing cabinet, and stretched her arms over her head, slowly. The beige suede screens that walled her off from the rest of the room were hardly more than a few feet away, just barely out of reach. There was very little in her tiny office-cubicle besides the desk, the filing-cabinet and the black leather chair she sat in — but unlike humans, she and her associates didn't need much in the way of paper records. The single three-drawer filing-cabinet served all their needs for storage, and all of one and a half drawers was taken up with reports on Fairgrove and the personnel there. The records for Adder's Fork Studios filled barely half of the bottom drawer.

But Adder's Fork didn't need much in the way of paper-trails and record-keeping. Customers came to find *them*, not the other way around. There was no need to go to any effort to keep track of accounting; payment was always in advance, cash only. And if the IRS or any other busy-body agency came looking for them, their agents would find — nothing.

Customers, on the other hand, could always reach them. Vidal saw to that.

Supply and demand, Aurilia mused, a little smile playing about her lips. *A small market, but a loyal one. And one with few options to go elsewhere. . . .*

She stood up, walking around the discrete beige partition to the space taken up by the studio. It was a good thing they didn't need to hire outside secretarial help. A mundane secretary would never be able to handle the environment.

Nearest to the office was the newest sound-stage. Tiny, by Hollywood standards, but quite adequate for the job, it looked very much like an old-fashioned doctor's office. Aurilia looked the new set over again, and decided it wasn't quite menacing enough. There was a definite overall impression of threat, but the customers weren't terribly bright sometimes; they needed things pointed out.

Circles, arrows, and underlinings.

She considered the doctor's examining table. The next film would be a period piece, of the 1800s, re-enacting a series of incidents that had taken place during the Chicago World's Fair. With liberal embellishments. The kind their customers really appreciated.

The lead character — one could hardly call him a "hero" — in this movie was a physician who had used the activity and bustle caused by the Fair to cover his own activities. He had lured in young women new to the city by advertising for secretaries, and offering a room above his office as an added incentive. With the Fair in full swing, rooms had been at a premium and were very expensive even in the poorest parts of town. Doctors were respected professionals — and in any case, he (supposedly) did not actually live in the same building as his office. Many young women applied whenever he posted his advertisement.

He only chose select individuals, however. Pretty girls, but ones with no family, or very far from home. Girls with no friends, and especially, no boyfriends. Girls with quiet, submissive natures.

He would scientifically discover their weaknesses, play upon them, and eventually, lure them down into his "special office," with the hidden door. Among other things, he had performed hack-abortions before he had hit on the secretarial scheme. Some of those secret patients had been his victims. It had been no problem to have any number of surprises concealed within the building; it had been constructed from his own plans. Once hidden behind the soundproof walls, he would overpower his girls with chloroform, then strap them to a special examining table —

And once he was finished with them — or even at the climax of his pleasures — he would behead them, with a special device he mounted onto the table.

The bodies he disposed of in various ways, none traceable at the time. Aurilia reflected that he had really been very clever, for a human. His downfall had come when he overestimated his invulnerability and grew careless, choosing a girl he thought fit the profile — who didn't.

But that was not what concerned the studio. They would use only the barest bones of the original story — and it certainly would not end in the doctor's capture.

Indeed, they were going to take extreme liberties in the matter of the victims' ages. None would be over the age of about sixteen. Most would be nine to thirteen, or at least, would look that young. Vidal already had several girls in mind, and there would, of course, be many constructs used to fill out the cast. Aurilia was considering a second version, employing young boys instead of girls, and a female "doctor" — or even a third and fourth with same-sex pairings. After all, why waste a perfectly good set?

But right now that set still needed a few modifications. Aurilia considered the examining table carefully. She couldn't make the restraints any more obvious. Perhaps —

Perhaps a change of color.

She reached out with her magic, and touching the aluminum with the hand of a lover, stroked the surface of the table, darkening it, dulling the shiny, stainless surface and changing its substance, until the tabletop had become a slab of dark gray marble.

That did it. That was exactly the touch the set had needed. Now the table called up images of ancient sacrificial altars, without the mind quite realizing it, or wondering why.

Of course, after the first victim, the audience would know what the table was for, and would simply be waiting for the "doctor" to lure another victim to his lair.

But the little touches and attention to detail was what had made Adder's Fork the leading producers of S and M, kiddie-porn, and snuff-films in the business. There was true artistry involved, and centuries of expertise.

Hmm. Perhaps an Aztec theme for the next group. Wasn't there a sect where the sacrifice was first shared by all the participants?

Aurilia busied herself with the rest of the set, checking the apparatus and the camera and sound set-ups, making certain that everything was in place for the shoot tomorrow. It was ironic that both the Unseleighe Court and the Seleighe Court had the same problem in dealing with the modern world. They both had to earn real money.

Different motives, and different ends, but the same needs. For Aurilia, Vidal, and Niall, it was money to pay for the private detectives and to buy property. Money to buy arms to ship to both sides of a fight, be it a simple gang-war or full-fledged terrorism. Money to bribe officials, or those whose power was not official but no less real. True money from human hands, not magic-made duplicates, for the underworld was cannier than the rest of human society and would catch such tricks quickly. The underworld preferred bills in denominations of less than a hundred dollars; preferred old, worn money rather than newly printed. They would not accept money with sequential numbers. The time it would take to gather single, old bills and duplicate them, or to duplicate a single, old bill and make enough changes in it to make every copy look different, was better spent in ways that simply earned that amount of money.

There are times in the humans' world when it is simpler and easier to do without magic.

That had left Aurilia with a few problems of logistics, but nowhere near as many as her opponents were forced to cope with. The Seleighe Court fools limited their ways of earning cash to legitimate means. Fools they were, because "legitimate" and "constricted" were one and the same. And when one reduced one's options, one halved one's income.

Anything illegal was *far* more profitable than anything legal. And, for all of its difficulties, moving and working in the shadow world of the underground was much simpler than coping with all the regulations and laws of the "honest citizen."

Look at everything Keighvin had gone through to establish Fairgrove Industries, for instance. He'd created something that could function totally within human parameters, and yet leave the nonhumans free to work. Resourceful he was, indeed, and though she hated him passionately, Aurilia could admire that much about him.

Whereas Adder's Fork had required only three things once Aurilia and Vidal had arrived at a plan; kenning an airplane and all the equipment they needed, making an underworld contact adept at forging records and getting their electronic copies into the proper systems, and installing a Gate into Underhill inside the plane.

The plane, a C-130 cargo craft, had taken six months to duplicate and another to modify so that it no longer looked like the craft it had been copied from. The lines had been subtlely changed, and the color turned to a light blue that blended in very well with the open sky. Being able to work Underhill had helped; magical energy was much more readily available there. But they had not been able to create the craft exactly; in point of fact, there was no iron or steel anywhere in it, it had no engine, and never needed refueling on mortal aviation gas. That was both an advantage and a disadvantage. There was nothing to break down, and they could land and take off from anywhere, at any time, but they dared not let inspectors or anyone with more than a cursory knowledge of aircraft anywhere near it. That flaw made a dreadful hole in their defenses. Aurilia would have liked a real engine — but the Unseleighe

Court shared their rivals' "allergy" to Cold Iron. How Keighvin and his crew could bear to work so near it was a mystery to her. And if they ever broke through the Fairgrove defenses, Cold Iron and humans wielding it would without a doubt be Keighvin's second line of defense. That was fine . . . she had a syringe of human blood with iron filings ready to inject into Keighvin when she had him. It would be very entertaining to watch his reactions to that.

But for that single technical flaw — the authenticity of the aircraft — Adder's Fork was completely in the clear. Gold coins — kenned copies of genuine Kruger-rands — had bought the records for plane and pilots, and had bought the human who inserted those records into the humans' computers. More coins, sold one at a time to dealers, had rented equipment long enough for Unseleighe Court mages to ken it. Aurilia had stock-piled many favors over the course of several hundred years; she cashed them all in on this venture.

Then it had only required time. Time to reproduce complicated gear and make sure that it worked; time to build the studio Underhill. Time to make more con-tacts in the human underworld, offering the kind of product certain humans would literally bankrupt themselves to own.

Adder's Fork did simple porn movies at first — well, relatively simple. All of their pictures had real, if un-adorned, plots, and most involved the occult. And every Adder's Fork film involved pain, bondage, S and M; these things raised power, energy the humans never used, energy that would ordinarily have gone to waste, so in addition to bringing in human money, the filming itself was a potent source of power. The favors Aurilia had cashed in were quickly replaced by other favors owed as the denizens of Underhill vied to be in at the filming, acting either on Vidal's direction as camera operators or other technicians, or as extras, if they were attractive enough. Not every creature of the Unseleighe Court was a boggle or troll. Some, like Aurilia and Vidal, were as lovely as any High Court elven lord or lady.

Now that they had both studios up and running, they still did produce that simpler sort of film, for over in Studio One, they'd finished one such film tonight. A gay-bondage party using the Caligula set, to be precise; one with a simple plot that was close to the reality of the situation — a group hires a strip-tease entertainer for the birthday-boy, then they all decide to take things a little farther. The "party-favor" had been a very pretty young male hooker, dark-haired and dreamy-eyed, who Aurilia thought they might use again some time. He was the only one who hadn't known the "party" was being filmed; he'd been plied with liquor at the bar where he had been picked up, and drugged in the cab on the way here. The set was a discreet one, the cameras mounted behind mirrors. The other five men, old customers, had been recruited with a cash bonus and a promise of whatever they wanted from the company catalog.

That was a formidable promise, and one that might have lured them more than the money. One thing that Adder's Fork had that no other pornshop possessed was an unbreakable copy-guard. Adder's Fork tapes could not be duplicated; attempts would only result in both tapes' signals breaking up — thanks to a special spell in the Underhill duplicating room. There was a warning to that effect at the front of each tape — and every time Aurilia received a request for a copy of something that duplicated an order to the same address, she smiled. Certain humans never could believe that there was something they couldn't get around.

High-tech meets high magic — and loses.

A more economic way to make ends meet. She considered her solution to the cash-flow problem to be just as clever and creative as Keighvin's. And far less work. His setup had taken decades to establish; hers mere months. His was rooted to one spot, and if there were ever troubles, he would have to vanish with no other recourse. Hers was as mobile as her "plane," for it did not matter where the Gate was located in the here-and-now of the humans' world, so long as it was rooted in something large enough to serve as an anchor. It was useful to have the studios Underhill, especially Studio Two. Screams couldn't penetrate the Gate, and even more Unseleighe Court creatures were vying for a chance to serve as extras in the films Two produced. Adder's Fork Studios had always been known for high-quality porn, but the Studio Two films, snuff-pictures with emphasized occult and satanic themes, really had the customers begging for more.

The customers raved about the "special effects," and it was not the deaths they were talking about. Vidal's careful camera work, showing every nuance of the snuff and lingering on the corpse afterwards, so that the customer could see for himself that it was neither moving nor breathing, made sure the customers knew they had gotten what they paid for. Most of the dead were magical constructs, who lived and breathed only long enough to scream and die, but there were enough true human deaths — and human reactions of fear and pain — to satisfy both the customers and the thirsts of Aurilia and her partners. No, the customers were talking about the "monsters" and "demons" that participated in the sexual rituals, and usually accounted for half of the deaths. Little did the clients know that these "monsters" were not humans in makeup and prostheses, but the Unseleighe Court creatures who thronged Aurilia's auditions every time she cast a picture.

And no one ever went away disappointed. Whoever didn't get on camera, got to help dispose of the corpse when Vidal didn't need it anymore. *Maybe we ought to film that next time*. . . . The Chicago doctor in this version was going to be a satanist as well, and at the moment

when the police broke down his door, would summon a
demon to carry him to (presumed) safety. On second
thought, Aurilia decided to leave the script the way it
was, with nothing other than the rituals and the half-
seen hints of "the Master," with the supernatural
actually entering the picture only at the end. Save all
the limb-chewing for the next flick.

It was ironic, Aurilia thought, that human religious
fanatics seemed convinced that there were so many truly
innocent activities that were inspired by their "Satan"
and created by evil, yet they didn't recognize true evil
when it walked among them. Adder's Fork was the
name of the studio that produced bondage, kiddie-
porn, and snuff-films. The holding company that
owned the airplane and (supposedly) produced training films was a respected member of the Chamber of
Commerce, incorporated as "Magic Mirror, Inc." Vidal
went to all the meetings and all the functions, smiled,
and passed among the foolish human sheep, even
donated money to some of the more fundamentalist
churches, and none of them ever guessed that beneath
his smooth, flawless exterior lay a creature that would
gladly have torn their hearts from their living bodies and
eaten them alive. In fact, he was praised by those fundamentalist leaders as a "true Christian businessman."

A shiver of energies touched her spine as the Gate let
someone through from the human world. She wasn't
worried; right now the Gate was keyed only to herself,
Vidal, and Niall mac Lyr. She waited a moment, dim-
ming the lighting with a thought. Vidal stalked
through the door from Studio One shortly thereafter,
closing it so carefully behind him that Aurilia knew he
was angry.

*Lovely. What sort of temper tantrum am I going to be treated
to this morning?*

She turned slowly to face him: He was still wearing
his human-seeming, which meant that although he
was angry, he had not been enraged so far as to lose

control. It was much the same as his true-shape; raven hair replaced the silver, though he wore it longer when he was not passing among humans. The pale skin had been overlaid with a golden tan. Brown eyes with round pupils substituted for the colorless, pale green, cat's eyes. . . . But the brow was just as high, the cheek-bones just as prominent, the eyebrows still slanted winglike towards his temples, and the body was still the wiry-slender build of a gymnast or a martial artist. His face wore a cool, indifferent expression, but his body betrayed him.

She, in her turn, did not pretend she did not notice his anger. She simply waited, smoothing the cream-colored silk of her skirt with one hand. She might be the head of this triad, the one with the plans, but he was the strength. He was only a little less intelligent than she, and a better, more powerful mage than she, and she had no intention of ever forgetting that fact. Only his hatred for Keighvin Silverhair kept him at her side, for normally Vidal worked alone. What Keighvin had done to him to warrant that undying enmity, Aurilia did not know and had never asked, but Vidal had tried to destroy the High Court lord for centuries. Until recently, he had rebuffed all efforts at recruiting his aid, even to eliminate Keighvin — but when she approached him with her plan, he had volunteered his help as soon as she had presented it all to him.

So now *she* waited for *him* to speak, and even though she felt a flash of irritation at his superior attitude, she suppressed it. She could not afford to lose him, and she would not antagonize him. Not yet, anyway.

He stalked past her, to the Roman orgy set; they'd finished the Caligula picture last week, but Aurilia hadn't broken the set down yet, because she'd planned to use it for the party picture. Vidal flung himself down on one of the stained cream satin-covered couches, and glared up at her through absurdly long lashes. She seated herself calmly, folded her hands in her lap in a position of calculated passivity, and waited for him to say something. It would have to be verbally; he would not deign to speak to her mind-to-mind. She was not of sufficient rank to warrant that intimacy.

"Keighvin's close to getting the engines into production," he snarled, finally. His command of human vernacular had improved out of all recognition in the past few months. Now it was almost as good as hers. "Very close. He's within weeks."

Aurilia frowned as she recalculated her original plan; she hadn't expected to have to put it into motion quite so soon. She crossed her legs, restlessly. "That's not good — but we've got a counter-plan already in place to discredit him." She blessed the day that she had watched that movie about Preston Tucker. It had given her everything she needed. . . .

"It won't fly," Vidal informed her, his black brows meeting as he scowled. "Somehow he's figured out his own weak spots, and he's ahead of you. He's got a human to front for him. A man with respect and reputation; a retired metallurgist who used to work for Gulfstream. This human knows his field, Aurilia, and he's got contacts we can't touch in the human world. He's going to be able to concoct an explanation that will hold up. And both Keighvin and that human mage of his have placed protections about this new man. I can't touch him magically, not with human and elven magic working against me. I couldn't even take down the first of his shields unless I could catch him Underhill."

That wasn't good; briefly she wondered if Keighvin or the human had seen the same movie she had. She would have to assume that they had, and plan accordingly. She closed her eyes for a moment, and thought. "This human, how old is he?" she asked, finally. "How healthy is he? Could we attack him physically?"

"Well, he's retired, so he's at least sixty-five," Vidal admitted. "He doesn't look terribly sturdy, but he's from the Old Country. You know those scrawny little men — they look fragile, but they're as tough as a briar root and twice as hard to break."

From the Old Country? Eire? Hmm — first generation immigrant? I can work with that. "But their meals are full of butter and eggs and fatty bacon," Aurilia said with a sly smile. "And they drink. That doesn't do a great deal for their hearts, their arteries, or their livers. By now, Keighvin has convinced him that all of his childhood tales are really true, and he's thinking of the things besides the Seleighe Court that might be real. He should have dredged up a tale or two from his memory about us — hopefully, a gory one. Why don't you go see if you can't frighten him into a heart attack?"

Vidal considered the idea for a moment, then smiled, slowly. His muscles relaxed, and the frown-line between his brows faded. "Now, that's not a bad notion — and it has a certain amount of entertainment value as well. A good thought, *acushla.* Well done."

That last was patronizing, a pat on the head, as one might pat a dog for a clever trick. Aurilia kept her temper, and smiled winsomely back at him. She was the mind, and he the strength; as long as she kept that firmly in mind, she remained in control of the situation, no matter what he might think. Let him break into a froth at every obstacle. She would keep her head, and guide them all through to the other side.

As she would keep careful track of every insult. She was not of high rank in the Unseleighe Court — but rank could be gained by toppling one higher. There would be an accounting when this was over.

Oh, yes.

Vidal lounged on his couch, perfectly at ease now, with a look in his eye as if he might well order Aurilia to wait on him in a moment. He could get away with that if he cared to, right now. He could order her to produce refreshment, or even to serve him in other ways, and she was bound by rank to do as he asked.

She had to sidetrack him, to remind him of her status

in the human world, where he depended on her plans and knowledge. He'd enjoyed working the Caligula picture; he didn't much like the Deadly Doctor concept, mostly because it wasn't decadent and luxurious enough. Aurilia sought for a distraction in plans for Adder's Fork to keep him from giving her orders — she wasn't sure she'd be able to keep her temper if he took the master-slave tone with her.

"What do we do after the Deadly Doctor?" she asked, innocently, looking around at the cream-and-red set, four couches, a couple of marble columns, and a lot of draperies and mirrors. And the series of red ropes lying about. It wasn't an elaborate set; the extras had provided much of the ornament on the Caligula film, and the party picture hadn't needed much more. "It ought to be something demonic. I'd thought Aztec — "

Vidal shook his head emphatically; the one place where she trusted his judgment over hers was in marketing. Somehow he always anticipated what the customers were going to buy. "Not yet. I don't think the customers are going to be ready for anything that exotic yet. It requires too much imagination, and the lead characters are the wrong color. We'll lose a lot of our Southern audience. They want handsome white men as their protagonists. We need something — steamy — decadent — depraved, debauched. Exotic, but not something where the customer can't identify with the master character — "

He shook his head, unable to come up with anything. On reflection, Aurilia agreed with him. She searched for a subject that might do, and suddenly a most unlikely source of inspiration flashed into her mind.

It was the rack of paperbacks at the airport; fully half of them were lurid romances, and she remembered thinking at the time that taken with a little less sugar and allowing the "villain" to win, the plots weren't all that different from Adder's Fork productions. *Passion's Frenzied Fury, Harem Nights, Wild Moon Rising,* they featured stupid, sweet and submissive heroines and some villains who certainly fit the "exotic, depraved, and debauched" description.

"What about a harem thing?" she asked. "We could re-use most of the Caligula set. . . . " But Arabs were not in particularly good odor at the moment, not even with the Adder's Fork customers. And the master character in a harem theme would have to be an Arab. "No, how about pirates; we could do the same there, use this set for the pirate captain's cabin, with one couch and a couple of sea-chests full of bondage gear. The customers won't know they didn't have reclining couches on ships, and frankly, I doubt they'll care. We can open with a boarding party, kill off a few constructs, lots of blood and guts there, take prisoners, and then cut to the cabin."

"Pirates," Vidal mused. "I like that. Snuff, or S and M?"

"Why not both?" she suggested. "A little torture, a little bondage, film from a couple of different angles, mix and match, and leave out the snuff scenes for the S and M flick. But what about the occult angle?"

Vidal grinned, pleased to come up with something she didn't know. "Voodoo, *acushla*. Everybody knows pirates were into voodoo. It's perfect; it's black magic on an exotic island setting, the white stud presiding over a harem of dusky priestesses on a moonlit beach . . . easy to reproduce Underhill with constructs doing all the extra parts. We can even use the arena set for the voodoo rituals, just grow a few palm trees, fill in the seats with foliage, and conjure a moon."

Aurilia felt that cold shiver again, but this time it was not due to someone using the Gate, but to a brush of fear. She did not care to meddle with alien magic — especially alien human magic. She'd had too many bad experiences in the past. . . .

"Be careful with that, will you? We can't afford to bring in something from real voodoo, even by accident. They might not be amused." *They weren't the last time.*

The Manitou was particularly displeased. If I hadn't been operating against whites, and not against the natives, I might not have survived his displeasure.

"True." Vidal frowned, this time absently. "I think it's worth it, though. Especially since I suspect we can get extra footage for another couple of flicks out of this. It's going to require some careful research."

By which he means I should take care of it, of course. Well, better research assistant than lowly handmaiden.

"Consider it done," she said, with a sweet smile. Vidal looked much happier, and she decided to broach her other idea. "What about making the Deadly Doctor into a foursome, with a female doctor in two of them?" This would be a chance for Aurilia to take her turn in front of the camera. Vidal got plenty of opportunities; even when there weren't any Unseleighe Court volunteers to act as technicians, he could control the camera magically even when he was being filmed by it, and his incredible — attributes — made him a natural for the master character. But they hadn't done anything with a Dominatrix for a long, long time. She'd wanted a chance to be in on the kills personally for weeks.

Vidal pursed his lips, looked sour, but nodded reluctantly. "Not a bad idea, I suppose. How many victims are we talking about? All told, I mean. It takes energy to make the constructs, and it won't be you who's doing it."

As if I didn't know that. "For the first film, I'd say six constructs and two real kills," she replied cautiously. "For the other three, I think the female-male needs a couple of extra real kills, otherwise the customer won't believe in the doctor's ability to overpower young men. But I wouldn't put real kills in the same-sex flick at all; the situation itself is going to be enough of a shocker."

Vidal nodded, after a moment of thought. "We ought to downgrade the same-sex encounters to bondage and torture. The fringe there is a lot smaller market, and I doubt it's worth going after."

She nodded, for once in complete agreement. "That

was what I thought — and there's more money available from the leatherboys than there is from the psychotics. The leather crowd never *will* believe that they can't find some way to break our copy-protection."

She rose, so that he followed her lead, subtly answering his superior attitude with body language of her own.

To recover his upper hand, he spoke first, with an order framed as a request. "Why don't you set up your casting-call while I go pay a visit to Doctor Kelly," he suggested. "And get me some parameters for the constructs. I'd prefer file personas, if you have some that will do; they're a lot easier to make than brand new. types."

"I don't know why file personas shouldn't work," she replied, already heading for the office and speaking over her shoulder as her cream-leather heels clicked against the marble floor. "I'll just modify the Submissive Secretary, the Street-Sparrows, the Victorian Hookers, and the French and Irish Maids. The hardest part will be the costumes, and I'm a good enough mage for that."

"Precisely," he said, not quite sneering. She ignored the implied insult that she was only a good enough mage to make clothing. He strode towards the door, his soft-soled shoes noiseless on the marble, already reaching for the knob.

"Bring me back some *good* news this time, all right?" she responded sweetly, with the implied insult that *she* was sending *him* out to do her bidding.

But the door closed on her words; he was already gone.

● CHAPTER SEVEN

Held aloft by good fellowship and excellent wine —
for Trish did, indeed, know her wines as well she knew
music — Sam deactivated his alarm system, unlocked
his door, and with a farewell wave to Tannim, slipped
inside. Thoreau had been waiting, and gave him a tail-
wagging welcome, then padded beside him with eager
devotion.

Sam smiled down at his faithful companion, and his
pleasure was not due just to the wine, the company, or
the greeting. This was going to work, this strange alliance of magic and technology, of the ancient Sidhe
and modern engineering. It was as real, and as heady a
mixture, as the odd gourmet dinner he'd just eaten.
And like the meal, it all meshed, so well that the various
parts might have been made for each other.

For all his skeptical, cynical words to young Tannim,
he'd seen a reflection of the elves' purported concern
for the welfare of children in the way Tannim had
treated the young prostitute. That hadn't been an act
of any kind; Tannim had been worried about the girl,
and had expressed that worry in tangible ways that
could help her immediately and directly. Money was
one thing, but giving her a way to eat regularly for a
while was a damned good idea.

*He could have bought her groceries — but that would have
entailed getting her into his car, and that could be trouble if the
police took an interest in the proceedings. And even if he'd
bought food for her, chances are she'd not have known how to
cook anything. Assuming she lives somewhere that she can cook
anything.*

It must be a hard, lonely way to live, now that he thought about it. Under the makeup, the child had been thin and pale, wearing a brittle mask of indifference that was likely to crack at any time. He'd always assumed hookers were too lazy to do any real work — but what place would hire a thirteen-year-old child? And what runaway would risk the chance of being caught by giving her real name to get a real job? Under the age of sixteen, you had to have a letter of parental consent to work, and if she was, indeed, a runaway, how would she ever get one?

Of course, she could have lied about her age, and forged a parental consent letter, but such fragile deceits wouldn't hold up to any kind of examination. Perhaps she had tried just that, and been found out. Perhaps she had discovered she had no other choice. Sex seemed less important these days than it was in his day; perhaps selling herself to strangers didn't seem that terrible.

Then again, perhaps it did, but there were no options for her, no way to go home.

He had never quite realized how relatively idyllic his own childhood had been. Why, he'd even had a pony — of course, most Irish children living in the country had ponies, but still . . .

Her life now must be hellish — but as Tannim had asked, if she was willing to continue with it, how bad must her home life have been that she chose this over it?

Sam resolved to start carrying books of fast-food gift certificates. That way, if they *did* run into the child again, or one like her, he'd have a material way to help as well.

And 'tisn't likely she'd find a dope dealer willing to trade drugs for coupons.

But there wasn't much he could do now, not without knowing all the circumstances, without even knowing the child's name and address. He had work to do; Tania's plight would have to wait.

He'd learned long ago how to put problems that seemed critical — but over which he had no control — in the back of his mind while he carried on with lesser concerns. He'd gotten several possibilities for the solution to Keighvin's needs last night, and he needed to track down the latest research, to see if anything new could eliminate his bogus "process" right off.

At least there's one problem I won't be having. The engine blocks will be there, and be everything I claim, pass every test. This won't be a cold-fusion fiasco — I've got real results, solid product that I can hand out to anyone who doubts. If the boys in Salt Lake City had just waited until they had working test reactors producing clean power before they went public, they'd have saved themselves a world of trouble. And if the process had worked the way they said it did, well, nobody would be arguing with their theory or their results, they'd just be going crazy trying to reproduce what they'd done. That's what's going to happen here.

He was looking forward to watching the other firms going crazy, in fact. This was almost like his college-prank days, on a massive scale.

Sam walked slowly down the hall, turning on lights as he passed. He intended to re-arm the security system as soon as he got to the office so that he couldn't be disturbed. His mind was buzzing with all of his plans, and he was so wrapped up in his own thoughts that he didn't even notice the stranger standing in his office until Thoreau stopped dead in the doorway and growled.

Perhaps the man hadn't been there until that very moment — for as soon as he saw the creature, Sam's own hackles went up. There was a curious double-vision quality about the intruder; one moment he was black-haired and dark-eyed, and as human as Tannim. The next moment —

The next moment he was as unhuman as Keighvin, and clearly of the same genetic background. But there the resemblance ended, for where there was a palpable air of power tempered with reason and compassion about Keighvin, this man wore the mantle of power without control and shaped by greed. Now Sam understood what his granny had meant when she had said that even with the Sight it was difficult for humans, child or adult, to tell the dark Sidhe from the kindly. If the creature had not been so obvious in his menace, he might have convinced Sam that he was Keighvin's very cousin.

Thoreau growled again, a note of hysterical fear in the sound; he backed up, putting Sam between himself and the Sidhe. Not very brave, certainly not the television picture of Lassie — but very intelligent. Sam was just as glad. He didn't want this creature to strike out and hurt his little companion. Sam had defenses; Thoreau had none.

"Samuel Kelly, do you see me?" the Sidhe asked flatly. It had the sound of a ritual challenge.

"I see you," Sam replied. "I see you as you are, so you might as well drop the seeming." Then he added, in a hasty afterthought, "You were not invited." Just in case recognition implied acceptance of the man's presence. Granny's stories had warned about the Sidhe and the propensity for semantics-games.

"I don't require an invitation," the Sidhe responded arrogantly, folding his arms over his chest as he dropped the human disguise.

One for me, Sam thought. The Sidhe played coupgames of prestige as well. Every time he surprised the creature, or caused it to do something, he won a "point." That intangible scoring might count for something in the next few moments. The higher Sam's prestige, the less inclined the thing might be to bother him.

"So what do you want?" Sam asked, tempering the fact that he'd been forced by the stranger's silence into asking with, "I'm busy, and I haven't time for socializing."

Again the Sidhe was taken aback — and showed a hint of anger. "I have come to deliver a warning."

To the stranger's further surprise, Sam snorted rudely. "Go tell it to the Marines," he said, hearkening back to his childhood insults. "I told you, I have work to do. I've no time for games and nonsense."

Inwardly, he was far from calm. Tannim had put some kind of arcane protection on him after dinner tonight, when he signed a preliminary agreement with Fairgrove. The young man had said that Keighvin would be doing the same, but how effective those protections would be, he had no idea. He knew *something* was there; he saw it as a glowing haze about him, like one of those "auras" the New Agers talked about, visible only out of the corner of his eye. How much would it hold against? Would it take a real attack if this stranger made one?

The Sidhe raised a graceful eyebrow, and the tips of his pointed ears twitched. "Bravado, is it?" he asked in a voice full of arrogant irony. "I should have expected it from the kind of stubborn fossil who would listen to reckless young fools and believe their prattle. Hear me now, Sam Kelly — you think to aid yet another rattle-brained loon, one who styles himself Keighvin Silverhair. Don't."

Sam waited, but there was nothing more. *"Don't?"* Sam said at last, incredulously. "Is that all you have to say? Just *don't?"*

"That is all I have to *say,"* the Sidhe replied after a long, hard stare. "But I have a demonstration for fools who refuse to listen — "

He didn't gesture, didn't even shrug —

Suddenly Sam was enveloped in flames, head to toe.

His heart contracted with fear, spasming painfully; he lost his breath, and he choked on a cry —

And in the next moment was glad that he hadn't uttered it. The flames, whether they were real, of magical energy, or only illusion, weren't touching him. There was no heat, at least nothing he felt, although Thoreau yelped, turned tail, and ran for the shelter of Sam's bedroom.

He remained frozen for a moment, then the true nature of the attack penetrated. *It can't hurt me, no matter what it looks like.* After a deep breath to steady his heart, Sam simply folded his arms across his chest and sighed.

"Is this supposed to impress me?" he asked mildly. A snide comment like that might have been a stupid thing to say, but it was the only attitude Sam could think to take. Tannim had warned him about lying to the Sidhe, or otherwise trying to deceive them. It couldn't be done, he'd said, at least not by someone with Sam's lack of experience with magic. And good or evil, both sorts took being lied to very badly. So — brazen it out. Act boldly, as if he saw this sort of thing every day and wasn't intimidated by it.

The Sidhe's face twisted with rage. *"Damn* you, mortal!" he cried. And this time he *did* gesture.

A sword appeared in his hand; a blue-black, shiny blade like no metal Sam had ever seen. A small part of him wondered what it was, as the rest of him shrieked, and backpedaled, coming up against the wall.

"Not so impudent now, are you?" the Sidhe crowed, kicking aside fallen books and moving in for the kill, sword glittering with a life of its own.

Sam could only stare, paralyzed with fear, as his hands scrabbled on the varnished wood behind him —

Tannim cursed the traffic as he waited at the end of Sam's driveway for it to clear, peering into the darkness. Something must have just let out for the night, for there was a steady stream of headlights passing in the eastbound lane — when he wanted westbound, of course — with no break in sight. And there was no reason for that many cars out here at this time of night. It looked for all the world like the scene at the end of *Field of Dreams,* where every car in the world seemed lined up on that back country road.

"So if he built the stupid ballfield out here, why didn't somebody tell me?" he griped aloud. "If I'd known the Heavenly All-Stars were playing tonight —"

He never finished the sentence, for energies hit the

shields he'd placed on Sam — which were also tied to *his* shields.

The protections about Sam locked into place, as the power that had been flung at the old man flared in a mock-conflagration of bael-fire.

Mock? Only in one sense. If Sam hadn't been shielded, he'd have gone up in *real* flames, although nothing around him would have even been scorched. Another Fortean case of so-called "spontaneous human combustion."

But Sam was protected — the quick but effective shielding woven earlier caught and held. Tannim had not expected those protections to be needed so soon.

He knew what the attacker was, if not who. Only the Folk could produce bael-fire. And the *hate-rage-lust* pulse that came with the strike had never originated from one of Keighvin's Folk. That spelled "Unseleighe Court" in Tannim's book.

All this Tannim analyzed as he acted. He jammed the car into "reverse" and smoked the tires. The Mustang lurched as he yanked the wheel, spinning the car into a sideways drift to stop it barely within the confines of Sam's driveway. He bailed out, grabbing his weapon-of-choice from under the seat and didn't stop moving even as he reached the door; he managed to force his stiff legs into a running kick and kept going as the door crashed open, slamming against the wall behind it.

He pelted down the hall, his bespelled, bright red crowbar clenched in his right hand, and burst into Sam's study. Sam had plastered himself against the wall nearest the door; Tannim flung himself between his friend and the creature that menaced him, taking a defensive stand with the crowbar in both hands, without getting a really good look at the enemy first.

He never did get a *really* good look. He saw only a tall, fair-haired man, a glittering sword, a scowl of surprised rage —

Then — nothing.

Only the sharp tingle of energies along his skin that told him a Gate had been opened and closed.

The enemy had fled. Leaving, presumably, the way he had arrived, by way of Underhill.

It's gonna be the last time he can do that, Tannim thought grimly, framing another shield-spell within his mind, setting it with a few chanted syllables. He dropped it in place over the body of the house, allowing the physical form of the house itself — and, more particularly, the electrical wiring — to give it shape and substance.

It was a powerful spell, and one of Tannim's best. Now no one would be able to pop in here from Underhill without Sam's express permission, nor would they be able to work magics against the house itself.

But it was draining, and Tannim sagged back against the wall when he was done, letting the crowbar slip to the floor from nerveless fingers. It fell on the carpet with a dull *thud,* and Tannim kept himself from following it only by supreme effort.

He looked up, right into Sam's face.

The metallurgist was reaching for his shoulder to help hold him up, such a mixture of expressions on his face that none of them were readable.

"I . . . don't suppose you have any Gatorade . . . ?" Tannim asked, weakly.

". . . and he set fire to me," Sam continued, after another sip of good Irish. After all the wine tonight, he was only going to permit himself one small glass — but by Holy Mary, he needed that one. His nerves were so jangled that he wasn't going to be able to sleep without it, and he didn't trust sleeping-pills. "He did, I swear it. Only the flames didn't burn. Scared the bejeezus out of poor Thoreau, though."

He reached down and fondled the spaniel's ears. Thoreau had emerged from the closet only after much coaxing, and remained half-hidden at Sam's feet, completely unashamed of his cowardice. Sam had praised the little dog to the sky for doing the right thing, though he doubted that Thoreau understood much of what he was saying; probably all Thoreau knew was that Daddy said he was a Good Boy, and Daddy was going to comfort him after the terrible fright he'd taken. Sam was quite glad that Thoreau had deserted him. One small spaniel was not going to make more than an indentation in a Sidhe's ankle — assuming the animal got that far before being blasted. He'd lost enough pets in his lifetime to old age and illness. He didn't want Thoreau turned to ash by a Sidhe with a temper.

"That was bael-fire, Sam," Tannim replied, refilling his cup from the bottle of Gatorade on the kitchen table. He'd already polished off one bottle, and Sam wondered where he was putting it all. "If you hadn't been protected, you'd have burned up like a match, but nothing around you would have been touched. Charles Fort had a lot of those cases in his books of unexplained phenomena. He called it 'spontaneous human combustion,' and thought it might have something to do with astral travel." The young man shook his head, much wearier than Sam had ever seen him. There were dark circles of exhaustion beneath his eyes, and his hair was limp and flattened-looking. "Nobody ever told Fort that going up in heatless flames is what happens when you get the Folk pissed off at you."

"But I was protected," Sam protested, sensing a flaw somewhere. "You said I had shields, and you said other mages would know that."

Tannim nodded, and rubbed his eyes. "Exactly. He *knew* bael-fire wasn't going to touch you. He'd have to be blind not to know those shields were there. I don't think he intended you to be hurt directly, Sam."

"What, then?" Sam asked in fatigue-dulled apprehension. What worse could the Sidhe have had in mind? "Or was that just intended as a warning? A bit extreme for a warning, seems to me."

"Heh. The Sidhe are always extreme." Tannim cocked his head sideways. "I think he was trying to scare you to death. I think he wanted it to look like you died naturally."

Sam took another sip of Irish, thinking about that for a moment before replying. "He did then, did he?" His apprehension turned to a slow, burning anger. "Sure, and that's a coward's way, if ever I saw one."

"Attacking a human with bael-fire is just as cowardly, Sam," the young man pointed out. "Or going after a human with elf-shot. In either case, it's like using grenades against rabbits. The target hasn't got a chance. I think he must have assumed that since you're retired, you're frail, and he was going to use that."

"Can I assume the blackguard was Unseleighe Court?" Sam asked, the anger within him burning with the same slow heat as a banked peat-fire.

Tannim nodded, and finished the last of his Gatorade. "That's their way, Sam. They never take on an opponent of equal strength if they can help it. I assume they came after you because you're hooked in with Fairgrove and Keighvin. I told you before that if you wanted to back out of this, you could." He capped the bottle and slowly tightened the lid down. "You're still welcome to. Nobody is —"

"Back out?" Sam exclaimed. "Bite your tongue! If the blackguards want a fight, they've come to the right place, let me tell you! Sam Kelly never started a fight, but he always finished them." He bared his teeth in a fierce smile. "I don't intend to let that change, no matter how old I might be."

Tannim's tired face lit up in a smile, and he clapped Sam on the shoulder. "That's the spirit! I was hoping we could count on you!"

Sam let the grin soften to something more wry than fierce. "They should have known better than to try and frighten an Irishman. We're stubborn bastards, and we don't take to being driven off. But come to think of it —

what the devil did you do to frighten *him* off? You just popped in the room, and he ran like a scalded cat."

"It wasn't what I did," Tannim replied, tapping the glass bottle on the crowbar that sat on the table between them. "It was what I had. This."

"Cold Iron?" Sam hazarded.

"Twenty pounds' worth, enchanted to a fair-thee-well," the young man told him, one hand still on the red-painted iron bar, a finger trailing along the gooseneck at one end, apparently remembering past uses. "One strong shot with this, and I don't care how powerful a mage he is, he'd have felt like he'd been hit by a semi. Eh heh . . . pureed by Peterbilt."

Sam snorted, then gazed at the bar with speculation. "Can anyone use one of those things? I used to be a fair hand with singlestick not long ago."

Tannim's eyes widened for a moment, then narrowed with speculation. "Huh. I never thought about that, but I don't know why not. I'll tell you what; I can't give you this one, but I can make one for you. And until I finish it, just remember that any crowbar is going to cause one of the Folk a lot of distress. If you'd had one in here tonight, it might even have disrupted the bael-fire spell."

Sam made a mental note to visit an auto-parts store tomorrow. He'd have one under his car seat and in every room in the house. "I'll get the one out of my car before you leave, and I'll pick up a few more tomorrow. You're sure nobody is going to be able to get back in here tonight?"

"Positive." Tannim took a deep breath, and held Sam's eyes with his own. "Absolutely positive. And as soon as I get back to Fairgrove and tie Keighvin's protections into yours, if the sorry sonuvabitch even tries, the Fairgrove Folk will know. If he brings in enough firepower to crack those shields, he'll touch off a war — "

"Not on my account!" Sam exclaimed with dismay.

That was far more than he'd bargained on . . . and something he did not want to have on his conscience.

Tannim grimaced, and now Sam realized that the young man had been a lot more shaken by the attack than he wanted to admit. "No — no, don't worry, they won't even try. They aren't any readier for open warfare than you and I are. But — you really can quit, Sam, and no one will hold it against you. . . ."

Sam shook his head emphatically. "I told you before, and I meant it. Tannim, the answer isn't 'no,' it's *'hell* no.' In fact — " he grinned, and discovered it was actually a real smile " — you couldn't get rid of me now if you paid me!"

Aurilia sighed, sipped her herb tea, and tried not to look at Niall mac Lyr. She concentrated instead on the delicate, fragile porcelain of her teacup, on the white satin tablecloth, and on the gray velvet cushions of her lounge chair. Normally she would have been enjoying a luxurious breakfast along with the tea, but her breakfast companion was not a creature designed to stimulate anyone's appetite.

The Bane-Sidhe squinted across the table at her, and glowered, its cadaverous face made all the more unpleasant by its sour expression. Every time Niall moved, a breath of dank, foul air wafted across the table toward her. Niall smelled like a fetid ditch — or an open grave. There had been times in Ireland when they were one and the same. The Bane-Sidhe did not at all match his surroundings in Aurilia's sybaritic sitting room of white satin and gray velvet. He looked like a Victorian penny-dreadful cover, for something entitled "Death and the Maiden," or "The Specter at the Feast." Aurilia sighed again, and pulled the gray silk skirts of her lounge-robe a little closer. She could only hope that when Niall left, he'd take the stench with him.

"Where is he?" Niall asked, for the seventh time. The

Bane-Sidhe's speaking voice was a hollow, unpleasant whisper; not even Vidal cared to hear its full-voiced cry. The wail of the Bane-Sidhe brought unreasoning terror even into the hearts of its allies.

Aurilia shrugged. It was no use answering him. She'd already told him she didn't know where Vidal was. The Bane-Sidhe was only interested in his own grievances.

"We have work to do," it continued, aggrieved. "Studio Two should be operational around the clock — *we* don't have to put up with union nonsense or mortal time-clocks. You promised me when I joined you that there would be enough nourishment for all of us. You told me — "

"I know what I told you," Aurilia snapped, her temper frayed by the Bane-Sidhe's constant whining. "I told you that *eventually* we'd have all the pain you could ever need or want. I didn't promise it immediately."

"Pah!" the Bane-Sidhe snorted, tossing its head petulantly. "That was a year ago! You could have had Studio Two in full production three months after you brought up Studio One. It's not as if we have to fret about the cost of sets or casts, or even equipment! But no, you had to chase after Keighvin Silverhair — you had to waste your time discovering what he was up to. And instead of being at full power, I must limp about on the dregs of energy a few paltry deaths supply, and Studio Two has produced only that puny little Roman fantasy — "

"You think humans come running to us to bare their throats to the blade?" Aurilia countered with justifiable irritation. Niall simply would not come to grips with the fact that the world had changed, and she had gotten tired of trying to convince him that things were different now than in 1890. "You think there's no *risk* involved in finding those 'paltry few victims'? This isn't the old days; when people die or disappear, even if they have no relatives to ask after them, someone generally notices! Take too many, and we'll be contending with mortal police at every turn! I'd rather *not* have to fly the anchor off if I don't have to, and if too many people come up missing, or we pick the wrong victims, Folk or not, we are going to be — "

"That is not the point," the Bane-Sidhe whispered angrily. "Your — " It turned, abruptly, its enshrouding wrappings flaring, sending a wash of dank stench over Aurilia, as the door to her sitting room opened and Vidal entered.

She assessed his expression, and her already-sour mood spoiled further. If Vidal had been unhappy before he left on his errand, he was livid now. Aurilia started to ask him what was wrong, then thought better of the idea. The rage that burned behind his thoughts was palpable even to her, and she was not particularly sensitive to emotion.

Well, this time she was not going to play scapegoat. Niall would undoubtedly want to know where Vidal had been and what he had been doing all this time. And just as surely, when the Bane-Sidhe learned of his errand, Niall would sneer at him.

Well and good. Aurilia would stay out of it. If anyone was to suffer Vidal's anger, let it be the Bane-Sidhe.

After all, she thought maliciously, *he spoiled my breakfast by arriving when he did. Let him take it in the teeth. I've had more than my share of My Lord Vidal's temper tantrums. Niall outranks him; let Niall exert himself for a change.*

"And where have *you* been?" Niall snarled. "I have things I wish to discuss — "

"And I don't give a damn!" Vidal exploded, his eyes black with rage, fists clenched at his sides. He turned pointedly away from Niall and snarled at Aurilia. "That thrice-damned human mage Keighvin has had his little protégé put *shields* on the old man. I couldn't touch him! And what's more, when I threw bael-fire at him, the old bastard *laughed* at me!"

The Bane-Sidhe rose to its full seven-foot height,

stood over Vidal, and glared down at the elven-mage, its tattered draperies quivering with anger. "Do you mean to say that you have been wasting your time trying to frighten Keighvin's pet mortals when you could have — "

"I'm doing what *you* should have been doing, you shabby fraud!" Vidal sneered. "You should have been the one trying to frighten the old man into a heart attack, not me! Not even a shield would have stopped your wail — right? Or — "

"Why? Why should I waste my time, waste the energy it takes to cross the Gate into the mortal world?" the Bane-Sidhe countered. "I've not enough to spare as it is!"

Vidal was not to be daunted by height or stench, Aurilia had to give him credit for that much. "Because Keighvin has to be stopped, or he'll stop us. Even *you* admit that! If you'd been here — "

The Bane-Sidhe's eyes flashed angrily, and Aurilia held her breath. If Niall grew enraged, he might lose control. "I would not have been wasting my time pursuing a dead-end vendetta when there are other options open!" Niall whined, his voice climbing dangerously in pitch and volume. "Humans are infinitely corruptible. Just look at the sheer numbers of them that are willing to pay to watch their fellows in torment! Look at our files! All we need do is find these foolish mortals' weaknesses and they will be our allies, not Keighvin's! It's simply — "

"A lot *you* know!" Vidal spat. "You haven't been Outside for a century! The mortals you knew are as dead as the creatures of Tam Lin's time! You can't corrupt a human by dangling a pretty piece of flesh in front of his nose anymore! And they aren't naive little village boys with shit on their shoes and not two thoughts in their heads. It's bad enough that we've got Keighvin against us, but now he has these human *mages* with him, and artificers, and they're not stupid, I'm telling you!"

The Bane-Sidhe grew another half a foot. "I have

taken the lives of more mortals than you ever dreamed of; I've the deaths of six knights of the Seleighe Court to my credit. That's more than you've ever *hoped* to do, you elven trash! Destroying the likes of you is less than a pastime — "

By the dark moon, this is getting serious — Aurilia clapped her hands together, distracting both of them for a moment.

"Niall, unless you really want a duel on your hands," she said coldly, "I think you'd better take back those last words to your *partner.*"

She had dealt with the Bane-Sidhe for so long now that she knew exactly what was running through its head, now that she'd sidetracked it. For all Niall's power — and he *was* powerful — he was old and afraid of losing any of it. He used his hoarded energies sparingly, and he lived in fear of finding himself in a duel of magics and coming out the vanquished. Vidal was young, as elves went, but he was powerful as well. Niall did not know *how* powerful, and that uncertainty would be enough. If he were forced to go head-to-head with the younger mage . . .

. . . who had done away with two of the Seleighe Court single-handedly, in the far past. . . .

"I beg pardon for those hasty words," the Bane-Sidhe whispered stiffly. "I am concerned that you seem to be wasting time better spent elsewhere."

Aurilia turned to Vidal, who stood, still rigid with anger, facing the Bane-Sidhe. "You should explain the problem to Niall, Lord Vidal," she said, in as close to a servile tone as she could manage, given how angry *she* was at both of the fools. "You are right in saying he is not familiar with the world outside the Gates today. You should tell him why Keighvin and his pets are dangerous to us."

Vidal's jaw tightened, but her subservient tone evidently mollified him enough to try to be polite. "Keighvin Silverhair is interfering directly in the world of mortals," he said, slowly, "as I have pointed out to you before. He will stop us in *our* quest for power if he can, for we are on directly opposing sides where mortals are concerned. But he has gone beyond simply interfering. Tonight I discovered that he is *using* them, recruiting and training them. And betraying our deepest secrets and weaknesses."

"What?" Niall and Aurilia both gasped. This was news to Aurilia; unpleasant news. If mortals knew how to meet the Folk in equal combat —

"The mage tonight had a bar of Cold Iron as a weapon," Vidal continued grimly. "Not steel — pure, forged Cold Iron, with Far-Anchored spells keyed to the Folk, and shieldings set specifically against our powers. The bastard *glowed* to the Sight, and he knew what he was doing, I tell you. Keighvin must have told him everything. He's going to be impossible to deal with. Another Gwydion, Merlin, Taliesen."

If Niall could have paled, he would have. Instead, he seemed to shrink, and he fluttered back into his seat, collapsing bonelessly with a moan.

"By the dark moon," the Bane-Sidhe groaned. "Why didn't you tell me this before? We must — "

Aurilia knew what the old coward was about to say — that they should leave, pack up in defeat and leave the ground to the enemy. Not a chance.

"Oh, no," she interjected sweetly. "He won't be impossible to deal with. I already have human informants following his movements. Before the week is out, I will know *his* weaknesses."

When the other two turned to stare at her in astonishment, she smiled, careful to cloak her triumph in modesty. "I simply don't have the power you have, my lords. I have learned to make do with the kind of weapons mortals use themselves. There are many ways to wound the human heart, and I have learned most of them. All I need to know is what the young man Tannim cares for — and he will be powerless against me."

She bowed her head a little, to hide the gloating in her eyes, for both the Bane-Sidhe and Vidal were still staring at her in a kind of awe. "You deal with the old man," she finished. "Leave the younger to me. I will deal with him, Cold Iron and all — for Cold Iron will not save him from a pierced heart."

● CHAPTER EIGHT

Tania sat in the farthest corner of Kevin Barry's and nursed her mug of hot, milk-laden coffee between hands so numb she couldn't even feel the cup. The weather had turned cold, out of nowhere, and despite Laura's repeated warnings, she had decided to take a chance and come to Kevin Barry's long enough to look for the strange young man again. The hundred he'd given her was long gone for rent; she'd been eating once a day here for the last week, trying to make the tab last a while, but she hadn't found a single trick in a week of walking the streets.

She had to admit, though, that she hadn't really been trying hard. Laura hadn't bothered warning her about Tannim after that first night; she had troubles of her own. Jamie was mixed up with something. He came home with less every night, and usually came home high. Laura was worried sick about the night he'd done the "party"; she'd gotten him to go to County Health and take the HIV test, but they wouldn't know what the results were for another couple of weeks.

And meanwhile, with Jamie getting high so often, it was only a matter of time before he slipped up again.

In a way, Tania didn't blame him for getting high; it might be the only way he could face what he had to do out there. But he was making Laura miserable.

And just maybe he's getting high because he can't face something else. Like his life. He isn't gonna be a cute young kid forever — and then what's he gonna do? He's already getting picked up by some really rough guys. He's come home with bruises or rope-burns the past three nights. The older he gets, the more of that kind he'll have to go with. And he says he'd rather die than get a MacDonald's job. He'd told Tania and Laura grandiose stories about getting a job at one of the country clubs, like waiting in the bar, and finding a rich old bored lady to support him, but he wasn't fooling anyone. Buses didn't run out there — and he wasn't exotic or talented enough. Tania had seen the kind of kids the "country-club women" picked up; they were generally very dark and latino-handsome, and they could dance, sing, and pay inventive flattering compliments. Jamie couldn't dance (at least not upright) and his most flattering compliment wasn't printable. "Escorts" were intelligent, and could make some kind of conversation. Jamie was stoned most of the time, and his brightest comments usually had to do with sports.

Tania studied the cream swirling slowly in the coffee. Ever since she'd met Tannim, Tania had felt like she'd gotten slapped awake, somehow. What she had now just wasn't enough anymore. She'd started looking ahead, planning for something besides the next trick, or the cheap TV set at the Goodwill. If Tannim was for real, and not just a pimp with a creative approach — well, maybe she'd see what he had to offer. She wasn't sure *why* she had decided to take the risk, and she wasn't sure why she'd decided to act against Laura's advice. In fact, she didn't really understand what was going on in her own head since she met the guy. But whatever it was, it kind of felt good — and it was a helluva lot better than sitting around listening to Laura try to cry without making any noise, or hustling the dirty old men in expensive suits.

Maybe all he wanted was her. That would be okay, too. She wouldn't mind going to bed with him. He was kind of cute, and was certainly nice. He'd promised not to hurt her; she trusted that promise.

She did know one thing: she'd made the decision to come here today at least in part because it had been too damned cold to trot around the street in nothing but

Spandex bike shorts and a halter. Now if Mr. Tannim would just show up. . . .

At least her hands were finally getting warm.

The pub had just opened for lunch a little while ago, but she really hadn't been that hungry when she first sat down. And in the last few minutes, as the place filled up, she noticed something kind of peculiar: although she'd have been glowered at for nursing a single cup of coffee instead of buying a meal or a drink anywhere else, no one was hassling her here. It had been that way every time that she had come in to get something on the tab; the girls smiled at her and were nice, and no one gave her any trouble, acted just like the night she'd been here with Tannim, in fact. Right now no one had even bothered her about getting something besides coffee. They acted like she was someone important; someone who should be given privacy and space, if that was what she wanted.

Maybe that man had something to do with it. Maybe because he had taken notice of her, they had extended that "courtesy to a good customer" umbrella he seemed to travel under to include her as well.

Every time someone darkened the doorway of the dining room, she looked up, squinting against the light, to see if it was him. As lunchtime filled the place up, she began to think she'd picked the wrong time, or day, or something. Even with the best wishes in the world, the waitresses were going to have to ask her to leave pretty soon, and let a paying customer have her table.

Of course, she could go ahead and order something. There was still enough cash left on the tab. And the aroma of the bean soup from the kitchen was enough to make a corpse hungry. Bean soup and bread — that wouldn't cost too much, and she could have some more coffee with lots of cream and sugar. . . .

She started to look for one of the waitresses, when movement at the door made her turn her head out of habit to see who it was. And there he stood, looking a lot like she remembered, only maybe cuter. A beat-up leather jacket this time, really nice Bugle Boy jeans and a hot brown-and-gray shirt — he could have been making an ad or something, he had that kind of style about him. She glanced down at her second-hand bike shorts and flushed a little. *She* was tacky. But it was the best she could do, and it was clean, anyway.

She looked up again. On second glance, the young man also looked tired, like he'd been working really hard.

Maybe he won't notice my clothes.

He squinted into the relative darkness, then started to turn away to go into the bar. She threw up her hand in an involuntary wave, then snatched it back, not certain now that she really *wanted* to talk to him again, after all. He might not be real happy to see her here, now. He might, in fact, be mad that she'd shown up, at least during the daytime.

Too late — he saw her signal, hesitant though it was; smiled and waved back, and started across the floor through the crowd.

But someone else had seen him too.

A really gorgeous dark-haired woman, dressed all in black leather and cream-colored silk, intercepted him at the entrance to the bar where she had just materialized as he crossed the room. Tania's heart sank. *This* must be who he was meeting. He hadn't come here looking for her. He hadn't even really seen her. He'd only seen the waving hand, and he'd thought it belonged to his lunch date. And God, she was incredible. The kind of woman Tania would have expected him to be seeing, not some tacky kid in Spandex.

She sidled up to him and put one hand on his shoulder, smiling brilliantly into his eyes. Her lips moved, although Tania couldn't hear what she was saying. He continued to scan the crowd in Tania's direction, a slight frown on his face. She blushed so hard she felt hot all over, and wanted to sink into the floor in embarrassment; her eyes burned, and her throat tightened. In another second, she was going to cry, she just knew it. And on top of looking tacky, she was going to get mascara smeared all over her face. She knew what he was looking for; now he wanted to know who had pretended to know him. Probably so he could make sure his lunch date with this fabulous babe wasn't interrupted by some scruffy little —

Abruptly, Tannim shook his head, said a few words, and brushed the woman's hand off his shoulder. His brow wrinkled just a little, and he stared directly into the woman's eyes. Then he drew his right hand up into a fist, slowly extended his thumb, and pointed it over his shoulder towards the door. The woman stood there, wearing the most stunned expression Tania had ever seen on anyone's face. He walked away from her as if she wasn't even there.

And as he got close enough to Tania to make out exactly who she was, his face broke out in a wide, welcoming smile, so warm it dazzled her.

Tannim had the feeling he really ought to go to Kevin Barry's for lunch today . . . it was a very strong feeling, and Tannim never, ever ignored those silent hunches of his.

So, although Keighvin had assigned him out to Roebling Road with a brake-mod this afternoon, Tannim decided to take a long lunch break.

Once again, he endured the bone-rattling cobblestones of River Street. He kept his "feelers" out for an incipient gap, then spotted one. He took instant advantage of the opening, shoving the Mustang into a parking space, right on the tail of a departing Caddy. He grinned at the driver of a Beemer, a suit-and-tie executive type, who scowled at him in frustrated annoyance.

Eat your heart out, buddy, he thought in smug satisfaction. *Here you are in your tie and execu-cut, and here I am in*

*my jeans and long hippie-freak hair — and I know I'm hap-
pier than you are. Why don't you just spend the rest of the
afternoon trying to figure out what I know that you don't?*

He felt just a little smug as he grinned into the yup-
pie-type's scowl. He'd gotten one of the primo spots,
too; hardly more than a wink and a nod from Kevin
Barry's. As the Beemer pulled away in search of another
place to park, he eased himself out of the car and headed
for the door to the gift shop — for the tiny gift shop let
directly out into the dining room side of the pub.

He waved at the lovely lass behind the counter of the
gift section, and looked over the new shawls, letting his
eyes adjust to the dim light. It was pretty dark in the
stage/dining area, and really crowded for a weekday; it
looked like half of Savannah had decided to hit the pub
for lunch. All of the tables were full, and there was a
line of about four people waiting for one to clear out.
But after a moment, that sixth-sense tingled again, and
he peered off into the far right-hand corner.

Someone waved tentatively at him from the very
back of the room. Tania?

It might be; whoever it was, she was female and
blond.

He started towards the corner, easing his way
around tables surrounded by people obliviously chat-
tering and munching away. But there was a huge
group in the very middle; they'd put three tables
together to form one big arrangement, and to get to
the rear he would have to go past the pub entrance on
the right-hand wall. Well, that was no problem, as long
as there wasn't anyone in *there* who wanted to have a
chat with him.

Just as he reached the double-doors into the pub,
someone pushed her way past the stand-up crowd at
the bar, and intercepted him at the doorway.

Before he realized she wanted *him*, she laid her hand on
his shoulder, forcing him to stop whether he wanted to or
not. He turned involuntarily to look at her; she smiled at

him as though she was an old friend. "Hello," she crooned, in a voice just loud enough for him to hear over the babble of voices in the pub. "I've been hoping you'd be here today; I'm glad to see my intuition is working."

She was stunningly beautiful: long, raven-black hair with a slight wave to it, huge brown eyes, sensuous lips and high cheekbones, and a flawless, rose-and-cream complexion. She was dressed in an ivory silk blouse and black leather skirt, both expensive, both understated in their elegance.

She was no one he'd ever seen before in his life.

Just before she'd touched him, all his internal alarms went off, for she had donned a glamorie that would have sent a Vulcan into heat. This was trouble, and all of his shields went up in full defensive mode.

While she spoke, he did a closer check, using mage-sight; as he had guessed, her appearance was nothing like her *real* self. There was no mistaking the white-blond hair, nor the cat-slitted, green eyes and the pointed ears.

Elven. One of the Sidhe. And since she was no one he knew, the odds were high that she was Unseleighe Court.

But she hadn't done anything to him but stop him — at least, not yet. So she wasn't declaring open warfare, not unless you counted attempted seduction as an aggressive act.

On the other hand, she could have assumed that Tannim was just as young and inexperienced as he looked.

I don't think so, lady.

But this was neither the time nor the place to answer her with a challenge. If that was Tania back there, he didn't want a kid to see him having even a verbal battle with a Sidhe. He calculated a dozen possible responses to her approach, trying to figure the one that would leave her the most stunned, and selected one by the time the last word had left her soft, wet lips.

He brushed her hand from his shoulder as if it was an inconvenient bit of dandruff.

"Your friends and mine don't get along, lady," he
said, without the least bit of inflection. "Run along and
we'll leave it at that."

He indicated the door, and watched the woman's
energy fields fluctuate wildly as she tried to process this
unexpected stonewalling. It was hard not to laugh,
even dire as the repercussions might be.

There was a split-second of astonishment before the
woman clamped down her mask of impassivity. He
could still see her body stiffen in the universal posture
of defensiveness.

*Score more status from the Bad Guys. She's trying to play it
off, but she's counting me as an equal, or a superior.*

He then moved past her as though she was not
there.

*I'll have to ask one of the girls what her face looked like to
them. Heh.*

Aurilia had perused the new agency's report very
carefully. *This* one had quite a bit of new information,
besides all the dossier nonsense that anyone with a
phone and a lot of patience could pull up out of public
records. According to the detective, young Tannim
favored one particular pub over every other establishment in Savannah: a pub called "Kevin Barry's."

Well, the lad was young, in his twenties, and if there
was one thing a young man was susceptible to, it was sex.
There hadn't been a young man yet that Aurilia hadn't
been able to lead about by the nose, sooner or later.
Generally sooner.

But just to make certain, she put a glamorie on herself that could make a corpse rise. Not even the pure
Sir Galahad could have withstood her now. And she
smiled to herself as she stood at the bar, sipping a glass
of *uiskebaghe*, and waiting for the youngster to make
one of his appearances. He would, too — she had that
feeling, and her premonitions were never wrong.

Those two fools were so busy persuading themselves that the only way they could dispose of the human was by combat that they never even bothered considering other options. Idiots. Why do anything with violence that can be accomplished subtlely?

She toyed with her glass, signaling the lady bartender for another, and considered what she would do when she had the mortal safely beguiled. *He might be useful, especially if he is any good as a mage. I could take him Underhill, to my own stronghold. . . . Yes, that might be the best solution. He'll be tended to in a gilded cage, and I can drain him slowly of power without the others knowing I have him.*

Movement of power at the edge of her shields alerted her that there was a mage within the confines of the pub; turning to check who had just entered, she saw to her immense satisfaction that the quarry had arrived. She left her glass, and quickly conjured a crumpled twenty, identical to the one she had kenned a few days ago, to leave beside the glass.

She intercepted Tannim just as he passed beside the door to the pub, placing one hand on his shoulder and whispering something innocuous while she exerted her glamorie. He stared at her for a moment, and she felt a flare of triumph. *I have him; I truly do. Now let's see what Vidal says about me —*

"Your friends and mine don't get along, lady," he said, brushing her hand off with an absent gesture.

He blew me off. I can't believe it. . . .

As she stared after him, stunned, he wound his way gracefully through the crowded dining-room without a single backward glance. He went all the way to the rear, where a tatty little teenager with badly bleached hair was sitting at a table for two —

Belatedly, she realized that not only had the young mage recognized her for what she was, he had broken her glamorie. Not only was she terribly conspicuous, he might well be watching her to see what she was going to do.

She melted back into the crowd as only a Sidhe could, and worked the opposite sort of glamorie — one to make her inconspicuous.

Then she retired to the gift shop and strained all her senses, trying to keep watch on him and his lunch guest.

In one sense she was frustrated; he had placed shielding about himself that he had extended to cover the table and the girl, so that she could not listen in on their conversation. But she could *watch* them, with a bit of the Sight.

After a moment she recognized the girl; she might have been the one in the blurred and darkened photo the new detective had included with his first report. Tannim had befriended the girl, who was evidently an underage prostitute, the first night the new man had been on duty. Then, as now, he had engaged her in conversation, and had bought her something to eat.

Well, that was interesting. What on earth could a teenage whore and a powerful young mage have in common? The report had been adamant that Tannim hadn't *done* anything with the girl, had in fact sent her on her way. Could it be possible that *this* was the weak point Aurilia had been looking for so fruitlessly?

The more she watched, the more certain she became. The girl did hold some kind of interest for him. Not sexual — but perhaps all the stronger for that. By the time the two of them paid the bill and left, she was filled with satisfaction. She had him. She had the vulnerable point. She didn't know exactly what she could do with it — yet — but she knew what it was.

Tania couldn't help herself; she smiled and blushed as the young man pulled up a chair and sat across the postage-stamp table from her. "Hey, kiddo," Tannim said, looking meaningfully at her coffee cup. "That doesn't look like a very nutritious breakfast." Before she could reply, he signaled one of the waitresses. "My usual," he said, "for two." And as the girl disappeared, he turned back to Tania.

"I've been watching for you," he said, "and I was kind of afraid I'd scared you off when you didn't show up."

She looked down at her cup in confusion. "Laura told me you were probably a — " She stopped herself just in time, appalled at the way she had let her mouth run without thinking. If the guy *was* a pimp, he might get angry and take it out on her, and Laura too. If he wasn't, he might get offended. " — Ummm — somebody I shouldn't get involved with."

"What, a pimp?" Tannim asked. "Or a pervert? Kiddo, you have to know that most of the guys who pick you up are perverts. Nobody really straight would want to make it with a kid as young as you are. And, Tania, the hair and the makeup job aren't fooling anybody."

The straightforward reply — too calm and matter-of-fact to be an insult — brought her up short. And before she could think of any retort, he continued.

"Look, I'm not interested in sex. I've got that elsewhere. I just want to talk to you — and not dirty, either." He looked ready to say more, but the waitress arrived with two club sandwiches and two colas, and he waited until she was out of hearing distance.

She eyed the sandwich dubiously, remembering what Laura had said. He caught her at it, and laughed a little. "Go ahead, Tania, it isn't drugged or anything, I promise." And as if to prove his point, he exchanged plates with her and bit into his sandwich with hungry enthusiasm. Feeling a little stupid, she did the same.

"Look," he said, when she'd finished half of her meal, gesturing with a potato chip, "I told you the other night that I liked seeing people able to dream — and I like it better when I can help them with those dreams. See, there's some weird shit going on out there, and helping you keeps me balanced. Keeps me in touch with the 'real world.' Dig?"

That was just a little too near the bone. "What are you," she asked defensively. "Some kind of Boy Scout or something?"

He sighed and shook his head. "I'm just a guy," he

replied. "A plain old human being. Eccentric. Obsessive. Imperfect. I can't do much, Tania — but I'd like to at least talk a while."

She shrugged, uncertain and trying to cover it with bravado. "I suppose. I'm not really busy right now. You're not my usual kinda client, but you ought to get something for your two hundred bucks, I guess —"

"Have you ever been on a picnic?" he interrupted. "A real picnic?"

Caught off-guard once again, she shook her head.

He took her hand and rose, pulling her to her feet. "Come on, then. Let's see if I can show you a good time."

Before she knew what he was doing, he had left money on the table for the bill, and led her outside into the bright sunlight. She squinted as he donned his Ray-Bans, and tugged her over to the River Street parking lot. The next thing she knew, she was sitting in the passenger's side of his car, while he buckled himself in on the driver's side, staring at a dashboard with more gadgets than a fighter-plane cockpit.

"Buckle up, kiddo," he reminded her. "What do you want to hear?"

She was dazed, and replied with the first thing that popped into her head. "That music the other night — here — is there anything more like that?"

"Good choice," he replied, popped in a cassette, then pulled out of the parking space before she had time to say anything else, like "where are you taking me" —

She could have hit herself in the head. If Tannim really was a pimp after all, in spite of all his talk about "dreams," she'd just put herself right into his hands. Willingly. How stupid could you get?

But he didn't pull out towards the worst part of town; he just drove up the ramp, onto President. They crossed a couple of bridges, while Tannim rattled on about music, and pulled up at a place called The Country Store. He left the motor running (and the tape playing) and dashed inside.

This is nuts — I could take the car right now, drive away. Take my chances —

But for some reason, she sat and waited, listening to Celtic harp and soulful voices as he returned with two white boxes, a large sack, and a couple of drinks in a paper carrier.

A faint aroma of food came from both boxes as he dropped them on the seat behind them, and Tania relaxed a little more. The idea of a pimp or drug-pusher buying a couple of box lunches was too ridiculous to contemplate. Maybe he was for real—

She yawned involuntarily while Tannim wedged the drinks into the center console. Last night had been long — and fruitless. She'd pounded the pavement until about four, then come home to find Laura in tears and Jamie too stoned to do anything but snore. Then she'd gotten up relatively early to come to Kevin Barry's—now the short sleep was catching up to her.

She must have dozed off anyway, for she came to herself with a start as Tannim turned the engine off. "Well, we're here," he said, with an expectant expression on his face.

She looked around, baffled. "Where's here?" she asked, not recognizing anything.

"It's a park, outside Fort Pulaski. This is a place I come with friends. That's one of the approaches to the docks — it's very deep here." He indicated the waterway before them. "See? There's one of the big container ships you see passing River Street." He opened the trunk of the Mustang and pulled out a familiar item: a cargo blanket like she used for bedding. Some pimp: blanket over one shoulder, white lunchbox in each hand, and a goofy grin.

She shivered in the sea breeze, and Tannim slapped his forehead after laying out the food and blanket. "I should have given this to you before," he explained sheepishly, handing her the sack. "Sorry . . . hope it fits."

Tania opened the sack, and pulled out — a sweat

suit. A *nice* one, with a puffy-ink Hilton Head logo and
. . . a unicorn.

*He knew. How could he know? Oh, God, it's beautiful . . .
it's better than anything I have now. I'd look like a tourist or a
college student. . . .*

She felt her eyes tearing up, and only her involuntary
shivering broke her out of it. Tannim stood with a self-
satisfied smirk, then sat on the blanket, his back to her.

*God, I'm a teenage hooker, and he gives me credit for modes-
ty. Incredible. . . .*

She slipped the suit on over her speedos and immediately felt warmer. It was thick fleece. "I look like . . . "
She let the sentence trail off.

"You look confident. " He grinned, looking her over.
"The unicorn design suits you. They're powerful
beasts, very, very magical, and as graceful as you are.
And just as capable of miracles."

Tania felt herself blushing. "I don't know . . . this is all
so weird, I mean, this feels like some movie. It's stupid,
this fairy-tale shit just doesn't *happen*."

"Mmm. No. Normally it doesn't. It doesn't make any
more sense than sunlight or trees. Or internal combustion." He gestured with a pickle spear. "You turn the
key, the car runs. Inside it, water runs through iron,
lightning sparks fire, thousands of tiny firestorms, and
all people ever think of is 'push the pedal and it goes.'
But, Tania, people are like that. Complex, but so taken
for granted, with all the powers of the elements in
them. Sooner or later, even we forget how wonderful
our internal machines are. All we need to be great is to
remember how amazing we really are."

"Oh, God, you're not one of those Scientologist
people, are you?"

Tannim nearly choked laughing. "Oh my God! Give
me some credit! I'm not *that* brain-dead!"

She smiled a little, sheepishly. "It's just that what you
keep saying all sounds like some feel-good pep talk to
fat executives."

The man had nearly stifled his laughing. He wiped his nose with a napkin. "All right. So it does. I just get enthusiastic sometimes. Guess I've gotten used to things working out."

Tania peered out towards the horizon again. The container ship there was four times larger, but still appeared no closer. "I haven't had that kind of luck lately. The street takes away dreams. Makes them hard to even remember. . . . "

Tannim nodded, as if he understood. Maybe he did. "Yeah. Yeah, I can imagine. But, well, like I said, sometimes all we need is a reminder that we can do about anything."

She shook her head stubbornly. "But how come you're doing all this for me? It doesn't make any sense! You've got to have something better to do than — "

"Than spend my day with a teenage hooker?" he interrupted. "If you were any such thing, maybe so. But I don't believe that any more than you *really* do. You know you hate it, but you think it's all you are. We both know better. And, well, yeah, I could be working. I've got testing to do, but, hell . . . the machines can wait. You can't. Not another day. Or else you wouldn't have shown up at Kevin Barry's looking for me."

They were both silent for a moment, watching the huge ship at last move into the channel. It was at least twelve stories high, marked in a language Tania couldn't identify. It bore a prancing horse atop a globe painted on one stack, above hundreds of multicolored boxes the size of tractor-trailers. Tannim stood up slowly and dusted his jeans off, then raised his arms and waved.

From beside a massive lifeboat a single figure waved back.

Tannim stood, grinning and satisfied, hands on hips. "There. A first welcome home."

*   *   *

Tania and Tannim talked for what felt like an hour. He was so easy to talk to, that by the time she realized what she'd done, she'd not only told him about herself, she was telling him about Laura and Jamie, too. She managed to keep from blowing everything, but from the bleak expression on his face, she guessed he was able to figure out most of it on his own. So she tried to change the subject —

But he changed it for her, asking her first about what she liked to read. That got her on the subject of fantasy, and *then* she was spilling the whole story about the night her mother found her book, and what had happened, and she was holding back tears with an effort. . . .

He patted her hand, but didn't try to touch her in any other way — which was just as well, really. She would have felt really stupid and afraid, both at the same time. Stupid, because she was crying over *books*, for chrissake; afraid, because if he touched her, he might try something more, and she *liked* him, she didn't want him to be like another trick. But she wanted someone to hold her and comfort her, wanted it so badly it was a dull ache deep down inside.

She stared out at the river as another ship appeared in the distance, and fought her tears down. Finally, after a long silence, he cleared his throat self-consciously.

"Don't you think maybe you ought to go back to your folks?" he said cautiously. "I know it was bad, but — "

She shook her head, angrily. "No!" she replied adamantly. "It was like being in jail all the time, except I hadn't done anything to deserve it! Hell, even in jail, people get to read what they want!"

"But — " he began. She cut him off with a look.

"I didn't deserve being treated like a criminal, and I won't go back to it," she said firmly, relieved that anger had chased away the incipient tears.

"All right, so you won't go back — but what about one of the shelters?" he replied. "That would get you out of that apartment into somewhere safe, and you could go back to school. You could even get a job if you wanted to; the shelter would help you."

She laughed, sourly. "Haven't been out on the street, have you?" she asked. He shook his head. "Well, the *good* shelters have waiting lists — or else they only let you stay a couple of weeks," she said, bitter memories of checking the places out still fresh in her mind. "And the rest of them either have churches running them, or they're always on your case about contacting your parents — and if you won't, they will, whether or not you like it."

He blinked. "Oh," he said. "But — don't you think it's still better than — "

"I don't need Jesus with my orange juice, thanks," she snapped in irritation. "I don't need getting told this was all my fault and I'm a sinful slut. I don't need getting nagged at, and told by some stupid psychologist who never met my parents how much they really do care about me. All *they* ever wanted was something else they could boast to the people at the club about. They never cared about me, they only cared about how good I could make them look." She shook her head. "By now they've probably put a Soloflex in my room. And they've figured out not having me around saves them enough for a weekend cruise to Bermuda every couple of months. I'll stay where I am, thanks."

Tannim just looked sad, and watched the ship grow nearer. "I never thought I'd wind up here," he said, after a while. "There was a time when I thought I'd stay in Oklahoma all my life. Now — sometimes I wonder if I'm ever going to really settle down in one place."

"Why?" she asked.

"Because I like traveling," he replied, and started off on a series of stories that lasted until the sun started to set. Some of them were so crazy they couldn't be true — and she wondered about the rest. It was weird, like he was talking around something half the time. Surely nobody as young as Tannim could have done so much in such a short time, could he?

On the other hand, why would he lie to her?

She let him talk; while he was telling her stories, he couldn't pry any more out of her. Finally, though, all the food had been eaten, all the stories seemed to have been told, and the sun was going down. She had work to do —

She found herself dreading it; going back onto the street seemed filthier than ever after this afternoon. But she didn't say anything, and when Tannim asked her if she wanted to go back to town, she just nodded and let him lead the way back to his car.

They were both silent on the way back to the city; it was as if they had forgotten how to talk to each other, or that they didn't know what to say. The silence was as awkward as the earlier conversation had been free. When Tannim asked her where she wanted to be dropped off, she replied, vaguely, "Wheaton Street, near Bee," and hardly noticed his wince.

But she did notice the worried look he wore when he pulled over to the curb and she got out.

"I wish you wouldn't," he said, and she didn't have to ask what he meant. She shoved her hands in her pockets, unable to look him in the eye —

And discovered that there was paper in there, paper that hadn't been there before.

She pulled it out. It was money, cash; several twenties. She wasn't sure how many, because she shoved it hastily back into her pocket before someone could see that she had it. "You believe in magic?" he asked. And before she could reply, continued, "Don't. It's unreliable. Make your own luck."

He smiled, reached over, and closed the door, then pulled out into traffic, leaving her standing on the corner.

With a pocket full of cash.

Make your own luck, he'd said. What was that supposed to mean? Or was it supposed to mean anything at all?

She turned to head down the street, pausing once in the shelter of a doorway to remove the cash again, and count it.

Five soft, old twenties. One hundred dollars. Exactly what he'd given her the last time.

Make your own luck.

Well, there was one thing she could do. She could get off the street for another night. Maybe even another week. That was luck enough for right now.

"Sam, old lad, could ye hand me that wee driver?" The Sidhe-mechanic put a hand out from underneath the computer-module, and Sam dutifully dropped a small screwdriver into it. An aluminum socket-wrench; Donal might be one of the three Sidhe at Fairgrove capable of handling Cold Iron with relative impunity, but it was only "relative." Right now Donal was doing something more than a bit dangerous: manipulating some of this computer equipment magically, altering it so that while it looked perfectly normal from the outside, and in fact would pass inspection by any licensed tech, what it would register was *not* what would be going on inside.

Which was, in fact, nothing at all.

But even the tiny amount of Cold Iron present in the screws holding various covers in place was enough to foul Donal's magic. Donal was taking them all out, placing them in an insulating container, then making his alterations according to Sam's instructions. The Sidhe's body twisted about for a moment as he squirmed to reach the tiny screws, then was still.

"There now," Donal said, his voice muffled, but the satisfaction coming through plainly. "That should do it. Turn it on, old lad, and let's see if it lies to us proper."

"Are you sure you want me to do that?" Sam asked anxiously. "You're still in there — that's a direct 220 feed — "

Rob, Donal's human shadow, snickered. "Ah, don't

worry about frying Donal's brains. He hasn't any to speak of. All you'll do is reinforce his perm."

"And who was it had to have his phone taken away, 'cause he'd order every damn thing K-Swell ever made?" Donal countered. "Who was it came t'me in mortal terror, 'cause he'd broken a chain letter? Who was it that told Keighvin he'd seen Elvis baggin' groceries at Kroger? Hmm?"

"Beats me," Rob said cheerfully, his round face shining with amusement.

"Well, Skippy, I think I'll take that as an invitation —" Donal started to emerge — fist-first — or at least made motions as if he might.

"All right, all right! So I get a little carried away!" Rob sighed dramatically.

"Turn on the juice, Sam," Donal repeated, suppressed laughter in his voice. "Ye needna worry about me. 'Tisn't electricity I need worry about; that I can handle — 'tis enough like magic as makes no nevermind."

Sam plugged the machine in and turned it on, setting it through its cycle, still worried despite Donal's assurances.

"Well?" came the muffled voice. "Is it lyin' to us the way it should?"

Sam nodded, forgetting that Donal couldn't see him. To all intents and purposes, there was a full-blown smelting operation going on — temperature was rising, the aluminum about to slag down, the vacuum building up preparatory to foaming the molten metal — even though there was nothing attached to the computer console.

Or maybe Donal *could* see him. "How much in the way of 'accidents' do ye want now an' again?" Donal asked.

Sam thought, making mental calculations. "With a process this complicated, I'd expect a fail-rate of fifty percent. I'd be really suspicious if it was less than that."

"Fifty percent it is," Donal answered. "Here, I'll gi' ye a taste of it." A moment later, alarms went off, indicating a catastrophic failure of the injection system. The system powered itself down.

Donal climbed out a moment later, and stood up, brushing his black coverall off. " 'Twon't always be the injection system," he said, full of happy pride at his own cleverness. " 'Twill alternate. And we may get five 'failures' in a row before we get a 'good casting.' Danaa's light, that's amusing! Wish I could do this sort of thing more often."

"What exactly *did* you do?" Rob asked. Donal smirked.

"Nothing you can dup, lad, nor your evil twin, neither. I just engraved a few extra circuits into the machine where they won't show; built 'em on the sensor-connections, then programmed 'em hard. So even if someone comes in an' changes the stuff they can see, 'twon't affect the outcome." Donal's grin got even wider. "Have t'say I'm right glad ye showed me how those computer-things work, now."

"Even though I had to drag you into computer literacy kicking and screaming," Rob taunted. "So, all we have to do is have one of the kenning Sidhe standing by to supply the evidence in the mold or in the furnace if we happen to have visitors, hmm?"

"Exactly," Sam said, feeling a wash of contentment come over him, despite the threats of the morning. Donal and Rob had told him, over and over again, that Donal could make these invisible mods to the computer-driven casting equipment, but until he'd seen it, he hadn't dared believe it.

"I hate to admit it, but you did good, *Conal*," Rob told the Sidhe.

"Thank ye kindly, *Skippy*," Donal replied, slapping the little mechanic on the back so hard he staggered. "Gents, I have t' be off; I've got mods to put in on m' brother's car."

"I don't think we'll need your particular expertise any more today, Donal," Sam said absently, as he ran another "casting" through the system, and this time got perfect "results." "Everything else Rob and I can fake without mucking with the computers."

Everyone was behaving perfectly normally; Sam was taking his cue from the rest, in spite of the fact that tonight would be anything but normal.

Assuming Vidal Dhu carried out his threats. He might not, according to Donal. He might simply have issued a challenge without intending to follow through on it seriously.

"He's done that before," Donal had said, sourly. " 'Tis worth it to him just t' muck us up for a night, make us waste energy and magical strength to counter a threat that was never real. Make us jumpy, make us chase our tails from midnight t'dawn, and all for naught."

The tall Sidhe (who reminded Sam strongly of G. E. Smith from the Saturday Night Live band) turned at the door and sketched a mocking salute before heading for the main shop building. As Sam and Rob finished setting up the rest of the equipment, with Rob running the fork-lift and Sam supervising the placement, Sam finally had the chance to ask a question that had been plaguing the life out of him all day.

"What's with this 'Skippy' business?" he asked, as they brought the second smelter up online and plugged its controls into the computer console.

Rob laughed, and rubbed his short black beard with a finger. "That's from when I first came into Fairgrove," he said. "They already thought I was nuts, 'cause I do imitations of televangelists and bad game-show hosts at the drop of a hat. But then I kept seeing this one Sidhe all over, like, within seconds of the time I'd seen him somewhere else. And half the time, when I'd call him 'Donal,' he'd glare at me like I was simpleminded and say his name was *Conal.* I thought I was going crazy. Then somebody finally told me that there were *two* of the bastards, they were twins, and they'd been having a good laugh at my expense." Rob chuckled. "I didn't mind, I mean, if they'd been human that's the first thing I would have thought, but who ever heard of twin Sidhe? The birthrate's so low I'd never have believed it."

"So?" Sam replied. "That doesn't explain 'Skippy.' "

"Well, I turned the tables on them. Half the time when one of them saw me and called me 'Rob,' I'd glare and say my name was Skippy. And when I was Skippy is when I'd do the really outrageous stuff, like try to sell Donal his own tool-kit or something." Rob's grin was so infectious that Sam found himself grinning in return. "They actually started to think I had a really crazy twin myself, named Skippy. It was weeks before anyone ever told them the human bad-movie joke about 'the evil twin, Skippy.' I thought when Dottie finally broke down and confessed that they were both gonna hang me right then and there."

Sam joined in Rob's laughter. "I'm surprised they didn't," he commented.

"I'd rather have been well-hung!" Rob grinned, and made sure the smelter was staying cold even though the computer console said it was red-hot. "Those two have a lot better sense of humor than anyone except Keighvin. I think it comes from hanging around Tannim so much."

Sam's response surprised even himself. "A lot of good things seem to come from hanging around Tannim," he said softly, half to himself. Then, a little embarrassed, he glanced over at Rob to see if the young man had overheard him.

Rob was nodding, uncharacteristically sober. "They do," he said, then —

"Sam, I have to tell you, I've got this *great* deal on a set of Ginsu steak knives, and if you order now, you get a free bamboo steamer — "

Sam chased him out of the building, brandishing a broom.

the sentient people, telling over and over again the old
with her own. Dreams were precious ... the rest were
content of the planet, and that this made them
remarkable ...

• CHAPTER NINE

Although she had every sense at her command locked onto her quarry, Aurilia "lost" the pair to everything
but sight the moment they entered Tannim's car —
and she lost the vehicle itself to President Street traffic
soon after. The protections on the vehicle might have
been set by Keighvin Silverhair, but Aurilia doubted it.
Whatever other powers the boy had, he certainly drove
like a demon. Once again she found herself forced to
admit to a kind of grudging admiration for one of the
enemy. . . .

But not for long. The aggravation of losing quickly
overwhelmed the admiration. *Damn him, anyway. Crafty
little monster. Where did he learn all that? Surely not from Silverhair. If I didn't know better, I'd suspect he'd managed to find
some devil actually interested in buying his skinny little
soul. . . .*

Still, Aurilia hadn't practiced her own particular
brand of subterfuge for so many centuries without
learning patience. She found herself an out-of-the-way
spot in one of the little "pocket parks" and sat in her
Mercedes. Tannim could cloak himself, and even his
car — but once the girl left his presence, she would
register to Aurilia's mage-senses. And the girl was really what Aurilia was after at the moment.

It took longer than Aurilia had thought it would, but
towards sunset, the girl finally "appeared" to Aurilia's
inner eye. She quickly triangulated with a mental map
of the town, and determined that the girl was at the
corner of Bee and Wheaton streets.

She reached out in thought, and seized mentally on

the nearest pigeon, taking over what little mind it had with her own. Pigeons were possibly the stupidest creatures on the planet, but that stupidity made them remarkably easy to enslave. When she was done with it, it would drop dead of shock, of course, but that didn't matter. One more dead pigeon on the sidewalk would excite no one except a feral cat or dog.

She sent the bird winging in a direct line to the area where the girl loitered. With sunset coming, a pigeon was perhaps not the best choice of slave-eyes, but it would do. A grackle would have been better, but like all the corbies, it would have fought back too much, wasting time and energy before she could take it. An owl was the best, but Silverhair used those, the bastard. And frequently owls were not what they appeared to be.

She caught only glimpses of what the pigeon saw; just enough to guide it to her target. Fortunately, the girl was fairly conspicuous with her bleached-blond hair, even from above. Though darkness had fallen, the shock of pale straw made a kind of beacon for the bird's dimmed eyesight. So although the pigeon was not much good at flying by street-lamps, once the bird had the girl in sight, Aurilia had it land on a rooftop, and follow her in short flights, from tree to phone-line, to rooftop again.

Even by daylight the pigeon's eyesight wasn't particularly good, as birds went, but Aurilia made out enough detail that she was forced to wonder what on earth Tannim saw in this appalling little creature. It certainly wasn't her looks. She was scrawny, underfed, a modern version of one of Aurilia's own Victorian Street-Sparrow constructs. Clean — well, Aurilia would give her that much. She was clean. And young, if your taste ran to children. But cheap, tacky — tasteless. Perhaps that was why her glamorie at the pub hadn't worked — maybe Tannim was only attracted to cheap tarts. Maybe he only enjoyed sex with hookers, children, or both. . . . But that didn't fit his profile, didn't fit anything she'd been able to learn about him.

Peculiar. Once she'd seen him, he hadn't struck her that way; in fact, his attitude towards the girl, so far as she had been able to make out, was positively chaste. In any case, the girl's parents had to know what she was doing, unless they were even stupider than the pigeon.

The girl wound her way farther and deeper into one of the bad areas off Wheaton. Well, now it wasn't much of a surprise that she'd had Tannim drop her back there on the corner. Aurilia didn't wonder now why the girl hadn't wanted Tannim to see where she lived; she was probably ashamed of her home. If she lived here, her parents couldn't be much better than what was locally termed "poor white trash." That might be why they didn't put any restrictions on her dress, her movement, or her behavior — they probably didn't care.

The girl suddenly dashed across a street and up an enclosed staircase, catching Aurilia by surprise. She sent the pigeon to perch in a tree outside the first lighted window she saw.

She peered short-sightedly at the window, trying to determine if the bird could get any closer, and discovered that luck was with her. The girl passed in front of it, showing it was the right one; and not only that, it was open, with no screen to keep her from perching on the ledge.

She moved the pigeon in a fluttering hop from branch to ledge, and poked the bird's head cautiously inside. The place was appalling: filthy, bug-ridden, falling to pieces, with the only furniture being pallets on the floor. There were two rooms to the place; the girl and two other youngsters were in this one, and voices from the door beyond proved that there were at least two more in the other room. There were no parents, no adults of any kind, anywhere in sight. Within moments of listening to the conversation between the children, it was clear to her that there were no adults in residence in the tiny apartment at all. There were perhaps a half dozen children living there, and now Aurilia knew exactly why the girl had looked and acted the way she did — for she recognized one of the other children. There was a girlishly-pretty young boy on a pallet at the side of the room, sleeping the profound sleep of the drugged with his face turned towards the window. Aurilia knew him very well indeed; she had just spent the past week editing film that had his face — and other parts — all over it.

It had been the "bondage-party" film (now called "Birthday Boy" and with three thousand copies already on order) that had featured five of their customers and one "pickup." The boy, called "Jamie," if she recalled correctly, was a free-lance hooker and a runaway.

Suddenly, given Tannim's notorious do-gooder impulses, many things fell into place. That was the attraction, then. *Tannim wants to save the girl if he can — and that fits right in with his profile. Meddling fool. Typical hero-wishing. Save her for what? A life of food-service?* Well, if he wanted to waste his time and resources on dead-end losers, Aurilia wasn't going to stop him. Particularly not when his little hobby fit right in with Aurilia's own plans. Not only her plans, but the current projects for Studio Two.

She withdrew her power in a burst of triumph, abruptly, allowing the pigeon to tumble unnoticed to the ground.

Tannim had expected Keighvin to jump all over him when he got back to the Fairgrove complex. After all, he had been scheduled to run test laps at Roebling, not spend the afternoon watching container ships and lolling around on the grass, however noble his motives.

Maybe if I just tell him the truth . . . edited. Emphasizing the need the child's in, and leaving out the lolling on the grass and the picnic dinner.

But as he wound his way through the offices, a change in the schedule posted beside the machine-shop door caught his eye. It would have been hard not to notice it; under the track schedule was a red-circled "canceled" notice.

When he read it, he had to grin. *The old luck comes through again. Excellent.* Some time between when he'd left for lunch and when he was supposed to return, Keighvin had changed the scheduling. The track had been closed this afternoon for repairs after some damage from a tire-test this morning.

A tire-test? What the hey?

He grabbed the first person he saw when he got into the shops. "What happened at the track this morning?" he asked.

The mechanic, Donal — one of Keighvin's Sidhe, and Tannim's oldest friend Underhill except for Keighvin — grinned wryly. "Hard to believe, eh? Wouldn't have believed it meself if I hadna seen it. We had a series of new tires for the GTP test mule — same mule you were supposed check brake mods and suspension geometry on. Well, seems our mods or the tires or both were a little *too* good." Tannim watched the elven man rock back on his heels, eyes glittering.

"So what happened?" he asked, since Donal was obviously waiting for him to make some kind of response.

"Well, the lateral gees put a three-inch ripple in the asphalt on one of the turns." Donal's grin got even wider, and Tannim didn't blame him; Donal was part of the crew responsible for the handling. This was something of a coup — for a mule to hug the track that hard on the turns said a lot.

But — a three-inch ripple? That was a lot of lateral. His expression must have said something of his surprise, as Donal held up a hand as if he was swearing to the fact.

"I promise; I measured it meself. We all saw it — a three-inch lump, plain as Danaa's light, ten feet long.

We had to hire a steamroller to flatten the track. Took us the rest of the day. Keighvin figured you'd see the posting and take off."

Now Donal raised an eyebrow, because Tannim *should* have known what had happened, since it had undoubtedly been all over the shop; Tannim just shrugged. He wasn't good enough to lie to a Sidhe, so he simply told part of the truth. "You know there's never anyone to answer questions around here in the afternoon. I had a picnic out at the Fort. So, where's Keighvin?"

"With Sam Kelly, at the forge-shop." Donal grinned again, showing gleaming white teeth, teeth that were a little feral-looking. "Now 'tis a 'forge' in more ways than one. Sam seems to have concocted a process that will pass muster, and he's moved that molten-metal equipment we kenned out to the other shop. Says we'll be ready for a cast of thousands."

"Ech, that's awful. 'Forged' engine blocks, hmm?" Tannim indulged the Sidhe; Donal was fond of puns. "And a 'forged' process. Well, I'd better get out there and see what Keighvin wants me to do now."

He wound his way through metal and machinery to the roofed passage that joined this shop to the formerly-empty forge building. He noticed along the way that a lot of the computer-driven equipment was missing; presumably it had been moved to its new home.

Keighvin *should* have been glowing with cheer; the mods that had warped the track had certainly proved successful, and now he had a "process" that would explain where his engine blocks and other cast-aluminum pieces were coming from. But when Tannim found him, supervising the set-up and activation of some arcane-looking machine by that insanely cheerful human tech-genius Skippy-Rob, he didn't look particularly happy.

Tannim wondered if something more had gone wrong than he'd been told, but it wasn't that kind of expression. He'd seen the Sidhe display all kinds of moods, and it was the "unreadable" ones that he feared the most. Keighvin was a gentleman by any creatures' standards, but he had his breaking points, and when he was near one . . . Keighvin looked up and saw him lurking out of the way, then beckoned the young mage over.

"What's cooking?" Tannim asked casually. "Anything wrong with Sam's phony process?"

"With the process — nothing," Keighvin replied, rubbing one temple distractedly. "But — Vidal Dhu showed up at Sam's this morning. Not inside the house, but he blocked Sam's driveway long enough to deliver a message."

"I think I can guess the message," Tannim said slowly.

Keighvin nodded, grimly. "A threat, of course. At least he didn't say, 'And your little dog, too.' The worrisome thing is that he's managed to recruit a corps of lesser nasties, and they're putting pressure on *our* boundaries. Nothing like overt warfare, but — don't go into the woods after dark."

"Any things we haven't taken out before?"

"Nothing any worse, so far as we can tell. I don't like it. And I don't like Sam being outside our hardened boundaries. I'm setting up our spare rooms here as sleeping-quarters for anyone who can't protect themselves, including Sam."

The man in question had come around the corner during Silverhair's little speech, and waited until he had finished before leaving the work crew and joining them.

"You're worrying too much, Keighvin," the old man said comfortably. "I've been going over my old gran's stories. I think I can hold off the boggles; enough to permit the cavalry to come over the hill to rescue me, anyway."

Tannim noticed that the old man was wearing what looked like an Uzi holstered at his hip; Sam patted it as he finished his statement.

Tannim frowned, rubbing his eyes. "Sam, I don't mean to rain on your parade, but plain old bullets aren't going to stop Vidal, and they certainly aren't going to do anything to a creature like a troll that can heal itself—"

Sam pulled the gun from the holster and handed it to him, wordlessly. Tannim took it — and it sloshed. It was one of the old Uzi-replica water-pistols, and not a real gun at all.

"One of your local geniuses prepared this for me," the old man said. "That's salt and holy water. That should take care of a fair number of yon blackguard's friends. I've got rosemary, rue, and salt in my pocket, and a horseshoe nail with them. There's an iron plate across every door and windowsill of the house, horseshoes nailed up over every door and the fireplace, and sprigs of oak, ash, and thorn up there with them. A lass here is preparing iron-filled .357 hollowtips for me Colt, and meanwhile, there's this—"

He touched the sheath on his other side, and Tannim saw the hilt of a crudely-forged knife. He had no doubt that it was of good Cold Iron. Sam wasn't taking chances on a *steel* blade.

"That's all very well," Keighvin warned, "but it won't hold them for long. They'll find ways around your protections and mine, eventually."

Sam holstered his water-pistol. "Doesn't have to keep them busy for long," he countered. "It'll hold them baffled for long enough. All I have to do now is supervise your setup, put my John Hancock to everything and write up my part in this deal. That's a matter of a couple of weeks at most. The rude bastard can bluster all he wants. Once I'm finished, you don't need *me* anymore. You just need my name."

"But what if something goes wrong?" Keighvin asked. "There's nobody here that knows the language—"

"But this Vidal character doesn't know that," Sam replied. "He's like some of the really old execs at

Gulfstream, the ones who didn't understand tech. He may even be a technophobe, for all we know. That kind thinks that once something technological is set in place, it sits and glowers and runs itself with no further help."

Both Keighvin and Tannim snorted; Sam shrugged. "I know it makes no sense, but that's the way these people think. All he'll see is me sitting back in my chair, and letting you run the show. He'll figure going after me is a waste of effort."

Keighvin shook his head doubtfully, and Tannim had to agree with the Sidhe. He wasn't convinced that Sam was right, either.

But Sam was an adult, and perfectly capable of making his own decisions. Besides, Tannim had other problems.

"Keighvin, I know this is coming at the worst possible time," he said, reluctantly, "but we've got another problem, too." Briefly he outlined Tania's situation, and the plight of the underage hookers she lived with. He hoped to catch Keighvin's interest, but the Sidhe-mage shook his head regretfully.

"Damn ye, Tannim, your timing sucks. I can't do anything for them right now," he said, plainly unhappy with the situation. "I'm sorry, but we're up to our pointy ears in alligators at the moment. I can't do anything for them out there — and you can't bring them here. I can't have a single non-mage mortal inside the boundary right now," he continued, frankly, laying the whole situation on the table so Tannim could see it. "And I'm stretching things to include Sam, because he believes and he's got a bit of the Sight himself. Who knows what these children would do if they saw a skirmish with one of Vidal Dhu's little friends out there? If they panicked, they could breach the shields. If they were taken in by appearances, they could actually bring Vidal inside."

Tannim had to admit, reluctantly, that Keighvin was right. He didn't want to say it out loud, though. *Maybe, just maybe, I can talk him into changing his mind.*

"If I let you bring them here, they'd at best be targets and weak spots," Keighvin continued. "Can't do that, no matter how desperate their situation seems to be, my friend. Keep siphoning them money; that's easy enough. They've kept their necks above water this long, Tannim, they can keep a little longer. When we've finished with Vidal Dhu, you can coax them in to us, but right now they'd just be in more danger with us than they are now."

Tannim grimaced. He didn't like it — but Keighvin was the boss at Fairgrove. This was his territory, and he knew the strengths and weaknesses better than anyone else.

So be it, Keighvin. I've got more to call on than spells. There's always the magic of folding green.

Keighvin eyed Tannim with a very readable expression — one of tired worry. He could read moods as well as minds. Tannim figured that Keighvin knew what his current expression meant. He met Keighvin's eyes squarely, and a little defiantly.

Yes, I am up to something.

But it was too late tonight to do anything about the situation. Tania was safe for the rest of the night, at least, and with any luck at all, that hundred would keep her off the streets for another couple of days. That would be long enough for Tannim to get Plan B into gear.

Assuming nothing happens between then and now. Like one of her friends getting tangled up with a pimp, or on the wrong side of a dealer, or —

He cut the thoughts short. There was no use worrying about the kids right now; he'd do what he could, when he could.

"Look," he said, running his hand through his hair, catching on more snags than usual, "I'm beat. If there isn't anything you need me for, I'm going home to get some shut-eye. Are we rescheduling those tests for tomorr— I mean, today? Or is it tomorrow?" He rubbed his eyes, wishing in a way that he could run them now. Although he was tired, he was also full of nervous energy, and he wished he had somewhere to go with it.

"No, Goodyear has the track," Keighvin said, his expression one of mingled relief and apprehension. Tannim had a shrewd idea of why the Sidhe wore the latter. Keighvin had to be wondering now just *what* it was Tannim had in mind to do about the kids.

Keep wondering.

"We have it after Goodyear," Keighvin added. "You *are* going to be fit to drive, I hope? And you don't plan on going anywhere tonight, do you? Sam should be safe enough here." The statement indicated that he wasn't necessarily worried about Tannim's involvement with the kids.

He thinks I'm going to go spend the rest of the night guarding Sam, or trying to hunt down Unseleighe creatures or something. Does he really think I'm that foolhardy?

"Don't worry, I don't plan on running out and hunting the kids — or Vidal Dhu — down tonight," Tannim replied with irritation. "I've got a little more sense than that. If the kids can wait, so can Vidal. He's not going anywhere. If he comes after us here, he's a fool, but you don't need me here to face him down."

Now the relief was so palpable on Keighvin's face that Tannim restrained himself from a sharp retort only by reminding himself that Keighvin didn't deserve it.

It's not his fault that you can't hit the broad side of a barn when you're tired. And it's not being paranoid on his part to worry about having you around when you're wonky. Conal may forgive you in a couple of hundred years, but what if you'd gotten more than his hair?

It was something Tannim didn't like to think about. And he hated being reminded of this new weakness of his. If only there was something he could do about it —

But Keighvin was waiting for him to say something;

he managed a tight smile, and flexed his shoulders. "I'm heading straight for bed," he said. "You know where to find me if you need me."

Keighvin was too aware of his own dignity to give him a comradely slap on the back, but Sam wasn't. "We'll be seeing you some time in the afternoon, then?" the old man asked, as Tannim staggered a little beneath Sam's heavy hand.

Keighvin lifted an ironic eyebrow. "Aye, do check in some time, won't you? So we can let you know what the schedule is."

Tannim controlled his expression carefully, so that none of his guilt would leak through. *He's got a suspicion I played hooky. It's a good thing this isn't your normal business.* . . . "I'll call when I wake up, but I'd like to come in after dark, if that's all right with you," he said. "It may take that long to get recharged."

This time he wasn't quite so irritated with Keighvin's reaction to his implied exhaustion, since it was working in his favor.

"Take all the time you need," the Sidhe replied quickly. "I'd rather have you take a couple more hours to get into top form than to come in at less than full strength."

Tannim nodded, trying his best to keep it from looking curt. "See you later, then."

He turned and walked out, back through the darkened office complex, back to the safe haven of the Mustang. It would take more than Vidal Dhu to get through the protections on the Mach 1, and he relaxed a little as he slid into the seat and shut the door.

There were times he wished that he'd taken Keighvin's offer of an elvensteed to replace the Mustang, especially when he was tired. It was a great honor for a mortal to be offered an elvensteed, and it would have been really nice to have a car that could find its own way home.

On the other hand, there was enough Cold Iron in the Mach 1 to give any Unseleighe Court critter more than it cared to handle. Keighvin couldn't even ride in it without pain. Tannim was glad of the new "plastic cars" for the sake of his friends, but when it came to keeping his own hide safe, arcanely and mundanely — he'd take good American sheet metal every time.

He thought, as he drove through the gates, that he sensed a lurking nastiness in the woods. But it was too dark to see much, even with mage-sight, and he was too tired to really want to risk a confrontation with anything. That nervous energy that had filled him was draining away a lot faster than he'd thought it would.

He drove carefully — and slowly, for him — back down the dark, near-deserted highway to his little rented house on the outskirts of Savannah. Normally he wouldn't have bothered renting anything as large as a house — but this place had some advantages that outweighed every other consideration. For one thing, it had a three-car garage almost as big as the house itself; whoever had built it must have been a real car-nut, or needed a hell of a workshop. The Mustang and all the gear Tannim needed to keep it in pristine condition no matter *what* he put it through fit comfortably inside.

But there were even more important considerations. The house and yard were hidden from the road by a thick ring of tall evergreens — which themselves were planted far enough from the house that while someone could have used them for cover, to get to the buildings an intruder would have had to cross a good-sized expanse of bare, weedy lawn, mowed short every week by the rental company.

The ring of evergreens was perfectly circular. It was, in fact, a Circle of the protective variety, and had been that way before Tannim moved in. Possibly even long before; the trees were old, fifty, maybe as much as a hundred years old. Had they been ensorceled that long? It was certainly possible. Sorcery invested in living things, unlike that invested in nonliving things,

tended to stick around long after the caster was dust —
and could even grow and flourish on its own.

The house itself was much younger, but it had been
built on an old foundation. Who had built the place this
way, Tannim had no idea. The rental agency simply ad-
ministered it, kept things repaired, collected his rent.
There had been protections on the house and garage,
too, but since they had been based on dead wood
rather than living, and the electricity had been off so
that the protections cast into the circuitry had drained
away, those shields had been faded by the time *he*
rented the place. The agency had been pathetically
grateful; evidently they'd had a hard time finding a
tenant.

Maybe the trees themselves kept out people they didn't like. It
was possible; there was the same feeling of semi-aware-
ness about the trees as there was to the Mustang. Odd
how he didn't even react to such things anymore.

Still, with the privacy and all, it was kind of odd that no
one had come along that wanted to rent it before he saw it.
On the other hand, for a house, the place was kind of
small; too small for a family, and yet the rent was a little too
steep for most single people. It was worth it — in an effort
to find a tenant, the agency had installed new appliances.
But the rent was still a little steep, even so.

For whatever reason, the place had stayed vacant for
a couple of years until Tannim came along. The little
one-bedroom cottage was perfect for him. The only
other thing he wished he had was a Jacuzzi — and if he
stayed, he could always install that in the garage.

He thumbed the garage-opener as he drove up the
drive; his electronics weren't quite as fancy as Sam's,
but then again, he wasn't as much of an engineer as
Sam was. Twin floodlights came on over the garage
door, two more went on inside, and the door rose
majestically on a miniature equivalent of the Fairgrove
shops.

The Mustang rolled inside, and the door descended

again, noisily. It was a little noisier than most, because it was heavier than most: five joined slabs of steel. Bombproof, he would have said. The door predated his occupancy, too.

Every so often he wondered what on earth the owner had been into that he needed a garage door that would withstand a B-52 strike.

He opened the Mustang's door, then paused, as all of the strain of the past week came down on him with a rush. Up until today, the test runs out at Roebling Road had alternated with sessions on the mods, all day and into the night. And when he hadn't been working on the mods, he'd been working, magically, on Sam's defenses. They weren't as good as the ones here, and he wasn't going to stop until they were —

Or until they buried Vidal Dhu and his friends.

He dragged himself up out of the bucket seat, and stumbled towards the door into the house. Fortunately, it led straight into the kitchen, and temporary salvation.

He leaned up against the fridge door for a moment, until the hum of the compressor starting up jarred him out of his tired daze. He pulled the door open and reached inside, blindly taking out a brand-new, unopened bottle of Gatorade with one hand. The other hand groped on top of the fridge and encountered crackling plastic. He brought down what he had found, and looked at it blearily as he shoved the fridge door shut with his hip.

Corn chips. Close enough to food.

He got as far as the tiny kitchen table, dropping down into the chair like a sack of deer antlers. There was an entire row of brown bottles and jars on the back edge of the table against the wall; vitamins, minerals, amino acids. He opened the bottle of Gatorade, ripped open the sack of chips, and began opening each of the bottles in turn, spilling out a couple of each until he had a little heap of pills in front of him. Then he began popping them into his mouth, methodically, washing

them down with swigs from the bottle of Gatorade, al-
ternating pills with a handful of chips until pills, chips,
and Gatorade were all gone.

Well, that takes care of the IOU to my body.

He thought about a hot bath, stood up, and decided,
when he went lightheaded, that the bath could wait.
He turned off the kitchen light and stumbled into the
bedroom, past the stark living room. The living room
always depressed him, anyway — it looked so empty.
There were two armchairs that had come with the
house, a floor-lamp, and his old stereo. The good rig
was in the bedroom; anyone who broke in would
probably figure Tannim didn't have anything worth
stealing. Which was mostly true; he hadn't accumu-
lated much in his years of traveling. *Moving fast keeps
you from hanging on to much.*

He flipped on the bedroom light; and there was The
Bed — the single piece of furniture he had acquired
and held onto through so many changes of address
that he'd forgotten half of them.

It was the size of two king-size beds put together, and
completely filled the bedroom. The basis for construc-
tion had been two orthopedic hospital beds, complete
with controls, with a flat section in between. The book-
case-headboard behind it went up to the ceiling, and
held mirrors, speakers, a lot of his audio gear, bed controls, and remotes for the TV and VCRs across the
room on the shabby bureau. Plus a tiny bar-fridge and
microwave. It had padded rails, and one section of the
padding on each side flipped up like the armrests on a
first-class airline seat; inside were tray-tables. When he
was really hurt or sick, he didn't even have to leave The
Bed except to hit the bathroom.

He'd found it (sans electronic gear, but wired with
four power-strips and its own pair of breaker-boxes) in
a Goodwill store in Dallas. It had been made in Ger-
many, and he'd always figured its previous owner was
one of the victims of the slump in oil prices. Occasional-

ly he looked at it, and wondered why he'd hung onto it with such tenacity. It was a stone bitch to move, and holding onto any piece of furniture was so completely unlike him that keeping this monster was insane. But then he'd get hurt, or he'd have one of his days when he'd wake up after a race or a fight hardly able to move, and he'd *know* why he kept it. He'd never find another like it. And it at least gave him one constant in all of his changes of address.

Too bad that he seldom had anyone to share it with.

He edged into the clear slot at the foot, and peeled off his shirt. Beneath it was his body-armor; one of the other reasons he hadn't been overly worried about an ambush by Vidal Dhu. It looked like a unitard, but it was composed of thousands of tiny hexagonal scales, enameled in emerald green. As he slid his pants off, the cool scales slipped smoothly, silkily, under his hands. It had been a project he and Chinthliss had worked on for three months, to the exclusion of everything else.

There were no seams. That was because every scale was joined magically to every other scale, and it could be opened where and when he chose. Though if he was ever unconscious, it would take someone like Keighvin to get it off him. . . .

So he just wouldn't get in any accidents.

Right.

He crooked one finger, which was the only component of the set-spell to open the suit, and ran the fingernail up the front. The armor opened and he shrugged it off, exactly like a dancer squirming out of a costume.

Beneath the armor were the scars.

Starting from the first, a knife-scar on the forearm he got protecting a potential mage, to the latest, teeth-marks that marked his leg from hip to ankle, his body was criss-crossed with a network of lines. They ranged from the thin white lines of old wounds, to the red of the newly healed.

I'm certainly not going to win any bikini contests.

Without the added support of the body-armor, his leg ached distantly, his shoulders felt like knotted wire ropes, and The Bed looked more inviting than ever.

But there was one more thing to do before he collapsed for the night.

He reached to the nearest shelf, and took out the tiny jar of Tiger Balm he kept there. Actually, he kept more than one in there — there was nothing worse than reaching for the only thing that could ease those constant aches only to find the jar empty.

He sat down on the edge of the bed, on the padded rail. With habit that had become ritualized, he applied the salve over every aching muscle. Before he had finished rubbing it into his shoulders, the heat had begun to soothe his aching leg.

He sighed, put the jar back, and crawled into the bed's embrace, fumbling for the light-switch and dropping the room into total blackness, without even a hint of outside light. The electronic clocks of the VCRs bothered him though, enough that he briefly considered flinging a towel over them before deciding he could just bury his head instead. His last conscious thought was to pull the blankets up over himself and burrow into them, before the exhaustion he had been holding off with both hands won the battle and flung him into sleep.

● CHAPTER TEN

Sam glanced over at Keighvin as Tannim retreated. The young man had looked tired and worried, and Sam knew the "why" of both. Tannim had put in several after-hours sessions reinforcing the protections on Sam's house; that took a lot more out of him than mere loss of sleep. And there was no doubt that he was worried about the kids, Tania especially.

He has reason to be. She takes her health into her hands every time she walks the streets, if not her life.

Sam had more immediate worries on his mind, and so did Keighvin. There was something Keighvin hadn't told Tannim. The Unseleighe Sidhe had shown up this morning outside Sam's house with more than a personal warning. He'd delivered a warning to Fairgrove as well, in the form of a challenge; time and place specified for tonight, at the Fairgrove boundaries. And despite Donal's attempts at reassurance, Sam trusted Keighvin's judgment, and Keighvin was worried.

"It's traditional," Keighvin had said. "You always warn your opponent before you attack — if they're of the Folk, that is." Then he'd smiled, but without humor. "Of course, the warning can consist of sending back the pieces of someone, appropriately gift-wrapped."

Sam had winced a little; it was one thing to hear about the bloodthirstiness of the Sidhe in a tale, and another to feel it so close to home. "What about mortals?" he'd asked. "Why did I rate a warning?"

Keighvin had pondered for a moment, as if the

question hadn't occurred to him. "Probably because you were protected too well to attack easily. Mortals — well, mortals in general just don't rate any courtesy, Sam. I'm afraid the Unseleighe Court deems mortals one short step above cockroaches."

At that Sam had grinned widely. "Could be they forget what good survivors cockroaches are," he had offered. Keighvin had laughed and slapped him on the back.

As soon as Tannim got out of earshot, he asked the question that he couldn't voice while Tannim was around. "Why didn't you tell young Tannim about the rest of the warning?" he asked the Sidhe. Keighvin shrugged.

"He's too tired to be of much use to us right now," Keighvin said with resignation. "He plays hero too much for his own good, and he'd be right here pitching levin-bolts, exhausted or no, if we'd told him. I'd rather not have the lad at my back when he's this worn down." Sam looked at him quizzically, and Keighvin coughed, embarrassed.

"Lately Tannim gets a little — erratic — when he's tired," the Sidhe said, carefully.

Erratic, hmm? Just what's that supposed to mean?

"How so?" Sam probed. "Level with me, Keighvin. What are we talking about here?"

Keighvin shook his head. "Truth to tell, Sam, I'd just as soon not have Tannim anywhere nearby when he's exhausted. His intended targets are safer than his allies. Lack of endurance, I fear."

Sam didn't know whether to be amused or alarmed. It was funny now, but it might not be that funny later, if he found himself having to dodge — what?

"Is this bad aim just with his magic?" Sam asked. Keighvin sighed.

"Magic, fisticuffs, guns, 'tis everything, anything that requires aiming." He spread his hands. "The last time it happened, we were picking slugs out of the walls for a fortnight, and poor Conal still hasn't regrown the hair Tannim scorched from his scalp."

Conal, a few feet away, looked up at the sound of his name, and scowled from under the brim of his baseball cap. Sam recalled now that the Sidhe-mechanic had looked rather odd when he'd removed the cap to scratch his head. He'd had a swath about two inches wide shaved from front to back, in a kind of reverse Mohawk. Sam had wondered at the time if it was some sort of new fashion — many of the younger elves had taken to punk and cutting-edge clothing with a glee unmatched by any human over eighteen. Now he knew better, at least in Conal's case.

"A near-miss," Keighvin continued, "and damned lucky it wasn't nearer than it was. Eh. Poor lad never was very sharp with a gun anyway." He shook his head again. "Wish we could get that glittery friend of his with the odd name to magic him up some endurance, but I fear that's asking for a miracle. He hasna been the same since he got that leg of his chewed on."

That explains the limp. Sam thought about asking about just what had been responsible for that injury, saw Keighvin's face, and decided against it. *There are some things man was not meant to know.*

Instead, he glanced at one of the many clock-calendars mounted around the shop. Not because anyone was on a timeclock, but because it was very easy to lose all track of time in here. Work continued every hour and day of the week — there were deadlines to be met, and later, once Sam and Keighvin had convinced the world that Fairgrove was a reliable, legitimate concern, there would be production schedules for outside clients as well.

It was ten-to-twelve. The Unseleighe Sidhe's challenge had specified midnight as the hour of attack.

And even as he looked up at the clock, folk and Folk all over the shop were putting up tasks and taking weapons from the unlikeliest hiding places. Conal

opened the top drawer of his rolling tool-chest and
produced a matched pair of filigreed swords; a pretty little human girl Sam had thought no more than eighteen
went to the first-aid kit on the wall and opened it up. She
took out a closely-wrapped bundle and unwrapped the
silk from what it contained: a gunpouch. Keighvin had
explained the insulating properties of silk when he'd
asked Sam to be sure and wrap anything of doubtful
content in a square of the stuff from a pile kept beside
the door before bringing it into the shop.

She opened the gunpouch itself, and the gleam of
more silk showed Sam that the pouches had also been
silk-lined, as double protection against the disruptive
effects of that much steel inside the shop. The pouch
contained a Glock Model 22. Everyone at Fairgrove
that was a marksman used these nine-millimeters; that
way all the ammo and magazines matched. Sam was
the only exception, and there hadn't been time to find
or get used to a new gun.

There was an entire row of those silk-wrapped
bundles in the kit. The girl handed one to another
mechanic, and slapped her acquisition into a shoulder
holster.

Sam patted his water-Uzi to be sure it was still with
him. His granny's tales had been very specific about
the effects of salt water on some creatures, like boggles
— and one of the mechanics, seeing what it was he had
on his hip, had stopped him long enough to put some
kind of pagan blessing on it. She'd said she'd made it
into "holy water" — and Sam's granny had been quite
adamant about how effective holy water was on the
"bad Sidhe." It made him a little uneasy, though; he
wasn't certain that was the kind of "holy water"
Granny'd had in mind.

But then, again . . . maybe it was.

He also had a silk-wrapped bag of iron filings in his
pocket, but unless he could find a way to use them safely, they were going to stay there. Using an area-effect

weapon like the iron filings could be as disruptive to his friends as to the enemy.

Like using a nuclear hand grenade.

Keighvin had spoken of the elven trouble with magic near iron earlier that day as they walked around the Fairgrove grounds. It had surprised Sam that he'd treated it like any other conversation topic, only wrinkling that smooth, passive brow when he mentioned the effects of iron's contact with elven flesh. He'd explained that the Sidhe's bodies thrived on magic itself, as well as food and drink, and the touch of Death Metal was a poison — a corrosive one. Then he'd gone on. The touch of iron was like a lens focusing light — to burn. It seemed that iron in its purer forms attracted the "frequency" of magical energy the elves used, much like a magnet, and warped it in ways that were often dangerous for the mage. Sam had said it was like a planet's gravity affecting every other heavenly body, always slightly tugging it off-target even from a distance, and Keighvin had nodded energetically. Then Keighvin leaned against a very thick fencepost, and said conspiratorially, "Therein's our advantage in the fight tonight. We've discovered that different iron alloys warp the magic in different ways — and we know how to *see* the alloys now. Magically."

Then he'd leaned back, very obviously smug.

Sam was not going to be in the front lines for this little confrontation; Keighvin had been quite firm about that. He was to be in the second rank, with the archers and others whose distance-weapons could not be fired from hiding. The humans on the crew who were good shots would be firing from cover, or protecting mages from physical attack. The others would be wading in hand-to-hand with weapons of steel and Cold Iron.

Keighvin had produced a shining, blue-sheened sword from out of nowhere (literally) and headed towards the outside entrance. Sam followed the Sidhe out, and stood behind him as he conferred with two

other Folk and an obviously retired GI employee. They
pointed out sections of Fairgrove on a map, and likely
avenues of attack. Sam got the impression they knew
the grounds very well, and had a few hundred dirty
tricks ready. They nodded to each other, traded code-
words, and checked radio headsets. Abruptly, the four
split up, and Keighvin motioned Sam to follow him,
speaking tersely into his mouthpiece.

   The two walked briskly into the parking area, where
Sam realized he wasn't quite *yet* used to the mixture of
machinery and magic at Fairgrove. Before him were a
half-dozen figures; a few humans in Cats Laughing and
Ian Falconer concert-tour sweatshirts and faded
jeans strapped on ballistic-cloth vests, and checked
magazines and radio earpieces. The rest of the group
stood among them, long hair in braids or falling like silvered snow over the intricate armor of the elven
Courts, settling the same sort of earpieces into gently
upswept, pointed ears. One of them carried a US
Army-surplus first-aid kit duct-taped to his enameled
armor; another swung a handful of aluminum baseball
bats as she warmed up for the coming battle. He
watched the Lamborghini and Dino ripple and shift
into a pair of tall, glittering "horses." They stamped,
and their hooves struck sparks.

   Keighvin swept the sword suddenly in a great vertical
circle, cutting a groove into the asphalt. Blue sparks
traced along its arc, and followed the blade up, leaving a
semicircular "mirror" suspended in midair. Images
showed within the mirror immediately, lit in tremendous contrast. "Here is where they are now," he said,
"and this is what we know of them. Janie on camera has
picked out five boggles, and three trolls on their front
line. Four rows of goblins, thirteen each, are after them,
Danaa only knows why. Here is their leader." The image
sharpened so quickly that a stab of pain shot through his
head behind his eyes, and Sam took an involuntary step
back from the thing he saw. One of the humans whistled

in mock appreciation and a little fear; another human female snorted and pulled the slide on her gun.

"You know the routine — we've gone over it before. Plug your other ear, or make enough noise to disrupt its effects. Dottie, you shouldn't have too much trouble doing that for all of us." The woman giggled and let the slide smack back into place. The rest laughed along as she stroked the extra five magazines she carried affectionately. "Donal, take Sam with you, watch him and watch your back. Dottie, Jim, Cuil, follow me and fan on my signal. Take the creek oak, Kieru. Anything goes sour, medical is here, and escape is by Thunder Road."

Sam ran through what he knew of Fairgrove. *Seven of the lot are medics; Thunder Road is what they call the driveway. Oh, Holy Mother.*

Two more elvensteeds appeared so suddenly that Sam was startled, and blushed in embarrassment over it. Donal jerked a thumb over his shoulder, and led the way inside again. He half-ran through the corridors to a well-lit room where scores of television screens glittered in the eyes of a single woman wearing a full headset, who spoke information so quickly it sounded like a chant.

"Keighvin, camera three shows the first and second ranks of goblins are splitting to let the leader advance. Two trolls are flanking, past camera six, coming into camera twelve. Wire shows crossing at the creek — camera six shows the other two trolls now, following the first two. Camera twenty has all of the boggles moving as one unit towards the forge. Carrie, you show clear to intercept from the other side. . . ."

Even an armchair general could see what was going on. *These bogeymen havena' plan at all that I can see. They've got a sorry lot to face these people.*

Donal leaned close to Sam and said, "Sarge Austin says a deployment like this shows the leader is such an egotist he thinks he can't be defeated."

"We still haven't seen his second rank, or his reserve. Maybe he's right," someone muttered, sounding nowhere near as confidant as Donal. Nods around the room echoed that sentiment.

On one screen, Sam saw Keighvin look directly into the camera, and unexpectedly smile and wave. He mouthed, "Hi, Mom!" and then moved on. It was obscenely absurd with the battle at hand and the odds so greatly against them, but despite himself, Sam smiled.

Donal only shook his head and said, "Danaa, he's been around that boy Tannim too long."

Janie paused for one long heartbeat, then spoke again: "Keighvin . . . their second rank just arrived. You aren't gonna like it."

Donal spat a curse in elven, and began running.

Panting and with a pain in his side, Sam came to a rest at Donal's back after a sprint through the offices and garages of Fairgrove. They had only paused for a moment in the body shop, so Donal could find an ear-piece for Sam; all they could find was an old, taped-up full headset with a battered power pack, stenciled with a SWAT logo. It crackled horribly when activated, but settled down after the initial protest, and then they were running again. Now they were outside, and Sam heard Keighvin's voice in his ears.

"Janie, dim the cameras in five, then hit the spots. Ready on the Pinball."

Donal crouched down and covered his eyes. Sam did the same, still wondering what this "Pinball" could be. An area-effect weapon? Some kind of spell? Keighvin had told him how all the iron around Fairgrove would disrupt any magic the elves used. . . .

The grounds lit up in brilliant light as hundreds of halogens came to life. Sam squinted against the glare and then gasped as he saw what they faced.

Oh Father who art in Heaven, hallowed be Thy name . . .

Caught in the daylike brightness were creatures out of his nightmares and old stories — although under that much candlepower, they looked only like so many special-effects puppets. All except their leader. It was unmistakably real, horrifyingly real, riding a creature that might once have been a horse, but now was tattered hide stretched over bone, fang-filled mouth, and evil, glint-of-fire eyes. The leader's ragged clothing whipped in a wind that seemed to blow from Sam's own soul, and he knew the Bane-Sidhe for what it was. Around it were rank upon rank of gray-and-green skinned goblins, wicked weapons drawn, and great shambling trolls with glistening knobby skin. Virtually all of them were cringing and clutching at their eyes. Behind them, in the second rank, were — Sidhe. Tall, silver-haired, dusky-eyed, identical to the Fairgrove Sidhe, and yet as different as a surgeon's scalpel and an assassin's dagger.

Unseleighe Sidhe. The first besides Vidal Dhu that Sam had seen. They carried some sort of weaponry that looked vaguely gun-shaped — all but four of the tallest. The quartet raised their arms and gestured, gathering sickly green light around their hands, and Sam knew the attack had begun.

"Come on, ye bastards," Donal muttered. "A little closer. Just a little closer — "

They didn't immediately oblige him; instead, some of the skinnier goblins peered, squinting, through the halogen glare, and the Unseleighe Sidhe raised crossbows. They looked odd; when they fired them into the trees where the hidden humans with firearms were waiting, Sam realized why.

Fairgrove wasn't the only group to have pirated technology, and although this was a simpler level of tech, it was no less deadly. The Unseleighe Sidhe had armed themselves with compound crossbows, and the bolts glowed with the same evil green as the mages were gathering about their hands.

"Shit," Donal spat. "Elf-shot. The pricks brought elf-shot."

And from the sudden cries of pain in the trees, those

bolts had found marks among the humans. Some shots rang out from the trees in answer, but the Unseleighe-mages cast a curtain of deflecting energy across their front ranks, and four boggle-mages emerged from the woods.

That'll be their attackers —

Encouraged by their success, the enemy leader gestured his troops to move forward under the crossbowmen's covering fire.

The boggle-mages gestured, as if about to throw something.

Keighvin's voice came clearly, calmly through the headphones: "Janie, Pinball now."

Then Sam realized why the elven leader had been so smug. The fencepost he'd leaned on earlier that day — and every other fencepost — cracked open along its top and revealed a dark metal bar, trailing shreds of silk cloth as they rose. The grounds-sprinklers popped up from the ground, refracting the artificial daylight in huge rainbows.

The tricky bastards!

The boggles unleashed their spells, and the bolts of searing energy careened madly across the field. One looped in a devastating arc, incinerating a half-dozen goblins before striking the boggle itself, who fell to the ground writhing in agony.

The beautiful, tricky bastards, they built silk-wrapped iron bars into the fenceposts! Sam's mind swam with amazement. *They ran lines to those posts when the sprinklers were installed, and it only takes turning one valve to raise the bars when you activate the sprinklers.* . . .

The bars themselves warped the paths of both the magical energy blasts and the enchanted elf-shot. And that was why it was called "Pinball," he realized, as he watched the spell-bolts the boggles had unleashed tear through their own ranks like silver balls in an arcade game, until they ran out of targets to burn.

He could see the flashes of gunfire around him, and felt the dull thuds muffled by the earphones. There were bodies down on their side, but most of them seemed to be moving, at least —

And now the odds looked to be even; tech on the Fairgrove side, numbers and bloodthirstiness on the Unseleighe side, as the crossbowmen changed from elf-shot to plain bolts with dark, glittering heads, that flew through the Pinball field with courses unaltered. Keighvin and Janie barked information to the team leaders, and the lines of tracer fire mixed with the enemy's spell-bolt trails. Donal stood behind a wild cherry tree and fired a longbow, measuring his shots very carefully, felling one goblin after another. Then the spells from Fairgrove began, and the odds altered again, this time in their favor.

Pinball. Good Lord, they're brilliant.

Keighvin had said that different iron alloys pulled elven magic — and Sam realized that those amounts could be *measured*. Like scientists used a planet's gravity to launch a satellite into orbit, the elven mages were *using* the known effect of iron on their spells to deflect their shots into their attackers, and destroy the enemy's accuracy!

Levin-bolts from human and elven mages lanced out from the buildings, the human ones tracking straight and true, the elven bolts arcing gracefully into their targets as they were pulled by the iron-alloy bars. The enemy's magickers launched spells back, and watched in horror as their attacks not only missed, but circled back out of control like unguided fireworks rockets inside the perimeter marked by the fenceposts. Keighvin ordered someone to fire "the magnet," and began counting backwards. When he reached two, the spellfire of the defenders halted, and Sam watched a crossbow bolt strike the ghastly horse their leader rode a moment later. Although he couldn't hear it, he could see Donal shout "Yes!"

Then the spells started up again, and Sam realized why the layout had seemed so familiar as the bolts disappeared around the other side of the buildings — and reappeared moving faster around the other side, racing around the inside of the fenceposts in a league-wide stream of death. They accelerated.

I'll be damned. Fairgrove's built like a simple electric motor — or a cyclotron. The posts are the electromagnets, the bolts the brushes. . . . I don't believe it! The more power you add, the faster the drum spins . . . and the magnet will —

Sam never even needed to finish the thought, as he watched the spell-bolts swirling around the complex track in, one by one, on the single solid iron bolt embedded in the Nightmare's chest. There was a silent explosion, and a great coruscating ball of fire spread for a hundred feet. When it cleared, there was a smoking pile of shredded flesh and rags marking what had once been a Nightmare.

But the rider was still moving, and had pulled back its hood.

Its face was a contorted image of pain, hatred, sadism, every vile emotion a human could possess, magnified a thousandfold. Its eyes glittered with cruelty and hunger, desiccated skin wrinkling around the sockets as it opened its mouth to scream. A low, painful sound built in Sam's ears, like bone scraping concrete. It rose in pitch as the creature wailed, giving him a shooting pain that ricocheted in his head like the spell-bolts racing around the complex. Sam tried to concentrate on what Keighvin and Janie were saying, not wanting to ponder the fact that a few dollars' worth of surplus police equipment was all that was saving him from the deadly wail of the Bane-Sidhe.

Sam and Donal broke from their cover and ran to crouch in the bushes around the forge building, but the creature lashed out at them with a whiplike tendril of crackling green fire. The blaze caught Donal in the chest, and heaved him off his feet. The Bane-Sidhe strode through the water-sprays, inside the lethal wall of spell-bolts, its head still tipped back in a wide-mouthed shriek.

Sam crouched over Donal while the monster approached, and saw that he was still breathing — but barely. The breastplate had been breached in three places he could see, twisted and seeping a bright red fluid that looked as human as any blood Sam had ever seen. Sam felt a dog-like growl of anger rumbling in his chest, and he stood and pulled the Uzi.

I'll be damned if ye'll get away with that, y'black bastard.

Narrowing his eyes, Sam trained the watergun on the horror stalking towards him, trigger pulled as he leveled it. It primed and fired when the Bane-Sidhe was only two arms-lengths from him, and the holy water struck and burned, burned like sulfuric acid. Its scream turned from one of attack to terror as it caught "fire," deep channels burning into its flesh where the water touched, black blood streaming, and the last thing Sam saw in its eyes before it turned to run — was fear.

In a little pocket of Underhill chaos, hastily built into an island of protection, Vidal conjured another torrent of water. Once again, he sluiced the Bane-Sidhe down. The liquid poured over Niall, who lay face-down on the rubbery, soft floor, in a quivering heap of pain and suffering, rags plastered to his unnaturally thin body. Niall's howl had died down to a whimper, which was a blessing. It wasn't the purposeful scream of a Bane-Sidhe's vocal attack, but Niall's cries of agony had called up corresponding pain in his ally, even through Vidal's hastily-conjured earplugs of wax.

The ultra-pure water, carefully warmed to blood-heat, was having an effect. Finally, Niall's whimpers faded and were replaced by hoarse, exhausted breathing.

Vidal conjured a warm breeze to dry the Bane-Sidhe. He hadn't bothered to remove the creature's rags — he hadn't dared. He didn't want to know what lay beneath them.

Slowly, the Bane-Sidhe uncurled, as the rags dried

and fluttered in his artificial wind. "Are you all right?" Vidal asked carefully.

"No," the Bane-Sidhe whispered raggedly. "But I shall mend." Then, as if the words had been dragged out of him unwillingly, "I thank you for your quick thinking. And you are right."

"Right?" Vidal replied, surprised. "About what, pray?"

"Keighvin Silverhair." There was no mistaking the venom in the Bane-Sidhe's voice now, the acidic hatred. "He has become contaminated with these mortals to the point that he is a great danger to us. He must be removed."

Vidal nearly lost his jaw. Those were the last words he expected to hear out of Niall; the Bane-Sidhe's stubborn refusal to admit he was ever wrong was legendary.

"I will help — when I have recovered," Niall concluded faintly. "But what do we do in the meantime? We have been routed."

"Not necessarily," Vidal said slowly, thinking of the silk-wrapped bundle he'd left Underhill. Aurilia had given it to him just this morning, after he'd issued the challenge.

"Keighvin and his fools have one strength," she'd told him, handing the tear-gas grenade to him, after showing him how to handle the weapon with silk-lined leather gloves, and how to pull the pin by means of the nylon cargo-tie she'd fastened to it in case he lost the gloves. "Their pet mortals know our weaknesses and exploit them, and they're using the mortals' weapons whenever they can. You'd best get ready to do the same if you want to defeat them."

He'd laughed at her at the time. Now —

Now he was coming to the reluctant conclusion that she was brighter than he had thought.

"I think I have a way to even the score a little," he said, slowly. "If nothing else — I think I can force one of the vermin out of its hole. The one, not incidentally, that got you."

The Bane-Sidhe's head turned sharply, and Vidal thought he saw the glitter of eyes inside the darkness of its hood, and despite himself, he shuddered.

"Do that," Niall said tersely, "and every power I have is at your call, without reservation."

Vidal held back the thrill of triumph, at least enough to keep it from showing on his face.

Sam unlocked the door and turned to lock it behind him — for although Vidal could not pop in magically, there was nothing stopping the Sidhe from walking in mundanely through the door unless Sam was very careful. The house was much too quiet without Thoreau padding up to greet him, but Sam was glad now that he had sent the spaniel to a kennel for safety until this was all over.

That's one non-combatant out of the way, anyway, he told himself. He'd done everything he could to cover his tracks, too; he'd paid in advance, then registered the dog under a neighbor's name, with her agreement, telling her he was going to be on a consulting job and might not be home for a while. It would take a great deal of investigation for the enemy to learn that Thoreau belonged to Sam. And by then, with luck, this would all be over.

He made sure that his new crowbar — one of six — was still in the umbrella stand by the door, and headed for the library. He still wanted to double-check something before he turned in for the night — what there was left of it.

Certainly the last thing he ever expected when he took this job was to get involved with elven warfare.

But the moment he reached the library door and turned on the light, something crashed through the window.

Glass shards flew everywhere. Something dark skittered and spun across the floor, banging into the furniture, skipping across the rug, spewing a yellowish gas from one end. It spun like a dervish, and Sam made the fundamental error of gasping in surprise.

The stinging of his throat and eyes told him how great an error that had been.

Tear-gas. Just like Belfast. Only this time he hadn't gotten such a big whiff of it.

Coughing and choking, Sam covered his nose and mouth with his hands, and ran, stumbling, for the door. His eyes burned painfully, streaming tears, making it hard to see; and his lungs felt as if someone had poured hot lead into them.

He fumbled at the lock and wrenched at the door handle until it opened, slamming it into the wall. He dove through it, tumbling out into the cool, fresh air and dropping to his knees on the concrete, his lungs screaming for oxygen.

Falling to his knees was all that saved him from the knife that thudded into the doorframe above him.

He started back, then jerked his head around in the direction of the curse that came out of the darkness, just as the house alarms — which he had not disarmed — started wailing, and all the exterior lights flared on as the second line of computer-driven defenses activated.

Peering through tears, he made out the dark shape of the enemy Sidhe, Vidal — and only that single foe — as the creature threw up its arm to protect its eyes from the wash of powerful light.

Vidal Dhu — you bastard.

He knew then that he had a few seconds before the Sidhe recovered and renewed the attack —

He was praying under his breath, the old litany of "Hail Mary," the words tumbling off his tongue in a high-speed gabble without his being aware of when he had started. And in the meantime, the rest of him was moving again, scrambling to his feet and making a desperate, tear-blurred, panting dash for the garage.

He reached it a breath ahead of the knife that clattered off the door, punched in a key-code on the pad to open it, and ducked another blade that landed somewhere in the darkened interior of the garage. If he could just reach the back —

He did, falling to his knees beside his goal, as the Sidhe came charging through the door behind him. Sam glanced over his shoulder, seeing only the upraised arms, and that black and glittering sword.

ThankyouMotherMary — Sam reached for the switch on the powerful box-fan in the middle of the floor with one hand, and the loosely wrapped packet of iron filings in his pocket with the other.

Just then the Sidhe spotted him, crouched on the floor. The enemy shouted with triumph, cries audible even over the sirens from Sam's alarm system, and raised his sword.

Sam switched on the fan, ripped the bag out of his pocket and dumped the double-handful of iron filings into the wind of its blades.

Howls of triumph changed abruptly to cries of pain, as thousands of tiny lances of Cold Iron bit into the Sidhe's face and hands, penetrating and catching even in its garments.

The Sidhe cried out again, threw his hands up to shield his face, and dropped the sword, which shattered into a thousand glassy bits on the concrete floor. Sam snarled, and rose to his feet, reaching blindly to the tool rack on the back wall, his breath wheezing in his lungs, his face still streaming tears.

Sam grabbed the first thing that came to hand; a solid, antique metal T-square, old and heavy enough to be made of steel.

He charged the Sidhe, swinging the implement viciously, like one of his peasant ancestors with a scythe. The Sidhe broke and ran, and Sam pursued, still swinging, to the end of his driveway. There he had to stop, for his lungs and legs both gave out — though he screamed hoarse curses at his enemy right up until the police first arrived in response to the commotion.

*   *   *

Neither Vidal nor the Bane-Sidhe were anywhere in the studio complex, which suited Aurilia just fine. She had work to do, and she couldn't do it if they were hanging around the studio or even the area of Underhill that had been sculpted to hold it. All they ever did was laze about, doing nothing useful, whining about some imagined grievance or other. Making constructs was tedious, exacting work, and she couldn't do it if there was someone distracting her, critiquing her, generally getting in the way.

The grunt work, of making the blanks, had already been done for her by an Unseleighe-mage who had gotten to play Messelina in the Caligula piece, trading work for the privilege of participation in their epic and a share in the results. They waited for her in their boxes in the Underhill workshop, in a work area Aurilia had pretty much to herself most of the time. The other two couldn't be bothered with sculpting constructs; Aurilia considered herself something of an artist in that area. It took skill to create something that would fool the clients into thinking it was a human being; skill and attention to detail. The latter required a patience neither Vidal nor Niall had, for all that they were powerful mages.

She hadn't planned on building her "extras" for another week, but the discoveries of this evening changed all that. She was working with a limited window of opportunity. Before too long, Tannim would extract his little pavement princess from her surroundings and get her away to safety. If he didn't succeed in that, the girl might be murdered by her own stupidity, or the kids might connect Adder's Fork with the young hookers who had already disappeared. The entire schedule for shooting "Deadly Doctor" would have to be moved up if Aurilia was going to be able to extract the maximum value from the potentials of the situation. That would take a lot of work on her part, but the end result would be worth it.

She opened the first coffinlike box. The creature waiting inside was not "alive" in the strictest sense. It was shaped rather like a store-front mannequin, the modern kind that was utterly featureless, with no eyes, ears, nose, mouth, or other orifices, just a blank face-shaped area. No hair yet, either, and it didn't breathe. If you cut it right now, it wouldn't bleed, for it had no circulatory system. It took all of its nourishment passively, like a plant, from the energy Aurilia channeled into it. If Aurilia didn't use it or feed it, within a month it would die of starvation and never even whimper in pain.

This construct was destined for another fate, however; one it would never understand.

Aurilia had already selected personas for this batch of constructs, and had clipped the pictures she wanted to use to the top of each box. This one would be a "Victorian Street Sparrow"; Aurilia's term for the underage thieves, pickpockets, and prostitutes that used to throng London's working-class districts.

And humans treat teenage prostitution as if it's something new because now there are mortals with PhDs writing about it.

She took the picture of the full-face shot in her right hand, and placed her left on the construct-blank's chest. The flesh was warm, but a little rubbery under her hand — and much too smooth to be human. That was all right; the clients weren't going to be paying much attention to the skin, after all. If it looked too perfect, they'd assume it was makeup or lighting.

The face would be the first; it was the hardest.   She chanted the first words of the spell, calling into being the features in the photograph she held: square chin, slightly undershot jaw, petulant lips. The flesh writhed and obeyed her, clearing away from jawline and neck, mounding up to form the lips, cheeks, and chin. The nose was next; nothing hard there, since the basic shape was already in place. Then the eye area. But there were no eyes there yet; the lids closed over round, featureless balls at the moment.

She selected another photograph and chanted to the body, giving it high, small breasts, a slightly protruding belly as if it was a little bit pregnant, broad hips. Then she sang hair into being, head and pubic; she had intended brown, but it grew up auburn. She decided to leave it the way it was. Sometimes the constructs took on slightly different characteristics than she had intended, though she never knew why.

What she had done up until now was pure sculpture. Now began the hard part; the part that required kenning. She removed her hands from the construct, and flexed them, then cupped them over the body in the box.

She sank herself into deep awareness and her chant changed; the rhythm pattern shifted, until it replicated the beat of the human heart. The words shifted, too, becoming heavier, more potent in sound if nothing else.

But they were potent in other ways.

Now the skin of the construct heaved and rippled, as beneath it, Aurilia created organs, bones, and a primitive nervous and circulatory system. The latter didn't have to actually do any work; its main job was to carry "blood" to places where the construct was going to be hurt. If Aurilia hadn't been in so much of a hurry, she could have created an exact duplicate of a human, something that would stand up to anything but a tissue analysis — but there was no point in being that thorough.

In the old days, that was why so many changelings sickened and died; no matter what they were fed, the food didn't nourish them and they wasted away. Why create something well made? We wanted the changelings to die. So did the Seleighe fools, though for entirely different reasons. . . .

Lungs were made the same way; mere bellows to simulate breathing and provide air for speaking and screaming. However, the construct *did* need a good pain-nerve net; it was going to have to react appropriately to painful stimuli. That meant a basic spine and some brain functions.

Within an hour, she had her "extra"; one of the creatures destined to die in front of the camera. She'd created dozens of constructs in her time; so long as the raw material was there, it was no effort anymore.

Bending over the box for a close look, she made the creature blink, simulate a variety of expressions, breathe. She fished a long, slender crystal from a pouch at her waist. It looked like a half-melted icicle, but was warm to the touch. This was the key to making her "extras" truly convincing; it was a condensed memory-crystal, containing the reactions of every human who had ever been inside either of the studios. She placed it point-down on the construct's forehead, and pushed it into the "brain." When her palm touched the skin of the forehead, the eyes suddenly snapped open.

The construct screamed itself awake.

She hushed it with a word and a motion.

The creature blinked, looked at her — and cowered away.

Satisfied, she put it to sleep with a thought, closed the lid on the creature's "coffin" and moved on to the next box.

She was half done when Vidal entered the complex, so immersed in her creations that she honestly didn't notice he was there until he knocked something over in the Studio Two bathroom and it broke. That startled her and broke her concentration, and she sensed his presence. She waited impatiently for him to put in an appearance and disrupt her work.

But he didn't; in fact, he stayed right where he was. She heard him moving about the bathroom, but very slowly — unnaturally so.

What on earth is wrong?

She finally left the workroom, too puzzled to continue working. When she entered Studio Two, she realized that the sound she had attributed to the background of disturbing noises that was a constant in the Underhill chaos-lands was actually nothing of the sort; it was the the sound of Vidal moaning.

She strode over to the bathroom door, her high-heels clicking on the stone of the floor, and jerked the bathroom door open.

She had half expected to find the Sidhe drunk, or otherwise incapacitated with self-indulgence. She certainly did not expect to find him wounded, bleeding, and suffering from Cold Iron poisoning. His face looked like a bloodied sponge.

"By the dark moon!" she exclaimed, shocked, and too startled to keep from showing it. "What happened to you?"

Vidal just groaned. She clamped her mouth shut on further questions, kicked off her shoes, and used the last of her energies to conjure handfuls of silk and bone instruments, tweezers and probes.

When she was finished, Vidal lay on the couch in the old Roman set, swathed in bandages, and she had a bloodstained, silk-wrapped bundle containing a handful of tiny iron fragments. She would have to take it across the Gate into the human side to dispose of it.

She shoved it aside for the moment with her foot. "What happened?" she asked flatly, fearing that Vidal had done something irrevocable. "I thought you and Niall were harassing Keighvin, I thought you'd issued a challenge—"

"We were," Vidal said, after a long moment of silence. "We were. But the bastard brought the humans into it, and the humans brought their own weapons. One of them got Niall with blessed water—the *old* blessing, the touch of the sun and the full of the moon—"

"What?" she exclaimed. "I didn't think anyone knew that this side of the ocean! Did he—"

"He's all right," Vidal said, sullenly. "He didn't get hit with a great deal, and I managed to get him back Underhill before it did too much damage to him. I—"

The shiver of Power behind her warned her of Niall's approach. "He did the best he could," the Bane-Sidhe said hoarsely, as she whirled on her knees to face him. Filmy white rags — much cleaner than they had been — fluttered as the creature gestured expansively. The charnel odor wasn't as bad, either.

Too bad he doesn't get doused with holy water more often.

"He did more than most. I pledged my full power if he could remove the mortal beast that struck me down. I had come to see if you had triumphed," Niall concluded.

"It was wiser than I had thought," Vidal said bitterly, raising himself up onto one elbow. "It was craftier."

A hiss of rage emerged from the hood cloaking the Bane-Sidhe's features. "So I see," it replied.

Aurilia held her breath. Uppermost in her mind was the fear that now the Bane-Sidhe would revoke its promise. Without Niall's aid and magic, she would not be able to restrain Vidal Dhu. He would fling himself at Keighvin's pet mortals until they destroyed him — and with him, her plans for vengeance.

The Bane-Sidhe raised itself up to its full height. Aurilia shrank into herself; Niall towered over her, emanating a kind of cold hatred. He seemed to pull all the light into himself — the very air grew dark, thick, and oppressive, while he himself glowed a faint, leprous blue-white. She shivered, and her breath caught in her throat. She had never experienced Niall's full power before this, and now she understood why mortals died of fright on simply seeing him.

"This cannot be borne," Niall said hollowly. "Mortals have never confronted us and won. This cannot be permitted. If more of them discover our weaknesses, they may learn also how to travel Underhill and confront us here as well."

That had never occurred to her, and the thought was as chilling as the full effect of the Bane-Sidhe's Presence.

Then she realized what Niall had not said. He was not removing himself and his power from their alliance. He was not insisting that they leave Keighvin and Fairgrove alone. In fact, he seemed to be advocating the very opposite. "But — " she began, feebly.

The cowl bent to regard her, and she shivered again. "We must eliminate Keighvin Silverhair and his mortal allies," the Bane-Sidhe said grimly. "He is the champion of those of the Seleighe Court who wish to integrate their society with that of the mortals. That must not be! I pledge to you, I shall drain every drop of my power to see him defeated and destroyed!"

"But we must be careful," she replied, quickly.

Niall paused for a moment, and then sighed, shrinking back to his normal size as he exhaled, releasing the light. Aurilia sighed with him, but with relief. If she never had to face the Bane-Sidhe in his anger again, it would be perfectly fine with her. "We must be careful," Niall agreed. "Our present state is the direct result of carelessness and overconfidence."

Vidal grunted; Aurilia assumed it was in grudging agreement.

"Thus far," Niall continued, shifting from side to side, restlessly, "the only one of the three of us who has brought plans to fruition scathlessly is you."

"Well," she replied, with a certain amount of hesitation, "I don't know about that."

If Vidal gets his nose out of joint about this —

"The Bane-Sidhe is right," Vidal growled. "It will take the three of us to achieve our goals, working together. We cannot afford to hare off with separate plans."

It's about time you figured that out, she thought sourly. *After all the work I've put in here.*

"Since you have been working here for hours, I assume you *have* a plan," Niall said pointedly.

Now, if ever, was the time to seize leadership, while momentum was behind her. Vidal was temporarily incapacitated and might be influenced; the Bane-Sidhe was already on her side. She gathered her composure, steadied her nerves, and nodded with all the authority she could command.

"Yes," she said. "I do."

● CHAPTER ELEVEN

Tannim woke three or four times during the night as random sounds threw him out of dreams, but that was all that they were, pure random sounds, and he drifted back into sleep again. When he finally woke for good, he lay watching the darkness for a while, thinking about getting up for a long time before doing anything about it. Bed felt wonderful, and he wished, selfishly, that he could stay there for the rest of the day. He felt rested, and at the same time, tired — as if he had gone off sleep-fighting, or something. He'd had some strange dreams last night; images of fairy-tale bogeymen mixed up with a Tokomak accelerator, of Nightmares getting hit with Cruise missiles and exploding, and of Sam on a S.W.A.T. team, guarding a rainbow.

Weird.

There was no light at all in the bedroom, other than the clock on the VCR. The lighted numerals said 4:23 — which meant it was about eleven. He hated having the damn thing blinking "12:00" at him, so he always reset it to some arbitrary time whenever the power went off or he had to unplug it.

There didn't seem to be any windows in the room. There was one, but he also hated daylight, which was why the floor-to-ceiling headboard blocked the window entirely, so that nothing could leak through.

So, it was about eleven. If he got up now, he could shower, shave, eat — pick out an appropriate outfit — and by one, when the people he wanted to see were in their offices, he'd be ready to see them.

He ran a systems-check on himself, first. About the

only thing still not right was his leg, which twinged a little when he flexed it. It had healed about as much as it was likely to, so it always felt like that, except when he was in a hot-tub, so he ignored it and reached for the light in the headboard.

He fumbled around a little before his hand encountered the proper little round knob. It was on a dimmer-switch, which he brought up in microscopic increments. His last live-in lover had hated that, insisting on having bright light instantly in the morning. It was one of the reasons they hadn't stayed lovers for long, although they had parted friends.

His stomach growled impatiently, reminding him that it had been a long time since lunch — most of which he'd pushed off on Tania — and that corn-chips and vitamins were not an adequate substitute for dinner. Chinthliss railed on him constantly about his admittedly horrible diet. He pried himself up out of the bed and headed for the bathroom.

Being a mage means you're never out of hot water. . . .

One very long, very hot shower later, he felt a little more like a human, but not up to choosing clothing. Magery was a very diverse avocation, and some mages could change their form with a thought — but Tannim was not one of them, and so clothing was the closest to shape-changing he was going to get on this world. His choice of garments today would make all the difference in the success of his still-nebulous plan, if he was going to get the maximum clout with a minimum of questioning. He put off the decision and pulled a Salvation Army print caftan over his head. Making a selection that important should be done on a full stomach. Time to invoke the spirit of the microwave.

His last lover *had* been an excellent cook, and had left the freezer full of marvelous microwavable goodies for him, knowing that he would never cook for himself, and knowing that he often forgot to shop as well. Tannim had been making them last for a while, but now, if ever, was the time to dip into the stash. He poked his head into the freezer and contemplated the neatly calligraphed labels.

Calzone, Chicken Kiev, Veal Scaloppini, Chicken Cordon Bleu, Gad. Eggplant Parmesan, ick. That can't have been meant for me. Unless I was out of everything else and couldn't move. Maybe that was the idea. Ah, Huevos Rancheros. Perfect. But it needs something to go with it. Should end in a vowel. . . . There, three-cheese zucchini. That'll do.

The microwave *beeped* five minutes later, and he fished clean dishes out of the dishwasher, poured himself a big glass of Gatorade, plucked an old t-shirt off the back of a chair and wrapped it around his hand, then pulled his breakfast out of the nuker. He took a forkful and blew on it to cool it, while he stared at the Ninja Turtles cavorting on his glass for a moment. *Maybe that's what I can tell my mother about what happened to the leg. "There was this glowing ooze, Mom, and —" Nah. She's probably seen the movies.*

Besides, right now he shouldn't be thinking about how to explain his scars to his mom. What he really needed was to figure out a persona for his meeting with the shelter directors. Something where he could plausibly fling money at them with a condition attached. They might not care for the condition — that they take in Tania (and her friends, if he could get them to come in with her) with no questions asked, and no pressure on any of them to contact parents. Counseling, yes; pressure, no.

And no sneaking off behind their backs, either. Whatever drove those other kids into hooking, it had to be worse than hooking. If it was, I'm not going to let them go back to it. Tania's folks were trying to make her into a good little Type-A overachiever drone by killing her spirit and imagination. She seems pretty sure it was worse for her than hooking. I don't know if they've learned their lesson yet, since she ran off, and I won't send her back to them until they have.

Getting them into a shelter would get them off the street long enough for Keighvin to clear up the little war with Vidal Dhu. Once that was taken care of, they could all go Underhill while Keighvin's spies found out whether the various parents were worthy of the privilege of having children. If not — Underhill they stayed, like half the humans at Fairgrove.

But meanwhile there was that matter of keeping them safe for a couple of weeks. The way he had it figured, if he threw enough cash at one of the shelters, more than enough to pay for the keep of Tania and all of her friends, they'd take in the strays just as fast as he could deliver them. The shelters were hard up for support; they couldn't afford to turn him down. But he needed that persona to make the offer.

It can't be a Suit. They'd smell Corporation and want to know too much, maybe get greedy, certainly want to see some I.D., which I don't have — except for Fairgrove, and I don't want to leave that kind of trail for Vidal Dhu to find. It can't be my usual look, or they'll want to know where I got all the cash, maybe call the cops on me, figuring me for a pimp or a pusher trying to recruit on their turf, or dumping some poor kid too gone to be useful anymore. He finished his breakfast quickly, hardly tasting it. Then he gulped the last of the Gatorade and went back into the bedroom, flung himself down on the bed, and turned it into a lounge chair while he pondered.

Teacher? No, where would a teacher get that kind of money? That lets out cop or social worker too, plus they'd want to see credentials; ditto psychiatrist or grad student doing research. I could try forging credentials, but if they double-checked, they'd find out I was phony.

He idly flicked on the TV to fill the silence; it was set on MTV already, and the picture and sound came up in the middle of the old "Take On Me" video from A-Ha, where the girl and her comic-book lover are being chased by the comic-book bad-guys. It was one of Tannim's favorites.

Now if life were just like a comic book —

Then it hit him. The perfect answer. He jumped out of bed and ran to the closet, ignoring the protests of his left leg, and dug through the jeans and soft cotton shirts until he came to an outfit he'd only worn once. He dug it out, and looked at it, then smiled.

Perfect.

Tannim lounged at his ease in the shabby waiting-room, his clothing at violent odds with the tacky plastic sofas. A young woman in her early twenties, with no makeup and her brown hair in a wash-and-wear bob eyed him warily from behind the shelter of her beat-up gray metal desk.

This was the first shelter on his list; the best, the cleanest, and the one least inclined to put pressure on kids. There were rules: you had to go to school, stay clean and off the street, do your homework, pass your courses. There were rules about boy- and girl-friends (group dates only), extra-curricular activities (supervised only), and sex (none). The kids got straightforward lessons in sex-education, and a thorough medical exam when they came in, including the HIV test. They had to spend time with a counselor every day. But if a kid couldn't bring himself to actually talk, he didn't have to — there were counselors who spent whole hours with utterly silent kids every damn day.

And the kids didn't have to give their real names until they wanted to. A big plus in Tannim's book. Understandably, this was the shelter with the longest waiting list. If they wouldn't go for his little bribe — well, then he'd try the next, then the next. . . .

If none of them swallowed the bait, he'd hit Keighvin up for some duplicated gold coins, cash them in with a collector who knew him, and come back to try again, with a new set of clothing, a new face, and a new story. Sooner or later, somebody was going to get bought.

Just as long as they're getting bought for a good cause, taking my conditions to have a chance to help more kids.

He settled the shoulders of his dark-red, full-length rayon jacket over his black silk shirt a little self-con-

sciously. This was a lot more flash than he usually wore.
So were the heavy silver-and-turquoise choker and
matching *ketoh* bracelet and concho belt. Those he
usually didn't wear at all except to pow-wows or when
he was with Mike Fighting Eagle and the rest of his
blood-brothers out in Arizona.

He watched the young woman at the desk without
seeming to look at her; it was easy enough, since she
couldn't see his eyes through his Ray-Bans. She was a
little nonplussed by his appearance; she obviously
wasn't used to having close to a thousand bucks worth
of clothing stroll up to the door of Shelter House unless
it was a pimp looking for a stray. She scraped the legs of
her plastic patio chair noisily against the worn brown
linoleum as she tried to find a comfortable way to sit.

Little does she know everything on my back was either con-
jured by elves or a gift. Never thought this outfit would come in
handy a second time.

"Mr. Cleveland will see you now, Mr. — ah — Burgundy," the case-worker currently manning the
front-desk said, with only the slightest hesitation. Tannim walked past her into the equally shabby, but
pleasant, office. The window blinds were wide open to
the sunlight, and there were plants in clumsy, hand-
made pots on the sill. The wallpaper had faded until the
yellow roses were a pale cream, and the leaves a ghost of
emerald. The decor was Goodwill-reject; the art on the
walls was all posters, posters of rock, sports, and movie
stars urging kids to stay in school, to stay off drugs, and
to read. The notepad was a giveaway from FedEx, and
the letterhead stationery on the man's desk had been
printed up on a very spotty dot-matrix printer, probably
donated. Obviously this place wasn't wasting money on
gold-embossed stationery and collector artwork — or
even interior decorating. The dark, harried-looking
man behind the desk stood up, surprise flashing briefly
across his face before he covered it with a smile. Obviously he wasn't used to seeing clothing like Tannim's,

either. He reached a hand across the desk to Tannim. "Alyx Burgundy," Tannim said, taking the hand immediately, and shaking it.

"Harold Cleveland," the director replied, with an equally firm handshake. "What can we do for you, Mr. Burgundy?"

Tannim sat down in one of the three visitors' chairs. Vinyl with an aluminum frame, they were as uncomfortable as they looked. "Mr. Cleveland, my boss sent me over here on his behalf. He's a horribly busy man, but he has the best of intentions. I'm sure you'll understand my being direct. I've got a donation with some strings attached."

Harold Cleveland eyed him with some suspicion. "What kind of strings?" he asked.

Tannim shrugged. "My boss wants to make sure that a little girl and maybe a couple of her friends have a safe place to go. You've got a waiting list — by the time you got around to them, they might be in real trouble. But — you also need money. My boss is very well-known in the music business, and very, very wealthy. He and the girl met after one of his shows, and they started talking. He likes her." Tannim paused for effect. "We'll take care of that money problem you've got right now if you'll move her and her friends to the top of the list." He presented the envelope of cash he'd withdrawn from his bank earlier, and fanned its contents on the desk — a thick stack of fifties and hundreds.

Harold blanched as he ran a quick mental count. Emotions warred on his face, and his hand flinched towards the money.

But the man had integrity. "I don't know," he said, slowly, controlling his immediate impulse. "I'd like to say yes — but we *do* have a waiting list. And I don't know where this money is coming from. . . . " He narrowed his eyes. "If your boss has this much to play around with, why isn't he taking care of this girl himself? Just because we're a charity, that doesn't mean we have no rules and no standards. If I may be so forward, Mr. Burgundy, why is he wanting *us* to take this girl in?"

Tannim sighed, as if exasperated. "My boss — and I'm sure you understand that I cannot reveal his identity — is in no position to do so. It's because she's underage — and as you probably figured out for yourself, right now, she's an underage hooker. My boss is in the public eye — every moment, you might say — and whenever he turns around there's somebody trying to come up with some kind of dirt on him. He feels sorry for the girl, but he can't risk some cop — or a smear sheet — putting two and two together and coming up with 'contributing to the delinquency of a minor' when all he wants to do is get her off the street and back in school."

He allowed his eyes to flicker up to one of the posters behind Cleveland's desk. There were several rock-music idols up there — but only one group was on tour in the area. He watched as Cleveland's eyes followed his "slip," and felt a bit of satisfaction as the man's mouth softened a moment. Good. Tannim hadn't lied. Let the man make his own conclusions — even if they were wrong. Given *that* particular star's reputation as a good-guy, Cleveland should now be very sympathetic. "The guy wants to get a good kid out of a bad situation, but you know what the tabloids would say if they found out."

He grimaced, and Harold Cleveland nodded.

"I see. This is a most . . . unusual proposal, Mr. Burgundy. On one hand, it's hardly fair to the children waiting that we take your three ahead of them. On the other hand, with just the money you have here — " he touched the stack " — we could afford to take in your three and a half-dozen more for a couple of months."

Tannim could see by his aura that he'd accepted the offer. Now it was only a matter of completing the dance.

"Mr. Cleveland, I appreciate your position. It's a tough call." He shrugged, making it look helpless.

Harold Cleveland sighed. "I don't see how we could

refuse, Mr. Burgundy. We've got no money to speak of, really. Too few donations, and the problems are getting worse. We'll take the offer."

Tannim nodded, then bowed his head.

"Good. Good. Her name is Tania, and she will be here with her friends within the next couple of days. I hope. She will have a lot to talk about — but nothing relating to my boss." He handed over a small polaroid. "If your outreach workers see her, I'd appreciate it if they talk to her. She might be shy about coming."

"Sworn to secrecy, I assume? To protect his reputation?"

Tannim looked back up, through the Ray-Bans.

"My boss is also my friend. When it comes to kids, he's a pushover. He's spent his life trying to understand them, and be like them, and make things easier for them. He said before I came over that he had a good feeling about this place. I am constantly amazed at his faith in human nature. Times like this — " he said, palming from a pocket " — I understand why. Thank you for being suspicious, Harold, and for being kind. This one's from me."

Tannim left a paper-clipped roll of twenties, stood and smoothed the jacket, and walked out smiling.

Tannim swung himself into his driver's seat, and indulged himself in a moment of self-satisfaction. *So much for Part One of Plan A. Now for Part Two.*

He closed the door and sat quietly in the Mustang for a moment, searching for a particular energy track, drawing on the energies stored in the car and on the faint traces still lingering about the passenger's seat. Negotiating with Harold Cleveland had taken longer than he expected, though it had been worth every second spent. Cleveland's outreach people would be looking for Tania now, as they made their rounds of Savannah. If they spotted her, they'd try to make contact and tell her there was a bunk for her and her friends. Tannim really didn't think they'd spot her before he found her, but there was always a chance, and one he couldn't pass up.

Sunset created a brilliant sky right out of a Maxfield Parrish painting over the marshes to the west. He sought through a maze of energy patterns as brightly and as subtly colored as the patterns in the sky, searching and discarding —

Then he found it; less red-tinged than before, and shading more towards the blue of intellect and acceptance, and away from the vermilion of anger and unreasoning emotion. But full of the warm gold of earthy good sense, too, which hadn't showed before, and the tingle of humor —

Tannim started the car, and pulled out of his parking place, which was filled as soon as the Mustang's tail cleared it. He scarcely noticed; he was too intent on tracing that energy trail back to its source, in the real world as well as in the spirit world. It wound through all the other traces, touching briefly at River Street before drifting on, heading off past the edge of Savannah.

After a little while, he got a sense of distance as well as direction, and realized where the trace was leading him. *Oatland Island, huh? Never figured Ross for a wildlife fancier. But then, I never picked him for a punster, either.*

Now that he knew where he was going, he was able to take a more direct route than following the trace through Savannah. By full dark, he was at the gates of the Oatland Island Education Center, parking before the carved wooden sign. A little conspicuous — but that could be remedied.

He turned off the engine and got out of the car; placed his hands palm-down on the warm fender, and frowned with concentration, activating one of the permanent spells that was as much a part of the Mustang now as its paint. He straightened after a moment, satisfied that the eyes of any passerby would simply slide right over the car without ever noticing it was there.

That spell — which he had dubbed "Hide In Plain Sight" — was one of the most useful he'd ever come up with.

He stretched, flexing finger and neck muscles, taking deep breaths of the cool, sweet, air. Ross Canfield wasn't likely to be as hard-nosed a negotiator as Harold Cleveland; with luck, he could get this over quickly and get back to Fairgrove before Keighvin started to get annoyed.

He pulled a sucker from the inner pocket of the expensive jacket, unwrapped it, and tucked the cellophane back into the pocket before stowing the candy in his cheek. The flavor startled him for a moment. *Pina-colada? Where'd I — oh, that's right. Donal thought I ought to have fancy suckers to match the jacket. Elves.*

He sat himself cross-legged on the warm hood while the crickets chirred in the grass beside the road, glad that the pants were a practical set of Bugle Boys instead of the unwashable dress-slacks Donal had wanted to put him into. One snag, and they'd have been ruined —

He relaxed all over, and began a low chant, drawing more power up from the stores invested in the Mustang. He had no intention of going for a spirit-walk this time, though. Not tonight, especially now that Vidal Dhu and company knew he was a player in the game. This time, all he intended to do was to call, sending out a very specific identity-sign along a specific trace. And if Ross Canfield was still willing to keep that promise he'd made —

The crickets stopped chirping. "Didja know that bluejays sing like damn canaries?" said a gleeful voice in his ear. Tannim jumped.

"Uh — " he said, cleverly, telling his rattled nerves that this had *not* been an attack and he didn't *need* all that adrenaline, thank you. And no point in yelling at Ross; the spirit didn't know about Vidal Dhu's vendetta, or that Tannim was one of his planned targets. "No, Ross, I didn't. I thought all they did was scream."

Ross sat himself down on the hood beside Tannim, a big grin on his face, oblivious to the shaking he'd just given the young mage. "They do," Ross said gleefully, as if he were imparting the greatest wisdom of the universe. "And starlings are 'bout the only birds that'll eat Junebugs an' Jap'nese beetles, an' bears have their cubs while they're hibernatin', an' there useta be cougars around here, an' gray foxes c'n climb trees —"

"Whoa!" Tannim held up his hand. "Now I know why you were hanging out here! Ross, why the sudden interest in wildlife? Or is it sudden?"

Ross grinned, not at all embarrassed. "Always wanted t' be a Park Ranger when I was a kid, but they gotta have college degrees an' my folks couldn't afford college. So —" He shrugged, then brightened. "Now, shoot, I can walk right up t' birds, sit practically on their tails an' watch 'em — found out about this place an' been hanging around listening t' everything. Better'n goin' t' college, 'cause there's nobody givin' tests! So, what can I do for you? I don't s'ppose this is a social call. Some'a my new buddies know you pretty good, an' they told me that when you said you was kinda busy, you weren't tellin' more'n half the truth."

Tannim blushed, unaccountably embarrassed. "Yeah, well, you can't believe all you hear, either. But no, this isn't a social call, I'm sorry to say. Wish it was, actually. I've got a favor to ask you."

Ross scratched his head, and Tannim noticed that he looked a lot younger — and definitely slimmer — than the last time they'd met. He'd noticed that effect before, with spirits that had adjusted well.

Being a ghost seems to be agreeing with him.

"Ask away," the ghost said. "I told you, I owe you."

"I don't know, Ross," Tannim replied slowly. "You might not want to do it once you've heard what it's all about."

"Try me," Ross suggested, and sat patiently while Tannim explained everything he knew about Tania, the trouble she was in, and how he needed someone to keep a close eye on her until he could get her into the shelter, and from there, to Keighvin and Fairgrove.

Everything was fine until Tannim worked up to telling Ross that the girl was a runaway—and a hooker. Then the ghost frowned, and scratched his head again. "I don't know, Tannim," he said, reluctantly, and Tannim's hope slipped a little. "I mean, that's the kinda kid I'd've said was a punk an' a tramp—before—but—"

That "before" gave Tannim reason to let his hopes rise again. "But?" he prompted.

Ross wrinkled his brow. "Well — I kinda found out somethin'. I can kinda see when people get worked up. I found out there's a lotta things goin' on, stuff I useta think were just media people makin' up stories t' sell papers. Lotsa kids in trouble out there, Tannim. Heard a couple of stories from ones that wound up—out here. They didn't have a reason t' make things up, y'know?"

Tannim nodded; Ross had changed, in more ways than showed in his aura. "She's not mixed up with drugs, Ross — and I don't think she will be — voluntarily. But if she gets picked up by a pimp before I can find her and talk her into the shelter—"

Ross scowled. "Yeah. That's what one of them kids out here said. Damn pimp picked her up at the bus stop, made all friendly, gave her what she thought was just grass — next thing she knows, she's hooked on crack with the bastard sellin' her for a hundred bucks a shot an' makin' her do all kindsa pervo kinky stuff—" He shook his head, and his aura swung into the bright, clear red of suppressed and controlled anger, anger carefully focused. Genuinely righteous wrath. "If I could make a ghost outa *that* bastard, I would."

"So would I," Tannim said sincerely. "I know it's not a lot of comfort—but you ever noticed there aren't a lot of *old* pimps and pushers? His lifestyle is real likely to get him killed — and Ross, when *he* comes over to your side, there are going to be a lot of things waiting for him. Remember what I told you about things that might try to eat you? Well, they think that low-lifes like him are mighty tasty, and they'll actually hang around, waiting, on the off chance that somebody'll put a hole in him."

"So that's what they were doin' — " Ross mused, half to himself. Then he shook his head. "Okay, Tannim, I'll see if I c'n find this girl an' keep an eye on her for you — though I don' know what help I could be if she got into trouble."

Tannim folded his arms over his chest, and grinned. "More help than you think, Ross. You been practicing what I told you about affecting the real world?"

Ross nodded. "Been learnin' some. Ain't fallin' through the hood, am I?" he replied, with a chuckle. "But that's *me* lettin' the real world affect *me*. When it comes t'me actually doin' things, I can't do much more'n flip a bottlecap."

"That could be enough," Tannim told him. "One thing you could do, you could come get me if the kid's in trouble. If you can't get me," he paused as he called up an image of Sam from an open palm, "you go to this man. His name is Sam Kelly, and he's a friend. He should be able to see you. But remember — not everybody can. Moving a bottlecap at the right time could make a big difference; you just have to start thinking on your feet."

"Easy for you to say," Ross grumbled, but he was smiling a little when he said it.

Tannim let out the breath he'd been holding in a sigh of relief. "Thanks, Ross," he said, sincerely. "When this is over and Tania's safe, I'll owe you."

But Ross shook his head emphatically. "No way, partner. I think I got one thing figgered. You kinda gotta earn your way upstairs. I didn' earn it when I was alive, so now I gotta do somethin' about it. What'd *you* think?"

Tannim had to shake his head, laughing. "Damn if I know. Never had a chance to talk to somebody who'd been there."

Ross laughed. "Well, if I turn up missin' when all this is over, you can figure I was right, huh? So show me what this kid looks like, and I'll get outta here."

Tannim called forth an image of Tania as he had last seen her and projected it into the spirit world. Bad bleach-job, too much makeup, Spandex shorts, and all. Ross studied the image for a moment, then nodded, and Tannim let it evaporate.

"Poor kid," the ghost commented. "Looks like trouble lookin' for a place t' happen."

"Yeah," Tannim said. "That's what I figured. Oh, and another thing. I have friends at the police department I give tip-offs to. You see anything from your side I could use, let me know."

Ross nodded, paused for a moment, then said, "Done. Well, I'm outta here. Got what I need. See you later, Tannim."

And with that, he was gone, instantly. Tannim stared at the place he had been, and snorted. The crickets started back up again.

" 'Been learnin' some,' my ass! That was a teleport, or I'm the Pope!" Then he chuckled. "Ross, you're a good man, and a sneaky bastard. Glad you're on my side."

Tannim stretched again, climbed down off the hood, started the Mustang and drove off into the night, heading for Fairgrove, and another set of duties.

Now if he could just keep them from becoming conflicting duties. . . .

Ross Canfield hadn't teleported, no matter what Tannim thought. He'd *translated* — or at least that was what The Old Man had called it, explaining that the literal meaning of "translate" was "to change one thing into another." What Ross had done was to change from being partially in the real world, to being completely in the spirit world. Or, one of the spirit worlds, anyway; he'd gotten the feeling from The Old Man that there was more than one, but this was the place that folks that were something like him wound up, until they were ready to go off elsewhere. Whatever, wherever "elsewhere" was. The Old Man wouldn't say anything more about that than Tannim would. Ross had started to think of it as being like tuning a radio station — sometimes you were right on the frequency, sometimes you drifted between them.

It was a peculiar sort of "place," not really a place at all. But it was a lot easier to find other ghosts from here. It was no use looking for The Old Man, though; Ross never found *him*, he found Ross, when and where he chose. Sometimes he taught Ross things; sometimes he just said something that only made sense a lot later. Sort of like that David Carradine movie his wife had liked so much. Ross was even starting to understand that now, though every time she'd played it on the VCR when he'd been alive, he'd gotten mad, 'cause it didn't make any damned sense.

He'd figured on doing what Tannim had suggested, looking her up, trying to come to terms with what had happened. And he'd run into her all right, but not when and where he'd expected. Turned out she was married to Marty now, looked happier and younger, more like the girl he'd married, and she had a kid, a little baby, about six months old. He hadn't thought he'd be able to forgive either of them, but they'd shown up at his grave and left flowers —

That was where he'd first seen them, as he was standing by the headstone, wondering what he should do next. It had been kind of a shock; he'd just stood there, staring at them, while they left the flowers and talked about him. And they hadn't said anything mean or spiteful, either. He'd listened to them for a long time, and had to conclude that the girl he'd thought he'd married, and the one he really *had* married, had been two different people.

He'd felt a lot better when he'd realized that, as if he'd got rid of a poison that had been in him. That was the first time The Old Man showed up, right after they left; taught him a couple of things, like how to *translate*, and vanished again. He'd left the grave and hadn't looked back.

Right now, Ross was looking for Vanessa, the kid-hooker he'd told Tannim about. He figured that if anyone knew where the other hookers would be operating, it would be her. Once he knew the streets to look on, he'd be a lot likelier to find this Tania kid.

When he'd first run into Vanessa, she'd been scared as a little baby bunny, with some of the annoying things that liked to pick on the weak and the frightened mobbing her. The damn things were cowards, even if they did look like some kind of deep-sea horror, and he and his new buddy Foxtrot Xray had scared them off. He wasn't sure what Fox was; he was native to the spirit world, and he changed his appearance all the time, sometimes more-or-less human looking, sometimes no more human than a ball of light. Called himself by that name 'cause it was military-talk for FX, and since he was kind of a spirit-soldier and kind of a special effect, it fit.

He wished he could enlist Fox's help on guarding Tania, but it wasn't Fox's kind of thing. Oh, Fox would be willing enough, but he could only operate in the spirit world, though, so he wasn't going to be any use on this job.

Not like when they'd found Vanessa under siege, and he and Fox had chased off the bullies. Ross had stayed around to give Vanessa a hand, and a shoulder to cry on; taught her about being newly-dead, like Tannim had done for him, and how it wasn't so bad.

He sometimes wondered if she thought of *him* as The Old Man. Maybe for her, he was.

Moving around in the spirit world was pretty easy;

you just had to think of who you wanted to be with, and unless they had you blocked out (which you did by thinking you wanted to be alone and felt like putting up walls), you were there. He found her wistfully hanging around a radio-station control-room, watching the DJ and listening to the music. He wrinkled his nose a little; not his kind of music at all, but it was making her happy, so what the hell.

"Hey, Vanessa," he said, quietly, so as not to startle her. She startled easily.

She looked up, big brown eyes wide, from under an unkempt mane of raven-black curls, her aura draining to muddy yellow-green. There was fear in her eyes which quickly faded, and she smiled shyly, the colors of her aura coming back. "Hi, Mr. Canfield," she said diffidently. "Mr. Xray, he was here an' showed me how t' find the radio station when I said I missed rock'n'roll."

"Honey, you c'n go backstage of every concert there is now, y'know," he reminded her gently. "No reason t' miss out on stuff now. Ain't nowhere y' can't go if y'want."

She shook her head. "I can't. Not yet. It just — reminds me too much — makes me mad 'cause all those kids are alive an' I'm not — "

He nodded, understanding perfectly. "When you're ready, honey. Listen, I got a question for you. Friend of mine needs t'find a girl, 'fore she gets herself inta trouble. You got any idea where the areas are that the hookers hang out?"

Vanessa's eyes widened. "Bull, President, an' the alleys between President an' River Street," she said promptly. "Mr. Canfield, she's not — anyone I know, is she?"

He shook his head. "Don't think so, honey. She's workin' alone, but she's just a little bitty baby, like you was, an' we need t'get her somewhere's safe." He didn't add, *before she winds up like you;* he didn't have to.

Vanessa's hands balled into fists, and tears welled up in her eyes. "I wanta help," she whispered hoarsely, "an' I *can't*. I wanta do somethin' an' whenever I try'n get near Bull, the world just sorta goes away —"

Fox said that Vanessa had died on Bull Street, victim of a heart attack brought on by one too many hits of crack. She still hadn't come to terms with her life, much less her death, and Ross sighed with helpless frustration.

"Look, honey, you just now helped, okay? An' someday you'll do better. Right now, you gotta learn to stand up f'r y'self, fight back, don't let nobody push you around. Then maybe you c'n do more."

Vanessa scrubbed at her eyes, and sniffed. And just when Ross began to feel really badly, wanting to comfort her, but needing to go find Tannim's girl in the real world, help showed up in the guise of Foxtrot. Today Fox looked like a cartoon hero, pipestem legs and wild hair. He just appeared out of nowhere, like always, and Vanessa looked up at him and smiled through her tears. Somehow they both always recognized Fox, no matter what he looked like.

"Heya, lady!" Fox crowed, as if there was nothing wrong. "Got something I want to show you." Then he looked over his shoulder at Ross, and grinned. "Sorry old man, no fossils allowed. It's just for people who believe in the magic of rock'n'roll."

"Ah, go on," Ross said, relieved. "You wouldn't know good music if'n it sat up an' bit your ass."

"That wouldn't be where I'd want something to bite me," Fox replied insolently, and reached for Vanessa's hand. She took it hesitantly, and they vanished in a glittering shower of sparks.

Fox was a pistol, all right. Maybe he'd picked Vanessa as his vixen of choice.

Ross smirked, then furrowed his brow in concentration, picturing Bull Street . . . building it up in his mind . . . then, *deciding* to be there.

Then he *was* there. Now *that* was a teleport.

He grinned widely. It was also his first teleport.

But there was no time to gloat about it; he had a girl

to find, one who might be getting herself into trouble she couldn't get out of right at this very moment.

He sharpened his real-world focus, bringing himself as far into the world of the living as he could without interacting with it; he wanted to be able to walk through people and things if he had to. He had noticed that he no longer had any trouble seeing even in the darkest places; the street was as bright as daylight to him, with every person on it outlined with his or her own little glow of colored light. The faces were the clearest, but it was as if every living creature carried its own little spotlight with him — and from the way the females tended to be dressed and act, it was pretty obvious that there was no lack of "professional ladies" on this section of Bull. They ranged in age from teenagers in punk gear to women with a fair amount of mileage on the meter. He noticed that their glows were all in muddy colors, sullen and angry; dirty red, murky yellow, dirt brown. Just like Vanessa, when she first came over. Her colors were clearing now, but she had a long way to go before she looked like Ross — and he was no match for the clear, blue-white light of Fox or The Old Man.

He spotted the pimps right away, too — and interestingly enough, the colors of their glows were sharp and less muddied, but acutely painful to look at. Reds and yellows that swirled together in eye-hurting combinations, screaming, clashing pinks and yellow-greens — and the intensity was somehow *too* much; a fluctuating, pulsing brightness, as if they were burning themselves out with every heartbeat. There were little ribbons of evil yellow connecting each pimp to his "ladies," and Ross wasn't sure just what that meant; was there some kind of emotional or mental dependency there? And if so, who depended on whom? And there was something else, too. Just as Tannim had said, there were *things* lurking about the pimps, vulturine creatures of shifting shape and shadow, watching and waiting with infinite patience. One of them looked in Ross's direction as if it felt his eyes on it, but its glance was indifferent, as if he was of no use to it. It blinked leprous-silver eyes and turned away, back to the pimp. He shuddered anyway. If these jerks only knew what was waiting for them. . . .

But none of the girls he saw, in their tinsel and flash, short skirts and glorified underwear, was Tania.

He drifted along Bull Street for about a mile, seeing no sign of her. When he noticed that the street had gotten emptier, that the girls he saw were no longer plying the trade, he realized he must have come to the end of the "district," and turned back, taking the opposite side of the street.

It all was pretty different from what he had expected. There were no "Irma la Douce" girls here, no "Pretty Women," or "Happy Hookers." This sure was a far cry from the way most movies portrayed street-walkers. There was nothing playful or cheerful here. Most of 'em looked like whipped dogs, spirits broken, minds numbed. Oh, there were a few who were different, but none of *them* were hooked up with pimps. It looked to Ross as if the best these kids could muster was the same blank business-like approach as the kids in the fast-food places, selling burgers. No wonder Vanessa had called a night on the job "hanging on the meat-rack."

Suddenly, his musings were broken into by a glimpse of blond hair with the streetlight shining off of it, and the arch of a nose and cheekbone that seemed familiar, an aura that wasn't as muddy as most. The girl moved, and he got a better look —

It was her, all right. Then something else caught his eye, and he realized that he wasn't the only person hunting her.

There was a man stalking her; a man in a suit, with an aura that was completely black, and a swarm of shadow-creatures around him that was three times the number around any of the pimps.

Ross moved in on the man, quickly, fearing the

worst. But before he could reach the girl's side, the man had already maneuvered so that he was between her and the rest of the people on the street. And just as he got within touching distance, the man managed to crowd her into an alcove, where she pressed herself back against a locked doorway, a look of fear and shock on her young face.

"What — " she said, her voice tight with panic. "What do you want? Leave me alone! I don't have any money, I don't have any drugs — "

Ross crowded in, trying to think of something he could do. He couldn't hit the guy, he couldn't drag him away, or even shout in his ear to distract him. And suddenly there didn't seem to be anyone else on this side of the street, as if the rest of the denizens of Bull had sensed the trouble and evaporated.

"It's you I want," the man said, in a cold, utterly expressionless voice. "If you come along, there won't be any trouble." He pulled back his coat, and terror spread across Tania's face as she saw the gun he was reaching for. "But if you won't be a good little girl — I'll have to — "

Ross didn't even think; he just grabbed for the gun, desperately, reaching right through the kidnapper's back and somehow getting his hands on the gun-grip and the trigger. And realizing that he couldn't take it away. That in fact, there wasn't much he could do. Except — maybe —

His next move was pure instinct. He cocked the hammer, and, as the kidnapper started in surprise at the telltale *click,* pulled the trigger.

The gun went off in the shoulder-holster, the bullet tearing its way through the leather and down his side, with a roar and a muzzle-flash that would have blinded and deafened Ross if he had been alive. The jacket blew away like a rag in a hurricane, and the man's body whip-cracked against the opposite wall of the alcove. Tania jerked back, screaming, then spun and bolted for the street.

The kidnapper clutched at his side, nearly doubling over as his legs and torso went slick with hot, red blood.

Tania made it across the street, just as the firefight began. Gunmen appeared from nowhere, the pimps and pushers he'd seen before, firing wildly; and Ross realized as he ducked out of sheer reflex that none of them knew why they were shooting. But they certainly knew what they were shooting at; the kidnapper, as the originator of the first shot.

The kidnapper went down, blood spraying, in the crossfire; Tania ducked into an alley, and sirens began to wail in the distance.

The firefight continued as Ross dashed across the street after her, while the red and blue flashes of approaching cop cars lit up the sky in both directions.

● CHAPTER TWELVE

Tania's side was afire, pierced with pain, but she ran anyway, gasping for breath as her lungs ached and her throat rasped. Behind her, sirens split the night air with unearthly wails, though the *crack* of gunfire no longer echoed down the alley. She didn't care; or rather, she had no room in her mind for anything but the desperate need to run, run until she was somewhere safe.

She couldn't see at all; her eyes were still dazzled by the flash when the gun had gone off. She lost her balance when she stumbled over a trash-can and fell face-first in the slimy alley, ripping the knees out of her tights and scraping the skin of both palms. She was up again in the next heartbeat — dashing out of the alley and into the lit street, across it, and into another alley again. She ran into a dumpster she hadn't even seen, pushed away from it, and stumbled off into the dark. At the end of this alley she slowed, then stopped, doubling over with one hand on the brick of the wall beside her, sucking in huge gulps of breath, her belly heaving as if a dull knife carved at it deeper every time she breathed.

Panic ebbed, slowly. Her palms burned, and so did her knees. She stood up, slowly, as the blinding white light of pure fear flickered and went out, freeing her mind, letting her think again.

This wasn't the first time she'd been approached by a pimp, but they'd never *come after her* before. No one had ever pulled a gun on her. If it hadn't gone off like that —

She started to shake, and not just from reaction to her

narrow escape. The gun — the gun had gone off, in the guy's holster — before he even touched it. He'd just pulled his jacket open to show it to her. He *had* been reaching for it, but he hadn't actually gotten his hand on it, when the hammer had gone *click*, he'd gotten a startled look on his face, and the gun had flashed and roared.

It had misfired. She had to think that. Anything else was too weird.

Besides, she didn't want to think about it at all. All she wanted, she realized desperately, was to get home. Back to the apartment, where she could soak her knees and hands before they got infected, soak her tired body in a hot bath, hide in her bed with a book, and never, ever come out again.

She stood up, still shaking but determined to get home, knees and palms sending little stabs of pain up her arms and legs every time the raw skin flexed.

She ignored that, and the distant ache in her side, and stepped out into the dim light from the streetlamp, trying to muster a show of courage. She couldn't help but glance over her shoulder, up and down the street; trying not to be obvious about it, but looking furtively to see if there was anyone else likely to make a grab for her. It wasn't just that she was afraid of another muscle-boy coming after her. In her current disheveled condition, she knew she looked like prey, easy prey. Even someone who might ordinarily leave her alone could be tempted to go for her the way she looked right now. And there were muggers, rapists, kids just looking to make some trouble, and she was all too obviously a good target. She started to shake again.

She saw only a couple of people on her side of the street, and neither of them looked terribly dangerous. One was an old bag-lady who tottered down the street peering into corners, clucking and muttering to herself; the other, of indeterminate gender, wandered all over the sidewalk, clutching a bottle in a paper sack.

That didn't mean there wasn't someone lurking

around the corner, or in the mouth of an alley; someone she couldn't see. But at least she'd see them and have a head start if they came after her. . . .

She started up the street, in the direction of the apartment, forcing herself to walk normally, with her head high. The wino stared at her as she passed him, but he didn't seem to really see her; the bag-lady ignored her entirely in favor of an old sneaker she'd just found.

Nothing happened; no one jumped out of shadowy doorways to grab her, and no one pulled any more guns. One or two kids, alone, dressed in variations on jeans and gang-jackets, looked her over carefully, but evidently decided she wasn't worth hassling.

By the time she made it back to the apartment, she was ready to pass out from fear and from exhaustion. But at least tonight there was a lightbulb illuminating the staircase, however faintly. There was no way that there could be anyone lurking on the landing, waiting to ambush her. She took the stairs slowly, carefully, pausing every few stairs to catch her breath. It took her a long time to fumble the key out of her tiny purse, and even longer to unlock the door.

The apartment was completely empty.

In a way, she was glad; that meant she wasn't going to have to explain what had happened to anyone until she'd managed to sort it all out herself. But the emptiness of the apartment meant she was going to be alone for a while. What if that pimp had friends? What if they knew where she lived? What if they'd been following her?

They couldn't know where she lived, she told herself, as she shut and locked the door behind her. All she had to do was stay away from the windows, and not turn on any extra lights that might be visible from the street. That wouldn't be too hard.

The sound of her own heart was so loud she was certain that if anyone did break in, they'd find her by that alone.

She edged her way around the first room. Tonio, Joe, and Honi were nowhere to be seen, and the bedding hadn't been slept in. She kept between the wall and the light, so that no betraying shadow could fall to tell anyone watching that there was now someone inside the apartment. The bathroom was dark, and once in its comforting shadows she heaved a sigh of relief. She stripped off the ruined tights, whimpering as she pulled the fabric away from abraded flesh. They were useless now; huge runs had already started unraveling the black knit, and by the time she got the tights off, there wasn't much left of them but a weblike snarl of threads.

My best tights, too, she thought, angrily, tears in her eyes. They'd cost her a full two dollars at Goodwill, and had been brand-new, out of a batch donated by some store or other. SCAD students had snapped up the rest; she'd practically had to fight to get this pair. And now some goon with a gun had ruined them. Her knees started bleeding again, and she caught the blood with a hastily grabbed wad of toilet tissue. She probably ought to let the scrapes bleed for a while, to clean them out.

She waited until the bleeding slowed, then wrung out a washrag in hot water, and sat on the toilet in her panties and cotton minidress, carefully dabbing at her knees and the palms of her hands, trying not to get any blood on anything else. Each touch of the damp cloth brought an involuntary hiss of pain from her, and she rinsed the cloth and wrung it out, over and over, then dabbed at her knees again, wondering if she ought to use the peroxide Laura did her hair with on the scrapes. But soap and water were free, and peroxide cost money.

Finally the scrapes looked pretty clean, and the bleeding stopped. Her knees looked awful, though. She could hide the palms of her hands, but how was she going to cover up her knees? She still had to hustle tomorrow, if not tonight.

She finally decided to wear the black garter-belt and the black opaque stockings for the next couple of days. Men never asked her to take those off, not even the suits. And if she never told them that the hose were a little old Italian lady's black support hose, they'd never guess. Those stockings were dark enough she could tape her whole leg and they'd never know it.

A great Goodwill find, courtesy of Laura, who could see potential in anything.

It was easier thinking about what to wear than it was to think about what had just happened. She filled the tub with hot water and slipped out of the rest of her clothing, then climbed in, hissing a little as the water set her knees and hands afire. The pain didn't stop, it only leveled off, and she relaxed back into the tub with a sigh and closed her eyes.

The pimp was dead; she had no doubt at all about that. The minute his gun had gone off, he had been dead. There were enough pimps and pushers nearby to start a small war; they all went armed, and they were all as paranoid as hell, especially the pushers. The minute a shot rang out, every muzzle on the street would have been pointed in her would-be kidnapper's direction, and a micro-second later, every one of the triggers would have been pulled. The law on the street was, "assume they're shooting at you." That was why she'd run for cover, hoping to reach the protection of brick and concrete before the fire-fight began.

She'd kept running once she was out of the line of fire because she also couldn't afford to get caught up with the dead, wounded, and witnesses when the cops came. Somebody might remember the guy was trying to grab her — might even finger her for the one who shot first. The Savannah cops were some of the best. They'd never let a private little war go on for long; she had to be out of there before they arrived and sealed the area off.

But who was that man, and *what* was he? Was he a pimp himself, or somebody's muscle? She didn't recognize him, but that didn't mean anything. New pimps moved in every week; he could have been someone new trying to expand his stable. She knew why he'd try for her; she was working alone, which made her a tempting target. Blondes, especially young ones, were always in demand. That was what Laura had told her when she'd insisted on bleaching Tania's hair.

But he hadn't looked or acted like a pimp; he'd had none of the flash, none of the surface style and smoothness. Hired heat was more like it — but if he'd been hired, who had done it? Why hire muscle to bring her in — was she that valuable, or was it just that there was just a scarcity of young blondes worth recruiting? And would they try again — or hunt her down and take the loss of the muscle-boy out on her?

Her head swam, and not just from the heat of the bath. It was all too complicated . . . and none of it made any sense.

She'd have to wait until Laura got home. Laura knew the street, Laura would be able to help her sort it out, and decide what to do.

I ought to at least change my territory, she thought drowsily. *That's a good idea. I could start working President Street.* It would be a little hazardous to move into a new area, since she'd be competing with girls who already had established territories, but maybe she could trade one of them for her old beat on Bull.

Or maybe she could see if she could hit Tannim up again —

But what if *Tannim* had sent the muscle?

The thought made her sit up straight for a moment. It was possible. He knew where her beat was; he knew when she worked. He'd already advanced her three hundred bucks and gotten nothing for it. Maybe he'd decided to collect. . . .

The thought made her sick. She'd trusted him. But wasn't that how the really sick people operated? They got you to trust them, and then they did horrible things to you.

Maybe *he* was the one behind some of the disappearances that had been going on for the past couple of months — the hookers that went off somewhere and never came back. The ones that weren't in the shelters, hadn't been busted, and hadn't moved to Atlanta. Maybe she wasn't the first kid he'd approached; maybe she was just the latest one in a series. She'd read a discarded newspaper's article about serial killers the other night; about how they always chose the same kind of people, that they seemed real nice until they were caught. Regular people; folks you'd never suspect.

She could only sit in silence and cry, her shivers making ripples in the steaming water.

The minute Tannim pulled up to the gate and keyed it open, he knew that there was something wrong. The radar detector on his dash whined as the gun hit it, but the run-lights didn't come on.

Suddenly he recalled his dreams last night; all of them had been about Unseleighe critters attacking and being countered. And he remembered the careful way Keighvin and the others had handled him before he'd left last night. There had been something about to go down — and they'd been keeping it away from him.

He flushed with anger, half tempted to turn the Mustang around and go home, his good mood vanishing. They were treating him as if he was some kind of invalid, a risk, just because he was a little tired and his aim got a little erratic —

Unbidden, the memory of Conal and the near-miss during the last little altercation rose up before his mental eye, and the flush turned to a blush.

He had been more than a "little" tired last night. It had been all he could do to get home and into bed. And his aim was worse than erratic when he was that weary. The last near-miss had been funny, but if someone from Fairgrove got plugged by Tannim's friendly fire, it would be a lot worse than Conal's hair-loss. Last night he'd been too exhausted to have been any use magically — it would have been firearms, then, and no mage-fire shield would deflect a steel-jacketed slug if the mage wasn't expecting one to come winging in.

But he was in good shape now . . . and he'd better get up there and see what Keighvin had for him.

The radio announcer finally ended his commercial spiel, and the first notes of the next half-hour's series of songs started.

There was no mistaking *that* horn riff, even without the lyrics. "Dead-man's Curve," by Jan and Dean.

With a shiver of ill-omen, Tannim snapped the radio off before the singing started.

The radar detector continued to whine as he pulled up the drive, at exactly two miles per hour under the posted limit of thirty. Whoever was on the cameras — probably Janie — would know by that speed that the car she was tracking was a friend and not a stranger or an enemy.

The glare beyond the trees told him that the parking lot was lit up like the yard of a maximum-security prison. In fact, all of the halogens were probably on tonight. Whatever had gone down, it must have been big. . . .

He cursed his own weakness. He should have been there. He should have. He longed to floor the Mustang and race up the drive, to get there all the sooner — but that would give Janie and everyone else heart failure.

Instead, he pulled sedately into a parking lot so brilliantly illuminated that every stray pebble showed clearly. It was a good thing the lot was square, or pilots would be mistaking it for the runway at the airport.

Sam's old Mark IV Lincoln presided over an otherwise empty lot. There were no other cars there, elvensteeds or otherwise. Of course, most of the other Fairgrove humans would be gone by now; the few that were left tended to have gift-steeds, presents from their foster-parents, like the Diablo and the Dino. And any elvensteeds would have gone back to native form for a fight. Still, the empty lot gave Tannim the shivers again.

He parked and locked the Mustang — normally he never locked it here, but there was no point in giving anything to the enemy. If the enemy was still here.

Once he was outside the Mustang's protective shields, there didn't seem to be any sign that the Fairgrove complex was still under siege. There was nothing in the air but the scent of honeysuckle and wet grass; no tremblings in the power-flows betrayed any disturbance of the protections around the place.

But out beyond the parking lot, there were more glares of halogen lights. The lights at the fence were blazing at full power, so there was something going on at the borders tonight.

He gave up on speculation and headed for the shop. Whatever had happened, he'd find it out a lot quicker by just going in.

The shop was quiet, with no one working on prototypes. No elvensteeds waited in car-form for someone to suggest modifications to their lines to add to verisimilitude. There was a huddle of bodies, standing and sitting, at the far corner, beside the prototype Victor he and Donal had been working on, and Tannim headed that way at a limping trot.

Sam looked up first, and his wide grin of relief was a welcome sight. Keighvin finished whatever he was saying to Sarge Austin, then turned his own emerald eyes up to greet the young mage.

"We had a visitor last night," the Sidhe said without preamble.

"And a fair horde of his friends," Conal said with a grimace of suppressed pain. "He'd sent a challenge with yon mortal, but we hadn't reckoned on his bringing as many as he did."

Tannim glanced around the circle, and came up quite a few names short. And there was a gloom about the Sidhe, combined with the reddened eyes of the humans, that spoke volumes.

We lost somebody. Shit.

"Casualties?" he asked carefully.

"Donal," his twin replied, and the lack of expression

in his voice told Tannim just how deep and raw the wound of loss was. Tannim closed his eyes briefly, and extended a tentative mental "hand" to his elven friend. It was clasped, and Conal accepted the comfort that flowed across the link.

"And one of the fosterlings," added Kieru. "Rob van Alman. Dinna fret yersel' lad, 'twouldn't have changed matters if you'd been here. The black bastard sent a Bane-Sidhe, an old, powerful one, and he'd gi'en his lesser Sidhe compound crossbows loaded wi' elf-shot. 'Twas the shot that got yon Rob, and the Bane-Sidhe that did for puir Donal. Ye'd ha' been no use 'gainst either one."

Tannim kept his eyes closed for a moment more, as he mentally ran through every swear-word he knew twice over. None of them were enough. Rob had been the most cheerful guy he'd ever known, always ready with a joke at his own expense, keeping the place laughing at the worst of times and under the most stressful conditions. And Donal — the Sidhe driver was Tannim's own replacement as mechanic on the SERRA team. He'd taught Donal everything he knew, and he could always count on Donal being there at the track whenever he ran — ready with a cold towel and a squeeze-bottle of Gatorade —

His throat tightened. He opened his eyes, and asked, hoarsely, "And wounded?"

"About a score," Keighvin replied with the carefully impassive expression of a war-leader. "We know that they're learning from us now; we won't underestimate them again."

Tannim took a deep breath to force his throat open, then another. He'd have his own private mourning session later. Maybe, once it was safe, he'd try to visit them on the other side. . . .

"What do you want me to do?" he asked.

"Mine-sweeping," Phil Austin said.

He blinked, puzzled. "But we don't — "

"What Sarge there means is that there's bits of steel

all over the grounds," Sam stuck in. "Bullets that missed, that kind of thing."

And none of the Folk would be able to do any precision magic except in the protected rooms until the stray metal was gotten rid of. He nodded. "And when I'm done?"

"Reinforcement on the perimeter," Keighvin replied decisively. "I want a shield ye couldna bring tank nor mouse through."

He nodded, and turned to go.

"Take Sam with you," Keighvin added. "There was enough ordnance flyin' about last night ye'll need four hands, an' he can tell ye the full of the story."

And that was definitely toned as a dismissal. Tannim's liege he was not, but the young man knew that the Sidhe's terseness was caused by pain, and not the arrogance of a nobleman. They walked out to the lighted perimeter, with Tannim stopping long enough to pick up a couple of chisels to dig bullets out of trees with, from the silk-lined tool locker where steel implements were kept. A half-dozen other humans prowled the grounds already, most of them sporting stained bandages, but none of them were mages. They were looking for bullet holes by eye alone; digging the steel-jacketed rounds out, and marking the hole with a splash of paint. Others were wrapping the Pinball bars in their special silk sheathes and shoving them down into the fence-posts. Someone with her face obscured by a bandage — Dottie, he recognized after a confused moment — came up and handed him a can of paint and a brush.

"Glad you're here now and not earlier," she said. "I just sent Fred home and you're the best mage we've got. Fred found all the easy ones; we know there's more out here, but they're probably buried in the dirt or twenty feet up in a tree."

Tannim nodded, a little relieved. He wouldn't have been any use, earlier. The presence of the other rounds would have obscured the ones that were harder to find.

"If you find something in a tree, dig it out, and slap

this stuff on it real good," Dottie continued tiredly.
"There's fungicide, wood-sealer, and growth-hormone
in it. The least we can do is make sure the poor trees
have a fighting chance after the way we damaged them."

"Are you all right?" Tannim felt impelled to ask.

"What, this?" she replied, touching the bandage.
"Just a graze. Bled like hell and hurts worse, but I'm
good for duty."

Unspoken — that there were plenty who weren't.
Tannim nodded again, and as she turned back to her
own task of putting the Pinball bars to bed, unfocused his
eyes and reached into himself for the spell that would let
him detect any amount of iron and steel, however small.

Sam asked quietly, "Uhm, lad, can you call up any of
your friends to help?"

Tannim absent-mindedly sniffed the paste, and
closed his eyes. "No . . . no, Sam. I'm not going to call in
any favors for something we can do ourselves."

We may need them later.

While Sam waited in silence, he gathered power from
inside himself, chanted in a mechanical drone to set the
spell in place, then triggered it with a hissed syllable only
Chinthliss would have recognized.

There was a bullet not ten feet from him — straight
up. It didn't take a prophet to predict a lot of climbing
tonight.

"So," he said, waving to Sam to follow him and handing the older man the paint and brush to hold as he
climbed the tree, "tell me what went down."

Sam took a visible breath, and began.

The tiny office was too small to contain Aurilia's rage.
"You *fool*," Aurilia stormed at Vidal. "You empty-
headed *witling*. I told you that I had a plan, that it
involved the child-whores, especially Tannim's chosen
slut; why couldn't you wait until I got the girl here?"

Vidal Dhu glowered and sulked, but Niall stood behind Aurilia, radiating cold anger, and finally Vidal

deflated, slumping down into his seat. "I thought it would be better to act directly," he muttered. "I thought that if we left the girl out on the street, anything could happen. She might decide to return home, she might decide to go into one of the shelters, she could even get herself killed being stupid."

"And *you* nearly got her killed!" Aurilia snapped. "Now you've frightened her; she'll be twice as wary as before! You've undone everything I built, in a single moment of genuine idiocy!"

"Maybe not," Niall rumbled thoughtfully. She turned to stare at him.

"How on earth can you say that?" she asked. "This — man — sent out a stupid human to kidnap the girl. He died trying to coerce her, and she was so frightened she ran, the gods only know where! You say he hasn't undone everything I worked towards?"

"Think a moment, child," Niall replied, as she chafed at being called a "child." "The girl has been affrighted, it is true. She may keep herself from the street for some time, it is also true. But you know who one of her friends is. And it seems to me that if she were offered a chance of employment that appears to be safer — at least, safer in the light of the attempted kidnapping — than whoring on the street, she may well take it."

Aurilia licked her lips thoughtfully. It was true, she did know the boy called "Jamie." It would be easy enough to find him in the course of a night. And if she offered him another "movie job," not only for himself, but for a female friend, he might bring in the girl. The ploy might not work the first time, but if Aurilia made it tempting enough, and added offers for other friends, sooner or later, she'd get Tannim's protégé, especially when the "movie work" was mild bondage, some sado-eroticism with only the trappings, not the actuality, or perhaps a staged "satanic ritual" before the cameras; nothing that would frighten them. It would mean a delay in her plans — for she had expected to go directly to where the girl was, and make the "movie offer" in person, but it wouldn't be too great a delay. Right now if anyone or anything approached the girl directly except her trusted friends, she'd bolt — and Aurilia wasn't certain she had the resources to try and catch a fleeing child without complications.

"I'm going to explain what I have in mind clearly this time," she said waspishly to Vidal Dhu, "so that there will be no mistakes, and no ill-advised attempts to anticipate the capture. I will find the boy I used in the party-film. He knows the girl. I will offer him more work, work for himself and a female friend. If he brings the girl in the first time, well and good — if *not*, we will be patient. We will offer him another night of work, this time with two females, and ask him if he has any more friends. Eventually, especially after we gain their trust, the girl will come of her own accord."

"Then we send Keighvin Silverhair a special little tape, or perhaps some pictures," Niall rumbled in satisfaction. "But — do we bring him here? That could be dangerous — this place is full of the kind of machinery and creations of Cold Iron his humans use so well. Even if it is on our own ground — "

Aurilia shook her head. "No, we will let him think that we have the children on our ground, Underhill. He will bring humans and Cold Iron weapons there trying to thwart us. We will ambush him, but more than that, we will portray him and his dogs to the Seleighe Court as a danger to us all. His position is tenuous enough; this violation of custom will have even his supporters against him. If he survives our ambush, he will never be allowed to set foot in the human world again."

"Leaving this place open to our hunting — " Vidal breathed in surprise. She nodded.

"And leaving us the children to dispose of in front of the cameras, accomplishing two tasks in one."

She smiled at Vidal's stunned expression. *You never gave me the credit for that much intelligence, did you?* she thought with viperish satisfaction. *When Keighvin is a memory, and I no longer need you, I think I shall challenge you, Vidal Dhu. With Niall's backing, I will not only humiliate you, I may even be able to destroy you.*

But she allowed no hint of her thoughts to appear in her speech or her body-language. Vidal studied her for a moment, but evidently read nothing, and shrugged.

"Very well then," he said. "I will go and prepare the ambush site. I can still conjure or cajole more than enough underlings to take on Keighvin and all of his allies—"

"Just be certain you do not underestimate him," Niall said coldly. His eyes glittered red within his pitted face. "As you did the last time."

Aurilia watched Vidal seethe with anger, but he held his tongue. "This time the confrontation will be on prepared territory of *our* choosing," he replied, just as coldly. "There will be no mistakes this time."

"I will find the children," Aurilia said quickly, sick to death of their posturing. "After all, I know what they look like."

Niall sighed gustily, breathing a wash of air straight from the grave over her. "And I shall ready the studio," he said. "I am weary, very weary. That is ample employment for me at the moment." Then he added as Vidal Dhu turned to go, as if in afterthought, "And Vidal, if we are able, I would like very much to have the destruction of Silverhair on videotape."

Vidal reddened again, but said nothing. Aurilia smiled.

George Beecher stared at the report on his desk and ground his teeth in anger and frustration. Bad enough that everything he'd collected on this "Tannim" character showed him to be the kind of guy George could easily have been friends with. But when he'd mentioned his client to an old buddy in Vice, hoping to find something that would make him dislike the guy, if not something he could take to the bitch, Terry had given him a strange look.

"You know I don't mix into your business, bud," he'd said, "but I think maybe you took the wrong client this time."

George had wondered about that remark — and now, today, *this* had arrived in the mail. A copy of a police file, with a note, "Burn this when you get done, okay? T."

Slim, as police files went, it nevertheless held more than enough to make George seethe with rage. His client, that charming, lovely young woman with the face of an old-world madonna, was up to her pretty little ear-lobes in a porn ring. And not just plain old garden-variety smut, either; George wouldn't have cared about that. She was definitely linked to S and M, B and D — and tentatively to kiddie-porn and snuff-films.

Whatever hold she wanted over Tannim, George wasn't about to give it to her. If he hadn't been dead sure that not even Terry could cover for him, he might have been tempted to go put some large-caliber holes in her wide, smooth forehead.

Now he was in an ethical quandary. He'd just gotten paid for his last invoice; he had a couple of days' worth of hours on the new one, but nothing he couldn't live without. If he hadn't already deposited the cashier's check, he'd have been in an even more serious quandary; as it was, the bills had all been paid and there was no way he was going to get the money back to throw in her face.

And I wondered why you always paid with a cashier's check. I thought it was so ex-hubby wouldn't know you'd hired me.

Bitch.

He chewed on his lip and stared at the police file lying in the pool of light cast by his desk lamp, and made some hard decisions.

He couldn't do what he *wanted* to do; go to her office, throw the file down on her desk, and tell her she could keep her damned filthy blood-money. For one thing, that would throw Terry's investigation. For another, these people never operated in a vacuum; she could have mob contacts and bosses, and certainly could hire muscle herself. If she knew *he* knew, it wouldn't take more than five hundred bucks to erase George Beecher, P.I., from the face of the earth.

So, no dramatic gestures.

No gestures at all, in fact.

With his jaw clenched, he swiveled his chair to face the old Smith-Corona on the typing stand beside his desk and laboriously typed out a letter on the agency stationery.

Ms. Morrigan: In light of the fact that I have uncovered nothing substantial in my investigations, I voluntarily dissolve our contract with no further payment expected. G. Beecher.

He dated it, folded it carefully, slipped it into an envelope, and left it for the secretary to mail in the morning.

And there was another thing he could do; he knew Tannim's address. Not that the kid hadn't lost him a million times when he'd tried to follow, but there were other ways of finding someone than tailing them. When the City Directory had come up dry, and the phone company proved uncooperative, he'd turned into a prospective creditor and called American Express. The kid had a Gold Card, after all. And he'd been oh, so puzzled, because Mr. Tannim didn't seem to have a first name . . . this amused the person on the other end of the line, who'd confided that Mr. Tannim was very eccentric in that regard.

Bingo; name, address, phone, current employer, and the fact that the kid paid all bills in full on time.

So he had Tannim's address. Now for a little anonymous letter to ease his conscience.

Sir: I wish to advise you that you are being investigated by a Ms. Aurilia Morrigan, of no known address, who operates a business from Hangar 2A at the Savannah Regional Airport. I do not know why Ms. Morrigan has chosen to have you investigated, but her motives are suspect, since confidential information given me reports she herself is under investigation for possible involvement in illegal activities, including child pornography. Please be advised that she may be dangerous, and take what seem to you to be sensible precautions.

There. That was all he could say without blowing his cover. This letter would not be entrusted to the secretary; it would be hand-delivered.

He folded it and inserted it into a plain, white envelope, turned off his desk lamp, and took his coat off the back of the chair. He knew where Tannim would be tonight: Kevin Barry's pub. He was probably looking for that poor little teenage hooker again. So, while Tannim was at the pub, George Beecher would be slipping this warning under his door.

It wasn't much, but it was something. And a damn sight better than doing nothing.

He flipped off the office lights and picked up the police file, leaving it and the copy of his letter to Aurilia Morrigan on the boss's desk. In the morning when he came in, there'd be a new case on his blotter, the files would have quietly disappeared, and no mention of the case would ever be made again. There was a little calligraphed piece in the boss's office, where he could see it when he sat at his desk.

Responsibility. Accountability. Integrity.

It wasn't the agency motto, but it might as well have been. Nice to work for someone with a bottom-line like that one. Yeah, the boss was a good man to work for. Even if sometimes it meant that you sweated a little at the end of the month. Better sweating a little money than not being able to sleep at night. Being a hardworking, average joe with a relatively clean conscience wasn't a bad way to live.

George flipped the latch and closed the door of the office quietly, patting his coat pocket to be certain that the letter was still there, and looking forward to a good night's sleep.

• CHAPTER THIRTEEN

Tannim drummed his fingers idly on the phone-tap detector, and waited for his police contact to pick up. There had been a few too many coincidences lately for comfort — and his nerves told him that anything could be a setup. This anonymous tip in his mailbox reeked of an inept trap.

On the other hand, why would any of his enemies be that inept? Unless it was to throw him off, and make him think it was too inept to be a trap —

Circular reasoning like that is gonna make me too dizzy to see in a minute.

At last a voice answered. The detector showed nil.

"Yeah?"

"Hiya, Terry? This is Greeneyes. Hey, look, you need a good bottle of scotch? I need a fingerprint check." He crossed his fingers and hoped Terry wasn't busy . . . or rather, *too* busy. Vice was always busy with something. Terry sounded annoyed, but not angry. "Aww, jeez man, you *know* I hate to do those! They take freakin' *forever*."

Tannim sighed. The balance sheet was a little too tilted in Terry's direction lately. He'd have to do something about that, later. Maybe when he got Tania safe he could talk her into fingering some pimps or pushers. "I know, I know, it's just that there's something weird going down, and there are a couple real young civilians in the middle of it. Dig?"

The growl Terry produced sounded only half-hearted. "Damn Boy Scout. All right, three bottles of Amaretto and a Bob Uecher card."

Well, that was an easy bribe, and just a little too quick

for something off the cuff. Tannim had always suspected Terry of keeping a list of items he wanted for doing favors. "Done. Thanks. Here's the story: got an anonymous letter in my mailbox, no address or postage, tipping me off to the whereabouts of Bad Guys. Letter says these Bad Guys are into everything that pushes my piss-off buttons. All I've got to go on is this letter, and I don't know if it's genuine. If it is, well . . . "

Terry snorted. "If it is, we'll find out about it after you've played vigilante, same as usual. Dammit, Greeneyes, this covert hero-crap of yours is going to sink us all. You and your friends're gonna get shot by a cop one of these days while you're out being white hats. You dig that?"

Tannim bit his lip. It was *not* the most encouraging thing he could have heard at the moment, but Terry had a good point. The police were damned good at their job in Savannah, and a lot of Tannim's activities could look mighty suspicious if someone that wasn't a friend happened upon them. He could picture it, too. His armor could stop a bullet, but he'd still lose a couple ribs from the impact, and then there were the explanations. . . .

And there was nothing armoring him from a head-shot.

"Greeneyes? You there?"

"Yeah . . . yeah, I'm here. I'll be careful, Terry. And look, you're right. If things get too rough, I'll call you for help."

Terry produced something that was closer to a bark than a laugh. "If it's that bad, I'll bring an ambulance."

Tania rubbed sleep from her eyes, her mouth tasting like her sweat-soaked, musty blankets. She'd tossed all night in half-sleep, haunted by images of gun-toting maniacs forcing her against grimy walls, and awakening was at best a hollow improvement. The creaking from the apartment's warped steps had snapped her into attentiveness — but she'd calmed as she heard a familiar voice. It was Jamie, high as a kite, staggering up the stairwell.

Oh, God. Not again. This is too much. . . .

Tania pulled the strands of hair from her mouth — that always seemed to happen when she slept, no matter how short her hair was. Jamie giggled uncontrollably, amused beyond belief by how difficult it was to get his key into the lock. Tania heard the unmistakable sound of his forehead thumping against the door, but the giggling didn't stop even then. He was wasted but good this time.

Laura was not waking as readily as Tania had; the two spent the wee hours hugging and comforting each other before finally crashing. Laura had seemed unusually tense over the threat to Tania, and it had amazed her no small amount that the normally suspicious, cynical girl could be so open about her fears when Tania'd confided in her. Both of them had talked about suicide as some solution to put the street out of their minds forever, but neither could do it. There was something, somewhere, to live for, and they could cry in hope over it — and if nothing else, they had each other.

And they both agreed that Jamie was in trouble. The drugs, the recklessness, his frailty . . .

By the time Jamie had gotten the door open, Tania had pulled her sweat suit top on, and was pulling the bottoms on over her still-stinging, scab-caked knees. Laura had roused, too, and had pulled on a tattered black shift. She'd obviously had better nights herself, and gave Tania a significant look as the door came open.

Jamie stumbled in, a red scarf around his neck despite the sultry night, tight jeans torn at the knees and a wad of something in his pocket. Dozens of rubber junk-jewelry bracelets covered his wrists, falling down his forearm as he hung his keys on an exposed nail. He turned heavily dilated eyes to his roommates.

"Heya! Miss me?" Another fit of giggling overtook him, and he made a great show of trying to control it. "Okay. Okay. Before you ask — no, I did not mug Ed McMahon." He turned his pocket inside-out, and a shower of crumpled twenties fell to the rotting floor.

With them fell a pair of tiny plastic bags full of white powder. Laura's breath hissed when she saw them. Tania's heart froze.

Jamie fished a last bill out of his pocket, smoothed it carefully, and dropped it onto the floor with the rest. He then tottered off into the kitchen and turned on the tap, and splashed his face obsessively. By the time he returned, Laura had picked up the money and counted. She'd avoided touching the bags as if they were pit vipers.

Three hundred forty dollars.

"Jamie, how'd you get this money?"

"You oughta be in pictures . . . you oughta be a star. . . . " Jamie sang off key. "I'm in show business, baby. Big time mooo-vie star. Want my autograph?"

Laura's brow was knotted up in rage. "What ah wanta know is what's goin' on, Jamie. What d'you do for all this cash?"

. . . And how much was there before you got stoned . . . ?

He gestured wildly. "I have starred . . . in a major motion picture, clothing optional. I agented myself and found my contract agreeable."

Laura's fist clenched, white-knuckled, on the cash.

"I was so very surprised to find that acting was so easy. Heels in the air and speak into the camera — it was so much like my day job I may go full-time." He snickered again, and bowed.

Tania tucked her knees up into her chest and rocked slowly on the mattress. This was the worst Jamie had ever come home wasted. It was like seeing your little brother slice at himself with a dirty knife, and laugh at the spectacle.

"Did they give you the drugs, Jamie?" Tania asked softly.

"Oh no. No. They don't like drugs on the set, baby.

They say it affects the quality of the performance. I got my buzz later. I like to celebrate. Party, 'arty, 'arty . . . " His voice trailed off.

Laura stashed the bills in Jamie's pocket and took his face in her hands. "You are effed-up, boy."

"Yeah, but I'm rich. Money, money, money for hooking easy." Jamie smiled, the kind of look he'd give with a birthday present. It was like sunlight through thundercloud. "And they want girls, too. Money for you, and it's in cash. Straight sex, some kink, a little bondage, but not worse than street johns, and they even call you a cab when you're done. You wanna come?"

Laura was still far from happy, but Tania knew that chilling look in her eyes. It was the same look she used sizing up johns, or buying clothes at Goodwill.

Tannim leaned back in the vinyl chair in Terry's office, and gazed in wonder at the hundreds of baseball and football cards in frames covering every wall. This was the first time he'd been allowed inside the Sanctum Sanctorum, but Terry had insisted he show up in person. Behind a coffee-stained desk cluttered with file folders, Terry jawed on the phone with one of his team. After a few minutes of mind-numbing technical talk, he insulted the caller's sexual prowess, then hung up grinning.

Tannim looked around conspiratorially, winked, and withdrew three bottles of Amaretto, a small paper bag, and the plastic-wrapped letter from his backpack. With a flourish, he opened the bag to reveal a colorful card between two thick slabs of Lexan.

"But it's not a bribe, of course," he said, grinning.

Terry nodded. "Of course not."

"That would be illegal." Tannim held it out. "I'd never do anything illegal, and if even if I thought about doing anything illegal, I'd never, ever ask you to do anything illegal."

"Heaven forbid." Terry leaned over the desk, took the

card-holder, and held it up to the light. "Thirty-proof Uecher." He put it down on top of the file-folders. "A token of your undying esteem, I'm sure."

"Naturally." Tannim somberly handed over the letter. "Here it is, pretty much as I found it. My prints are on it, of course."

Terry took it out of the plastic and unfolded it with a pair of tweezers, and glanced at the contents. Then he snorted and passed the note back to him without taking the same elaborate precautions. "Greeneyes, I don't have to run prints to know who sent you that. It's legit, from one of the most principled P.I.'s I know. He's a buddy, and he managed to acquire a little confidential information from the usual impeccable sources. And he was really pissed off about working for this woman once he had the dope on her."

Tannim raised an eyebrow. "The impeccable source was someone for whom I have undying esteem? You're investigating her?"

Terry went stone-faced. "Can't answer that. You just watch yourself if you go anywhere near her. She's not only pretty poison, she's gonna find herself hip-deep in alligators real soon now. And I'd hate to see a friend caught in the alligator pit."

Tannim nodded. He knew Terry had grown up on cop shows where the good guys worked outside the letter of the law. That was the only thing that had kept the cop in him from pushing Tannim away for interfering in police business, any number of times. Terry knew there was something strange about his friend "Greeneyes," and that favors could one day be called in. After all, he'd tipped off Terry to some goings-on around town before, ones that by-the-book police work would never have revealed. The baseball card bribes were only part of the dance.

But that meant there was another debt that needed to be put to rest. "All right, credit where it's due. He take a personal check?"

Terry opened a worn Day-Timer, then scribbled on stationery marked "From The Desk Of Hank Aaron." "Here's his address. His rate is fifty-eight an hour plus expenses, and he has a car to pay off. You were never here, I never saw you, pay no attention to the cop behind the curtain. Later."

Tannim took the note. "Just let me know when you're in need of another token of my admiration."

"Out," Terry ordered. "Let an honest cop get some work done. Go."

Tannim went, whistling "Take Me Out To The Ball Game."

Tania tried, but couldn't erase the image of twenties falling to the floor. They fell in slow motion, or in sharp detail, and crept back into her thoughts no matter how hard she tried to forget them by reading.

Laura and Jamie were her family now, like it or not. All three of them knew they were too young to be trying to survive out here on their own, that the world was a cold, uncaring place that made no allowances for their weaknesses. It was never more plain than the past few days, and going through all of the old magazines she'd collected only reinforced how hopeless the future looked for her almost-family. Page after page showed perfect teeth, made-up faces, clothes that cost more than Tania had made in a year. Here on one page was a cigarette-smoking model, showing how glamorous a stick of burning weeds could be. On this page was a bare-chested Adonis in designer jeans. On this page . . . Tania closed the magazine on the camper ad. Was this the way the real world was, or was this what the advertisers expected people to be? The Suits at the ad agency hyped what their demographics told them to: that upper middle-class whites were their target audience, blue-eyed, clean-cut, blond. . . .

Like my family . . . was. . . .   And there they were, laughing and happy, in their pressed slacks and forty-dollar haircuts, mocking the decay around Tania from glossy pages.

Tania chewed on her lower lip. That, among other things, was something her mother had nagged her about constantly, calling it a "bad habit," or "unladylike."

I wonder if she chews on her lip now when she thinks of me. She probably told the social clubs that I was kidnapped, and milked her grief for the attention. The neighborhood probably used my disappearance as an excuse to double their security patrols, while setting up a politically-correct fund to find me. Papa probably bought that third BMW he wanted with it, and the money he's saved on my French tutor and racquetball coach....

It all would have been so much better with one less imported luxury car, and a camper instead, out in the woods once in a while, where there were no neighbors to impress.

It seemed like a ragged lifetime ago, those days when her posture and manners were always on her mind for fear of verbal punishment later. There could always be somebody watching, her parents had drilled her, and looking like you were everything they wanted to be would make them do exactly what you wanted. Now, Tania was in a world where invisibility was what one desired most; trying to be unnoticeable to the ravagers.

Money was one thing her parents had that she envied — but all that ready cash hadn't kept her from running. If money hadn't kept the all-American yuppie dream family together, how could it help a trio of tramp runaways?

It hadn't escaped Tania that their shared poverty was the glue that kept them together. If each of the three had enough money to live independently, wouldn't her new family dissolve?

God, I wish they were back.

The other three roommates hadn't returned yet, either. In fact, they hadn't been seen in a couple of days, not here, nor on the street. Tania's imagination painted grisly images of what had happened to them, none of which were likely, but still — they had probably only hopped a train, or stolen a car, and were in another state by now.

Or gotten shot by a —

Enough. Worry about how to pay the rent if they'd gone for good, not about what might have happened to them. You couldn't worry about everybody. *Save the worrying for the people you care about.*

Tania opened one of the books in her small stack of paperbacks. She was bright enough to know that escapism was a myth; she read now to find solutions. The science fiction and mystery writers she loved the most were the ones who taught as well as they entertained, and whose characters understood human nature. There were heroines and heroes, aliens with kind eyes, fire-breathing dragons and silver unicorns. . . .

Like the one on the sweat suit Tannim gave me. . . .

And there *he* was in her thoughts again. Maybe she had believed a few too many fantasy stories. Maybe she'd been tricked by her own wounded heart into believing there could be someone who did good things for no other reason than that they needed to be done. Why would anyone do that? It didn't make any sense at all. . . .

No more sense than treating a kid as property.

There was the burden of proof: if her world were cruel enough to make her an alien to her own blood, then it had to have another extreme to the good. One crusty, drunken old john had babbled about odds last week, saying that if something hadn't happened yet, it was statistically likely to happen soon. He called himself a gambler, but he'd never gambled with disease and death the way a streetwalker did. Maybe Tannim was the long-awaited proof that a human being could be kind for kindness' own sake in a risky world full of self-serving pricks.

If her world was one of insane gambles, then Tannim's brand of insanity was the better.

And, no matter how restricted she had been in Research Triangle Park, her life had never been in
danger. Her folks had always seen to it she'd had the
best health care their money could buy. She'd never
had to worry about guys with guns coming after her on
the street . . . or someone with a knife waiting for her on
the landing with the lights out.

Maybe they'd changed once they'd lost her. Maybe.
People changed — God, people changed. Maybe they'd
welcome her back and have things her way, now that
they knew what assholes they'd been. They'd forced her
to run by not giving her enough credit, but Tania was
damned if she'd be that insulting even to them. Anyone
could change if they were kicked hard enough.

And that, Tania knew, was the single good thing that
being on the street had done for her. She wasn't the
mewling brat she saw herself as a couple of months
ago, she was a hardened survivor. If they were going to
get her back, it would be on her terms. She'd have her
privacy, her room inviolate, her own choice of clothes,
her own choice of books. . . .

And their love. . . .

Tania sat a few minutes, and realized a smile had
come to her face. The dream the ads showed could be
real, if everyone loved everyone else, and gave them
the choice to be themselves.

Her brow furrowed as she realized that was why
Jamie had gotten the way he had, though — she and
Laura had wanted so much to stay out of his business
that they'd let him get progressively more out of control. He was just as much a kid as she was, and he
needed someone to say "no, stop that, you're screwing
up" once in a while. The three all loved each other,
even though they'd never said it. The way Laura and
Jamie had insisted she stay home until whoever was
looking for her got tired of looking was proof of that.
And, as his family, the two girls were obligated to help
him out of the drugs and danger, just as they were

obligated to help each other improve their lives. Maybe the money could keep them together after all.

A car engine outside roused her from her thoughts. She rose, knees protesting, and edged next to the window. She peeked around the frame, and saw a glossy yellow taxi at the broken curb. Jamie and Laura were getting out, wearing new outfits, and laughing. The taxi left as they climbed the stairs, and Tania met them at the door, an expectant look on her face.

Laura arrived, sailing through the door like Marilyn Monroe at the premiere of *The Seven Year Itch*, her face aglow. "Hey, sugah! We're baaack! Jamie here picked a good one, honey. Ah been keepin' his sweet tush outta trouble."

Jamie blushed, and giggled a little self-consciously. Laura got in his face and pinched his cheeks, saying, "Jamie-wamie, you'se the best lil' studmuffin ah ever been gigged by."

Tania stammered, taken aback by their happiness. And Laura being sexed by Jamie? That was a first — none of the three had ever had sex with each other. It must have been some gig indeed. "S-so, what was it like? You both okay?"

Laura twirled in place, making her bright red miniskirt flare. "Honey, we're better than okay. It's easy tricking, soft kink, and they'se payin' enough I ain't gonna rag on 'em about rubbers, 'specially since it's with mah Jamie, an' we know he's clean. Lookie lookie."

Laura opened her clutch purse and thumbed open a roll of twenties. "Three hundred *each*, sugah. And they need another girl." She licked her lips and winked. "Baby-doll, I think you're exactly who they're looking for."

"She turned about her milk-white steed, and took True Thomas up be'hind, and aye whene'er her bridle rang, the steed flew swifter than the wind. For forty days and forty nights he wade thro red blood to the knee, and he saw

neither sun nor moon, but heard the roaring of the sea."

Tannim lay back in the worn driver's seat of the Mustang, hands caked with dirt, clutching the three dozen or so slugs he and Sam had dug out of the trees and grounds. "The Ballad of True Thomas" came unbidden to him, one of many songs and fables he'd learned to fascinate and entertain the Folk Underhill. He closed his eyes, seeing neither sun nor moon, and the breeze washing over the car sounded like the sea.

"For forty days and forty nights, he wade thro red blood to the knee. . . ."

It hadn't just been fatigue that had kept him down the night before, he'd surmised. Conal or Keighvin had no doubt influenced his sleep, playing on his own desires to deepen it. He remembered, now, the other elements of his dreams: the lover that had come with him into a room of green and gold, and laid him down . . . they had no doubt arranged that, too, to occupy him, keep him in the dream for as long as it took for his body to heal itself of the strain he'd been putting on it. And in the room with them had been a sleeping golden eagle, and a tapestry of a kind dragon holding a child, gently, as a parent would.

Oh, the dreams of mages. They were sharp and powerful, second only to the waking world, but just as real in their influence on the mage. The lover had been that *woman* that had plagued his dreams for so long; the one he'd seen while with Chinthliss, so far away. He had seen her a half-dozen times, but never spoken to her; black hair, green eyes, grace beyond words, cheekbones. . . .

Little wonder he had been enthralled by her, and by the dream. Even with all that had just happened, she still could dominate his thoughts.

The Queen of Air and Darkness. . . .

But she wasn't Sidhe, he was certain of that, not even Sidhe in disguise; there was too much of mortality

about her, a mortality that made her beauty all the
sweeter. . . .

More to be done.

With the slugs in the car's protective envelope, the
Sidhe could resume their great magics on the grounds,
and safely call up the Lesser Folk to assist. The grounds
would be changed, from above and below. Although it
might look the same to a casual observer, below the surface would be thousands of tricks and traps that not
even the souls at Fairgrove would know completely.
That was for the better, too — anyone could be broken,
and made to betray their friends, when magic and guile
were involved. Tannim didn't *want* to know the place's
secrets; he had too many weak spots that could be
manipulated. Chinthliss had laid him bare one time, to
show him how easily it could be done, then helped him
build up defenses against the most likely attacks. Tannim had countered by dissecting him with words. The
great creature had twitched uncomfortably as he
repaid the test, using no magic at all. It had been the
most trusting moment of Chinthliss' life, and his best
friend had never forgotten the lesson his human friend
had taught him.

There were many ways to destroy someone — with
magic, knives, or scalpels of language. Nothing could
save a victim from a determined and resourceful
enough foe. Nothing could save a human trapped by
the Unseleighe Court. Or one of the Seleighe Sidhe,
for that matter.

It couldn't save . . .

Enough.

There were two boxes still in the back seat, aside from
the tape case; both of them had been gifts from Donal.
One was a CD player that Tannim hadn't had time to install since it had been given to him eight months ago.

*"So that you may stop fearing for your precious songs, my
friend. These little disks cannot be harmed by the passing of
spirits."*

Oh, Donal.

The other was . . .

He reached back with one hand, cupping the spent slugs in his lap, and brought the small box up into the front with him. He thumbed it open, and pulled from it an emerald green silk scarf with edges of silver and gold. A birthday gift from one of the Fair Folk, one that showed great trust and friendship. Silk, spun and woven Underhill, with all of the magic of Underhill twined in its warp and weft. A single shred of this could open doors into Underhill for Tannim that few mortals had even guessed at.

God, Donal, this is never what you intended it for. Danaa watch over you, dear friend. Tannim solemnly placed the bullets on the scarf and tied it into a bundle, then nestled it on the dashboard.

A reminder to me of what you have to pay for, Vidal Dhu.

Tannim drew the crowbar from its resting place, and slipped it into its leather and silk sheath. The gooseneck crowbar was one of the most elegant designs ever, he'd always thought. A single piece of simple formed iron, direct and unadorned, flat blade at one end, strong hook at the other. No one he knew of besides himself had ever used that hook quite the way he did. He'd found that it would fit comfortably over a shoulder, and never be noticed under a loose jacket even when you were shaking someone's hand.

Chinthliss and his other friends had warned him about his temper. Told him how mages affected everything in the area when they became emotionally upset. How he had to be in control all the time. How he couldn't let revenge be a motivator.

Good thing they can't see how much I want to crease Vidal Dhu's skull with this crowbar right now.

But they were right, and he knew it. If he let the rage inside him take over, let the grief overwhelm him, he would be operating at less than peak performance. Vidal Dhu was a past master at seeing weaknesses that were waiting to be exploited, and his own anger was just such a weakness.

"When you're angry, you aren't thinking, you're feeling," Chinthliss had said. *"That's all well and good when you're putting power behind something, but it spells disaster in a fight."*

Yeah, well, the old lizard was right. He ran his hand through his sweaty hair. He had to calm down; he had to. He wasn't ready for any kind of a fight in this state.

Drive. He could just drive, and let the thrum of motor and highway be his absolution. Actually, that was not such a bad idea — there was tension by the bucket at Fairgrove right now, and some of it might be the result of ordinary hunger. A quick burger run might do everyone a lot of good.

Tannim started the car with the key and the foot-switch under the brake pedal, and pulled onto Thunder Road, not even thinking of making a speed run. His head was filled with replays of what had happened lately — the fights and intimidations, the pain of little Tania. Vidal Dhu's incessant vendettas. The dreams. Donal. There they were again — Donal and Rob. Damn. So much of this could be dealt with by calling Chinthliss and teaming up with him, but his friend and mentor had problems of his own, and was just as likely to call for Tannim's help. So, no dice there. That familiar feeling was back — of having all the pieces but not *quite* fitting them together yet.

Keighvin's building like a volcano. Conal's suppressing his grief for his brother, but it won't hold for long. Skippy-Rob's death is hurting us all, and Dottie's out of it along with a half-dozen more, easy. Sam's turned out to be stronger than we'd thought, but Vidal knows it too — plus, whatever's left of the Bane-Sidhe will want a piece of him. The production schedule's at a complete standstill. Janie's probably been on the phone all day letting the rest of SERRA know what's happened, so there'll be help soon, but if anything happens before then, we're sucking fumes.

The overcast skies didn't help his mood any, and the

drive-through burger order was in a monotone, not his usual cheerful banter. The girls at the window, who usually flirted with him, could tell there was something wrong, and mercifully said nothing while Tannim sat and stared through the Mustang's front glass, eyes unfocused, chewing on his knuckles in concentration.

That's not even considering what this is doing to me. My concentration is going straight to hell. Fighting Eagle could probably snap me back into shape with a sweatlodge, but that's a couple thousand miles away. I'll have to call in allies before this is done, and I'm running out of bribes for them. No Guardians around either. I'd call that P.I., but he's a civilian. First sign of magic and he'd freak. Can't call in cops, or Terry would catch it but good, plus they're civvies too, at least where magic is concerned. My power reserves are okay, plus what's in the car, but against pissed-off Sidhe? Hard to say.

A polite cough startled him out of his thoughts. The cheeseburgers and chicken were ready, and the drive-through girl waited patiently with all six bags. Tannim sheepishly took the bags, and used the old trick of seat-belting them in place before driving back towards Fairgrove.

Get a grip, man. You could be broadsided by a Peterbilt and never see it coming in this state. He shook his head and began paying more attention to the road, before he ran into someone. *Never drive angry or distracted. Rule one, boy. Innocent people out there . . .*

Innocent people. Damn, with all of this going on, he hadn't had time to get word to Kevin Barry's about Tania and her friends having a place at the shelter! Tannim again regretted not having installed a cellular phone — it would have made that a moment's work. Instead, he had to pull over to a pay phone and root through the phone book for the number.

Before his hand could touch the receiver, a psychic blow slammed against his shields. He whirled and flared out his shields into a barrier, scintillating and probing in the light ranges humans couldn't see.

Before him stood Ross Canfield, hands curled into fists, ready to strike at Tannim's shields again. Tannim leveled a blade of magical force at the ghost's throat, and held it there until Ross relaxed.

"Jeez, boy, come on! Just trying to get your attention. Ya couldn't seem t'hear anythin' else I tried!"

"You got it, Ross. Bigtime. What's the damned problem?"

Ross backed off — evidently, the young mage was projecting irritation like a bad country station. Tannim reduced his shields after checking Ross over, and nervously ran a hand through his hair for the umpteenth time that night.

"It's your little girl, Tannim. She's in bad trouble. She . . . "

Tannim looked around a moment, then gestured at the car with a thumb. "Get in."

The shields around the car turned transparent for a moment, and Ross slipped into the passenger's seat and waited, food-sacks visible through his body. Tannim sat down next to him and fastened his harness, then started the engine and pulled away from the pay-phone.

"Sorry, Ross. Lost a couple friends last night. Still on edge over it."

Ross nodded; could be the news of the fight had made it over to his side.

"Tania?"

"I've been following her. Last night, a real nasty fella tried to kidnap her. I stopped him. Today, she's gone off with her friends to be in a porn movie. A limo picked them up, and as soon as they stepped in, I couldn't see them anymore. There was just something about it that wasn't right — a wall, like you've got on this car."

"Oh, shit." Pieces were falling into place. The car accelerated.

"Fox is watching her now. Last time he talked, he was furious. I haven't heard from him in a couple'a minutes, though an' I'm startin' t' worry. She's— "

"Fox? Who's this Fox?"

"A friend of mine from the other side. Foxtrot Xray, he calls himself. Smartass shapechanger. Powerful. Anyway, the limo lost me, but Fox could follow it. I came to you, soon as I could."

The gates of Thunder Road were coming into view. As the Mustang rolled up, Tannim could see that there were three of the Fairgrove crew, including Conal, standing around a foot-wide smoking hole. They turned at the sound of Tannim's approach, and Conal walked a few steps to stand next to the open driver's window.

"What's the burn-spot?"

"A messenger," he spat. Conal peered into the Mustang, noting the burgers and the ghost at once, and appeared unimpressed by either.

"The ghost is with me. That" — nodding at the hand — "must be bad news."

"Aye, you can bet your last silver on that." He handed the envelope to Tannim. It bore the black seal of Vidal Dhu.

The main bay was eerily quiet. There were no screams of grinders, no buzz of technical talk or rapping of wrenches. There was no whine of test engines on dynos coming through the walls. Instead, there was a dull-bladed tension amid all the machinery, generated by the humans and the Sidhe gathered there.

Tannim laid the envelope on the rear deck of the only fully-operational GTP car that Fairgrove had built to date, the one that Donal had spent his waking hours building, and Conal had spent track-testing. He'd designed it for beauty and power in equal measure, and had given its key to Conal, its elected driver, in the same brother's-gift ceremony used to present an elvensteed. Conal now sat on its sculpted door, and absently traced a slender finger along an air intake, glowering at the envelope.

Tannim finished his magical tests, and asked for a knife. An even dozen were offered, but Dottie's Leatherman was accepted. Keighvin stood a little apart from the group, hand on his short knife. His eyes glittered with suppressed anger, and he appeared less human than usual, Tannim noticed. Something was bound to break soon.

Tannim folded out the knifeblade, slit the envelope open, and then unfolded the Leatherman's pliers. With them he withdrew six Polaroids of Tania and two others, unconscious, each bound at the wrists and neck. Their silver chains were held by some*things* from the Realm of the Unseleighe — inside a limo. And, out of focus through the limo's windows, was a stretch of flat tarmac, and large buildings—

Tannim dropped the Leatherman, his fingers gone numb. It clattered twice before wedging into the cockpit's fresh-air vent. Keighvin took one startled step forward, then halted as the magical alarms at Fairgrove's perimeter flared around them all. Tannim's hand went into a jacket pocket, and he threw down the letter from the P.I. He saw Conal pick up the photographs, blanch, then snatch the letter up.

Tannim had already turned by then, and was sprinting for the office door, and the parking lot beyond.

Behind him, he could hear startled questions directed at him, but all he could answer before disappearing into the offices was "Airport!" His bad leg was slowing him down, and screamed at him like a sharp rock grinding into his bones. There was some kind of attack beginning, but he had no time for that.

Have to get to the airport, have to save Tania from Vidal Dhu, the bastard, the son of a bitch, the —

Tannim rounded a corner and banged his left knee into a file cabinet. He went down hard, hands instinctively clutching at his over-damaged leg. His eyes swam with a private galaxy of red stars, and he struggled while his eyes refocused.

Son of a bitch son of a bitch son of a bitch. . . .

Behind him he heard the sounds of a war-party, and above it all, the banshee wail of a high-performance engine. He pulled himself up, holding the bleeding knee, and limp-ran towards the parking lot, to the Mustang, and Thunder Road.

Vidal Dhu stood in full armor before the gates of Fairgrove, laughing, lashing out with levin-bolts to set off its alarms. It was easy for Vidal to imagine what must be going on inside — easy to picture that smug, orphaned witling Keighvin Silverhair barking orders to weak mortals, marshaling them to fight. Let him rally them, Vidal thought — it will do him no good. None at all. He may have won before, but ultimately, the mortals will have damned him.

It has been so many centuries, Silverhair. I swore I'd kill your entire lineage, and I shall. I shall!

Vidal prepared to open the gate to Underhill. Through that gate all the Court would watch as Keighvin was destroyed — Aurilia's plan be hanged! Vidal's blood sang with triumph — he had driven Silverhair into a winless position at last! And when he accepted the Challenge, before the whole Court, none of his human-world tricks would benefit him — theirs would be a purely magical combat, one Sidhe to another.

To the death.

Keighvin Silverhair recognized the scent of the magic at Fairgrove's gates — he had smelled it for centuries. It reeked of obsession and fear, hatred and lust. It was born of pain inflicted without consideration of repercussions. It was the magic of one who had stalked innocents and stolen their last breaths.

He recognized, too, the rhythm that was being beaten against the walls of Fairgrove.

So be it, murderer. I will suffer your stench no more.

"They will expect us to dither and delay; the sooner we act, the more likely it is that we will catch them unprepared. They do not know how well we work together."

Around him, the humans and Sidhe of his home sprang into action, taking up arms with such speed he'd have thought them possessed. Conal had thrown down the letter after reading it, and barked, "Hangar 2A at Savannah Regional; they've got children as hostages!" The doors of the bay began rolling open, and outside, elvensteeds stamped and reared, eyes glowing, anxious for battle. Conal looked to him, then, for orders.

Keighvin met his eyes for one long moment, and said, "Go, Conal. I shall deal with our attacker for the last time. If naught else, the barrier at the gates can act as a trap to hold him until we can deal with him as he deserves." He did not add what he was thinking — that he only hoped it would hold Vidal. The Unseleighe was a strong mage; he might escape even a trap laid with death metal, if he were clever enough. Then, with the swiftness of a falcon, he was astride his elvensteed Rosaleen Dhu, headed for the perimeter of Fairgrove.

He was out there, all right, and had begun laying a spell outside the fences, like a snare. Perhaps in his sickening arrogance he'd forgotten that Keighvin could see such things. Perhaps in his insanity, he no longer cared.

Rosaleen tore across the grounds as fast as a stroke of lightning, and cleared the fence in a soaring leap. She landed a few yards from the laughing, mad Vidal Dhu, on the roadside, with him between Keighvin and the gates. He stopped lashing his mocking bolts at the gates of Fairgrove and turned to face Keighvin.

"So, you've come to face me alone, at last? No walls or mortals to hide behind, as usual, coward? So sad that you've chosen *now* to change, within minutes of your death, traitor."

"Vidal Dhu," Keighvin said, trying to sound unimpressed despite the heat of his blood, "if you wish to duel me, I shall accept. But before I accept, you must release the children you hold."

The Unseleighe laughed bitterly. "It's your concern for these mortals that raised you that have *made* you a traitor, boy. Those children do not matter." Vidal lifted his lip in a sneer as Keighvin struggled to maintain his composure. "Oh, I will do more than duel you, Silverhair. I wish to Challenge you before the Court, and kill you as they watch."

That was what Keighvin had noted — it was the initial layout of a Gate to the High Court Underhill. Vidal was serious about this Challenge — already the Court would be assembling to judge the battle. Keighvin sat atop Rosaleen, who snorted and stamped, enraged by the other's tauntings. Vidal's pitted face twisted in a maniacal smirk.

"How long must I wait for you to show courage, witling?"

Keighvin's mind swam for a moment, before he remembered the full protocols of a formal Challenge. It had been so long since he'd even seen one. . . .

Once accepted, the Gate activates, and all the Court watches as the two battle with blade and magic. Only one leaves the field; the Court is bound to slay anyone who runs. So it had always been. Vidal would not Challenge unless he were confident of winning, and Keighvin was still tired from the last battle — which Vidal had not even been at. . . .

But Vidal must die. That much Keighvin knew.

● CHAPTER FOURTEEN

There could be no mercy this time. Those mortal folk who had raised Keighvin in the tradition of the mortals' forgiving God had been wrong — there came a time when there could be no more forgiveness.

But neither could Keighvin afford to accept Vidal's Challenge. In a straight mage-duel right now, he was no match for Vidal; and in his current state of physical exhaustion he could not even best his enemy blade-to-blade.

That left only one thing he could do: stall for time, trigger the trap when Vidal was not looking, and hope that someone or something would intervene and tilt the balance back his way.

Pray for luck, in massive quantities — to Danaa and the humans' God, who also cherished children — that all the pieces could somehow come together at once and Keighvin could save himself, Fairgrove, and the hostage children.

"Why here, Vidal?" he asked, keeping face and voice impassive. "Why now?"

"To prove to Seleighe and Unseleighe Courts alike that you're a fool, a brain-sick, soft-headed fool, Keighvin Silverhair," Vidal snarled, scarlet traces of energy crackling down his hands as he clenched them, his pitted face twisted with sick rage. "You and your obsession with these mortals, with their works and their world, when you should be exploiting them!"

So far he hadn't noticed that Keighvin hadn't formally accepted the Challenge. Until the Challenge was accepted, with the proper words, any means of defeating

Vidal was legal. Until Vidal noticed, Keighvin intended to keep stalling, while he tried to think of some way of alerting his people back at the complex to his need.

From a half mile away, his sharp hearing picked up the burbling growl of a high-performance engine; a particularly odd growl, closer to the sound of a racing plane than a car. Long familiarity let him identify it instantly as Tannim's Mustang. And a plan occurred to him with a blinding flash of insight.

All he had to do was keep stalling, for a little longer. The trap would not be needed after all.

Blessed Danaa, thank you. Sacred Mother of Acceleration be with us. . . .

He swept his arms wide, flinging his cloak to either side as if he had unfurled wings; at the same time he magically keyed the gate-control behind Vidal, so that the twin panels receded and locked in the "open" position.

"Oh, impressive," Vidal mocked. He had not noticed that the physical gates behind him were open; all his attention had been centered on Keighvin's extravagant gesture — precisely as Keighvin had hoped.

Behind Vidal, the engine-sounds screamed and dopplered as Tannim gunned the Mustang and turned her. Vidal Dhu had not noticed the telltale noises at all; or if he had, had thought it was another car on the highway somewhere in the distance.

Or perhaps, in his arrogance, he accounted the things that mortals did of no importance.

He sneered, and the vermilion glow about him increased. "What is your next trick, Keighvin Witling? Do you make an egg appear from your mouth? Or a coin from your ear?"

The engine's growl pitched up; and behind Vidal's back, the speed-run lights flashed from green, to yellow, to red.

Pain from Tannim's abused knee sent streaks of red

lightning across his vision. It felt as if someone had driven a glass knife into his kneecap, and his leg got heavier with every step he took. Very much more, and his leg wasn't going to hold him.

Just a few more steps. . . .

Light. Light from the parking lot ahead of him, through the office windows. The Mustang was close enough to "hear" the remote now.

The keys were in his right hand, although he didn't remember groping for them. With his left hand clutching his thigh just above the knee, he thumbed the remote while staggering for the door, and was rewarded with the growl of the engine.

A few more steps. . . .

The door, the last barrier between himself and the Mach 1. He hit it, hoping it would open, hoping it hadn't quite caught the last time someone had come through. It flew wide, spilling him onto the concrete outside. He tried to roll, but didn't quite make it, and his left knee struck concrete, leaving a red splotch of blood where he'd hit.

JEEEEsus!

Gasping for air, he got to his feet again, and made the last few steps to the Mustang. He fell inside, sobbing, unashamed of the tears of pain.

He hauled himself into place with the steering wheel, and stole a precious few seconds to jerk the harness into place, yanking it tighter than he ever had before. As he reached over for the door-handle and slammed it closed, he averted his eyes from the hole in his jeans and the mess underneath. If he didn't look at it, it might not hurt so much.

Oh God, don't let me have taken my kneecap off, please. . . .

And he was profoundly grateful he'd followed an old cop friend's advice — that he "couldn't shoot and drive" without an automatic tranny. Right now, there wasn't enough left of his leg to manage a stick-shift.

He reached blindly for the T-shifter and threw it into

reverse, gunning the engine at the same time. The rear of the car slewed wildly, spinning in a cloud of exhaust and tire-smoke and a screech of rubber, until the nose of the Mustang faced the driveway.

He smoked the tires.

Gees threw him back into his seat, and his leg howled in protest; tears blurred his sight, but he knew Thunder Road like he knew the colors of his magic, and he kept it straight down the middle.

Fifty. Seventy. Ninety.

The Mustang thundered defiance, getting louder as it built up to speed, the war-cry of the engine thrumming through the roll-cage, vibrating in his chest, filling his ears to the exclusion of any other sound. The trees to either side were a blur, made so as much by acceleration as by his watering eyes.

Hundred ten.

The road narrowed, and he felt every tiny irregularity in the asphalt in his tailbone — and his knee. The passing-lines down the middle started to strobe — then seemed to stop — then appeared to pull away from him. It was one of the most unnerving optical illusions of high-speed driving, daring the driver to try and catch them. He clamped his hands on the steering wheel so hard they hurt, and still the tiny corrections he was making sent him all over the road like a drunk.

And the road got awfully narrow when you were going this fast. . . .

The Mach 1 shuddered and vibrated, as its spoiler and ground-effects fought against lift. Now would not be the time to research a Mustang's airspeed velocity.

One thirty.

The trees on either side seemed closer — much closer. The speed made them bend right over the road, cutting off the stars above the road. There was light from the streetlamps at the end of the tunnel of trees. The gates were open. He keyed in his mage-sight.

His mouth was dry. His knee still screamed pain at

him, but *he* was no longer capable of feeling it. Somewhere, deep inside, he knew he was going to pay for this later — but that was later and this was now, and he was in the grip of his own adrenalin.

The speedometer had already pegged, and he was going to run out of road in a few seconds.

Keighvin counted under his breath, keeping himself and Rosaleen squarely in front of the gates, occupying Vidal's complete attention. The Unseleighe Sidhe was still blissfully unaware of the engine-howl behind him, but Keighvin saw the tiny dot of Tannim's Mustang growing larger, and knew that his timing would have to be exquisite.

He's going to have to start braking soon . . .

One heartbeat too soon, and Vidal would escape the trap, for Keighvin's jump would warn *him*. One too late, and he and Rosaleen would go down with the enemy.

Better too late than too soon, he thought, and felt Rosaleen, the darling of his heart, agreeing silently with him.

:I could jump for *him,:* she added, mind to mind.

Blessed Danaa. . . . It was a brilliant notion. Vidal would probably not interpret *that* as either an attack or an attempt to escape something coming up behind him. It would certainly get his attention. And it might look as though Rosaleen had bolted out of nervousness or battle-anger her rider couldn't control.

But Rosaleen, as strong and clever as she was, would not be able to make the jump in one bound. She would have to take a second leap at the very last instant to clear the Mustang, and that would leave her wide open to an attack by Vidal.

:So be it,: she said, and then it was too late for second thoughts — the Mustang was braking, the engine-howl was near enough that even Vidal was likely to sense something wrong, and there were only seconds left —

Rosaleen leapt.

Vidal started; shouted in contempt. "Idiot! It'll take more than one horse to — "

Rosaleen gathered herself a second time, muscles bunching beneath Keighvin's legs, and Keighvin heard Tannim inexplicably hit the gas — again.

Rosaleen threw herself into the air, as high as she could, flinging herself *over* Vidal, and over the Mustang. But the Mach 1's sudden acceleration threw her timing off —

She strained — tucking her hooves as high as she could —

One trailing hoof caught on the Mustang's roof, sending a shower of sparks up, just as Vidal whirled, and saw a silver horse below two flaring nostrils — framed by a hood the deep red of heart's blood — and his mouth formed a scream he never had time to voice.

Tannim pumped the brakes furiously, pleading with all powers that they wouldn't lock up. He looked *past* the gates for the first time.

There was something blocking his way.

The glow of magic — flavored unmistakably with the screaming scarlet of Vidal Dhu.

Screw it.

The foot went down again — on the accelerator. Vidal turned, sensing something wrong — his eyes grew wide in horror —

And Tannim saw, over the tied bundle on his dashboard, the final moment of Vidal Dhu's life.

The Mach 1 impacted his body squarely, as Tannim used the hood's air-intakes to sight on his hips — and Vidal folded, his face mating with the Mach 1's hood in a soggy, splintering crash like a melon below a hurtling cinder-block.

Suck sheet metal!

Tannim threw a burst of reinforcing energy into the windscreen just as they hit, praying the glass wouldn't shatter. The pyrotechnic-glare blazed out from the car's every seam, as long-stored energy was tapped, obscuring Vidal's impact on the windshield. Then Vidal was flung up in the air like a rag doll. The glass held, then cleared enough to reveal the next problem.

Tannim had just run out of road.

Oh shit. . . .

Rosaleen stumbled, throwing Keighvin against the saddle-bow; recovered, stumbled again, and went to her knees. Keighvin thanked Danaa that Rosaleen was not a horse; the first stumble would have broken her legs off like twigs; the second would have broken her neck *and* his.

The elvensteed lurched to her feet and whirled. Keighvin heard the whine of another car approaching, registered it absently as Conal's Victor, and leapt from Rosaleen's back, his hands clenched into fists as he watched Tannim's Mustang slewing sideways.

Dear Danaa, let him pull this off —

Tannim didn't have the room to brake; instead, he slung the car around, gunning the throttle to break loose the drive-wheels, putting the tail squarely in the direction of momentum, with the still-spinning wheels now working to arrest the car's movement.

The tires smoked like an erupting volcano, with a scream like the death-wails of four Bane-Sidhe. The cloud of smoke and dust hid the Mach 1 from view, and Keighvin held his breath —

The screaming stopped; it did not end in a crash of sheetmetal and glass. The smoke and dust lifted, to reveal the Mustang sitting beneath the streetlight, with steam and smoke coming from the wheel wells, its tail tucked neatly into the embankment on the opposite side of the road.

Blessed Danaa — he did it. In all of his long lifetime, Keighvin had not seen a piece of driving to match it. He sucked in a deep breath, only now aware that he had forgotten to breathe entirely.

Before Keighvin could take a single step towards the Mustang, the engine coughed and roared, and with another screech of tires, Tannim pulled the Mach 1 back onto the road and screamed off towards the airport . . .

. . . Just as Conal braked the Victor beside Keighvin. Conal took in the entire scene in a single glance, swore a paint-blistering oath, and burned rubber in hot pursuit of the human mage.

Keighvin took another deep breath and walked, slowly, to what was left of Vidal Dhu.

The Unseleighe Sidhe was still alive. His body was a broken wreck, his face a shapeless ruin, but he still breathed, and Keighvin could Feel the hatred rising from him like the stench of decaying flesh.

He looked down at his lifelong enemy, and knew that Vidal was still conscious, could still hear every word he spoke.

He stared down at the body for a long time, then chose his words with precise care. "Once before I left you for dead, Vidal, and once before you returned to make war upon me. Once I gave you mercy and let you live — and you repaid my mercy with blood." He drew the tiny, hand-forged *skean dhu*, the little "black knife," from its silk and leather sheath at his belt. Fitting that it should be a gift from Tannim, who never believed the gift of a knife severed a friendship. This stroke would be from both of them. "No more mercy, Vidal Dhu."

With a curious lack of passion, he drove the knife of Death Metal home to the hilt and stood, leaving it buried in what was left of Vidal's twisted heart.

Tannim's leg felt as if he'd been soaking it in lava, but it was bearable. The hood of the Mach 1 bore a huge dent where Vidal Dhu's face had made its first impression. Tannim wanted to hammer the dent out with what was left of that face.

But that could wait until later. Right now, there were three kids in trouble, and personal vendettas could wait — assuming Keighvin left anything of the Un-seleighe Sidhe for anyone to play with. He didn't think Keighvin Silverhair had even an atom of mercy left for Vidal Dhu.

And, of course, before Tannim could get any more licks in, there were others with more right than he had to dance on Vidal's little corpse. Conal, most notably.

Tannim still wasn't certain how he'd pulled that slingshot maneuver off, and he wasn't sure he'd ever be able to duplicate it.

Then again, I devoutly hope I'll never have to....

He looked reflexively in the rear-view mirror, not ex-pecting to see anything, but as an automatic reaction — and saw the front end of the Victor filling the rear windscreen, with Conal, helmeted as if he was on the track, grimly clutching the wheel. For one startled moment, it felt as if his earlier thought had summoned the Sidhe.

Conal?

The Victor was so close he could hear the high-pitched whine of its engine over the brawling thunder of the Mach 1's.

Jeez — the radio!

If Conal had his helmet on, he *might* have plugged in his radio-mike. Tannim reached over and flipped on the FM scanner between two four-wheel drifts; it hit two broadcasts too faint to hold, then stuck on —

". . . . *Tannim will ye turn yer bloody damned receiver on, I've been...*"

". . . tryin' t' raise ye fer the past five friggin' minutes, ye demon-blasted muddle-headed excuse fer — " Conal broke off his tirade as Tannim waved frantically.

"It's about damned time!" the Sidhe exploded. "Keighvin's bringin' up th' rear-guard; the rest is most-ly behind me. I don't s'ppose ye've got a plan?"

While waiting for a reply, Conal cursed under his breath, as between the tight suspension and the low ground clearance, the Victor bottomed out for the thousandth time since this desperate run began. He was certain they were leaving a trail of sparks and grooved pavement. Not to mention what this run was doing to the undercarriage of Donal's precious car —

Donal. Sweet Danaa. . . .

Tannim stuck his hand out the window, miming shooting a gun. Repeatedly. "Ah, blessed Danaa, th' boy thinks he's Mel Gibson now," Conal muttered. " 'Tisn't a plan he's got, 'tis a deathwish." He raised his voice a little. "Yon Sam's wi' Dottie an' her 'steed. You an' I have th' only real metal beasties, an' we're leadin' the pack. They should be on my tail in a trice. An' *you're* leadin' *me* b'cause I don't have any bleedin' headlights!"

Plan, we need a plan . . . there's going t' be damn-all interference at the airport. Conal thought fast, speaking his thoughts aloud, and watching the mage-sight-enhanced silhouette of the young man ahead of him for any signs of agreement or disagreement.

Staying right on Tannim's tail was no easy feat — it was a good thing the Victor had better brakes than the Mustang. "We're goin' t' have t' breach th' mage-shields on their stronghold — an' we're goin' t' have t' break down a fence there too, if I recollect. Now, the shields, they're likely t' be just like any *reg'lar* Sidhe defenses — an' that's pure Sidhe magery, w'out any human backup. So if you an' me should happen t'hit it wi' all that sheet metal, seems t' me it should go down. . . ."

Tannim nodded vigorously, and raised a clenched fist in the air.

Conal continued to think aloud. "That still leaves th' fence. But if we put our magics t'gether, you an' meself, an' armored up th' point on yon Mustang — ye think it'll fly, lad?"

There was no doubt that Tannim thought it would fly. Conal grinned in savage satisfaction, even though it included a twinge of guilt.

The Mustang was Tannim's pride, joy, and precious baby. He was going to have to spend weeks on it as it was, repairing the damage that had already been done to it. Conal hated to ask him to put the Mach 1 on point — but there wasn't much choice. "I know how ye feel 'bout that car, old son. But ye've got 'bout twenty-five thousand worth there, an' *I'm* pilotin' near half a mil. I promise, ye'll have every tiny atom of magery I got on that nose. So — do we brace for rammin' speed?"

In answer, magic energy flared up all over the Mustang, a vivid coruscating aurora of every color Conal could name and some that had no names, as Tannim released more of the energies he had invested in the Mach 1's body, adding his own to them. After the initial flare, they settled into a thin skin of light, with a vivid blue-white glow somewhere near the front end. Conal unleashed his own powers, letting them meld with the human's work. He Felt Tannim direct the shape and force of it, as Donal and the young mage had so often when working on the Victor. . . .

He choked back a sob, and shook his head to free his eyes of of the stinging tears that threatened to obscure his sight.

This one's for you, Donal.

He let his grief and anger build, containing them within himself until they were too painful, too powerful to hold back any more. And *then* he added both to the mixture, strengthening it as only emotion could, giving it a wild power no dispassionate, cold, controlled magery could ever hope to rival. *Oh aye, my brother, my friend. This one is for you. . . .*

Tannim triggered the remainder of the Mach 1's defenses, letting the energy run wild for a moment before shaping it into a pointed ram over the Mustang's nose. To his mage-sight it outshone the headlights — and when he added in his own, personal power, it flared again with arc-light brilliance.

One eye on the tach to keep her from red-lining, one eye on the road — he needed a third eye for the magic —

Well, he could manage that by inner eye and feel; he

waited for Conal's input, and it came to him, smooth and controlled, from the hand of an expert. And so like Donal that his eyes stung with unexpected grief.

Christ.

He and Donal had worked so closely together on that vehicle behind him, working complex collaborative magics. The Victor wasn't pretty, not yet; the bodywork was immaculate, but the paint job was hardly more than a promise, and it still had tech-bugs to work out. No, it wasn't pretty. But it was beautiful, a work of pure art and genius, magic on four wheels.

A complete whole, in its own way. Even if it didn't have headlights yet.

A lump of sorrow threatened to choke him; just before he could swallow it down, he felt another surge of energy coming down the link. This one was pure emotion, and the feelings matched his own. Grief. Rage. A burning need for vengeance.

He gave in to his mourning, to his anger, and let his emotions join with Conal's to reinforce the magery they had just created. He rode it like a wave, then wrenched the wave into a coruscating barrier/weapon sheathing the front chrome.

Never fight when you're angry. Chinthliss had told him that, over and over. But there was a counter to that. Yes, anger destroyed control, disturbed the ability to think. But it *granted* a force that no controlled magic could match; and this, if ever, was a situation that called for that extra edge.

Deliberately Tannim forgot everything except the road ahead and his memories of Donal and Rob; and of little Tania, somewhere ahead, in mage-forged chains.

In the hands of people who tortured and killed children, and filmed it for profit.

He linked himself into the mage-ram, and filled it, laying its channels so the ram would dispel moments after impact with the fence, exposing the steel of the Mustang's nose.

Finally, when he had to dim his own mage-sight because the front of the Mach 1 had gotten too bright for *him* to bear, he became aware that Conal was trying to get his attention.

"Tannim! Wake up lad! Th' rest of th' cavalry's behind, an' Keighvin says ye're lightin' up th' sky like a bloody fireworks display!"

He shook himself loose, and took the eye he'd had on the tach and spared a glance for the rear-view mirror. Yeah, they were behind him, all right. All the elvensteeds were in car-shape, and they streamed behind him as if he were a demented pace-car driver, in a LeMans race to hell.

It wouldn't be long now; the beacon from the airport was on the horizon.

"Tannim! Sarge says Hangar 2A is second off the commercial access road!"

He hadn't noticed any civilians on the road — either they'd been lucky, or —

"By the way, ye've run a brace a' station wagons an' a Miata off onto th' shoulder. We better get there pretty quick-like, or th' next lad ye run off is likely t' be a black'n'white."

And he hadn't noticed. *Great. Just great.*

Then he knew where his other-worldly allies were — they were ahead of him, forcing people off the road so they wouldn't be hit. Bless them, bless them, and thank God for mage-sight — there was the sign for commercial air. It couldn't be far now. . . .

Hang on, Tania. Help's on the way —

The movie people sent a limo; that alone impressed Tania. She and Laura got in the forward-facing seat, while Jamie (wired and irritable, and in need of a fix) bounced into the rear-facing bench. The driver closed the doors, and Tania ran her hand over the armrest, only to discover that it was really a cellular phone. Intrigued, she and Laura began exploring all the amenities this rolling room offered.

The dark blue upholstery hid a myriad of surprises: a TV and radio, wet bar and a little refrigerator, and —

She looked up at Jamie's sudden exclamation of pleasure, and lurched across the intervening space between them. Too late; he'd not only gotten one of the little bags of white powder open, he'd stuck his nose inside it and snorted directly from the packet.

As she and Laura stared at him, appalled, he lay back in the embrace of the seat-cushions and grinned at them. "Oh, chill out," he said, mockingly. "It's no big deal. I just need it for the shoot — "

Then he stuck his nose in it and sniffed *again.*

Oh God — how much of that has he done —

That was when the driver turned to look at them, and something odd about his eyes made Tania glance at him.

She froze, as his glowing, red eyes glared at them through the glass of the screen and the growing darkness of the interior. Eyes like two little candle-flames in the middle of a completely featureless face.

Tania screamed; Laura jumped and gurgled — Jamie started to turn —

And then, with no warning, everything went black.

She woke to moaning, in the dark, with her hands cuffed behind her back. She held absolutely still for a moment, wondering if she was stuck in the trunk of a car, or in a completely darkened room.

Her left arm was numb where she was lying on it, her legs knotted with cramps, and she was horribly cold. She stretched out her legs, tentatively, and encountered no resistance, rolled, and learned she was on some kind of hard, cool, stone-like surface; probably a cement floor.

Somewhere off in the darkness, someone was cursing. Someone else was moaning, crying. After a moment, she recognized the voice. Laura.

Oh God —

At just that moment, lights came on again in the darkness off beyond her. The huge bulk of something was between her and the light, and it took her a moment to recognize it as an airplane.

The moment the lights came on, Laura stopped moaning and started to scream, cry, beg her unseen captors to leave her alone, to let her loose. The sharp *crack* of a hard slap echoed across the building, but Laura didn't stop.

"Get her inside and across the Gate," said another female voice. A cold hand of fear clutched Tania's throat; *these* must be the people who'd sent that thug out after her! Whatever they'd done to Laura so far, what they were about to do must be much, much worse for her to be shrieking like that. They must be monsters —

Then she remembered the faceless thing in the limo. Maybe they really were monsters, and Laura was screaming in mindless fear because the limo-thing — or something worse — was what had hold of her.

Oh, God — The ice of fear threatened to paralyze her, but right now nobody seemed to be watching her. She might have a chance to get away, get help. She rolled over, whimpering with the effort and pain it cost her, closing her eyes to concentrate on moving quietly —

And when she opened them, she was staring straight into Jamie's dried, wide-open eyes.

She couldn't help it; she screamed, and kicked away reflexively, pushing herself across the concrete away from the corpse, which gazed at her with a frozen expression of horrified pain. There was no doubt that Jamie was dead; he never blinked, never moved, never took a breath; his body was twisted up in a careless heap — a discarded puppet, with the ghastly evidence of violations no sane mind could inflict.

"What's that?" the female asked. Footsteps out of the dark heralded the arrival of someone. A moment later, a hand caught a fistful of Tania's hair and pulled her face up. She just caught a glimpse of a blond man, handsome in a movie-star way, before he slapped her hard enough to lose his own hold on her hair and she dropped back down to the concrete, too much in shock and pain even to cry out.

"Just the little bitch, my lady," the man called out, staring down at her and smiling. "She seems to have been startled by her bedmate. I think she'll be quiet now." He leaned down and crooned, softly, "Won't you?"

She nodded, tears cutting their way down her cheeks. *He has pointed ears. And green eyes —*

"Fine," the woman snapped. "Come give me a hand with this one."

The man smiled and locked eyes with her, and Tania shuddered at the promises in that smile. With a toss of his head, he flung his long mane of blond hair over his shoulder, and walked off again, turning only once to say, "He's sure to be hard for you now."

He had pointed ears. First the monster, then this — elf? He matched all the descriptions of elves — at least, the evil ones. . . .

They killed Jamie. The tears fell harder; she put her bruised cheek down on the concrete, and sobbed. *They killed Jamie, they're going to kill Laura, and then they're going to kill me —*

At that precise moment, the lights went out with an explosive flash; Laura screamed again, high and shrill, and the woman cursed.

"Hold still, little lady," came a harsh, Louisiana-accented whisper in her ear.

She jumped, and stifled a yelp.

"Come on, now, I cain't help ya if ya won't hold still," the voice scolded. *"It's hard 'nough doin' this shit without ya'll movin' around."*

"Who are you?" she whispered back, unable to hear or feel anything behind her, in spite of the fact that the whisperer must be on top of her. "What — "

"Ross Canfield, honey," he whispered back. *"I'm tryin' t' get these damn cuffs unlocked. I'm a friend'a Tannim."*

Her heart leapt and pounded, and she started to try to struggle, then remembered to hold still. "Tannim? Oh God, does he know what's happening? Mr. Ross, they killed Jamie, they've got Laura —"

"I know, honey," came the grim reply. *"Tannim's comin' as fast as he can, but there's a couple miles between him an' us, an' a lotta things c'n happen in a couple'a minutes. I keep puttin' out th' lights t' kinda delay 'em, an' now that you're awake, I'm gonna try and get you loose."*

"Don't bother about *me,* get to Laura before they do something horrible to her!" she said, hysterically.

"Honey, I cain't help Laura," Ross replied. *"There ain't a lot I can do, but I'm doin' all of it right now."*

"Why not?" she whispered through her tears, as Laura screamed again. "Who are you? Why won't you let me see you?"

There was a *click* behind her, a grunt of satisfaction, and the handcuffs suddenly loosened. She jerked her hands, freeing them, and pushed herself into a sitting position, feeling frantically for her rescuer.

"Ya cain't see me 'cause I couldn't get visible an' work on th' damn cuffs at th' same time," said Ross, from right in front of her, where her hands were groping. She blinked; a glowing shape was forming in front of her. *"I'm sorry, honey,"* he continued, apologetically. *"There's only so much a ghost c'n do."*

As he finished his sentence, the glow took shape and sharpened — and she sat there with her hands buried to the wrist in the chest of a transparent redneck.

She jerked her hands back, and stuffed them in her mouth, choking on another scream.

● CHAPTER FIFTEEN

Five thousand, six thousand, seven thousand, hold on, hold on ...

Tannim's eyes flicked from the road to the tach to his mirrors, each split-second's attention divided. The RPM needle swept up as the engine's exhaust note built to a lusty whine, but Tannim refused to lift. He wanted every ounce of power he could get from the 351, and he was timing its peak torque to coincide with the impact on the fence. There were only a few hundred feet for the Mustang and the Victor to build up speed once the last turn was made. Then, the fence faced them: chain link and pipe.

This isn't a movie; they don't just break away, Tannim thought grimly, at last slapping the T-bar up into drive and stroking the throttle. Four hundred horses' strength thrust the car forward and pressed Tannim back into the seat as the distance to the fence closed —

— and the chainlink disintegrated, shattering like crystal shards as the magical field disrupted it and cast flaming shrapnel high into the air. The Mustang exploded through it onto the tarmac, and barely a breath behind it came the Victor. Crackling sheets of flame swept over the Mustang and then curled off into nothingness, exposing unscorched paint and chrome and four headlights stabbing the darkness.

Mage-sight showed flickering patterns of energy all over the hangar door, and more beyond — there was no doubt this was the right place. Any hope of surprise would be lost, though, if the field could not be breached all at once — and doing that meant punching a hole.

I'm going to miss you, old car, really — it's been good. . . .

Tannim braced himself as the RPMs climbed again, and the hangar door swept inexorably closer.

Alarms and klaxons burst into life, while rotating scarlet lights sent flashing signals of danger.

Oh shit. The cops will be here any minute. We'd better get this over with fast.

The bulk of Hangar 2A loomed ahead, the alarmlights strobing against its flat metal sides. It looked locked up tight from where Tannim sat. He went through a very short list of bones he could afford to have broken, but still, there seemed to be no other way to sunder the magical defenses against elven magery. Lacking a helmet to protect his eyes, Tannim used the only defense he had against the inevitable flying, shattered glass from the windshield. He drew the Ray-Bans from his jacket and flipped them open, raised them to his eyes. . . .

A sliver of light grew from the ground as the main door of Hangar 2A rose, clanking and protesting.

What in —

"*Hurry up, hotshot,*" came a voice so close to his ear it might have been from the passenger's seat. "*I hit th' damn door button, but I ain't gonna promise it'll stay that way fer long!*"

"Ross!" Tannim could have kissed the ghost. "You ever-lovin' *genius!*"

"*Save it,*" Ross said shortly. "*You got a reception committee. An' I ain't up t' arrow-catchin'.*"

Tannim backed off the throttle. For once, he had all the concrete he needed, and guided the Mustang into a wide arc which would very soon place him at the tail of the aircraft he saw inside the hangar. The Victor didn't need to follow, not with its superior handling. Conal gunned the beast and pulled up alongside, then ahead of him, the elvensteeds overtaking both of them, having no need to conform to the apparent laws of physics. The steeds streamed into the open hangar, a fantasy of black, white, and screaming scarlet Ferrarris, Lotuses, Jags, show cars, all bearing inhuman warriors in enameled armor and humans with high-powered firearms.

Every light in the place came up full, much to the obvious surprise of those inside, giving the Fairgrove team a clear view of their enemies. The enemies ran for what little cover the hangar and the C-130 inside provided —

And one small peroxide-blonde in a torn taffeta minidress spotted the Mach 1, lurched to her feet, and stumbled to a run. And a silver-haired Sidhe darted out of cover, in hot pursuit of *her,* hands stretched to seize and hold her.

Aw shit — Tannim hit the door-release keypad on the console and yanked the wheel sideways, so that the momentum of his spin swung the passenger door wide open just as the Mustang came to rest a few feet from Tania. She flung herself in the general direction of the passenger's seat, crying hysterically, her face streaked with mascara and tears. Tannim leaned as far over as his race-harness would allow, offered his right hand, grabbed her outstretched hands and dragged her the rest of the way inside. Then he gunned the engine again, slewing the car to the right on the slick concrete, and as the pursuing Sidhe came charging, glittering blade drawn, Tannim opened the driver's door right in his path.

The side window shattered as the Unseleighe Sidhe went down and the rear tire rolled over him. Tannim jammed on the brakes and bailed out, forgetting his bad knee —

Which promptly collapsed under his weight, with a stab of agony that made all the previous pain seem like a day at the dentist's. He fell, mouth gaping; saved himself from complete collapse by grabbing the door, and hauled himself back up. Tania stared in shock, tears still pouring from her eyes.

"Shut the damn door!" he yelled. Galvanized by his angry command, she reached over and shut her side,

head snapping back to face him instantly. *"Lock* them," he continued. "Please! Stay down, and *don't move!"*

She stared at him dumbly, as if she had seen too much for her brain to take in. *Aw hell, she's probably seen Ross, boggles, trolls, God knows what —*

"Look," he said pleadingly, taking his crowbar out as the firefight erupted all around him. "When this is over, I promise I'll show you a unicorn. Just *lock* the doors, *stay* down, and *don't move."*

She nodded, and he slammed the door, waiting just long enough to see her push the lock down and duck under the safety of the dash next to the battered CD-player box before turning to stumble into the fray.

Dottie let the elvensteed do the driving; she simply checked over her ammo and the rest of her gear as best she could with only one unbandaged eye. The headset looked very odd, wired in place over the bandages. She had assured Sam that the damage was slight, just a cut eyelid rather than a gouged eye, but it meant she couldn't use that eye until the lid healed. Sam noticed, however, that she had *not* mentioned the rest of the cut, a slash that continued up over the top of her head and had taken forty-seven stitches to close.

She finally took her main weapon onto her lap, and patted it the way Sam patted Thoreau. He stared at it, and her, still fascinated and taken a bit aback by the mere existence of a shotgun with a bore the size of the Holland Tunnel, never mind that it was tiny Dottie who was toting the thing. And then there were the shells, in double bandoleers that made her look like a Mexican bandit. She smiled gleefully when she noticed the direction of his stare.

"Triple-aught steel shot and salt," she said fondly. "Packed 'em myself. Forget the Force. Trust in the spread of the gauge, Sam."

He took a mental inventory of his own weapons. He'd left the water-Uzi behind, figuring that the enemy already knew of that, and were expecting it. *Two-penny nails, Colt revolver and steel-jacketed bullets, six-inch circular saw blades . . . good thing Thoreau and I play frisbee a lot.*

He'd been saving the damn sawblades for months, collecting them from all his friends, since his neighbor Mary had started painting daft little landscapes on them and peddling them at craft fairs. He'd not trusted her around even a dulled edge, and he'd ground every bit of sharpness off, lest she slice open a finger while dabbing paint.

Still, dull or not, they'd play merry cob with an Unseleighe Sidhe's day when thrown hard enough.

I d'know about that baggy of iron filings, though, he worried. *Is the plastic likely to break on impact or not?* He wanted to have at least one weapon that couldn't possibly harm anyone but a Sidhe. There were three children in there, who might still be alive. If one of the nasties grabbed one to use as a shield . . .

Ahead of them, the Mustang impacted the gate with a fiery crash that sent sparks in a thousand directions, and lit up the place with every alarm known to the mind of man. Dottie only sighed. "So much for subtlety," she muttered, then frowned as she listened to something on her headset.

"Sam, Keighvin wants us to check the offices and make sure nobody gets out that way," she said absently, after a moment. Sam nodded, though Dottie looked a little disappointed as her elvensteed made an abrupt direction change, throwing him against the door, then screeched to a halt outside the darkened glass of the office entrance.

The doors dissolved and he and the mechanic bailed out like a pair of commandos. The elvensteed waited until it was obvious that they weren't going to need it in its current form — then it rippled, transforming into horse-shape, before rearing, pivoting on its hind hooves, and shooting off through the night towards the open hangar door.

Dottie moved in fast, blasting the thick glass door open with a single shell and darting through to throw herself against the wall. Sam followed, Colt in his hand and heart in his mouth, plastering himself to the wall on the side opposite her.

Nothing: desk, chairs, a painting on the wall behind the desk, now all full of holes. Typical receptionist area. But two hallways branched from it — one to the right, and one to the left. Glass crunched under their feet. Dottie jerked her head leftwards; Sam nodded, and eased into the hall to the right, ripsaw blade from the ammo-box at his side in his odd hand. Funny thing, that. Even though he was right-handed, he'd always been ambidextrous at frisbee. Thoreau had no idea at all what a good doggie he'd been.

He inched along the hallway with his back against the wall. When he reached a door, he opened it from the side; waited, then felt along the wall for the lightswitch and flicked it on before poking his nose and the barrel of the Colt inside. The first two doors he encountered led to storage rooms full of cardboard boxes. He checked one box that was open; it was full of videotapes in blank plastic holders. The third, however, was a little different.

He blinked in astonishment; this was a reception area that would have done justice to any of Gulfstream's high-powered execs. In one corner was a wide-screen TV with a discreet VCR on top; surrounding it were couches covered in what Sam was willing to bet was black leather. Matching black leather chairs were arranged in little conversation circles, each centered on a stylish walnut table. A wet bar took up one entire side of the room. Sam licked his lips, and tried not to think how much money was invested in the plush gray carpet, the black marble of the bar, the lush seating and furniture.

He eased along the wall to make sure no one was hiding behind the bar, sliding on the soft cushion of the bag of iron dust in his pocket. If only he'd had time to think of a better delivery system for it. . . .

The bar itself was magnificent: rare scotch and decanters of cut crystal, goblets, stem glasses, silver-chased antique seltzer bottles, shot glasses. . . .

Holy God, I could use a whiskey and soda right —

He froze. Soda. Seltzer bottles — the old fashioned, rechargeable kind — their nozzles were big enough that *nothing* would clog them — not even iron dust. At least not right away — and the seltzer would make a good vehicle for the dust.

Now if the bastards had just gone all the way with this yuppie image of theirs, and had really invested in expensive crystal seltzer siphons and not the fake kind, the kind that could be opened and recharged at the bar, instead of the sort that took refills of cheap canned soda-water. . . .

He stuffed his gun back in the holster and dropped the sawblade into the ammo box, and began rummaging through the stock under the bar itself.

Armed with overcharged seltzer bottle in one hand, sawblade tucked under that thumb, and Colt in the other hand, Sam resumed his explorations.

There wasn't much else to find. The rest of the suite was one enormous room, with tables piled high with videotapes, mailing boxes, and more supplies beneath the tables. Two postal machines graced the far end of the room.

He started to cross it — and Dottie's personal Howitzer thundered from across the hall.

He sprinted back the way he had come; it was longer, but this way he'd be coming up from behind her, not arriving in the line of fire.

This side of the office complex was a set of small, empty rooms, barren even of furniture. The shotgun spoke twice more as he passed them. He began to pant as he reached what would have been the executive lounge; he was an old man, and not used to running so much —

The shotgun roared again as he reached the door

and flattened himself to one side of it. It looked as if this place was set up as a kind of rudimentary video studio. He couldn't see Dottie at all —

But he *could* see the back and shoulders of a tall, slight young man hiding behind a screen with a crossbow in his hands: blond-haired —

— pointy-eared —

He didn't even think; he just acted. He dropped to the floor, putting the seltzer bottle aside, drew up the sawblade and pitched it — then dodged aside without waiting to see if it hit. The worst it would do would be to distract him.

The Sidhe must have seen the movement out of the corner of his eye, for he turned just as Sam dropped, reflexively firing the crossbow.

The bolt *thud*ded into the wall above his head — just as the sawblade hit the Sidhe in the neck.

He shrieked and gurgled, and fell back into the screen, knocking it over, and Dottie's shotgun thundered again.

There wasn't much left of either Sidhe or screen when Sam got to his feet again. With the screen gone, the rest of the room was in plain view, and it was pretty evident that Dottie didn't miss with that thing.

And the bodies of the Sidhe — were smoking and evaporating.

Sam stared at them, repulsed, but unable to look away. The bodies were literally dissolving, leaving only the sprinkles of iron buckshot behind. Dottie stood up from her hiding place behind an overturned sofa across the room, and made her way across the smashed lights and broken video equipment to his side, absently reloading from her bandoleer.

"Why are they *doing* that?" Sam asked, fighting down nausea. "Our people didn't — "

"Our people weren't killed by Cold Iron, holy herbs, and blessed rock-salt," Dottie said. "It's mostly the iron that does it — " She caught sight of what Sam had in his right arm and frowned. "Sam, this is a bad time for cocktails."

He took his eyes off the remains soaking into the industrial-brown carpet. "Here," he said, thrusting it at her. "Put that pagan blessing of yours on it, like you did with me watergun."

She raised an eyebrow, but freed her right hand to cup over the bottle. She whispered a few words, then sketched a sign in the air over it —

And this time Sam saw for certain what he hadn't quite caught the first time. A flash of light traveled from her hand to the bottle, and the water lit up for a moment. Her brows furrowed.

"There's Cold Iron in the water in that thing!" she exclaimed, half in accusation, half in admiration. "How in hell did you manage that?"

Sam just grinned. "Never piss off an engineer."

Ross was livid, and ready to murder — if he could. They'd already tortured and killed the boy. One of the bastards had taken the other girl, the dark one, across the Gate into Underhill before he could do anything about it. That was Foxtrot's territory; he'd have to handle it now. But Ross had managed to get the hangar door open, and to keep it open, long enough for everybody to get inside.

The little blonde was safe inside Tannim's car — or at least, as safe as any physical body was going to be with all that steel-jacketed lead and those magic lightning bolts in the air. The firefight was spectacular, and the Bad Guys were losing it. . . .

Ross decided he'd better go keep an eye on Miss Bad News, the one duded up like a fashion model who seemed to be in charge. If she had any rabbits to pull out of her pert little hat, now would be the time.

He scanned the area for her aura, a peculiar purple-black like a fresh bruise. It was easy enough to spot; she was heading straight for the C-130 — or whatever it was. It wasn't exactly a plane, although it used the electronics of one. The engines didn't run on any fuel *he* was familiar with. There weren't any fuel cells in the wings, just peculiar spongy things filled with sullenly glowing energy.

He blinked himself into the body of the plane, avoiding the dead-black area of the Gate in the tail. He didn't know where that led, and Foxtrot had whispered into his head that he didn't *want* to know where it went. For a moment he was afraid that Queen Bee there was going through —

But no; instead of turning towards the tail, as soon as she climbed the stairs to the side entrance, she turned towards the cockpit, taking strides as long as that tight executive skirt of hers would permit, her high-heels clicking determinedly on the flooring. He followed her, growing more and more alarmed.

Jeez. She got a gun up there or somethin'? She can't be plannin' t' take this thang off —

But that, it seemed, was precisely what she intended to do.

She dropped herself down into the pilot's chair, and reached for the controls. Ross looked around, frantically, for a way to stop her — he was just a plain old country boy — he didn't know anything about gear like this, not like Tannim did.

But that reminded him of what Tannim had told him about how he could glitch gear — and none of this stuff was armored against spirits. In their arrogance, the Bad Guys must never have counted on finding a ghost ranged up against them.

As the motors caught, and the rotors started to turn, Ross grinned savagely, and began taking a walk through the control panels.

Aurilia strapped herself into the pilot's seat and reached for the controls, glad she'd taken the time to rob that young pilot of his memories. It was time to cut her losses and run for it. Vidal was gone, and since the

Fairgrove hosts were *here* instead of at the ambush site, presumably they had either killed or captured him. She'd already lost personnel, including some lesser Sidhe. Since the hangar door had malfunctioned and let the enemy *in,* she might as well take advantage of the situation and fly the plane, Gate and all, *out.* There were other cities to exploit; Atlanta wasn't that far away. She could return one day in force, and take Keighvin at her leisure.

She heard the first engine catch; the second. All the instruments were green —

She'd take the aircraft out on the runway, and too bad for anything that happened to be in the way. Maybe she'd waggle the wings at the Fairgrove idiots shaking their fists down on the ground. Then head for new, fresher meat —

The engines coughed once, twice — the rotors slowed — and the engines died. Lights began flashing all over the cockpit, and warning buzzers whined like hornets in a blender.

She stared at the instrument panel, which now displayed readings that made no sense at all. The oil-pressure was off-scale; an engine was overheating. One had never started. Five airplanes were about to hit her according to radar. The airspeed read one hundred twenty knots. The altimeter showed her to be in a steep climb.

She pounded her fists on the panel, but succeeded only in hurting her hand. Somehow, *something* had glitched the electronics. And as she stared at the display panels, movement ahead of her caught her eye.

The hangar door was closing. Even if she could fix what had just been done, she'd never get the plane started and moving before the door was closed.

She snapped the belts off and flung herself out of the seat. *Niall,* she thought, a red rage beginning to take hold of her, making her shake. *Niall will have to go call in his debts, the stinking corpse. If Keighvin wants a war, a war he'll get!*

*   *   *

The girl lay where one of the Sidhe had flung her, on the couch in one of the movie-sets, too hysterical and fear-crazed to touch. Foxtrot left her alone. He couldn't do anything for her mental state, and at the moment she wasn't in any physical danger.

There wasn't a *lot* he could do in this Sidhe-built pocket of Underhill, anyway. His realm was a different sort of space. Right now he was little more than a glowing spark, hovering at about eye-level for a human, beside one of the video cameras. Still, whatever he could do to help the cause — though he couldn't do much here, at least he could do *something*. He couldn't even enter the human plane at all, not like Ross and the true ghosts could.

Changes in the energy level rippled across him, alerting him to the fact that something had just crossed the Gate. He bounced in place, torn between the urge to see what had crossed it, and the fear that if he left the girl alone, something would happen to her. Finally he gave in to the former, and raced across the studios to the staging area in front of the Gate. It didn't look like much; just an expanse of flat, brown stone, walled on one side by the studios, on two sides by the gray, swirling chaos of Unseleighe Underhill, and on the fourth side by the utterly featureless, black void of the Gate. The two pillars that held it in place on this side glowed an eye-jarring blackish-green. If Fox forced himself, he could see through to the other side, very dimly, as if he was peering through dark smoked glass.

The Bane-Sidhe paced impatiently on the other side, rags fluttering as he moved. *It* must have been what caused the disturbance in the Gate energies, Fox reasoned. But — why?

Movement in the gray chaos caught his attention. There was someone out there — coming in response to a call?

No —

There were *hundreds*. Lesser Sidhe atop Nightmares, trolls and goblins and boggles and redcaps and worse — every variety of Underhill nasty Fox had ever seen — headed this way —

Making for the Gate.

If they came through, Ross's friends would be outnumbered and outclassed. He had to stop them, somehow. All he had here in the way of special effects was the power of pure illusion. . . .

And there was only one entity powerful enough in and of himself to stop an army of the Unseleighe Court. It would be a gamble; they might not believe the illusion. They might decide to take him on anyway. By his reckoning, the trick had only a fifty percent chance of working.

Well, that was what being a shapechanger and a trickster was all about, and he'd played worse odds happily.

He took his most recent memory of the High King and held it up before his mind's eye. The memory was about five hundred years old, but it would do. That wasn't so long in the lives of the Sidhe.

He Manifested in a flash of light, calculated to blind and surprise them, and when they recovered from the blaze, they saw the majesty of King Oberon striding towards them.

As he raised his remembered image of Oberon's sword in a threatening sweep, the foremost riders pulled their beasts up on their haunches, pure fear on their faces. As he took one step forward, they turned tail and ran, panicking the ones behind them, until the entire army was in flight.

Fox howled with maniacal glee, conjured the illusion of an elvensteed below him, and gave chase.

Aurilia snarled with impatience, kicked off her high heels, and summoned her armor and arms. She ran down the stairs of the plane and headed aft, wondering what could be holding up Niall. Surely it didn't take *that*

long to summon his followers! And while the Bane-Sidhe
dawdled, the last of Vidal Dhu's flunkies were falling, and
her own troops were coming under fire. *Fatal* fire too;
most of Keighvin's people were armed with a variety of
Cold Iron weapons, and those that weren't were using
the presence of the two steel-bearing cars to bend the
trajectories of their magics in unexpected ways.

Damn them!

She could hardly see, she was so angry. The feel of
the hilt in her hand was not enough; she wanted to
slash something with it —

Just as she reached the tail of the plane and the ramp
down onto the concrete, the Bane-Sidhe let out a wail
of despair and stumbled down the ramp to cling to her
with both skeletal hands, babbling, desiccated eyes
wide in horror.

"What?" she shouted at him, daring to shake him,
hard. *"What?* What's the matter?"

"Oberon!" Niall wailed. "It's Oberon! He's here, he's
on Keighvin's side, he — chased off the army — he
might return —"

Oberon! For one moment, she panicked as
thoroughly as Niall. But then —

"It can't be Oberon, you fool!" she said fiercely. "He's
vowed to stay clear of things involving mortals!" Niall
continued to babble, and she pushed him away from
her in disgust. "Come on, you worm," she snapped,
turning, and hoping the insult would wake some sense
in the Bane-Sidhe's skull. "There's still time to —"

She froze. There was a mortal between her and the
battle; an old man brandishing a gun — and a seltzer
bottle.

While Dottie marched straight into the fray, pump-
ing her shotgun and picking off targets as calmly as if
she was shooting skeet, Sam worked his way around
the edge of the hangar towards the C-130. The
sawblade-frisbees proved lethal indeed; by the time he

was twenty feet from the tail-ramp, he'd used them all, and to good effect. Dull or not, they *acted* as if they were sharp when they hit any of the enemy — and even if all his hits did was to wound the creatures, that gave one of the other Fairgrove Folk a chance to get in a killing blow.

He made a dash from cover to the tail-ramp of the plane without getting worse than his hair scorched — and a steel-jacketed round into his attacker's face took care of hazard from that quarter. That was when he heard voices — and recognized one of them for the Bane-Sidhe by the evil whine under its words.

Blessed Mother Mary — if that thing starts to howling, in here, with all the echoes —

He froze with fear and indecision. He remembered all too well his last encounter with the thing. And that was with the protection of his ear-pieces. Here, at short range, the thing could fry his brain.

You're for it, lad. This is it. It's you between that thing and all your friends. He squared his shoulders. He was the only one within striking distance of it. And if it took him down — well — there were worse ways to go.

He stood up and walked calmly around the ramp; the Bane-Sidhe was there, all right — and curiously shrunken. It clung to the shoulders of a stunning woman in dark, shining armor, and babbled fearfully at her. She pushed it away, and turned. And froze as she saw him. He brought up both his weapons to bear.

The Bane-Sidhe took one look at the bottle in his hand, and stood paralyzed with fear, unable to speak, much less howl.

The woman stared at him — then began to laugh. "What *is* this?" she said scornfully. "Which are you, Moe, Larry, or Curly?"

The Bane-Sidhe pawed her shoulder and babbled something about "It's him, it's him, Holy Water." She shoved the thing rudely away and began walking toward Sam. "You're a fool, mortal," she said, her eyes narrowing as she slowly unsheathed her sword. "I know all about guns and gunpowder." Her free hand sketched a symbol in the air, where it glowed between them for a moment. "There," she continued, "your gun is useless. Go ahead, try it — "

He did, he couldn't help himself; he pulled the trigger convulsively, and the hammer simply *click*ed. She laughed.

"I don't necessarily have to play by elven rules any more than Keighvin does. What my magic can't touch, the magic of an elemental can. And as for that silly little water bottle you have, it might give Niall problems, but it won't hurt me. Holy Water is only good against the Bane-Sidhe, not a full-Sidhe. I might even find it — refreshing — "

He shook the bottle frantically to get the maximum amount of spray, as she neared him, forcing him to back up against the corrugated metal wall of the hangar. She raised her sword. "Good night, court jester," she said —

And he hit her full in the face with the metal-charged water.

She screamed; he raised the stream above her as she dropped to her knees, pawing at her face, and sprayed the Bane-Sidhe. It opened its mouth to shriek, and he directed the stream into its mouth — saw it splash out for a moment — and then come out the back of the Bane-Sidhe's head, boiling the decayed skin off of its bones.

The nozzle clogged, then, but it didn't matter. Both the woman and the Bane-Sidhe were out of the battle and no hazard to anyone. The woman knelt, keening in pain; the Bane-Sidhe writhed on the ground unable even to do that.

I did it. By God, I did it. . . .

He took one step to the woman, raised the seltzer bottle, and brought it crashing down onto her skull. His old legs gave out, then, and he sat down on the concrete, and waited for the rest to find him.

• CHAPTER SIXTEEN

Tannim limped away from Tania and the Mustang, crowbar unsheathed and at the ready. Three black elvensteeds thundered past him, ridden by spell-casting Sidhe in cobalt blue armor. They cut across his path, in pursuit of two red elvensteeds ridden by gray-clad Unseleighe, whose armor already showed burn marks and holes from bullets and elven arrows. As he watched, the three chasing split into an inverted vee, one to each side and one pulling back between them. Seeing they had been flanked, but not immediately noticing the third fighter, the Unseleighe slowed and whirled, to be caught in the throats by that third Fairgrove warrior sweeping a silver longsword in a massive arc. Both riders fell, and the Fairgrove fighters dispatched the red 'steeds with swordstrokes. Then the three turned as one, seeking new targets. *Padraig, Sean, and Siobhan,* Tannim noted absently. *I guess polo is good for something after all.*

And so the battle went; the Lesser Sidhe their Unseleighe opponents had rallied were being steadily routed by Keighvin's tactical skill — and the unpredictability of the magical and technological weapons brought to bear against them.

Tannim had not yet engaged any Unseleighe in hand-to-hand combat since leaving the car — but he held no illusions that his freedom would last. For now, he was taking the lay of the situation magically, while he had the time to do so. He Felt the hangar's defensive net being drained away around the battle; someone had given up on this place, and was going to use its energy elsewhere. The airplane's engines had started a moment earlier, but had then gone silent, propellers seizing. Maybe Ross had glitched the airplane, and now whoever had been trying to escape was gathering power for a last stand. Maybe it was one of the Fairgrove mages stealing the power away.

Maybe it was part of a trap.

In any case, the flow was heading in the general direction of the airplane; he narrowed his eyes to home in on the focal point—

And was struck sharply from behind, strongly enough to go to the concrete.

Dammit! I missed one . . . ?

A heavy arrow clattered to the ground beside him, from where it had struck him in the back. Its tip smoldered — elf-shot, made to kill humans instantly by disrupting their tissues and lifeforce at once. It had not penetrated, thanks to Chinthliss' armor, but left a ragged, seething hole in his beloved jacket. He whirled, hands blazing with energy, to face a seven-foot-tall Unseleighe who had fired point-blank at him from behind several huge wooden crates.

The bow was raised again, arrow leveling at Tannim's face this time — and Tannim took three stumbling steps towards him and lashed out with the crowbar's hook. He caught the bow, which splintered as if touched by an arc-welder.

Enchanted. Damn, I've got a good one here. . . .

The Sidhe's face contorted with a snarl; apparently he had felt about the bow much the way Tannim felt about his jacket. Tannim looped the crowbar's path up over his head and brought it down on the Sidhe's upraised arm, where sparks flew again.

Enchanted armor, too? Oh, hell, I don't need this right now.

Tannim's shoulder blades ached from where the arrow had hit; the armor had done *nothing* to arrest the shaft's momentum. The knee, and now the entire leg, were threatening to freeze up, and only dogged determination was keeping him on his feet. That, and a strong sense of self-preservation.

The Sidhe staggered back, and dug his fingers into the crate beside him, coming away with a two-by-four the size of Detroit. He clearly intended to beat Tannim into a liquid with it. The fellow hadn't drawn his sword, doubtless assuming that Tannim was armored the same as he, but like as not, he'd noted that the arrow's impact alone had hurt the human. The young mage could only limp backwards, mind working furiously to find an easy save — or *any* save! — while the towering Unseleighe stalked him.

The two-by-four swung; Tannim deflected it downwards with the crowbar. Its owner brought it back around much faster than Tannim would have thought possible and swung again, too fast to deflect, this time just catching Tannim in the left side above the kidneys. He flew sideways, landing on his back, and the crowbar slipped from his fingers and clanged against the concrete.

The visor on the Sidhe's helm was down now, a silvery metal skull shadowing slit-pupilled eyes. He stepped swiftly to the downed human, drawing the board up over his head for the final blow, one to Tannim's skull. Tannim's fingers grasped the pointed end of the crowbar as he propped himself up with his left arm, and he did the only thing he could —

The crowbar struck again, this time hooking the Sidhe's right ankle, and Tannim put all his weight into pulling on it. The warrior went off-balance and toppled back, as Tannim recovered and leapt to the warrior's chest, pressing the crowbar's point under the visor and prying up. The metal skullface bent until the bone underneath gave. The body twitched once, then fell still.

Tannim withdrew the dripping bar and staggered back, falling against the crate he'd nearly body-slammed a moment before. The three riders shot past him then, one raising a high-sign to him before decapitating another Lesser Sidhe, and then all three disappeared behind another stack of crates. Above them, a flash of white — a barn owl, no doubt giving aerial information to Keighvin. To his right, shotgun blasts and other gunfire marked Dottie's arrival with a pair of mechanics. And at the tail of the airplane was —

Tannim broke into as good a run as he could manage, sending out a desperate mental call to all of his allies, and even Chinthliss. He'd spotted the focus of the tapped energy—and she was just about to unleash it on Sam Kelly.

Sam backed away from what he'd done, inching on his buttocks like a kid in a sandbox. This was all so absurd, and so deadly — maiming fairy tales with a slapstick gag. At his age, anyone else would be sipping prune juice and weeding petunias in Florida, not acting like Batman in mail-order slacks. It was ridiculous, all of it, but there it was — a gibbering, discorporating Bane-Sidhe scratching its last moments on the tail-ramp of a C-130 with no throat or mouth left to scream with, and at the foot of the ramp, a former Joan Crawford look-alike knelt, doing the ultimate death scene.

He could hear her sucking breaths, sobbing, and despite what she'd no doubt done, it was a heart-rending sound — that of a near-immortal dying. Funny, he'd never thought of it that way before — it made him shudder. Or *was* that the reason his skin was prickling . . . ?

The woman raised her head, and gazed hatefully up at him with a marred, bloodied, but by no means dissolved face. She clenched her fists. Sam's heart froze.

Bloody hell, her makeup. It wasn't water-based, God help me — the iron-water didn't touch her skin enough to kill her —

Tannim kept a weather-eye on all sides while running, not wanting to be blindsided again. And much as he liked Sam, if there was a greater danger to be met, he'd have to answer that first. But as far as he could tell, the Unseleighe were at fourth and ten, with no kicker and no linebackers left. The hangar door was closed now, and they weren't going to be able to escape—what was left of them, anyway, unless they had a Gate up their sleeves. Tania was still in the Mustang; the Victor was still in one piece. Keighvin was on the farthest side of the hangar, astride Rosaleen. With no other threats apparent, he allowed himself to narrow in on the one immediately before him.

The woman Sam had been backing away from was standing now — the primal energy building up in her like floodwater against a dam. It did not Feel exactly like Sidhe magic, either — this was something Tannim knew well, something he was familiar with himself — it was elemental magery. It swirled about her in a sullen eddy as she raised her hands to spell-cast.

And where in hell did she get that? *The Sidhe don't do elemental stuff* —

Well, evidently this Sidhe did. But there was something wrong with the flavor of it.

Never mind that; right now Sam was a sitting duck — literally, so far as the sitting part went — and the Unseleighe was about to let loose. He couldn't deflect it, and he couldn't shield Sam from it — he had his hands full keeping his own shields up. There was only one thing handy.

He threw the crowbar.

It wasn't exactly made for throwing, and Tannim was badly off balance. *He* went down on his ass, as his leg gave out altogether — and the bar just barely hit the woman's upraised hands, knocking them aside, aborting the spell she had been about to cast. She whirled and saw him — and he recognized her as the woman from Kevin Barry's — probably the same "Aurilia Morrigan" that had sicced the P.I. on him. And she recognized him, too; though her face was red and swollen, blistered in places from what could only have been Cold-Iron contagion, she snarled with an unmistakable rage and turned her attention towards *him*.

He clasped his hands, arms braced towards her in a desperate warding-spell, and cowered inside his shields as she unleashed a deadly combination of Sidhe and elemental magic on him. She overloaded his mage-sight; his eyes burned with the raw power flung at him. He Felt his shields eroding, being peeled away a layer at a time. He kept throwing more of them up, but he was quickly running out of energy. He'd pumped too much into the ram, and he'd already drained all the reserves in the Mustang.

A lick of fire got through, and he cried out as it scorched his cheek before he managed to cut it off. She was just throwing too much at him — it kept changing with every second — forcing him to change his protections just as quickly. He couldn't see anything; he was trapped in the heart of a swirling maelstrom of multicolored magics, all of them subtlely wrong, but enough so to make his stomach churn with distress and his eyes ache and water.

Another lick of flame came through, touching his legs. It burned away patches in his jeans, but could not eat through further. His armor was proof against that, but not against everything, as the Sidhe with the two-by-four had figured out. The argument his knee had lost with the file cabinet had bruised or broken his kneecap — and had torn newly-healed gashes open again. There was blood seeping through the armor there — if Aurilia saw that and figured out the implications, she could call up a stone elemental to pulverize him, and his friends would bury him in the armor because it would be the only way to keep him from oozing all over the bottom of the coffin....

There were two determined firelords and an air elemental striking at him, relentlessly. They were beginning to hurt him seriously — all of his magical deflections were being undermined second by second. He'd never been oriented towards force-versus-force war — all his life he'd been the clever one using a tiny bit of leverage in the right place. Like the crowbar — but it was likely slag by now, and soon there would be nothing left of him but smoldering ashes in green-scaled armor. He was nearly blind, crippled, and thoughts of submission or suicide lanced his mind....

No! There's gotta be a way I can turn this stuff against her

— there's always a way. She's got the elementals Bound — if I can break the coercive spells, the elementals will —

The Hammer of God crashed down about ten feet from him. He clapped his hands to his ears; a reflex, it was too late to effectively protect them.

The magics around him swirled and evaporated —

Aurilia stood with hands outstretched, a look of complete surprise on her face, and a hole in her chestplate. As she crumpled, her eyes left Tannim and tracked to his right —

Where Sam was getting slowly to his feet, smoking Colt revolver in his hand, an expression of grim satisfaction on his face. He walked wearily to where Aurilia lay, and stared down at her for a moment.

Then, slowly and deliberately, he sighted down the barrel of the Colt. This time Tannim had enough warning to cover his ears and look away to protect his eyes from muzzle-flash. Sam Kelly planted a second steel-jacketed round right between Aurilia's eyebrows.

Tannim's ears were ringing; ringing hard enough to make him dizzy. Or maybe that was the pain in his knee. When he looked back, Sam had holstered the gun and was walking towards him.

"Why — why in hell didn't you use that before?" he said in frustration.

"What?" Sam's voice sounded very faint and far away through the cacophony in his ears.

Right. Neither of us can hear after two shots from the Colt.

"I said," he shouted, "why didn't you use that before?"

"She got me damn bullets!" Sam shouted back. "They wouldn't fire!"

"So?" Tannim yelled.

"I guess she saw too many movies!" Sam screamed, with smug, self-satisfied anger.

"What?"

"Guess she never heard of speed-loaders!" Sam laughed.

So. She'd neutralized the bullets in the gun with her

elementals, but not the ones in Sam's speed-loaders. That was the drawback of coercing elementals; whenever they had the option of taking you literally — if it was to your disadvantage — they would. They had done *exactly* what she told them to, and had not touched one bullet more than that.

Tannim felt his lips stretching in a grin; a feral grin that Sam answered with a nod. She'd underestimated Sam, too. She'd surely thought that once the old man was down, he was helpless.

"I saw you were in trouble, so I took a chance!" Sam continued; his voice seemed a little louder over the ringing. Maybe their ears were starting to recover. "I figured the gun might fire with fresh bullets — an' if that hadna worked, I'd've clubbed th' bitch with it!"

He offered Tannim a hand; the battered mage took it, and hauled himself to his feet. Or rather, foot — his left leg flatly refused to bear his weight. With Sam's help, he limped over to get his crowbar to use as a makeshift cane.

"That's what happens when ye piss off an engineer, lad," Sam continued, at a slightly lower volume. "We keep pitchin' things at ye until something works."

"So you do," Tannim observed, with a smile. "So you do."

Their troubles weren't over yet, however; for although the Unseleighe Sidhe and their troops had been destroyed to the last troll, there was a mundane problem still out there. Dottie galloped up on the back of her 'steed, shotgun still smoking, to remind them of just that.

"Tannim!" she shouted. The 'steed's hooves skidded on the concrete when she reined it up abruptly beside them. "Tannim, Conal says the cops are outside! We've got them barricaded out for the moment, but how are we gonna get out of here?"

"Oh, shit." The rest were pulling up beside him or running to meet him, including Keighvin and Conal in the Victor. He looked about frantically for an avenue of escape, but couldn't think of anything. "Keighvin, there isn't any time to build a Gate, is there?"

"Large enough to take the 'steeds — and especially, the cars?" Keighvin shook his head. "And we dare not leave them. They would point straight to us and Fairgrove."

Tannim tugged at his hair, frantically, trying to think. "Can't you transform them or — "

"Hey, hotshot!" A familiar misty form, visible only to mage-sight, appeared at his elbow.

"Not now, Ross — " He wondered, briefly, if they could all pile into the plane and fly off—

"Hey!" The ghost slammed into him, jarring what was left of his shields, shaking him. He turned to glare, but Ross ignored it. *"If you want a goddamn Gate, I got one for ya!"*

Those beside Tannim who could hear the spirit stared at Ross. Keighvin seized him by the insubstantial arm. Ross started, and stared back at the elven lord in shock. Keighvin was probably the first real-world creature Ross'd met who could grab and hold a ghost when he chose.

"A Gate? Where, man!" Keighvin demanded.

Ross pointed at the tail-section of the C-130. *"Right in there. That was how they was bringin' in reinforcements, until Fox scared 'em off. You could bring the cars up the ramp, see?"*

Keighvin started to smile, for the first time in this long, harrowing day-and-night. "Fitting," he said, with great satisfaction. "Fitting, that we should use *their* Gate." He looked about him, and began issuing orders. "Dottie, get Tannim back to his car; you and Frank armor it to protect Underhill from it. Conal, you and Kieru do likewise with the Victor. Deirdre, Siobhan, Padraig, Sean — you help me incinerate the corpses that are left. The rest of you, collect the wounded, and up through the Gate! We'll gather on t'other side and make our way home at leisure — *after* we destroy the Unseleighe holdings Underhill!"

Keighvin set the last of his spells in place, and double-checked them. He glanced around the hangar once to make certain that there were no further signs of Sidhe or Fairgrove or anything out of the "ordinary" —

Though he doubted that the police would think what they found was ordinary. Hundreds of porn-tapes, including several of kiddie-porn and snuff-movies. One young man, obviously tortured to death—

And a hard time we had getting young Tania to turn loose of the body, too. He shook his head in pity; he hadn't blamed her for not wanting to leave Jamie's corpse here for the police to find, but he'd convinced her that it was the only way to cover the Fairgrove trail and give the police enough to think about that they wouldn't look for complications.

The complete sets and equipment from the Underhill Studios, dumped near the crates, including what they had used on Jamie — and what few records the trio had kept.

Danaa only knew what the police would make of it all. There would be no bodies save that of Jamie; nothing but the wreckage of the offices and hangar, evidence of a fight — and a mystery.

Yon Tannim thinks that the police will assume that some organized-crime contract went sour, and this was the result. Well, I care not.

All the preparations had taken less than fifteen minutes; meanwhile, the police were outside, trying to find a way to crack the wall of protections on each doorway, and shouting to them to come out and surrender on their bullhorns. Keighvin heard them through the corrugated metal walls — but while he stood here, this place was made of sterner stuff than corrugated aluminum.

Let the police concoct an explanation for how a fight took place, but bodies and survivors vanished. So long as there is nothing linking this place to Fairgrove or the Sidhe, it matters not to me what they say.

Well, he was ready. Siobhan was the last of the

cleanup crew, and she had gone through the Gate a moment ago. It was time.

He mounted Rosaleen, and galloped up the ramp. As soon as he passed across the Gate boundary, the spells he had set activated; the substance of the plane, of Underhill itself, tried to go back to Underhill through the only portal available.

The Gate.

Let them explain this.

The plane imploded, taking the Gate with it, and leaving nothing of itself behind.

The protections on the outside walls collapsed.

Tannim's Mustang was the first up the ramp, with Sam in the seat beside him, and Dottie and Frank in the passenger's bench. Dottie's 'steed — transformed into a proud, ethereal unicorn, a glowing snowy white, with silken mane and tail, silver hooves and horn, and golden eyes — was right behind with Tania on her back. The Mach 1 was doing a good job of glowing itself, from all the magics Dottie and Frank had layered on, insulating Underhill from the devastation so much Cold Iron could cause.

Riding just ahead was Kieru, with his 'steed back to its normal shape — though not even for Tania's sake could Kieru convince it to put on a horn.

Kieru vanished into the dead-black nothingness at the end of the ramp, dissolving into what appeared to be a hard, solid wall. Tannim shuddered, and tried not to look — but his turn was next, and he sent his much-abused American-built steed following in Kieru's wake. He closed his eyes, slowing to a crawl as the Gate sucked up nose, hood, and approached the windscreen —

There was a shiver of energy all over his body as he passed through, and every hair on his body stood on end for a moment. When the feeling had passed he opened his eyes again —

There, Kieru had pulled up, his mouth agape with

astonishment and a little fear. Just beyond him stood a
tall Sidhe; blond hair streaming to his waist, armored
with gold-chased silver, brandishing a sword. His face
was — impossible. *Too* beautiful, even for the Sidhe —
and he was crowned.

"The High King," Kieru said aloud, as his elvensteed backed. "Danaa! 'Tis High King Oberon —"

Then, before either Tannim or Kieru could do or say
anything else, the High King shifted shape —

And in place of the breathtakingly handsome
Oberon, there was a red-haired young man in black
coveralls, with an aircraft carrier flight-crew cap, mir-
ror-shades, ear-protectors, and a pair of aircraft batons
— who began directing the new arrivals, as if he was
parking fighter planes.

Tannim looked at Sam; Sam shrugged. "Do what the
man tells ye," Sam suggested.

Seeing no reason why he shouldn't, Tannim did,
eventually parking at the edge of the "pavement" that
marked the end of the Unseleighe-built area and the
chaos of the unclaimed places of Underhill. He turned
the engine off, pivoted, and watched the stranger.

The red-haired youth walked up to the Mustang,
saluted with a baton, and vanished — leaving only the
afterimage of an embroidered chest-patch on his flight
suit, which read "FX."

● CHAPTER SEVENTEEN

It had been a long few months of healing and rebuilding. Conal, thorough as ever, had stroked every last bit of information out of the Victor's diagnostic computer after returning to Fairgrove, and had already forged enough redesigned parts to keep the crew busy testing for a year. The local and national news had enjoyed a field day with the high-visibility "Mystery of Hangar 2A" — no doubt Geraldo was plotting an exposé by now.

Tannim had mentioned to Keighvin that someone would eventually discover the Fairgrove link, possibly even one of the few Fed-employed mages he'd run around with a couple times, but reassured the elven lord that they were generally pretty cool, and cynical in the way only Government employees could be.

They also knew when to leave things mysteries.

It was no mystery, though, how well Tania had recovered from her ordeal. She and he had talked often, and she admitted to having lost faith in Tannim before her kidnapping — but Tannim suspected seeing him coming to her rescue had helped restore her faith in other things, too. And being brought to the wonderland of Underhill, astride what at least *looked* like a unicorn — that is, before meeting a real one — had jolted her from her fears. Her friend, Laura, had been badly broken by what had happened, but was being cared for Underhill by the Court. It was certain that when she was seen again, she would be strong and well, and had promised Tania to be her friend always.

Then Tania had been advised to go to the counselors

at the Shelter House back in Savannah, to talk out what
the people of Fairgrove could not help with. Her heart
of hearts had healed well in her talks with the counselor — and that had led to today.

Tannim bent forward in the seat, pressing the scan
button on the new CD/FM/AM tuner, installed at long
last. It skipped from WRDU in Raleigh to WYRD in
Haven's Reach. Haven's Reach was a tiny community
with one of the highest per-capita counts of mages in
the United States, right between Raleigh and Fayet-
teville. Somehow, WYRD stayed on the air year after
year regardless of its eclectic playlist.

Now it played Icehouse: "Hey Little Girl." The DJ
must be psychic. Actually, in that town, he probably was.

Tannim's left knee hardly ever hurt anymore;
Chinthliss had finally showed, embarrassingly
apologetic that he hadn't come to Tannim's aid. His
dear friend had finally, apparently, had a romantic encounter, and was *very* distracted when Tannim had
screeched for help. To make up for it, he'd called in a
favor from a Healer-friend — now the knee moved just
fine, and the muscles had finally gotten the detailed attention they'd needed for months.

That had made the drive to Research Triangle Park
bearable physically — but he was still on edge emotionally over what was happening now.

The counselors had been more than professional —
they had sincerely worked for the girl's best interests,
and Tania decided, after going over all of her options,
that this meeting would be best. So, her parents had
been contacted, and Tannim had driven here here, to
her old home, to see if the pieces could be fit together
anew. She'd told him on the way there that she'd know
the moment she saw her parents whether it was right or
not, and if she was going to stay, she'd turn and wave.

Tania was walking up the steps, across a yard that
had at one time been perfectly manicured. Now it
showed signs of neglect, at odds with the *Architectural*

Digest showpieces to either side of it. In the looping driveway was a gold BMW with a "For Sale" sign on the dash. And in one window of the house, a crystal suncatcher glittered, etched with a white horse sporting a single spiraling horn.

That was a good sign. The DJ segued from Icehouse to a-ha: "Out of Blue Comes Green."

The door opened, and two figures rushed out, embracing her for one glorious minute. They stood at the door, then motioned for her to come inside with them. Tania stepped towards the threshold, stopped, and slowly faced the Mustang. Her arm raised, trembling, and Tannim could see tears streaming down her face even from this far. She shakily waved, smiling sweetly but obviously choking back more tears.

Tannim slipped the Mustang into drive and pulled away slowly from the curb. Tania was going to be all right, that much he knew. She had loving parents who had finally learned what raising a child was about, and she would be just fine.

After all, once touched by a unicorn, growing up couldn't be too hard.

AFTERWORD

Tania's story is, unfortunately, not unusual. In fact, Tania got out of her troubles relatively easily. If your situation is like Tania's — alone, out on the street, with nowhere to go and afraid to go home, there *is* help for you. *Real* help; not elves, not magic, and you don't even need a quarter to get it.

Call 1-800-999-9999 for the Runaway Hotline. There are people on the other end of that phone that will help you: they'll find you a safe place to stay, they'll help you with any other problems you might have, from drugs to getting away from a pimp, and they'll get you back with your parents if that's the right thing for you.

You can call an 800 number from most payphones for *free*. Check the instructions on the front of the phone; you shouldn't even need a quarter to use it. Just wait for the tone, and dial the number. You won't be sorry.

Make your own luck — and your own magic. And then go and build yourself a good life.

High Flight
Larry Dixon
Mercedes Lackey

Baen Books
Jim Baen
Toni Weisskopf

FALLEN ANGELS

Two refugees from one of the last remaining
orbital space stations are trapped on the North
American icecap, and only science fiction fans
can rescue them! Here's an excerpt from *Fallen
Angels*, the bestselling new novel by Larry
Niven, Jerry Pournelle, and Michael Flynn.

*   *   *

She opened the door on the first knock and stood out of
the way. The wind was whipping the ground snow in swirling circles. Some of it blew in the door as Bob entered. She
slammed the door behind him. The snow on the floor
decided to wait a while before melting. "Okay. You're here,"
she snapped. "There's no fire and no place to sit. The bed's
the only warm place and you know it. I didn't know you
were this hard up. And, by the way, I don't have any
company, thanks for asking." If Bob couldn't figure out
from that speech that she was pissed, he'd never win the
prize as Mr. Perception.

"I am that hard up," he said, moving closer. "Let's get it on."

"Say what?" Bob had never been one for subtle technique, but this was pushing it. She tried to step back but his
hands gripped her arms. They were cold as ice, even through
the housecoat. "Bob!" He pulled her to him and buried his
face in her hair.

"It's not what you think," he whispered. "We don't have
time for this, worse luck."

"Bob!"

"No, just bear with me. Let's go to your bedroom. I don't
want you to freeze."

He led her to the back of the house and she slid under
the covers without inviting him in. He lay on top, still
wearing his thick leather coat. Whatever he had in mind,

she realized, it wasn't sex. Not with her housecoat, the comforter and his greatcoat playing chaperone.

He kissed her hard and was whispering hoarsely in her ear before she had a chance to react. "Angels down. A scoopship. It crashed."

"Angels?" Was he crazy?

He kissed her neck. "Not so loud. I don't think the 'danes are listening, but why take chances? Angels. Spacemen. *Peace* and *Freedom.*"

She'd been away too long. She'd never heard spacemen called *Angels*. And— "Crashed?" She kept it to a whisper. "Where?"

"Just over the border in North Dakota. Near Mapleton."

"Great Ghu, Bob. That's on the Ice!"

He whispered, "Yeah. But they're not too far in."

"How do you know about it?"

He snuggled closer and kissed her on the neck again. Maybe sex made a great cover for his visit, but she didn't think he had to lay it on so thick. "We know."

"We?"

"The Worldcon's in Minneapolis-St. Paul this year—"

The World Science Fiction Convention. "I got the invitation, but I didn't dare go. If anyone saw me—"

"—And it was just getting started when the call came down from *Freedom.* Sherrine, they couldn't have picked a better time or place to crash their scoopship. That's why I came to you. Your grandparents live near the crash site."

She wondered if there was a good time for crashing scoopships. "So?"

"We're going to rescue them."

"We? Who's we?"

"The Con Committee, some of the fans—"

"But why tell me, Bob? I'm fafiated. It's been years since I've dared associate with fen."

Too many years, she thought. She had discovered science fiction in childhood, at her neighborhood branch library. She still remembered that first book: *Star Man's Son,* by Andre Norton. Fors had been persecuted because he was different; but he nurtured a secret, a mutant power. Just the sort of hero to appeal to an ugly-duckling little girl who would not act like other little girls.

SF had opened a whole new world to her. A galaxy, a

universe of new worlds. While the other little girls had played with Barbie dolls, Sherrine played with Lummox and Poddy and Arkady and Susan Calvin. While they went to the malls, she went to Trantor and the Witch World. While they wondered what Look was In, she wondered about resource depletion and nuclear war and genetic engineering. Escape literature, they called it. She missed it terribly.

"There is always one moment in childhood," Graham Greene had written in *The Power and the Glory*, "when the door opens and lets the future in." For some people, that door never closed. She thought that Peter Pan had had the right idea all along.

"Why tell *you*? Sherrine, we want you with us. Your grandparents live near the crash site. They've got all sorts of gear we can borrow for the rescue."

"Me?" A tiny trickle of electric current ran up her spine. But . . . *Nah.* "Bob, I don't dare. If my bosses thought I was associating with fen, I'd lose my job."

He grinned. "Yeah. Me, too." And she saw that he had never considered that she might not go.

'Tis a Proud and Lonely Thing to Be a Fan, they used to say, laughing. It had become a *very* lonely thing. The Establishment had always been hard on science fiction. The government-funded Arts Councils would pass out tax money to write obscure poetry for "little" magazines, but not to write speculative fiction. "Sci-fi isn't literature." *That* wasn't censorship.

Perversely, people went on buying science fiction without grants. Writers even got rich without government funding. *They couldn't kill us that way!*

Then the Luddites and the Greens had come to power. She had watched science fiction books slowly disappear from the library shelves, beginning with the children's departments. (That wasn't censorship either. Libraries couldn't buy *every* book, now could they? So they bought "realistic" children's books funded by the National Endowment for the Arts, books about death and divorce, and really important things like being overweight or fitting in with the right school crowd.)

Then came paper shortages, and paper allocations. The science fiction sections in the chain stores grew smaller. ("You can't expect us to stock books that aren't selling." And they can't sell if you don't stock them.)

Fantasy wasn't hurt so bad. Fantasy was about wizards

and elves, and being kind to the Earth, and harmony with nature, all things the Greens loved. But science fiction was about science.

Science fiction wasn't exactly outlawed. There was still Freedom of Speech; still a Bill of Rights, even if it wasn't taught much in the schools—even if most kids graduated unable to read well enough to understand it. But a person could get into a lot of unofficial trouble for reading SF or for associating with known fen. She could lose her job, say. Not through government persecution—of course not—but because of "reduction in work force" or "poor job performance" or "uncooperative attitude" or "politically incorrect" or a hundred other phrases. And if the neighbors shunned her, and tradesmen wouldn't deal with her, and stores wouldn't give her credit, who could blame them? Science fiction involved science; and science was a conspiracy to pollute the environment, "to bring back technology."

Damn right! she thought savagely. We do conspire to bring back technology. Some of us are crazy enough to think that there are alternatives to freezing in the dark. *And some of us are even crazy enough to try to rescue marooned spacemen before they freeze, or disappear into protective custody.*

Which could be dangerous. The government might declare you mentally ill, and help you.

She shuddered at that thought. She pushed and rolled Bob aside. She sat up and pulled the comforter up tight around herself. "Do you know what it was that attracted me to science fiction?"

He raised himself on one elbow, blinked at her change of subject, and looked quickly around the room, as if suspecting bugs. "No, what?"

"Not Fandom. I was reading the true quill long before I knew about Fandom and cons and such. No, it was the feeling of hope."

"Hope?"

"Even in the most depressing dystopia, there's still the notion that the future is something we build. It doesn't just happen. You can't predict the future, but you can invent it. Build it. That is a hopeful idea, even when the building collapses."

Bob was silent for a moment. Then he nodded. "Yeah. Nobody's building the future anymore. 'We live in an Age of Limited Choices.'" He quoted the government line without cracking a smile. "Hell, you don't *take* choices off a list. You *make* choices and *add* them to the list. Speaking of which, have you made your choice?"

That electric tickle . . . "Are they even alive?"

"So far. I understand it was some kind of miracle that they landed at all. They're unconscious, but not hurt bad. They're hooked up to some sort of magical medical widgets and the Angels overhead are monitoring. But if we don't get them out soon, they'll freeze to death."

She bit her lip. "And you think we can reach them in time?"

Bob shrugged.

"You want me to risk my life on the Ice, defy the government and probably lose my job in a crazy, amateur effort to rescue two spacemen who might easily be dead by the time we reach them."

He scratched his beard. "Is that quixotic, or what?"

"Quixotic. Give me four minutes."

PRAISE FOR
LOIS MCMASTER BUJOLD

What the critics say:

The Warrior's Apprentice: "Now here's a fun romp through the spaceways—not so much a space opera as space ballet.... it has all the 'right stuff.' A lot of thought and thoughtfulness stand behind the all-too-human characters. Enjoy this one, and look forward to the next."   —Dean Lambe, *SF Reviews*

"The pace is breathless, the characterization thoughtful and emotionally powerful, and the author's narrative technique and command of language compelling. Highly recommended."   —*Booklist*

Brothers in Arms: "... she gives it a geniune depth of character, while reveling in the wild turnings of her tale. ... Bujold is as audacious as her favorite hero, and as brilliantly (if sneakily) successful."   —*Locus*

"Miles Vorkosigan is such a great character that I'll read anything Lois wants to write about him. ... a book to re-read on cold rainy days." —Robert Coulson, *Comics Buyer's Guide*

Borders of Infinity: "Bujold's series hero Miles Vorkosigan may be a lord by birth and an admiral by rank, but a bone disease that has left him hobbled and in frequent pain has sensitized him to the suffering of outcasts in his very hierarchical era.... Playing off Miles's reserve and cleverness, Bujold draws outrageous and outlandish foils to color her high-minded adventures."   —*Publishers Weekly*

Falling Free: "In *Falling Free* Lois McMaster Bujold has written her fourth straight superb novel. ... How to break down a talent like Bujold's into analyzable components? Best not to try. Best to say 'Read, or you will be missing something extraordinary.'" —Roland Green, *Chicago Sun-Times*

The Vor Game: "The chronicles of Miles Vorkosigan are far too witty to be literary junk food, but they rouse the kind of craving that makes popcorn magically vanish during a double feature."   —Faren Miller, *Locus*

MORE PRAISE FOR
LOIS MCMASTER BUJOLD

What the readers say:

"My copy of *Shards of Honor* is falling apart I've reread it so often.... I'll read whatever you write. You've certainly proved yourself a grand storyteller."
—Liesl Kolbe, Colorado Springs, CO

"I experience the stories of Miles Vorkosigan as almost viscerally uplifting.... But certainly, even the weightiest theme would have less impact than a cinder on snow were it not for a rousing good story, and good storytelling with it. This is the second thing I want to thank you for.... I suppose if you boiled down all I've said to its simplest expression, it would be that I immensely enjoy and admire your work. I submit that, as literature, your work raises the overall level of the science fiction genre, and spiritually, your work cannot avoid positively influencing all who read it."
—Glen Stonebraker, Gaithersburg, MD

" 'The Mountains of Mourning' [in *Borders of Infinity*] was one of the best-crafted, and simply best, works I'd ever read. When I finished it, I immediately turned back to the beginning and read it again, and I can't remember the last time I did that."   —Betsy Bizot, Lisle, IL

"I can only hope that you will continue to write, so that I can continue to read (and of course buy) your books, for they make me laugh and cry and think ... rare indeed."   —Steven Knott, Major, USAF

What do you say?

Send me these books!

Shards of Honor • 72087-2 • $4.99 _____
The Warrior's Apprentice • 72066-X • $4.50 _____
Ethan of Athos • 65604-X • $4.99 _____
Falling Free • 65398-9 • $4.99 _____
Brothers in Arms • 69799-4 • $4.99 _____
Borders of Infinity • 69841-9 • $4.99 _____
The Vor Game • 72014-7 • $4.99 _____
Barrayar • 72083-X • $4.99 _____

Lois McMaster Bujold:
Only from Baen Books

If these books are not available at your local bookstore, just check your choices above, fill out this coupon and send a check or money order for the cover price to Baen Books, Dept. BA, P.O. Box 1403, Riverdale, NY 10471.

NAME: _____

ADDRESS: _____

_____

I have enclosed a check or money order in the amount of $ _____.

MAGIC AND *COMPUTERS* DON'T MIX!

RICK COOK

Or . . . do they? That's what Walter "Wiz" Zumwalt is wondering. Just a short time ago, he was a master hacker in a Silicon Valley office, a very ordinary fellow in a very mundane world. But magic spells, it seems, are a lot like computer programs: they're both formulas, recipes for getting things done. Unfortunately, just like those computer programs, they can be full of bugs. Now, thanks to a *particularly* buggy spell, Wiz has been transported to a world of magic—and incredible peril. The wizard who summoned him is dead, Wiz has fallen for a red-headed witch who despises him, and no one—not the elves, not the dwarves, not even the dragons—can figure out why he's here, or what to do with him. Worse: the sorcerers of the deadly Black League, rulers of an entire continent, want Wiz dead—and he doesn't even know why! Wiz had better figure out the rules of this strange new world—and fast—or he's not going to live to see Silicon Valley again.

Here's a refreshing tale from an exciting new writer. It's also a rarity: a well-drawn fantasy told with all the rigorous logic of hard science fiction.

69803-6 • 320 pages • $3.50